Total-E-Bound Publishing books by Lynne Connolly:

Unbroken
Temporary Spy

Tom Jones: Part One

A Clandestine Classic

HENRY FIELDING and
LYNNE CONNOLLY

Tom Jones: Part One
ISBN # 978-1-78184-568-4
©Copyright Lynne Connolly 2013
Cover Art by Posh Gosh ©Copyright January 2013
Interior text design by Claire Siemaszkiewicz
Total-E-Bound Publishing

Published in 2013 by Total-E-Bound Publishing, Think Tank, Ruston Way, Lincoln, LN6 7FL, United Kingdom.

Tom Jones:
Part One

Dedication

To the Universal Register, without which this book
might not have been written

Preface

To the Honourable George Lyttleton, Esq
One of the Lords Commissioners of the Treasury

Sir,
Notwithstanding your constant refusal, when I have asked leave to prefix your name to this dedication, I must still insist on my right to desire your protection of this work.

To you, sir, it is owing that this history was ever begun. It was by your desire that I first thought of such a composition. So many years have since passed, that you may have, perhaps, forgotten this circumstance, but your desires are to me in the nature of commands, and the impression of them is never to be erased from my memory.

Again, sir, without your assistance this history had never been completed. Be not startled at the assertion. I do not intend to draw on you the suspicion of being a romance writer. I mean no more than that I partly owe to you my existence during great part of the time which I have employed in composing it—another matter which it may be necessary to remind you of, since there are certain actions of which you are apt to be extremely forgetful, but of these I hope I shall always have a better memory than yourself.

Lastly, it is owing to you that the history appears what it now is. If there be in this work, as some have been pleased to say, a stronger picture of a truly benevolent mind than is to be found in any other, who that knows you, and a particular acquaintance of yours, will doubt whence that benevolence hath been copied? The world will not, I believe, make me the compliment of thinking I took it from myself. I care not. This they shall own, that the two persons from whom I have taken it, that is to say, two of the best and worthiest men in the world, are strongly and zealously my friends. I might be contented with this, and yet my vanity will add a third to the number, and him one of the greatest and noblest, not only in his rank, but in every public and private virtue. But here, whilst my gratitude for the princely benefactions of the Duke of Bedford bursts from my heart, you must forgive my reminding you that it was you who first recommended me to the notice of my benefactor.

And what are your objections to the allowance of the honour which I have solicited? Why, you have commended the book so warmly, that you should be ashamed of reading your name before the dedication. Indeed, sir, if the book itself doth not make you ashamed of your commendations, nothing that I can here write will, or ought. I am not to give up my right to your protection and patronage, because you have commended my book. For though I acknowledge so many obligations to you, I do not add this to the number, in which friendship, I am convinced, hath so little share, since that can neither bias your judgement, nor pervert your integrity. An enemy may at any time obtain your commendation by only deserving it, and the utmost which the faults of your friends can hope for, is your silence, or, perhaps, if too severely accused, your gentle palliation.

In short, sir, I suspect, that your dislike of public praise is your true objection to granting my request. I have observed that you have, in common with my two other friends, an unwillingness to hear the least mention of your own virtues—that, as a great poet says of one of you, he might justly have said it of all three, you "do good by stealth, and blush to find it fame".

If men of this disposition are as careful to shun applause, as others are to escape censure, how just must be your apprehension of your character falling into my hands? Since what would not a man have reason to dread, if attacked by an author who had received from him injuries equal to my obligations to you?

And will not this dread of censure increase in proportion to the matter which a man is conscious of having afforded for it? If his whole life, for instance, should have been one continued subject of satire, he may well tremble when an incensed satirist takes him in hand. Now, sir, if we apply this to your modest aversion to panegyric, how reasonable will your fears of me appear!

Yet surely you might have gratified my ambition, from this single confidence, that I shall always prefer the indulgence of your inclinations to the satisfaction of my own. A very strong instance of which I shall give you in this address, in which I am determined to follow the example of all other dedicators, and will consider not what my patron really deserves to have written, but what he will be best pleased to read.

Without further preface then, I here present you with the labours of some years of my life. What merit these labours have is already known to yourself. If, from your favourable judgement, I have conceived some esteem for them, it cannot be imputed to vanity, since I should have agreed as implicitly to your opinion, had it been given in favour of any other man's production. Negatively, at least, I may be allowed to say, that had I been sensible of any great demerit in the work, you are the last person to whose protection I would have ventured to recommend it.

From the name of my patron, indeed, I hope my reader will be convinced, at his very entrance on this work, that he will find in the whole course of it nothing prejudicial to the cause of religion and virtue, nothing inconsistent with the strictest rules of decency, nor which can offend even the chastest eye in the perusal. On the contrary, I declare, that to recommend goodness and innocence hath been my sincere endeavour in this history. This honest purpose you have been pleased to think I have attained. And to say the truth, it is likeliest to be attained in books of this kind. For an example is a kind of picture, in which virtue becomes, as it were, an object of sight, and strikes us with an idea of that loveliness, which Plato asserts there is in her naked charms.

Besides displaying that beauty of virtue which may attract the admiration of mankind, I have attempted to engage a stronger motive to human action in her favour, by convincing men, that their true interest directs them to a pursuit of her. For this purpose I have shown that no acquisitions of guilt can compensate the loss of that solid inward comfort of mind, which is the sure companion of innocence and virtue, nor can in the least balance the evil of that horror and anxiety which, in their room, guilt introduces into our bosoms. And again, that as these acquisitions are in themselves generally worthless, so are the means to attain them not only base and infamous, but at best uncertain, and always full of danger.

Lastly, I have endeavoured strongly to inculcate, that virtue and innocence can scarce ever be injured but by indiscretion, and that it is this alone which often betrays them into the snares that deceit and villainy spread for them. A moral which I have the more industriously laboured, as the teaching it is, of all others, the likeliest to be attended with success, since, I believe, it is much easier to make good men wise, than to make bad men good.

For these purposes I have employed all the wit and humour of which I am master in the following history, wherein I have endeavoured to laugh mankind out of their favourite follies and vices. How far I have succeeded in this good attempt, I shall submit to the candid reader, with only two requests. First, that he will not expect to find perfection in this work, and secondly, that he will excuse some parts of it, if they fall short of that little merit which I hope may appear in others.

I will detain you, sir, no longer. Indeed I have run into a preface, while I professed to write a dedication. But how can it be otherwise? I dare not praise you, and the only means I know of to avoid it, when you are in my thoughts, are either to be entirely silent, or to turn my thoughts to some other subject.

Pardon, therefore, what I have said in this epistle, not only without your consent, but absolutely against it, and give me at least leave, in this public manner, to declare that I am, with the highest respect and gratitude,

Sir,

Your most obliged,

Obedient, humble servant,

Henry Fielding.

BOOK ONE

Containing as much of the birth of the Foundling as is necessary or proper to acquaint the reader with in the beginning of this history.

Chapter One

The introduction to the work, or bill of fare to the feast

An author ought to consider himself, not as a gentleman who gives a private or eleemosynary treat, but rather as one who keeps a public ordinary, at which all persons are welcome for their money. In the former case, it is well known that the entertainer provides what fare he pleases, and though this should be very indifferent, and utterly disagreeable to the taste of his company, they must not find any fault. Nay, on the contrary, good breeding forces them outwardly to approve and to commend whatever is set before them. Now the contrary of this happens to the master of an ordinary. Men who pay for what they eat will insist on gratifying their palates, however nice and whimsical these may prove, and if everything is not agreeable to their taste, will challenge a right to censure, to abuse, and to damn their dinner without control.

To prevent, therefore, giving offence to their customers by any such disappointment, it hath been usual with the honest and well-meaning host to provide a bill of fare which all persons may peruse at their first entrance into the house, and having thence acquainted themselves with the entertainment which they may expect, may either stay and regale with what is provided for them, or may depart to some other ordinary better accommodated to their taste.

As we do not disdain to borrow wit or wisdom from any man who is capable of lending us either, we have condescended to take a hint from these honest victuallers, and shall prefix not only a general bill of fare to our whole entertainment, but shall likewise give the reader particular bills to every course which is to be served up in this and the ensuing volumes.

The provision, then, which we have here made is no other than *Human Nature*. Nor do I fear that my sensible reader, though most luxurious in his taste, will start, cavil, or be offended, because I have named but one article. The tortoise — as the alderman of Bristol, well learned in eating, knows by much experience — besides the delicious calipash and calipee, contains many different kinds of food. Nor can the learned reader be ignorant, that in human nature, though here collected under one general name, is such prodigious variety, that a cook will have sooner gone through all the several species of animal and vegetable food in the world, than an author will be able to exhaust so extensive a subject.

An objection may perhaps be apprehended from the more delicate, that this dish is too common and vulgar, for what else is the subject of all the romances, novels, plays, and poems, with which the stalls abound? Many exquisite viands might be rejected by the epicure, if it was a sufficient cause for his contemning of them as common and vulgar, that something was to be found in the most paltry alleys under the same name. In reality, true nature is as difficult to be met with in authors, as the Bayonne ham, or Bologna sausage, is to be found in the shops.

But the whole, to continue the same metaphor, consists in the cookery of the author, for, as Mr Pope tells us —

"True wit is nature to advantage drest,
What oft was thought, but ne'er so well exprest."

The same animal which hath the honour to have some part of his flesh eaten at the table of a duke, may perhaps be degraded in another part, and some of his limbs gibbeted, as it were, in the vilest stall in town. Where, then, lies the difference between the food of the nobleman and the porter, if both are at dinner on the same ox or calf, but in the seasoning, the dressing, the garnishing, and the setting forth? Hence the one provokes and incites the most languid appetite, and the other turns and palls that which is the sharpest and keenest.

In like manner, the excellence of the mental entertainment consists less in the subject than in the author's skill in well dressing it up. How pleased, therefore, will the reader be to find that we have, in the following work, adhered closely to one of the highest principles of the best cook which the present age, or perhaps that of Heliogabalus, hath produced.

This great man, as is well known to all lovers of polite eating, begins at first by setting plain things before his hungry guests, rising afterwards by degrees as their stomachs may be supposed to decrease, to the very quintessence of sauce and spices. In like manner, we shall represent human nature at first to the keen appetite of our reader, in that more plain and simple manner in which it is found in the country, and shall hereafter hash and ragoo it with all the high French and Italian seasoning of affectation and vice which courts and cities afford. By these means, we doubt not but our reader may be rendered desirous to read on for ever, as the great person just above-mentioned is supposed to have made some persons eat.

Having premised thus much, we will now detain those who like our bill of fare no longer from their diet, and shall proceed directly to serve up the first course of our history for their entertainment.

Chapter Two

A short description of squire Allworthy, and a fuller account of Miss Bridget Allworthy, his sister

In that part of the western division of this kingdom which is commonly called Somersetshire, there lately lived, and perhaps lives still, a gentleman whose name was Allworthy, and who might well be called the favourite of both nature and fortune, for both of these seem to have contended which should bless and enrich him most. In this contention, nature may seem to some to have come off victorious, as she bestowed on him many gifts, while fortune had only one gift in her power. But in pouring forth this, she was so very profuse, that others perhaps may think this single endowment to have been more than equivalent to all the various blessings which he enjoyed from nature. From the former of these, he derived an agreeable person, a sound constitution, a solid understanding, and a benevolent heart. By the latter, he was decreed to the inheritance of one of the largest estates in the county.

This gentleman had in his youth married a very worthy and beautiful woman, of whom he had been extremely fond. By her he had three children, all of whom died in their infancy. He had likewise had the misfortune of burying this beloved wife herself, about five years before the time in which this history chooses to set out. This loss, however great, he bore like a man of sense and constancy, though it must be confessed he would often talk a little whimsically on this head. For he sometimes said he looked on himself as still married, and considered his wife as only gone a little before him, a journey which he should most certainly, sooner or later, take after her, and that he had not the least doubt of meeting her again in a place where he should never part with her more—sentiments for which his sense was arraigned by one part of his neighbours, his religion by a second, and his sincerity by a third.

So fond was he of his wife that on her demise he had vowed never to marry again, for he would not allow another woman to take the place she had occupied so assiduously and completely. However, a man must have some pleasures of the flesh, his health depended on it, so the squire had a number of arrangements with women who were perfectly content to continue their association without benefit of contract or ceremony.

He now lived, for the most part, retired in the country, with one sister, for whom he had a very tender affection. This lady was now somewhat past the age of thirty, an era at which, in the opinion of the malicious, the title of old maid may with no impropriety be assumed. She was of that species of

women whom you commend rather for good qualities
than beauty, and who are generally called, by their
own sex, very good sort of women—as good a sort of
woman, madam, as you would wish to know. Indeed,
she was so far from regretting want of beauty, that she
never mentioned that perfection, if it can be called
one, without contempt, and would often thank God
she was not as handsome as Miss Such-a-one, whom
perhaps beauty had led into errors which she might
have otherwise avoided.

Miss Bridget Allworthy—for that was the name of
this lady—very rightly conceived the charms of
person in a woman to be no better than snares for
herself, as well as for others. And yet so discreet was
she in her conduct, that her prudence was as much on
the guard as if she had all the snares to apprehend
which were ever laid for her whole sex. Indeed, I have
observed, though it may seem unaccountable to the
reader, that this guard of prudence, like the trained
bands, is always readiest to go on duty where there is
the least danger. It often basely and cowardly deserts
those paragons for whom the men are all wishing,
sighing, dying, and spreading, every net in their
power, and constantly attends at the heels of that
higher order of women for whom the other sex have a
more distant and awful respect, and whom—from
despair, I suppose, of success—they never venture to
attack.

Reader, I think proper, before we proceed any
further together, to acquaint thee that I intend to
digress, through this whole history, as often as I see
occasion, of which I am myself a better judge than any
pitiful critic whatever. And here I must desire all those
critics to mind their own business, and not to
intermeddle with affairs or works which no ways

concern them. For till they produce the authority by which they are constituted judges, I shall not plead to their jurisdiction.

Chapter Three

An odd accident which befell Mr Allworthy at his return home. The decent behaviour of Mrs Deborah Wilkins, with some proper animadversions on bastards

I have told my reader, in the preceding chapter, that Mr Allworthy inherited a large fortune, that he had a good heart, and no family. Hence, doubtless, it will be concluded by many that he lived like an honest man — owed no one a shilling, took nothing but what was his own, kept a good house, entertained his neighbours with a hearty welcome at his table, and was charitable to the poor, i.e. to those who had rather beg than work, by giving them the offals from it — that he died immensely rich and built an hospital. Always considerate of his health and the people around him, the squire conducted his more interesting business away from home, where his reputation should not be sullied by any rumour that he was less than upright at all times. Indeed, according to the ladies, his uprightness was never in doubt.

And true it is that he did many of these things, but had he done nothing more I should have left him to have recorded his own merit on some fair freestone over the door of that hospital. Matters of a much more extraordinary kind are to be the subject of this history, or I should grossly misspend my time in writing so voluminous a work, and you, my sagacious friend, might with equal profit and pleasure travel through some pages which certain droll authors have been facetiously pleased to call *The History of England*.

Mr Allworthy had been absent a full quarter of a year in London, on some very particular business, though I know not what it was, but judge of its importance by its having detained him so long from home, whence he had not been absent a month at a time during the space of many years.

This enabled him to pay attention to a lady he had been acquainted with for a long time, but had sadly neglected of late, business having kept him in the country.

Mrs Dickinson was the relict of a city businessman and had a very fine sort of lodging in Red Lion Square, so good that when she invited Mr Allworthy to save the cost of an inn and stay with her in comfort, he accepted with a grateful heart and voluminous thanks.

So pleased was the estimable lady to see him that she found great difficulty in keeping her fichu in place, a matter the squire was only too pleased to assist her with, and the fichu disposed of, a great expanse of cleavage came into view, something Mr Allworthy took advantage of with both hands.

On tumbling her back onto the sopha, the squire animadverted on the size of her breasts, which had become bountiful in his absence. "Mr Allworthy, I have had nothing to do but eat and visit the establishments that cater to my requirements," the lady said. "I have long been in need of more vigorous exercise."

A gleam came into the good squire's eyes when the lady announced that fact. "I believe I can help you with that ambition, my dear madam."

So saying, he swept up her skirts, finding the lady, having anticipated his visit, had little more than a hooped petticoat and a shift between her decency and her total exposure to the squire's appreciative eyes. "My word, madam, you have spent a long time without a man," he said, gratefully fingering her slit, which had gathered copious moisture to guide his way. Not that he needed such guidance, his experience having given him much knowledge in the matter of women and what they required.

"I'm a respectable woman, sir, and I do not lift my petticoats for a man unless I can also enjoy his company out of the bedroom. I have a reputation to consider."

The squire glanced up from his absorbing pursuit. "I hope I have not sullied your reputation. I would not wish to damage what you have taken so long to develop." But he was gratified by the widow's words and appreciated her welcome.

Taking some of her welcome, he tasted it and found it good. Having done so, he hungered for more and bent his head to her welcoming amplitude. At the first application of his tongue, the lady shuddered and begged him not to stop this side of Christmas. While he doubted he could accomplish that feat, being comparable to the marathon races accomplished by the ancient Greeks, he assured himself that he was capable of achieving the lady's good favour.

Mr Allworthy was proved correct in his assumptions, and applied himself assiduously to his self-imposed task, reflecting that he had not tasted a woman in a considerable time, being too taken up with matters of work and his duties in the country. A clean, respectable woman could produce a nectar a man could appreciate, even incorporate into his daily absorption, and Mrs Dickinson proved extremely generous in her offering, as she was in every aspect of her life.

Mr Allworthy tasted, and found good enough to continue until the lady's screams and gratified murmurs gave him permission to expose his desire for her, which he did without further discussion.

His rod proving adequate to the occasion, he plunged deep inside her, mingling their essences with a satisfaction that nearly overcame his vow to bring her to the gates of heaven more than once. Burying his face in her breasts, which she generously gathered in her own hands to offer him, he thought it only good manners to accept and make himself at home in her warm welcome.

His roaring was enough to provide entertainment for the populace passing outside, but they remained hidden to the world at large, as Mrs Dickinson had received him in her first floor salon, using the ground floor of her snug house mainly for business. He had completely omitted to take the servants into his consideration, but fortunately the lady was a good mistress, and he would also see they did not go out of pocket.

Plunging inside the lady's sweet quim, he did not ask for permission, taking the lady's sighs as abundant invitation. Only then did the good squire realise how much he had imperilled his health by leaving such exercise too long, for he had a strong belief in the power of good fresh country air and vigorous exercise to prolong a man's health and happiness.

The lady seemed of similar mind, because she applied herself to the course of physical prowess with great enthusiasm and abandon, having a mind to contest the squire's ability to keep his course for more than a short span of time.

Indeed, in a matter of moments, the squire gave a great bellow and flooded the lady with all the gratitude she might have wished for, except that her sopha might not be the best place for such action, because it squeaked and groaned with every thrust, accompanying their already loud serenade with a different counterpoint.

They lay, panting and laughing, the lady a willing participant for a second course, once the squire had regained his senses and control over his respiratory faculties.

With such activity, and the business that had drawn him to the city, the squire was well content, but as time passed he hankered for his home, and having satisfied the lady and himself on numerous occasions, in and out of bed, he bade her a lingering farewell and commanded his horse to be brought to the door. In fact, he was looking forward to a period of peace and tranquillity, without the need to service a woman before he could get some rest, because the lady's enthusiasm for the task occasionally outweighed his willingness to give it.

* * * *

He came to his house very late in the evening, and after a short supper with his sister, retired much fatigued to his chamber. Here, having spent some minutes on his knees — a custom which he never broke through on any account — he was preparing to step into bed, when, upon opening the bedclothes, to his great surprise he beheld an infant, wrapped up in some coarse linen, in a sweet and profound sleep, between his sheets.

He stood some time lost in astonishment at this sight, but, as good nature had always the ascendant in his mind, he soon began to be touched with sentiments of compassion for the little wretch before him. He then rang his bell, and ordered an elderly woman-servant to rise immediately, and come to him, and in the meantime was so eager in contemplating the beauty of innocence, appearing in those lively colours with which infancy and sleep always display it, that his thoughts were too much engaged to reflect that he was in his shirt when the matron came in.

She had indeed given her master sufficient time to dress himself, for out of respect to him, and regard to decency, she had spent many minutes in adjusting her hair at the looking-glass, notwithstanding all the hurry in which she had been summoned by the servant, and though her master, for aught she knew, lay expiring in an apoplexy, or in some other fit. She was not to know that the squire had already satisfied his carnal appetites for some time to come, or that he made a point of never taking advantage of those who worked for him, considering it a pastime of his betters, or perhaps of those people with little care to what their neighbours thought of their conduct.

It will not be wondered at that a creature who had so strict a regard to decency in her own person, should be shocked at the least deviation from it in another. She therefore no sooner opened the door, and saw her master standing by the bedside in his shirt, with a candle in his hand, than she started back in a most terrible fright. She might perhaps have swooned away, had he not now recollected his being undressed, and put an end to her terrors by desiring her to stay without the door till he had thrown some clothes over his back, and was become incapable of shocking the pure eyes of Mrs Deborah Wilkins, who, though in the fifty-second year of her age, vowed she had never beheld a man without his coat. Sneerers and profane wits may perhaps laugh at her first fright, yet my graver reader, when he considers the time of night, the summons from her bed, and the situation in which she found her master, will highly justify and applaud her conduct, unless the prudence which must be supposed to attend maidens at that period of life at which Mrs Deborah had arrived, should a little lessen his admiration.

When Mrs Deborah returned into the room, and was acquainted by her master with the finding the little infant, her consternation was rather greater than his had been. Nor could she refrain from crying out, with great horror of accent as well as look, "My good sir! What's to be done?"

Mr Allworthy answered, she must take care of the child that evening, and in the morning he would give orders to provide it a nurse.

"Yes, sir," said she, "and I hope your worship will send out your warrant to take up the hussy its mother, for she must be one of the neighbourhood, and I should be glad to see her committed to Bridewell, and whipped at the cart's tail. Indeed, such wicked sluts cannot be too severely punished. I'll warrant 'tis not her first, by her impudence in laying it to your worship."

"In laying it to me, Deborah!" answered Allworthy. "I can't think she hath any such design. I suppose she hath only taken this method to provide for her child, and truly I am glad she hath not done worse."

"I don't know what is worse," cries Deborah, "than for such wicked strumpets to lay their sins at honest men's doors, and though your worship knows your own innocence, yet the world is censorious. It hath been many an honest man's hap to pass for the father of children he never begot, and if your worship should provide for the child, it may make the people the apter to believe. Besides, why should your worship provide for what the parish is obliged to maintain? For my own part, if it was an honest man's child, indeed – but for my own part, it goes against me to touch these misbegotten wretches, whom I don't look upon as my fellow-creatures. Faugh! How it stinks! It doth not smell like a Christian. If I might be so bold to give my advice, I would have it put in a basket, and sent out and laid at the churchwarden's door. It is a good night, only a little rainy and windy, and if it was well wrapped up, and put in a warm basket, it is two to one but it lives till it is found in the morning. But if it should not, we have discharged our duty in taking proper care of it, and it is, perhaps, better for such creatures to die in a state of innocence, than to grow up and imitate their mothers – for nothing better can be expected of them."

There were some strokes in this speech which perhaps would have offended Mr Allworthy, had he strictly attended to it, but he had now got one of his fingers into the infant's hand, which, by its gentle pressure, seeming to implore his assistance, had certainly out-pleaded the eloquence of Mrs Deborah, had it been ten times greater than it was. He now gave

Mrs Deborah positive orders to take the child to her own bed, and to call up a maid-servant to provide it pap, and other things, against it waked. He likewise ordered that proper clothes should be procured for it early in the morning, and that it should be brought to himself as soon as he was stirring.

Such was the discernment of Mrs Wilkins, and such the respect she bore her master, under whom she enjoyed a most excellent place, that her scruples gave way to his peremptory commands. And she took the child under her arms, without any apparent disgust at the illegality of its birth, and declaring it was a sweet little infant, walked off with it to her own chamber.

Allworthy here betook himself to those pleasing slumbers which a heart that hungers after goodness is apt to enjoy when thoroughly satisfied. As these are possibly sweeter than what are occasioned by any other hearty meal, I should take more pains to display them to the reader, if I knew any air to recommend him to for the procuring such an appetite.

Chapter Four

The reader's neck brought into danger by a description, his escape, and the great condescension of Miss Bridget Allworthy

The Gothic style of building could produce nothing nobler than Mr Allworthy's house. There was an air of grandeur in it that struck you with awe, and rivalled the beauties of the best Grecian architecture, and it was as commodious within as venerable without.

It stood on the south-east side of a hill, but nearer the bottom than the top of it, so as to be sheltered from the north-east by a grove of old oaks which rose above it in a gradual ascent of near half a mile, and yet high enough to enjoy a most charming prospect of the valley beneath.

In the midst of the grove was a fine lawn, sloping down towards the house. Near the summit rose a plentiful spring, gushing out of a rock covered with firs, and forming a constant cascade of about thirty feet, not carried down a regular flight of steps, but tumbling in a natural fall over the broken and mossy stones till it came to the bottom of the rock, then running off in a pebbly channel, that with many lesser falls winded along, till it fell into a lake at the foot of the hill, about a quarter of a mile below the house on the south side, and which was seen from every room in the front. Out of this lake, which filled the centre of a beautiful plain, embellished with groups of beeches and elms, and fed with sheep, issued a river, that for several miles was seen to meander through an amazing variety of meadows and woods till it emptied itself into the sea, with a large arm of which, and an island beyond it, the prospect was closed.

On the right of this valley opened another of less extent, adorned with several villages, and terminated by one of the towers of an old ruined abbey, grown over with ivy, and part of the front, which remained still entire.

The left-hand scene presented the view of a very fine park, composed of very unequal ground, and agreeably varied with all the diversity that hills, lawns, wood and water, laid out with admirable taste, but owing less to art than to nature, could give. Beyond this, the country gradually rose into a ridge of wild mountains, the tops of which were above the clouds.

It was now the middle of May, and the morning was remarkably serene, when Mr Allworthy walked forth on the terrace, where the dawn opened every minute that lovely prospect we have before described to his eye. Now, having sent forth streams of light, which ascended the blue firmament before him, as harbingers preceding his pomp, in the full blaze of his majesty rose the sun, than which one object alone in this lower creation could be more glorious, and that

Mr Allworthy himself presented—a human being replete with benevolence, meditating in what manner he might render himself most acceptable to his Creator, by doing most good to his creatures.

Reader, take care. I have unadvisedly led thee to the top of as high a hill as Mr Allworthy's, and how to get thee down without breaking thy neck, I do not well know. However, let us e'en venture to slide down together, for Miss Bridget rings her bell, and Mr Allworthy is summoned to breakfast, where I must attend, and if you please, shall be glad of your company.

The usual compliments having passed between Mr Allworthy and Miss Bridget, and the tea being poured out, he summoned Mrs Wilkins, and told his sister he had a present for her, for which she thanked him— imagining, I suppose, it had been a gown, or some ornament for her person. Indeed, he very often made her such presents, and she, in complacence to him, spent much time in adorning herself. I say in complacence to him, because she always expressed the greatest contempt for dress, and for those ladies who made it their study.

But if such was her expectation, how was she disappointed when Mrs Wilkins, according to the order she had received from her master, produced the little infant? Great surprises, as hath been observed, are apt to be silent, and so was Miss Bridget, till her brother began, and told her the whole story, which, as the reader knows it already, we shall not repeat.

Miss Bridget had always expressed so great a regard for what the ladies are pleased to call virtue, and had herself maintained such a severity of character, that it was expected, especially by Wilkins, that she would have vented much bitterness on this occasion, and would have voted for sending the child, as a kind of noxious animal, immediately out of the house. But, on the contrary, she rather took the good-natured side of the question, intimated some compassion for the helpless little creature, and commended her brother's charity in what he had done.

Perhaps the reader may account for this behaviour from her condescension to Mr Allworthy, when we have informed him that the good man had ended his narrative with owning a resolution to take care of the child, and to breed him up as his own. For, to acknowledge the truth, she was always ready to oblige her brother, and very seldom, if ever, contradicted his sentiments. She would, indeed, sometimes make a few observations, as that men were headstrong, and must have their own way, and would wish she had been blessed with an independent fortune. But these were always vented in a low voice, and at the most amounted only to what is called muttering.

However, what she withheld from the infant, she bestowed with the utmost profuseness on the poor unknown mother, whom she called an impudent slut, a wanton hussy, an audacious harlot, a wicked jade, a vile strumpet, with every other appellation with which the tongue of virtue never fails to lash those who bring a disgrace on the sex.

A consultation was now entered into how to proceed in order to discover the mother. A scrutiny was first made into the characters of the female servants of the house, who were all acquitted by Mrs Wilkins, and with apparent merit. For she had collected them herself, and perhaps it would be difficult to find such another set of scarecrows.

The next step was to examine among the inhabitants of the parish, and this was referred to Mrs Wilkins, who was to enquire with all imaginable diligence, and to make her report in the afternoon.

Matters being thus settled, Mr Allworthy withdrew to his study, as was his custom, and left the child to his sister, who, at his desire, had undertaken the care of it. He deemed it highly unlikely that anyone would be found to claim the child, and informed anyone who cared to ask that he had no notion how the infant had come to take up residence in his bed, but felt obliged to give charity to a poor, unfortunate being unable to care for itself.

Chapter Five

Containing a few common matters, with a very uncommon observation upon them

When her master was departed, Mrs Deborah stood silent, expecting her cue from Miss Bridget. As to what had passed before her master, the prudent housekeeper by no means relied upon it, as she had often known the sentiments of the lady in her brother's absence to differ greatly from those which she had expressed in his presence.

Miss Bridget did not, however, suffer her to continue long in this doubtful situation. For having looked some time earnestly at the child, as it lay asleep in the lap of Mrs Deborah, the good lady could not forbear giving it a hearty kiss, at the same time declaring herself wonderfully pleased with its beauty and innocence. Mrs Deborah no sooner observed this than she fell to squeezing and kissing, with as great raptures as sometimes inspire the sage dame of forty and five towards a youthful and vigorous bridegroom, crying out, in a shrill voice, "O, the dear little creature! The dear, sweet, pretty creature! Well, I vow it is as fine a boy as ever was seen!"

These exclamations continued till they were interrupted by the lady, who now proceeded to execute the commission given her by her brother, and gave orders for providing all necessaries for the child, appointing a very good room in the house for his nursery. Her orders were indeed so liberal, that, had it been a child of her own, she could not have exceeded them. But, lest the virtuous reader may condemn her for showing too great regard to a base-born infant, to which all charity is condemned by law as irreligious, we think proper to observe that she concluded the whole with saying, since it was her brother's whim to adopt the little brat, she supposed little master must be treated with great tenderness. For her part, she could not help thinking it was an encouragement to vice. But she knew too much of the obstinacy of mankind to oppose any of their ridiculous humours.

Reflection on the part of many of Mrs Deborah's many acquaintances may have indicated relief that throwing her energies into the welfare of the child rather than the pleasures of the table appeared to the benefit of her form and her complexion.

With considerations of this nature Miss Bridget usually, as has been hinted, accompanied every act of compliance with her brother's inclinations. And surely nothing could more contribute to heighten the merit of this compliance than a declaration that she knew, at the same time, the folly and unreasonableness of those inclinations to which she submitted. Tacit obedience implies no force upon the will, and consequently may be easily, and without any pains, preserved. But when a wife, a child, a relation, or a friend, performs what we desire, with grumbling and reluctance, with expressions of dislike and dissatisfaction, the manifest difficulty which they undergo must greatly enhance the obligation.

As this is one of those deep observations which very few readers can be supposed capable of making themselves, I have thought proper to lend them my assistance, but this is a favour rarely to be expected in the course of my work. Indeed, I shall seldom or never so indulge him, unless in such instances as this, where nothing but the inspiration with which we writers are gifted, can possibly enable anyone to make the discovery.

Chapter Six

Mrs Deborah is introduced into the parish with a simile. A short account of Jenny Jones, with the difficulties and discouragements which may attend young women in the pursuit of learning

Mrs Deborah, having disposed of the child according to the will of her master, now prepared to visit those habitations which were supposed to conceal its mother.

Not otherwise than when a kite, tremendous bird, is beheld by the feathered generation soaring aloft, and hovering over their heads, the amorous dove, and every innocent little bird, spread wide the alarm, and fly trembling to their hiding-places. He proudly beats the air, conscious of his dignity, and meditates intended mischief.

So when the approach of Mrs Deborah was proclaimed through the street, all the inhabitants ran trembling into their houses, each matron dreading lest the visit should fall to her lot. She with stately steps proudly advances over the field. Aloft she bears her towering head, filled with conceit of her own pre-eminence, and schemes to effect her intended discovery.

The sagacious reader will not from this simile imagine these poor people had any apprehension of the design with which Mrs Wilkins was now coming towards them. But as the great beauty of the simile may possibly sleep these hundred years, till some future commentator shall take this work in hand, I think proper to lend the reader a little assistance in this place.

It is my intention, therefore, to signify, that, as it is the nature of a kite to devour little birds, so is it the nature of such persons as Mrs Wilkins to insult and tyrannise over little people. This being indeed the means which they use to recompense to themselves their extreme servility and condescension to their superiors. For nothing can be more reasonable, than that slaves and flatterers should exact the same taxes on all below them, which they themselves pay to all above them.

Whenever Mrs Deborah had occasion to exert any extraordinary condescension to Miss Bridget, and by that means had a little soured her natural disposition, it was usual with her to walk forth among these people, in order to refine her temper, by venting, and as it were, purging off all ill humours. On which account she was by no means a welcome visitant. To say the truth, she was universally dreaded and hated by them all.

On her arrival in this place, she went immediately to the habitation of an elderly matron, to whom, as this matron had the good fortune to resemble herself in the comeliness of her person, as well as in her age, she had generally been more favourable than to any of the rest. To this woman she imparted what had happened, and the design upon which she was come thither that morning. These two began presently to scrutinise the characters of the several young girls who lived in any of those houses, and at last fixed their strongest suspicion on one Jenny Jones, who, they both agreed, was the likeliest person to have committed this fact.

This Jenny Jones was no very comely girl, either in her face or person, but nature had somewhat compensated the want of beauty with what is generally more esteemed by those ladies whose judgement is arrived at years of perfect maturity, for she had given her a very uncommon share of understanding. This gift Jenny had a good deal improved by erudition. She had lived several years a servant with a schoolmaster, who, discovering a great quickness of parts in the girl, and an extraordinary desire of learning—for every leisure hour she was always found reading in the books of the scholars—had the good-nature, or folly—just as the reader pleases to call it—to instruct her so far, that she obtained a competent skill in the Latin language, and was, perhaps, as good a scholar as most of the young men of quality of the age. This advantage, however, like most others of an extraordinary kind, was attended with some small inconveniences. For as it is not to be wondered at, that a young woman so well accomplished should have little relish for the society of those whom fortune had made her equals, but whom education had rendered so much her inferiors. So is it matter of no greater astonishment, that this superiority in Jenny, together with that behaviour which is its certain consequence, should produce among the rest some little envy and ill-will towards her. And these had, perhaps, secretly burnt in the bosoms of her neighbours ever since her return from her service.

Their envy did not, however, display itself openly, till poor Jenny, to the surprise of everybody, and to the vexation of all the young women in these parts, had publicly shone forth on a Sunday in a new silk gown, with a laced cap, and other proper appendages to these.

The flame, which had before lain in embryo, now burst forth. Jenny had, by her learning, increased her own pride, which none of her neighbours were kind enough to feed with the honour she seemed to demand. And now, instead of respect and adoration, she gained nothing but hatred and abuse by her finery. The whole parish declared she could not come honestly by such things, and parents, instead of wishing their daughters the same, felicitated themselves that their children had them not.

Hence, perhaps, it was, that the good woman first mentioned the name of this poor girl to Mrs Wilkins. But there was another circumstance that confirmed the latter in her suspicion, for Jenny had lately been often at Mr Allworthy's house. She had officiated as nurse to Miss Bridget, in a violent fit of illness, and had sat up many nights with that lady. Besides which, she had been seen there the very day before Mr Allworthy's return, by Mrs Wilkins herself, though that sagacious person had not at first conceived any suspicion of her on that account. For, as she herself said, she had always esteemed Jenny as a very sober girl—though indeed she knew very little of her—and had rather suspected some of those wanton trollops, who gave themselves airs, because, forsooth, they thought themselves handsome.

Jenny was now summoned to appear in person before Mrs Deborah, which she immediately did. When Mrs Deborah, putting on the gravity of a judge, with somewhat more than his austerity, began an oration with the words, "You audacious strumpet!" in which she proceeded rather to pass sentence on the prisoner than to accuse her.

Though Mrs Deborah was fully satisfied of the guilt of Jenny, from the reasons above shown, it is possible Mr Allworthy might have required some stronger evidence to have convicted her. But she saved her accusers any such trouble, by freely confessing the whole fact with which she was charged.

This confession, though delivered rather in terms of contrition, as it appeared, did not at all mollify Mrs Deborah, who now pronounced a second judgement against her, in more opprobrious language than before. Nor had it any better success with the bystanders, who were now grown very numerous. Many of them cried out, they thought what madam's silk gown would end in, others spoke sarcastically of her learning. Not a single female was present but found some means of expressing her abhorrence of poor Jenny, who bore all very patiently, except the malice of one woman, who reflected upon her person, and tossing up her nose, said, "The man must have a good stomach who would give silk gowns for such sort of trumpery!" Jenny replied to this with a bitterness which might have surprised a judicious person, who had observed the tranquillity with which she bore all the affronts to her chastity. But her patience was perhaps tired out, for this is a virtue which is very apt to be fatigued by exercise.

Mrs Deborah, having succeeded beyond her hopes in her enquiry, returned with much triumph, and at the appointed hour, made a faithful report to Mr Allworthy, who was much surprised at the relation. For he had heard of the extraordinary parts and improvements of this girl, whom he intended to have given in marriage, together with a small living, to a neighbouring curate.

His interest may have extended to the hope that a small, discreet arrangement could have benefited all parties concerned, but his resolve to remain chaste and beyond reproach in his own county prevailed and nothing came of his proposal. At least, he never admitted to any such ambitions when Jenny bewailed his lack of interest in her mind, rather, his fascination with her comely form. The squire was never a man to indulge his appetites with anyone unwilling to receive them, so, relieved by her response and her moral character, he left her alone and had nothing but kind words for her and anyone who spoke of her. His concern, therefore, on this occasion, was at least equal to the satisfaction which appeared in Mrs Deborah, and to many readers may seem much more reasonable.

Miss Bridget blessed herself, and said, for her part, she should never hereafter entertain a good opinion of any woman. For Jenny before this had the happiness of being much in her good graces also.

The prudent housekeeper was again dispatched to bring the unhappy culprit before Mr Allworthy, in order, not as it was hoped by some, and expected by all, to be sent to the house of correction, but to receive wholesome admonition and reproof, which those who relish that kind of instructive writing may peruse in the next chapter.

Chapter Seven

Containing such grave matter, that the reader cannot laugh once through the whole chapter, unless peradventure he should laugh at the author

When Jenny appeared, Mr Allworthy took her into his study, and spoke to her as follows. "You know, child, it is in my power as a magistrate, to punish you very rigorously for what you have done, and you will, perhaps, be the more apt to fear I should execute that power, because you have in a manner laid your sins at my door.

"But, perhaps, this is one reason which hath determined me to act in a milder manner with you. For, as no private resentment should ever influence a magistrate, I will be so far from considering your having deposited the infant in my house as an aggravation of your offence, that I will suppose, in your favour, this to have proceeded from a natural affection to your child, since you might have some hopes to see it thus better provided for than was in the power of yourself, or its wicked father, to provide for it. I should indeed have been highly offended with you had you exposed the little wretch in the manner of some inhuman mothers, who seem no less to have abandoned their humanity, than to have parted with their chastity. It is the other part of your offence, therefore, upon which I intend to admonish you, I mean the violation of your chastity – a crime, however lightly it may be treated by debauched persons, very heinous in itself, and very dreadful in its consequences.

"The heinous nature of this offence must be sufficiently apparent to every Christian, inasmuch as it is committed in defiance of the laws of our religion, and of the express commands of Him who founded that religion.

"And here its consequences may well be argued to be dreadful, for what can be more so, than to incur the divine displeasure, by the breach of the divine commands, and that in an instance against which the highest vengeance is specifically denounced?

"But these things, though too little, I am afraid, regarded, are so plain, that mankind, however they may want to be reminded, can never need information on this head. A hint, therefore, to awaken your sense of this matter, shall suffice. For I would inspire you with repentance, and not drive you to desperation.

"There are other consequences, not indeed so dreadful or replete with horror as this, and yet such, as, if attentively considered, must, one would think, deter all of your sex at least from the commission of this crime.

"For by it you are rendered infamous, and driven, like lepers of old, out of society, at least, from the society of all but wicked and reprobate persons, for no others will associate with you.

"If you have fortunes, you are hereby rendered incapable of enjoying them. If you have none, you are disabled from acquiring any, nay almost of procuring your sustenance, for no persons of character will receive you into their houses. Thus you are often driven by necessity itself into a state of shame and misery, which unavoidably ends in the destruction of both body and soul.

"Can any pleasure compensate these evils? Can any temptation have sophistry and delusion strong enough to persuade you to so simple a bargain? Or can any carnal appetite so overpower your reason, or so totally lay it asleep, as to prevent your flying with affright and terror from a crime which carries such punishment always with it?

"How base and mean must that woman be, how void of that dignity of mind, and decent pride, without which we are not worthy the name of human creatures, who can bear to level herself with the lowest animal, and to sacrifice all that is great and noble in her, all her heavenly part, to an appetite which she hath in common with the vilest branch of the creation! For no woman, sure, will plead the passion of love for an excuse. This would be to own herself the mere tool and bubble of the man.

"Love, however barbarously we may corrupt and pervert its meaning, as it is a laudable, is a rational passion, and can never be violent but when reciprocal. For though the Scripture bids us love our enemies, it means not with that fervent love which we naturally bear towards our friends, much less that we should sacrifice to them our lives, and what ought to be dearer to us, our innocence. Now in what light, but that of an enemy, can a reasonable woman regard the man who solicits her to entail on herself all the misery

I have described to you, and who would purchase to himself a short, trivial, contemptible pleasure, so greatly at her expense! For, by the laws of custom, the whole shame, with all its dreadful consequences, falls entirely upon her.

"Can love, which always seeks the good of its object, attempt to betray a woman into a bargain where she is so greatly to be the loser? If such corrupter, therefore, should have the impudence to pretend a real affection for her, ought not the woman to regard him not only as an enemy, but as the worst of all enemies, a false, designing, treacherous, pretended friend, who intends not only to debauch her body, but her understanding at the same time?"

With tears pouring down her face, Jenny cried out that she begged his pardon, and would not repeat the offence.

Mr Allworthy hung his head. "Indeed, child, I had decided on a different future for you, but you have decided on your own. Please right yourself, for your distress has caused you to lose control of your clothing."

And indeed, to some extent, it had. Jenny, crimson-faced, but with a mischievous edge to her mien, straightened the voluminous fichu that had loosened in her distress, but somehow her efforts only made it looser, and she lost the garment altogether. In bending to retrieve it, her sweetly curved breasts made a concerted effort to escape her tight-laced silk gown, leaving its protection entirely and providing the good squire with evidence of the beauties of a form that had tempted the infant's unknown father to sin.

"Jenny, your sin is great, not only in bearing the child, but in tempting men to forget themselves in pleasure with you. I am forced to punish you for your transgressions, but I will not use the whip, which would deliver blows you would bear the scars of for a lifetime." With a nod of his head, he indicated the horsewhip he kept in his study, which was more usually put to the use its maker intended. However, when he watched Jenny bend over the substantial wood of his desk, her breasts grazing the pad on which he customarily composed his correspondence, if he had not done so before, now he understood the appeals of such a woman. The excitement he had seen in her face before she turned around, at the interest he showed in her display of her form had encouraged him to believe that she would not entirely dislike what he was about to deliver.

For when he raised her skirts to prepare her for the punishment he intended to deliver, the sight that met him, so round, so sweet, undid his intentions to remain stern with her, and he considered setting her up in a snug little cottage.

But that would not do, despite the girl having the roundest and softest arse it had been his pleasure to view. Removing his coat and rolling up his sleeves, the squire listened to her pleas for mercy with understanding and mighty anticipation.

Here, Jenny expressing great concern, Allworthy paused a moment, and then proceeded. "I have talked thus to you, child, not to insult you for what is past and irrevocable, but to caution and strengthen you for the future. Nor should I have taken this trouble, but from some opinion of your good sense, notwithstanding the dreadful slip you have made, and from some hopes of your hearty repentance, which are founded on the openness and sincerity of your confession."

He delivered the first slap with precision and care, allowing his hand to linger on the scene of his punishment. The girl squealed, but he took care that her distress would not outweigh the lesson he was about to give to her.

"If these do not deceive me, I will take care to convey you from this scene of your shame, where you shall, by being unknown, avoid the punishment" — and here, another slap, landing with resounding success on her left cheek—"which, as I have said, is allotted to your crime in this world, and I hope, by repentance, you will avoid the much heavier sentence denounced against it in the other."

Two smacks now, one on each side, giving the girl a pleasingly matching set of handprints. The squire stopped to admire his handiwork, stopping to cup her buttocks to ensure they were not overmarked. For he wished to teach her a lesson, not behave with brutality.

His treatment was having the opposite effect, it seemed, for Jenny widened her stance, and in doing so gave him a glimpse of paradise, which, on this occasion, was pink and gleaming with the natural essence a woman will deliver when in a state of arousal.

Allworthy had no intention of going further, but the enticing sight gave him pause. He tested the girl's cunt, pushing his finger into her snug hole. Jenny was no virgin, that was for sure. The discovery made him determined on his course. With two fingers in her now, he continued to admonish her.

"Be a good girl the rest of your days, and want shall be no motive to your going astray, and believe me, there is more pleasure, even in this world, in an innocent and virtuous life, than in one debauched and vicious."

Having worked her to a state of interest, the squire removed his fingers and tasted them. The girl was ready, he considered it a shame to waste what was so freely offered. He delivered another smack, her cheeks quivering deliciously under the blow, reddening in a way that distracted him from his task.

"As to your child, let no thoughts concerning it molest you. I will provide for it in a better manner than you can ever hope. And now nothing remains but that you inform me who was the wicked man that seduced you, for my anger against him will be much greater than you have experienced on this occasion." Anyone who abandoned such a sweet creature deserved more punishment than he was prepared to give to Jenny.

Jenny slid to the floor, her submission of great interest to the squire. She took care that her skirts did not impede the view he had of her body, offered up to him as gratitude for his merciful treatment of her, and her humble request for forgiveness.

Jenny now lifted her eyes from the ground, and with a modest look and decent voice thus began.

"To know you, sir, and not love your goodness, would be an argument of total want of sense or goodness in anyone. In me it would amount to the highest ingratitude, not to feel, in the most sensible manner, the great degree of goodness you have been pleased to exert on this occasion." As she spoke, the squire raised her, gently, and draped her over a substantially built stool set by the fire. He stepped back to admire his handiwork. Jenny remained in the position he had set her, her arse tipped up for his inspection and her breasts dangling free over the other side of the stool, the tight-lacing of her form creating a pleasing picture. The squire walked around her as she continued her speech, wondering which part of her to begin his true punishment.

"As to my concern for what is past, I know you will spare my blushes the repetition. My future conduct will much better declare my sentiments than any professions I can now make."

Allworthy grasped her nipples, watching the smooth skin become sharp little points under his tugs and nips. This girl preferred a rough lover, he thought. He could only give her a taste, but this, he considered, her transgressions deserved giving her a punishment she would remember. Jenny's voice quivered with emotion. "I beg leave to assure you, sir, that I take your advice much kinder than your generous offer with which you concluded it, for, as you are pleased to say, sir, it is an instance of your opinion of my understanding."

He moved around to her back end and thrusting his fingers in her most intimate orifice, commenced to delivering the spanking she deserved with his other hand. Hardened by hunting and good country living, his hand bore witness in the form of callouses and hard skin that seemed only to increase the flow of liquid bathing his digits.

She gasped and paused while he determined the exact level of her pain, and decided she would suffer in another way. Here, her tears flowing apace, she stopped a few moments, while he prepared himself for her by undoing the fall of his breeches with a greater dispatch than he had donned them a few hours earlier, and then proceeded thus. "Indeed, sir, your kindness overcomes me." He entered her with a mighty thrust, his organ finding its way inside her as if it had been there before. Jenny exclaimed, then moaned in a way that drove the squire to further efforts, holding her breasts in his hands to assist her balance on the stool. Jenny continued gamely with her speech while he ploughed his own path within her. "I will endeavour to deserve this good opinion, for if I have the understanding you are so kindly pleased to allow me, such advice cannot be thrown away upon me." With each "me" he drove hard within her, her voice rising each time. "I *thank* you, sir, heartily, for your intended *kind*ness to my poor *helpless* child—he is innocent, and I *hope* will live to be *grateful* for all the *favours* you shall show him. But now, sir, I *must* on my *knees* entreat you not to *persist"*—here she stopped and cried out, as the slapping of flesh against flesh brought her to temporary oblivion—"in asking me to declare the *father* of my infant."

The squire effectively silenced her then, by increasing the power of his strokes, tweaking and pulling her breasts to a level he would consider, in most women, to be painful, but in Jenny it produced only sighs and moans. He removed one hand from the torment to deliver more blows to her posterior, now plump and red from his attentions. She would bear the marks of his fucking for some time to come, but by the time she left the village for her new life, no signs would remain. He could only hope that any man fortunate to obtain her favours in the future would appreciate the preferences of the girl.

It surprised him that one so young should appreciate the power of a little pain with pleasure, but she undoubtedly did so. Regretfully, he could not keep her by, for such behaviour would inevitably come to the notice of his friends and neighbours, but he would not expose her to such approbation.

His thrusts increased with the heaviness of his hand on her buttocks, and he groaned at the apogee of his pleasure, only remembering to draw out of her and hold his member against the loose tails of his shirt to contain the evidence of his passion at the last moment. He could not give her another mark of shame, or he might find himself the recipient of another mewling infant in his bed.

Jenny put herself to rights and he did the same, neither remarking on what had just occurred until, fully dressed once more, Jenny sank to her knees. "I wish to thank you, master, for your mercy."

He had thought himself spent, but at the words the squire came to full attention once more. Although he had only recently restored himself, he watched her unbutton his breeches and reach inside, loosening the string of his drawers to once again release the principal perpetrator of punishment.

She studied it for a moment, and wet her lips. Squire Allworthy groaned and gripped her head. "If you do not consume what you have in your hand in the next moment, then have the great mercy to restore it to its hiding place, for I have no more resistance to give you."

The girl opened her mouth, showed her tongue, and bent forward, taking him in fully with an expertise that surprised him. Whoever the father of her child was, he'd taught her well.

Jenny teased and played, her tongue an exquisite instrument, until he was forced to take hold of her head and force her down, so that she took him in and then she began to move.

How he could have come to such hardness in so short a time eluded the good squire, but ready he was, and she swallowed him all. He had never known a woman who could lick and suck to such good effect, and within a short space of time she was drawing him up, and he could not remember what he meant to admonish her for, much less what he would do with her once she had confessed all to him.

Her lips, softly surrounding him, gave him a taste of paradise, but then he was giving it back to her, because, with a barely suppressed shout, his essence shot from his body into hers.

She drank him down, every drop, with every evidence of satisfaction, and then leant back on her heels and carefully restored him to respectability, before he stroked her hair and asked, in a gentler tone of voice, "Won't you tell me the father of your infant, so he may be brought to bear the results of his acts?"

Jenny gazed up at him worshipfully. "I promise you *faithfully* you shall one day know, but I am under the most solemn ties and engagements of honour, as well as the most religious vows and protestations, to conceal his name at this time. And I know you too well, to think you would desire I should sacrifice either my honour or my religion."

Mr Allworthy, whom the least mention of those sacred words was sufficient to stagger, hesitated a moment before he replied, and then told her, she had done wrong to enter into such engagements to a villain, but since she had, he could not insist on her breaking them. He said, it was not from a motive of vain curiosity he had inquired, but in order to punish the fellow, at least, that he might not ignorantly confer favours on the undeserving.

As to these points, Jenny satisfied him by the most solemn assurances, that the man was entirely out of his reach, and was neither subject to his power, nor in any probability of becoming an object of his goodness.

The squire was sorry to hear it, and wondered if the man knew what a treasure he had thrown away by abandoning such a passionate woman as Jenny Jones.

The ingenuity of this behaviour and the demonstration of her passion had gained Jenny so much credit with this worthy man, that he easily believed what she told him. For as she had disdained to excuse herself by a lie, and had hazarded his further displeasure in her present situation, rather than she would forfeit her honour or integrity by betraying another, he had but little apprehensions that she would be guilty of falsehood towards himself.

He therefore dismissed her with assurances that he would very soon remove her out of the reach of that obloquy she had incurred, concluding with some additional documents, in which he recommended repentance, saying, "Consider, child, there is one still to reconcile yourself to, whose favour is of much greater importance to you than mine."

Chapter Eight

A dialogue between Mesdames Bridget and Deborah, containing more amusement, but less instruction, than the former

When Mr Allworthy had retired to his study with Jenny Jones, as hath been seen, Miss Bridget, with the good housekeeper, had betaken themselves to a post next adjoining to the said study, whence, through the conveyance of a keyhole, they sucked in at their ears the instructive lecture delivered by Mr Allworthy, together with the answers of Jenny, and indeed every other particular which passed in the last chapter.

To be sure, they learned a very great deal from the informative lesson the good squire delivered, and vowed to keep the details to themselves.

This hole in her brother's study door was indeed as well known to Mrs Bridget, and had been as frequently applied to by her, as the famous hole in the wall was by Thisbe of old. This served to many good purposes. For by such means Mrs Bridget became often acquainted with her brother's inclinations, without giving him the trouble of repeating them to her.

It is true, some inconveniences attended this intercourse, and she had sometimes reason to cry out with Thisbe, in Shakespeare, "O, wicked, wicked wall!" For as Mr Allworthy was a justice of peace, certain things occurred in examinations concerning bastards, and such like, which are apt to give great offence to the chaste ears of virgins, especially when they approach the age of forty, as was the case of Mrs Bridget. However, she had, on such occasions, the advantage of concealing her blushes from the eyes of men, and *de non apparentibus, et non existentibus eadem est ratio* – in English, "when a woman is not seen to blush, she doth not blush at all".

They had rarely seen a demonstration the like of which the squire had shown to Jenny Jones, but they had both lived long and interesting lives, so they were far from shocked. Merely surprised at the invention of the participants.

Both the good women kept strict silence during the whole scene between Mr Allworthy and the girl, but as soon as it was ended, and that gentleman was out of hearing, Mrs Deborah could not help exclaiming against the clemency of her master, and especially against his suffering her to conceal the father of the child, which she swore she would have out of her before the sun set.

At these words Mrs Bridget discomposed her features with a smile, a thing very unusual to her. Not that I would have my reader imagine, that this was one of those wanton smiles which Homer would have you conceive came from Venus, when he calls her the laughter-loving goddess. Nor was it one of those smiles which Lady Seraphina shoots from the stage-box, and which Venus would quit her immortality to be able to equal. No, this was rather one of those smiles which might be supposed to have come from the dimpled cheeks of the august Tisiphone, or from one of the misses, her sisters.

With such a smile then, and with a voice sweet as the evening breeze of Boreas in the pleasant month of November, Mrs Bridget gently reproved the curiosity of Mrs Deborah, a vice with which it seems the latter was too much tainted, and which the former inveighed against with great bitterness, adding, that, among all her faults, she thanked Heaven her enemies could not accuse her of prying into the affairs of other people.

She then proceeded to commend the honour and spirit with which Jenny had acted, if not her absolute probity, which they would speak of another time, when they had more leisure to discuss the finer details of the scene. She said, she could not help agreeing with her brother, that there was some merit in the sincerity of her confession, and in her integrity to her lover — that she had always thought her a very good girl, and doubted not but she had been seduced by some rascal, who had been infinitely more to blame than herself, and very probably had prevailed with her by a promise of marriage, or some other treacherous proceeding.

This behaviour of Mrs Bridget greatly surprised Mrs Deborah, for this well-bred woman seldom opened her lips, either to her master or his sister, till she had first sounded their inclinations, with which her sentiments were always consonant. Here, however, she thought she might have launched forth with safety, and the sagacious reader will not perhaps accuse her of want of sufficient forecast in so doing, but will rather admire with what wonderful celerity she tacked about, when she found herself steering a wrong course.

"Nay, madam," said this able woman, and truly great politician, "I must own I cannot help admiring the girl's spirit, as well as your ladyship. And, as your ladyship says, if she was deceived by some wicked man, the poor wretch is to be pitied. And to be sure, as your ladyship says, the girl hath always appeared like a good, honest, plain girl, and not vain of her face, forsooth, as some wanton hussies in the neighbourhood are."

"You say true, Deborah," said Miss Bridget. "If the girl had been one of those vain trollops, of which we have too many in the parish, I should have condemned my brother for his lenity towards her and his weakness in succumbing to temptation. I saw two farmers' daughters at church, the other day, with bare necks. I protest they shocked me. Church is not the place for displays of flesh, such events should always be conducted in privacy. If wenches will hang out lures for fellows, it is no matter what they suffer. I detest such creatures, and it would be much better for them that their faces had been seamed with the smallpox, but I must confess, I never saw any of this wanton behaviour in poor Jenny. Some artful villain, I am convinced, hath betrayed, nay perhaps forced her, and I pity the poor wretch with all my heart."

Mrs Deborah approved all these sentiments, and the dialogue concluded with a general and bitter invective against beauty, and with many compassionate considerations for all honest plain girls who are deluded by the wicked arts of deceitful men.

Chapter Nine

Containing matters which will surprise the reader

Jenny returned home well pleased with the reception she had met with from Mr Allworthy, whose indulgence to her she industriously made public, if not the more particular matters of the interview, partly perhaps as a sacrifice to her own pride, and partly from the more prudent motive of reconciling her neighbours to her, and silencing their clamours.

But though this latter view, if she indeed had it, may appear reasonable enough, yet the event did not answer her expectation. For when she was convened before the justice, and it was universally apprehended that the house of correction would have been her fate, though some of the young women cried out "It was good enough for her," and diverted themselves with the thoughts of her beating hemp in a silk gown, yet there were many others who began to pity her condition. But when it was known in what manner Mr

Allworthy had behaved and spoken to her, the tide
turned against her. One said, "I'll assure you, madam
hath had good luck." A second cried, "See what it is to
be a favourite!" A third, "Ay, this comes of her
learning."

Every person made some malicious comment or
other on the occasion, and reflected on the partiality of
the justice. But none suspected the passions that ruled
Jenny, that she vowed to conquer. However, she
considered the slight discomfort in sitting down for
the next few days a small price to pay for the mutual
pleasure it had brought herself and the good squire.

The behaviour of these people may appear impolitic
and ungrateful to the reader, who considers the power
and benevolence of Mr Allworthy. But as to his power,
he never used it, and as to his benevolence, he exerted
so much, that he had thereby disobliged all his
neighbours. For it is a secret well known to great men,
that, by conferring an obligation, they do not always
procure a friend, but are certain of creating many
enemies.

Jenny was, however, by the care and goodness of Mr
Allworthy, soon removed out of the reach of reproach,
when malice being no longer able to vent its rage on
her, began to seek another object of its bitterness, and
this was no less than Mr Allworthy, himself, for a
whisper soon went abroad, that he himself was the
father of the foundling child.

This supposition so well reconciled his conduct to
the general opinion, that it met with universal assent,
and the outcry against his lenity soon began to take
another turn, and was changed into an invective
against his cruelty to the poor girl, although Jenny had
never spoken a word about the scene in the study, and
the two witnesses kept their secret to themselves, to

discuss over the comfort of tea. Very grave and good women exclaimed against men who begot children, and then disowned them. Nor were there wanting some, who, after the departure of Jenny, insinuated that she was spirited away with a design too black to be mentioned, and who gave frequent hints that a legal inquiry ought to be made into the whole matter, and that some people should be forced to produce the girl.

These calumnies might have probably produced ill consequences, at the least might have occasioned some trouble, to a person of a more doubtful and suspicious character than Mr Allworthy was blessed with. But in his case they had no such effect, and being heartily despised by him, they served only to afford an innocent amusement to the good gossips of the neighbourhood.

But as we cannot possibly divine what complexion our reader may be of, and as it will be some time before he will hear any more of Jenny, we think proper to give him a very early intimation, that Mr Allworthy was, and will hereafter appear to be, absolutely innocent of any criminal intention whatever. He had indeed committed no other than an error in politics, by tempering justice with mercy, and by refusing to gratify the good-natured disposition of the mob, with an object for their compassion to work on in the person of poor Jenny — whom, in order to pity, they desired to have seen sacrificed to ruin and infamy, by a shameful correction in Bridewell.

So far from complying with this their inclination, by which all hopes of reformation would have been abolished, and even the gate shut against her if her own inclinations should ever hereafter lead her to choose the road of virtue, Mr Allworthy rather chose to encourage the girl to return thither by the only possible means. Too true I am afraid it is, that many women have become abandoned, and have sunk to the last degree of vice, by being unable to retrieve the first slip. This will be, I am afraid, always the case while they remain among their former acquaintance. It was therefore wisely done by Mr Allworthy, to remove Jenny to a place where she might enjoy the pleasure of reputation, after having tasted the ill consequences of losing it.

To this place therefore, wherever it was, we will wish her a good journey, and for the present take leave of her, and of the little foundling her child, having matters of much higher importance to communicate to the reader.

Chapter Ten

The hospitality of Allworthy, with a short sketch of the characters of two brothers, a doctor and a captain, who were entertained by that gentleman

Neither Mr Allworthy's house, nor his heart, were shut against any part of mankind, but they were both more particularly open to men of merit. To say the truth, this was the only house in the kingdom where you was sure to gain a dinner by deserving it.

Above all others, men of genius and learning shared the principal place in his favour, and in these he had much discernment. For though he had missed the advantage of a learned education, yet, being blessed with vast natural abilities, he had so well profited by a vigorous though late application to letters, and by much conversation with men of eminence in this way, that he was himself a very competent judge in most kinds of literature.

It is no wonder that in an age when this kind of merit is so little in fashion, and so slenderly provided for, persons possessed of it should very eagerly flock to a place where they were sure of being received with great complaisance, indeed, where they might enjoy almost the same advantages of a liberal fortune as if they were entitled to it in their own right. Mr Allworthy was not one of those generous persons who are ready most bountifully to bestow meat, drink, and lodging on men of wit and learning, for which they expect no other return but entertainment, instruction, flattery, and subserviency—in a word, that such persons should be enrolled in the number of domestics, without wearing their master's clothes, or receiving wages.

On the contrary, every person in this house was perfect master of his own time. And as he might at his pleasure satisfy all his appetites within the restrictions only of law, virtue, and religion, so he might, if his health required, or his inclination prompted him to temperance, or even to abstinence, absent himself from any meals, or retire from them, whenever he was so disposed, without even a solicitation to the contrary. For, indeed, such solicitations from superiors always savour very strongly of commands. But all here were free from such impertinence, not only those whose company is in all other places esteemed a favour from their equality of fortune, but even those whose indigent circumstances make such an eleemosynary abode convenient to them, and who are therefore less welcome to a great man's table because they stand in need of it.

Among others of this kind was Dr Blifil, a gentleman who had the misfortune of losing the advantage of great talents by the obstinacy of a father, who would breed him to a profession he disliked. In obedience to this obstinacy the doctor had in his youth been obliged to study physic, or rather to say he studied it, for in reality books of this kind were almost the only ones with which he was unacquainted, and unfortunately for him, the doctor was master of almost every other science but that by which he was to get his bread, the consequence of which was, that the doctor at the age of forty had no bread to eat.

Such a person as this was certain to find a welcome at Mr Allworthy's table, to whom misfortunes were ever a recommendation, when they were derived from the folly or villainy of others, and not of the unfortunate person himself. Besides this negative merit, the doctor had one positive recommendation — this was a great appearance of religion. Whether his religion was real, or consisted only in appearance, I shall not presume to say, as I am not possessed of any touchstone which can distinguish the true from the false.

If this part of his character pleased Mr Allworthy, it delighted Miss Bridget. She engaged him in many religious controversies, on which occasions she constantly expressed great satisfaction in the doctor's knowledge, and not much less in the compliments which he frequently bestowed on her own. To say the truth, she had read much English divinity, and had puzzled more than one of the neighbouring curates. Indeed, her conversation was so pure, her looks so sage, and her whole deportment so grave and solemn, that she seemed to deserve the name of saint equally with her namesake, or with any other female in the Roman calendar. Her secret vices were for her eyes only, and purely for the purpose of self-education, for she would not want to go to her husband completely ignorant of the ways of the bedchamber. That would be impolite.

As sympathies of all kinds are apt to beget love, so experience teaches us that none have a more direct tendency this way than those of a religious kind between persons of different sexes. The doctor found himself so agreeable to Miss Bridget, that he now began to lament an unfortunate accident which had happened to him about ten years before, namely, his marriage with another woman, who was not only still alive, but, what was worse, known to be so by Mr Allworthy. This was a fatal bar to that happiness which he otherwise saw sufficient probability of obtaining with this young lady, for as to criminal indulgences, he certainly never thought of them. This was owing either to his religion, as is most probable, or to the purity of his passion, which was fixed on those things which matrimony only, and not criminal correspondence, could put him in possession of, or could give him any title to, and a snug little property in the country could serve him well.

He had not long ruminated on these matters, before it occurred to his memory that he had a brother who was under no such unhappy incapacity. This brother he made no doubt would succeed, for he discerned, as he thought, an inclination to marriage in the lady, and the reader perhaps, when he hears the brother's qualifications, will not blame the confidence which he entertained of his success.

This gentleman was about thirty-five years of age. He was of a middle size, and what is called well-built. He had a scar on his forehead, which did not so much injure his beauty as it denoted his valour—for he was a half-pay officer. He had good teeth, and something affable, when he pleased, in his smile, though naturally his countenance, as well as his air and voice, had much of roughness in it. Yet he could at any time deposit this, and appear all gentleness and good humour. He was not ungenteel, nor entirely devoid of wit, and in his youth had abounded in sprightliness, which, though he had lately put on a more serious character, he could, when he pleased, resume.

He had, as well as the doctor, an academic education, for his father had, with the same paternal authority we have mentioned before, decreed him for holy orders, but as the old gentleman died before he was ordained, he chose the church military, and preferred the king's commission to the bishop's.

He had purchased the post of lieutenant of dragoons, and afterwards came to be a captain, but having quarrelled with his colonel, was by his interest obliged to sell, from which time he had entirely rusticated himself, had betaken himself to studying the Scriptures, and was not a little suspected of an inclination to methodism.

It seemed, therefore, not unlikely that such a person should succeed with a lady of so saint-like a disposition, and whose inclinations were no otherwise engaged than to the marriage state in general. But why the doctor, who certainly had no great friendship for his brother, should for his sake think of making so ill a return to the hospitality of Allworthy, is a matter not so easy to be accounted for.

Is it that some natures delight in evil, as others are thought to delight in virtue? Or is there a pleasure in being accessory to a theft when we cannot commit it ourselves? Or lastly, which experience seems to make probable, have we a satisfaction in aggrandising our families, even though we have not the least love or respect for them?

Whether any of these motives operated on the doctor, we will not determine, but so the fact was. He sent for his brother, and easily found means to introduce him at Allworthy's as a person who intended only a short visit to himself.

The captain had not been in the house a week before the doctor had reason to felicitate himself on his discernment. The captain was indeed as great a master of the art of love as Ovid was formerly. He had besides received proper hints from his brother, which he failed not to improve to the best advantage.

Chapter Eleven

Containing many rules, and some examples, concerning falling in love, descriptions of beauty, and other more prudential inducements to matrimony

It hath been observed, by wise men or women, I forget which, that all persons are doomed to be in love once in their lives. No particular season is, as I remember, assigned for this, but the age at which Miss Bridget was arrived, seems to me as proper a period as any to be fixed on for this purpose. It often, indeed, happens much earlier, but when it doth not, I have observed it seldom or never fails about this time. Moreover, we may remark that at this season love is of a more serious and steady nature than what sometimes shows itself in the younger parts of life. The love of girls is uncertain, capricious, and so foolish that we cannot always discover what the young lady would be at—nay, it may almost be doubted whether she always knows this herself.

Now we are never at a loss to discern this in women about forty, for as such grave, serious, and experienced ladies well know their own meaning, so it is always very easy for a man of the least sagacity to discover it with the utmost certainty.

Miss Bridget is an example of all these observations. She had not been many times in the captain's company before she was seized with this passion. Nor did she go pining and moping about the house, like a puny, foolish girl, ignorant of her distemper. She felt, she knew, and she enjoyed, the pleasing sensation, of which, as she was certain it was not only innocent but laudable, she was neither afraid nor ashamed. She applied herself assiduously to those books she had obtained over the years, in order to obtain the greatest knowledge, so her studies of great sermons occasionally had a smaller volume secreted in its voluminous size, and she found the illustrations most instructive.

In most of them, the lady was entertaining a gentleman with shift awry and frequently in undress, but Miss Bridget assumed she could both retain her modesty and titillate the man, who would, naturally, be her husband.

And to say the truth, there is, in all points, great difference between the reasonable passion which women at this age conceive towards men, and the idle and childish liking of a girl to a boy, which is often fixed on the outside only, and on things of little value and no duration—as on cherry-cheeks, small, lily-white hands, sloe-black eyes, flowing locks, downy chins, dapper shapes—nay, sometimes on charms more worthless than these, and less the party's own. Such are the outward ornaments of the person, for which men are beholden to the tailor, the laceman, the periwig-maker, the hatter, and the milliner, and not to nature. Such a passion girls may well be ashamed, as they generally are, to own either to themselves or others.

The love of Miss Bridget was of another kind. The captain owed nothing to any of these fop-makers in his dress, nor was his person much more beholden to nature. Both his dress and person were such as, had they appeared in an assembly or a drawing-room, would have been the contempt and ridicule of all the fine ladies there. The former of these was indeed neat, but plain, coarse, ill-fancied, and out of fashion. As for the latter, we have expressly described it above. So far was the skin on his cheeks from being cherry-coloured, that you could not discern what the natural colour of his cheeks was, they being totally overgrown by a black beard, which ascended to his eyes. His shape and limbs were indeed exactly proportioned, but so large that they denoted the strength rather of a ploughman than any other. His shoulders were broad beyond all size, and the calves of his legs larger than those of a common chairman. In short, his whole person wanted all that elegance and beauty which is the very reverse of clumsy strength, and which so agreeably sets off most of our fine gentlemen, being partly owing to the high blood of their ancestors, viz., blood made of rich sauces and generous wines, and partly to an early town education.

Though Miss Bridget was a woman of the greatest delicacy of taste, yet such were the charms of the captain's conversation, that she totally overlooked the defects of his person. She imagined, and perhaps very wisely, that she should enjoy more agreeable minutes with the captain than with a much prettier fellow, and forewent the consideration of pleasing her eyes, in order to procure herself much more solid satisfaction.

Indeed, she began to imagine that his more powerful form would suit her much better, as she required a man of strength to undertake some trifling duties around the house such as would take him into neglected and overlooked rooms, some of which had not been opened for years.

The captain no sooner perceived the passion of Miss Bridget, in which discovery he was very quick-sighted, than he faithfully returned it. The lady, no more than her lover, was remarkable for beauty. I would attempt to draw her picture, but that is done already by a more able master, Mr Hogarth himself, to whom she sat many years ago, and hath been lately exhibited by that gentleman in his print of a winter's morning, of which she was no improper emblem, and may be seen walking—for walk she doth in the print—to Covent Garden church, with a starved foot-boy behind carrying her prayer-book.

The captain likewise very wisely preferred the more solid enjoyments he expected with this lady, to the fleeting charms of person. He was one of those wise men who regard beauty in the other sex as a very worthless and superficial qualification, or, to speak more truly, who rather choose to possess every convenience of life with an ugly woman, than a handsome one without any of those conveniences. And having a very good appetite, and but little nicety, he fancied he should play his part very well at the matrimonial banquet, without the sauce of beauty.

To deal plainly with the reader, the captain, ever since his arrival, at least from the moment his brother had proposed the match to him, long before he had discovered any flattering symptoms in Miss Bridget, had been greatly enamoured — that is to say, of Mr Allworthy's house and gardens, and of his lands, tenements, and hereditaments, of all which the captain was so passionately fond, that he would most probably have contracted marriage with them, had he been obliged to have taken the witch of Endor into the bargain.

As Mr Allworthy, therefore, had declared to the doctor that he never intended to take a second wife, as his sister was his nearest relation, and as the doctor had fished out that his intentions were to make any child of hers his heir, which indeed the law, without his interposition, would have done for him, the doctor and his brother thought it an act of benevolence to give being to a human creature, who would be so plentifully provided with the most essential means of happiness. The whole thoughts, therefore, of both the brothers were how to engage the affections of this amiable lady.

But fortune, who is a tender parent, and often doth more for her favourite offspring than either they deserve or wish, had been so industrious for the captain, that whilst he was laying schemes to execute his purpose, the lady conceived the same desires with himself, and was on her side contriving how to give the captain proper encouragement, without appearing too forward, for she was a strict observer of all rules of decorum. In this, however, she easily succeeded, for as the captain was always on the look-out, no glance, gesture, or word escaped him.

The satisfaction which the captain received from the kind behaviour of Miss Bridget, was not a little abated by his apprehensions of Mr Allworthy, for, notwithstanding his disinterested professions, the captain imagined he would, when he came to act, follow the example of the rest of the world, and refuse his consent to a match so disadvantageous, in point of interest, to his sister. From what oracle he received this opinion, I shall leave the reader to determine. But however he came by it, it strangely perplexed him how to regulate his conduct so as at once to convey his affection to the lady, and to conceal it from her brother. He at length resolved to take all private opportunities of making his addresses, but in the presence of Mr Allworthy to be as reserved and as much upon his guard as was possible, and this conduct was highly approved by the brother.

He soon found means to make his addresses, in express terms, to his mistress, from whom he received an answer in the proper form, viz. the answer which was first made some thousands of years ago, and which hath been handed down by tradition from mother to daughter ever since. If I was to translate this into Latin, I should render it by these two words, *nolo episcopari*, a phrase likewise of immemorial use on another occasion.

On the first occasion, she required him to help unhang a painting from the wall of the winter parlour, which was not often used at this time of year. The captain, not unwilling, accompanied Miss Bridget to the room, where, disdaining the use of servants, who she declared had better things to do with their time, he strode to the wall and stared at the painting, so obscured by time as to be almost unviewable.

He took the lady's word that the work was a particularly fine example of a Dutch landscape, much admired in the previous century, and reached up to hook it down. The painting was not a large one, and the captain did not need the services of the stepladder which someone had thoughtfully placed in the room, but he took great care bringing down the work, which had, in the fashionable style, been attached by a long string to the top rail, a string which must once have been gold, but had faded to a pale colour, attesting to the ancient nature of the painting in question.

The task accomplished, Miss Bridget asked him if the view from this window was not a fine one. The captain, with the vision that the view might one day belong to him readily agreed, and stood next to her, so that when she stumbled, he handily rescued her from an ignominious fate on the floor, much as Vulcan rescued Venus from tumbling into the pit.

Miss Bridget appeared in no hurry to escape his clutches, which, while not a fine, respectful hold, seemed to appeal to her in another way, for she immediately turned up her face for his kiss, which was not long in appearing, the captain pressing his lips to her like a starving dog falling upon a disregarded morsel.

Not averse to such rough handling, Miss Bridget returned the kiss in full measure, and even allowed her suitor to rescue her fine bosom from its casing of fichu and corset, admiring the pearl clasp he had to perforce unfasten to reach the treasures beneath.

Barely touched by any man before him, the captain fell to admiring the soft skin and sweet pink and he became overcome by a desire to taste what he had so lately uncovered.

The lady gave a most unladylike groan, and allowed the liberties which properly should belong to one person alone, and since she had not yet acquired the services of a husband, the captain would, perforce, suffice.

"Oh, Miss Bridget, you have such a beautiful form you would tempt a saint to sin!" the captain exclaimed, much to the satisfaction of the lady, who gripped the back of his head, though whether to bring him closer to his target or to hold herself steady, none could tell.

Her utterances of "Oh, sir! Oh, sir!" did not serve to explain the mystery, but when he laid a hand on her skirts and began to haul them up, she broke away, giving a shaky protest. "Sir, I think you forget yourself."

The captain, eager to redress his fault, but pleased with the progress he had made, readily assisted Miss Bridget to restore her person to respectability, although he found himself loath to hand over the pretty brooch he'd rescued for her from where it had tumbled to the floor.

Taking advantage of his position, he handed her the brooch and made the remark, "I would rather be kneeling here before you in supplication for an entirely different matter. Madam, I have become enamoured of you, and I would ask you a question that, if you replied in the negative, I would find it hard to accept."

After puzzling out this rodomontade, Miss Bridget went off into a peal of girlish laughter, one she had cultivated on first leaving the schoolroom and had never amended since.

"Dear sir, while I find your words flattering, I can by no means accept that you wish for such a lifelong attachment after having known me so little time."

The captain prepared himself for a siege, although his preference was for hard-fought, but short battles.

The captain, however he came by his knowledge, perfectly well understood the lady, and very soon after repeated his application with more warmth and earnestness than before, and was again, according to due form, rejected, but as he had increased in the eagerness of his desires, so the lady, with the same propriety, decreased in the violence of her refusal.

Not to tire the reader, by leading him through every scene of this courtship—which, though in the opinion of a certain great author, it is the pleasantest scene of life to the actor, is, perhaps, as dull and tiresome as any whatever to the audience—the captain made his advances in form, the citadel was defended in form, and at length, in proper form, surrendered at discretion.

During this whole time, which filled the space of near a month, the captain preserved great distance of behaviour to his lady in the presence of the brother, and the more he succeeded with her in private, the more reserved was he in public. And as for the lady, she had no sooner secured her lover than she behaved to him before company with the highest degree of indifference, so that Mr Allworthy must have had the insight of the devil—or perhaps some of his worse qualities—to have entertained the least suspicion of what was going forward.

By the occasion of the final assault, Miss Bridget had exhausted excuses to find the captain in a place in the house little frequented, and had suggested a walk in the garden, it being a fine day, and the extensive garden having a few private places where nobody could see them from the house.

She led him to a large oak with wide-spread branches, at the base of which some ancestor had erected a fine, sturdy bench.

No sooner were the two ensconced on the sturdy seat than the captain had his hands on her clothing, and divested her of the impediments that lay between him and the object of his attentions. Soon after he discovered that she wore a gown simply hooked down the front, as the lady had decided against the open gown and stomacher she affected on most days. Easier and simpler to unfasten, and to lay her quivering bosom open to his eyes and his tongue. He tasted the bounties as if he had not eaten for a month, making appreciative sounds as if consuming the most exquisite joint of beef.

This approach did not go amiss with the lady, who sighed and moaned his name. Miss Bridget was mightily pleased with her campaign, and for a military gentleman he had been remarkably easy to lead, but she knew that the time to end it was nigh. She would surrender and allow him to believe he had everything to gain from this alliance and she everything to give.

Consequently, she allowed him liberties she had forbidden before. While he made himself comfortable with her breasts and knew them as well as she did, he had little knowledge of what lay beneath her skirts, although a time or two she had forced herself to be patient and take her lesson from Queen Anne Boleyn, who had made her king wait for five years before surrendering.

Miss Bridget decided that a month would be adequate for her siege, since she had every intention of bringing the courtship to the conclusion desired by both parties, so that when the captain slid his large hand under her skirts, she did little more than increase her sighs and allow her legs to fall open a trifle, as if by nature and not design.

Her reward came soon enough, for he insinuated one finger, and then two into that happy heaven men sometimes call paradise in their more imaginative moments.

The Captain had no such poetical language, and merely praised Miss Bridget for her bravery, assuring her, "Of such mettle are good soldiers made. I have longed to touch your quim, and I find myself enchanted by the quantity of love-juice I find there. Men sometimes taste as well as touch, but at this moment, ma'am, with your permission, I'll introduce another part of my body there."

"Oh, Captain, whatever can you mean?"

"Allow me to teach you the joys of love, my dear."

If her education, although self-taught, had not been so extensive, she would have considered him the most skilful of men. As it was, he released his member from his breeches, and guided her hand to it, inviting her to acquaint himself with its size and form. He was very proud of what he had to show her, but Miss Bridget had seen larger, in the pictures she owned. She might have put that down to the vivid imagination of the artists, had she not observed one or two other pricks in her life, and this one was modest.

Quelling her disappointment, for the size of the rest of her swain had persuaded her that his offering would be generous, she allowed him to mount her. Although the sturdy bench made its presence felt against her back, making her sure she would sustain bruises from the encounter, she suffered his entry and cried out at the appropriate moment.

Although a rough man, the captain treated her gently, at first, praising her once more and assuring her she would enjoy the practice much more as she rehearsed the act. "After all," he said with a whimsical smile, or as whimsical as the man with the mien of a pirate could affect, "Garrick must rehearse for weeks before he is happy with his latest stage creation."

Miss Bridget, who had had the fortune to see Mr Garrick perform at Covent Garden, could attest to that. She could also attest to the Captain's performance being adequate. After a few moments of gentle tuition, the Captain seemed to forget she was there, and it was fortunate that she knew which part of her cleft to agitate with her fingers, because if she had not, she would have received precious little satisfaction from this first encounter. Taking consolation from the Captain's remarks about Garrick, she allowed him to plunge deeply and cry her name in a loud voice as he erupted inside her body. She allowed that, too, although her studies had reminded her that the chance of getting with child were increased that way.

She had already made up her mind to receive his addresses and bring them to a positive outcome, so a child could only be welcome.

So under the branches of the great oak, the matter was decided between them.

Chapter Twelve

Containing what the reader may, perhaps, expect to find in it

In all bargains, whether to fight or to marry, or concerning any other such business, little previous ceremony is required to bring the matter to an issue when both parties are really in earnest. This was the case at present, and in less than a month the captain and his lady were man and wife.

The great concern now was to break the matter to Mr Allworthy, and this was undertaken by the doctor.

One day, then, as Allworthy was walking in his garden, the doctor came to him, and with great gravity of aspect, and all the concern which he could possibly affect in his countenance, said, "I am come, sir, to impart an affair to you of the utmost consequence, but how shall I mention to you what it almost distracts me to think of!" He then launched forth into the most bitter invectives both against men and women, accusing the former of having no attachment but to their interest, and the latter of being so addicted to vicious inclinations that they could never be safely trusted with one of the other sex. "Could I," said he, "sir, have suspected that a lady of such prudence, such judgement, such learning, should indulge so indiscreet a passion! Or could I have imagined that my brother—why do I call him so? He is no longer a brother of mine—"

"Indeed but he is," said Allworthy, "and a brother of mine too."

"Bless me, sir!" said the doctor. "Do you know the shocking affair?"

"Look'ee, Mr Blifil," answered the good man, "it hath been my constant maxim in life to make the best of all matters which happen. My sister, though many years younger than I, is at least old enough to be at the age of discretion. Had he imposed on a child, I should have been more averse to have forgiven him, but a woman upwards of thirty must certainly be supposed to know what will make her most happy. She hath married a gentleman, though perhaps not quite her equal in fortune, and if he hath any perfections in her eye which can make up that deficiency, I see no reason why I should object to her choice of her own happiness, which I, no more than herself, imagine to consist only in immense wealth. I might, perhaps, from the many declarations I have made of complying with almost any proposal, have expected to have been consulted on this occasion, but these matters are of a very delicate nature, and the scruples of modesty, perhaps, are not to be overcome. As to your brother, I have really no anger against him at all. He hath no obligations to me, nor do I think he was under any necessity of asking my consent, since the woman is, as

I have said, *sui juris*, and of a proper age to be entirely answerable only, to herself for her conduct."

The doctor accused Mr Allworthy of too great lenity, repeated his accusations against his brother, and declared that he should never more be brought either to see, or to own him for his relation. He then launched forth into a panegyric on Allworthy's goodness, into the highest encomiums on his friendship, and concluded by saying, he should never forgive his brother for having put the place which he bore in that friendship to a hazard.

Allworthy thus answered. "Had I conceived any displeasure against your brother, I should never have carried that resentment to the innocent, but I assure you I have no such displeasure. Your brother appears to me to be a man of sense and honour. I do not disapprove the taste of my sister, nor will I doubt but that she is equally the object of his inclinations. I have always thought love the only foundation of happiness in a married state, as it can only produce that high and tender friendship which should always be the cement of this union, and in my opinion, all those marriages which are contracted from other motives are greatly criminal. They are a profanation of a most holy ceremony, and generally end in disquiet and misery. For surely we may call it a profanation to convert this most sacred institution into a wicked sacrifice to lust or avarice. And what better can be said of those matches to which men are induced merely by the consideration of a beautiful person, or a great fortune?

"To deny that beauty is an agreeable object to the eye, and even worthy some admiration, would be false and foolish. Beautiful is an epithet often used in Scripture, and always mentioned with honour. It was my own fortune to marry a woman whom the world thought handsome, and I can truly say I liked her the better on that account. But to make this the sole consideration of marriage, to lust after it so violently as to overlook all imperfections for its sake, or to require it so absolutely as to reject and disdain religion, virtue, and sense, which are qualities in their nature of much higher perfection, only because an elegance of person is wanting. This is surely inconsistent, either with a wise man or a good Christian. And it is, perhaps, being too charitable to conclude that such persons mean anything more by their marriage than to please their carnal appetites, for the satisfaction of which, we are taught, it was not ordained.

"In the next place, with respect to fortune. Worldly prudence, perhaps, exacts some consideration on this head, nor will I absolutely and altogether condemn it. As the world is constituted, the demands of a married state, and the care of posterity, require some little regard to what we call circumstances. Yet this provision is greatly increased, beyond what is really necessary, by folly and vanity, which create abundantly more wants than nature. Equipage for the wife, and large fortunes for the children, are by custom enrolled in the list of necessaries, and to procure these, everything truly solid and sweet, and virtuous and religious, are neglected and overlooked.

"And this in many degrees, the last and greatest of which seems scarce distinguishable from madness — I mean where persons of immense fortunes contract themselves to those who are, and must be, disagreeable to them — to fools and knaves — in order to increase an estate already larger even than the demands of their pleasures. Surely such persons, if they will not be thought mad, must own, either that they are incapable of tasting the sweets of the tenderest friendship, or that they sacrifice the greatest happiness of which they are capable to the vain, uncertain, and senseless laws of vulgar opinion, which owe as well their force as their foundation to folly."

Here Allworthy concluded his sermon, to which Blifil had listened with the profoundest attention, though it cost him some pains to prevent now and then a small discomposure of his muscles. He now praised every period of what he had heard with the warmth of a young divine, who hath the honour to dine with a bishop the same day in which his lordship hath mounted the pulpit.

Chapter Thirteen

Which concludes the first book, with an instance of ingratitude, which, we hope, will appear unnatural

The reader, from what hath been said, may imagine that the reconciliation—if indeed it could be so called—was only matter of form. We shall therefore pass it over, and hasten to what must surely be thought matter of substance.

The doctor had acquainted his brother with what had passed between Mr Allworthy and him, and added with a smile, "I promise you I paid you off— nay, I absolutely desired the good gentleman not to forgive you. For you know, after he had made a declaration in your favour, I might with safety venture on such a request with a person of his temper, and I was willing, as well for your sake as for my own, to prevent the least possibility of a suspicion."

Captain Blifil took not the least notice of this, at that time, but he afterwards made a very notable use of it.

One of the maxims which the devil, in a late visit upon earth, left to his disciples, is, when once you are got up, to kick the stool from under you. In plain English, when you have made your fortune by the good offices of a friend, you are advised to discard him as soon as you can.

Whether the captain acted by this maxim, I will not positively determine. So far we may confidently say, that his actions may be fairly derived from this diabolical principle, and indeed it is difficult to assign any other motive to them. For no sooner was he possessed of Miss Bridget, and reconciled to Allworthy, than he began to show a coldness to his brother which increased daily, till at length it grew into rudeness, and became very visible to everyone.

The doctor remonstrated to him privately concerning this behaviour, but could obtain no other satisfaction than the following plain declaration. "If you dislike anything in my brother's house, sir, you know you are at liberty to quit it." This strange, cruel, and almost unaccountable ingratitude in the captain, absolutely broke the poor doctor's heart, for ingratitude never so thoroughly pierces the human breast as when it proceeds from those in whose behalf we have been guilty of transgressions. Reflections on great and good actions, however they are received or returned by those in whose favour they are performed, always administer some comfort to us — but what consolation shall we receive under so biting a calamity as the ungrateful behaviour of our friend, when our wounded conscience at the same time flies in our face, and upbraids us with having spotted it in the service of one so worthless!

Mr Allworthy himself spoke to the captain on his brother's behalf, and desired to know what offence the doctor had committed, when the hard-hearted villain had the baseness to say that he should never forgive him for the injury which he had endeavoured to do him in his favour, which, he said, he had pumped out of him, and was such a cruelty that it ought not to be forgiven.

Allworthy spoke in very high terms upon this declaration, which, he said, became not a human creature. He expressed, indeed, so much resentment against an unforgiving temper, that the captain at last pretended to be convinced by his arguments, and outwardly professed to be reconciled.

As for the bride, she was now in her honeymoon, and so passionately fond of her new husband that he never appeared to her to be in the wrong, and his displeasure against any person was a sufficient reason for her dislike to the same.

The captain, at Mr Allworthy's instance, was outwardly, as we have said, reconciled to his brother. Yet the same rancour remained in his heart, and he found so many opportunities of giving him private hints of this, that the house at last grew insupportable to the poor doctor, and he chose rather to submit to any inconveniences which he might encounter in the world, than longer to bear these cruel and ungrateful insults from a brother for whom he had done so much.

He once intended to acquaint Allworthy with the whole, but he could not bring himself to submit to the confession, by which he must take to his share so great a portion of guilt. Besides, by how much the worse man he represented his brother to be, so much the greater would his own offence appear to Allworthy, and so much the greater, he had reason to imagine, would be his resentment.

He feigned, therefore, some excuse of business for his departure, and promised to return soon again, and took leave of his brother with so well-dissembled content, that, as the captain played his part to the same perfection, Allworthy remained well satisfied with the truth of the reconciliation.

The doctor went directly to London, where he died soon after of a broken heart, a distemper which kills many more than is generally imagined, and would have a fair title to a place in the bill of mortality, did it not differ in one instance from all other diseases — viz., that no physician can cure it.

Now, upon the most diligent enquiry into the former lives of these two brothers, I find, besides the cursed and hellish maxim of policy above mentioned, another reason for the captain's conduct. The captain, besides what we have before said of him, was a man of great pride and fierceness, and had always treated his brother, who was of a different complexion, and greatly deficient in both these qualities, with the utmost air of superiority. The doctor, however, had much the larger share of learning, and was by many reputed to have the better understanding. This the captain knew, and could not bear, for though envy is at best a very malignant passion, yet is its bitterness greatly heightened by mixing with contempt towards the same object, and very much afraid I am, that whenever an obligation is joined to these two, indignation and not gratitude will be the product of all three.

BOOK TWO

Containing scenes of matrimonial felicity in different degrees of life, and various other transactions during the first two years after the marriage between Captain Blifil and Miss Bridget Allworthy.

Chapter One

Showing what kind of a history this is, what it is like and what it is not like

Though we have properly enough entitled this our work, a history, and not a life, nor an apology for a life, as is more in fashion, yet we intend in it rather to pursue the method of those writers, who profess to disclose the revolutions of countries, than to imitate the painful and voluminous historian, who, to preserve the regularity of his series, thinks himself obliged to fill up as much paper with the detail of months and years in which nothing remarkable happened, as he employs upon those notable eras when the greatest scenes have been transacted on the human stage.

Such histories as these do, in reality, very much resemble a newspaper, which consists of just the same number of words, whether there be any news in it or not. They may likewise be compared to a stage coach, which performs constantly the same course, empty as well as full. The writer, indeed, seems to think himself obliged to keep even pace with time, whose amanuensis he is, and like his master, travels as slowly through centuries of monkish dullness, when the world seems to have been asleep, as through that bright and busy age so nobly distinguished by the excellent Latin poet —

Ad confligendum venientibus undique poenis,
Omnia cum belli trepido concussa tumultu
Horrida contremuere sub altis aetheris auris,
In dubioque fuit sub utrorum regna cadendum
Omnibus humanis esset, terraque marique.

Of which we wish we could give our readers a more adequate translation than that by Mr Creech —

When dreadful Carthage frighted Rome with arms,
And all the world was shook with fierce alarms,
Whilst undecided yet, which part should fall,
Which nation rise the glorious lord of all.

Now it is our purpose, in the ensuing pages, to pursue a contrary method. When any extraordinary scene presents itself — as we trust will often be the case — we shall spare no pains nor paper to open it at large to our reader. But if whole years should pass without producing anything worthy of his notice, we shall not be afraid of a chasm in our history, but shall hasten on to matters of consequence, and leave such periods of time totally unobserved.

These are indeed to be considered as blanks in the grand lottery of time. We therefore, who are the registers of that lottery, shall imitate those sagacious persons who deal in that which is drawn at Guildhall, and who never trouble the public with the many blanks they dispose of, but when a great prize happens to be drawn, the newspapers are presently filled with it, and the world is sure to be informed at whose office it was sold. Indeed, commonly two or three different offices lay claim to the honour of having disposed of it, by which, I suppose, the adventurers are given to understand that certain brokers are in the secrets of Fortune, and indeed of her cabinet council.

My reader then is not to be surprised, if, in the course of this work, he shall find some chapters very short, and others altogether as long – some that contain only the time of a single day, and others that comprise years – in a word, if my history sometimes seems to stand still, and sometimes to fly. For all which I shall not look on myself as accountable to any court of critical jurisdiction whatever, for as I am, in reality, the founder of a new province of writing, so I am at liberty to make what laws I please therein. And these laws, my readers, whom I consider as my subjects, are bound to believe in and to obey, with which that they may readily and cheerfully comply, I do hereby assure them that I shall principally regard their ease and advantage in all such institutions. For I do not, like a *jure divino* tyrant, imagine that they are my slaves, or my commodity. I am, indeed, set over them for their own good only, and was created for their use, and not they for mine. Nor do I doubt, while I make their interest the great rule of my writings, they will unanimously concur in supporting my dignity, and in rendering me all the honour I shall deserve or desire.

Chapter Two

Religious cautions against showing too much favour to bastards, and a great discovery made by Mrs Deborah Wilkins

Eight months after the celebration of the nuptials between Captain Blifil and Miss Bridget Allworthy, a young lady of great beauty, merit and fortune, was Miss Bridget, by reason of a fright, delivered of a fine boy. The child was indeed to all appearances perfect, but the midwife discovered it was born a month before its full time. Mrs Blifil praised the Lord and the great oak for her good fortune.

Though the birth of an heir by his beloved sister was a circumstance of great joy to Mr Allworthy, yet it did not alienate his affections from the little foundling, to whom he had been godfather, had given his own name of Thomas, and whom he had hitherto seldom failed of visiting, at least once a day, in his nursery.

He told his sister, if she pleased, the newborn infant should be bred up together with little Tommy, to which she consented, though with some little reluctance — for she had truly a great complacence for her brother, and hence she had always behaved towards the foundling with rather more kindness than ladies of rigid virtue can sometimes bring themselves to show to these children, who, however innocent, may be truly called the living monuments of incontinence.

The captain could not so easily bring himself to bear what he condemned as a fault in Mr Allworthy. He gave him frequent hints, that to adopt the fruits of sin, was to give countenance to it. He quoted several texts — for he was well read in Scripture — such as, *He visits the sins of the fathers upon the children, and the fathers have eaten sour grapes, and the children's teeth are set on edge*, etc. Whence he argued the legality of punishing the crime of the parent on the bastard. He said, though the law did not positively allow the destroying of such base-born children, yet it held them to be the children of nobody — that the Church considered them as the children of nobody — and that at the best, they ought to be brought up to the lowest and vilest offices of the commonwealth.

Mr Allworthy answered to all this, and much more, which the captain had urged on this subject, that, however guilty the parents might be, the children were certainly innocent. That as to the texts he had quoted, the former of them was a particular denunciation against the Jews, for the sin of idolatry, of relinquishing and hating their heavenly King, and the latter was parabolically spoken, and rather intended to denote the certain and necessary consequences of sin, than any express judgement against it.

But to represent the Almighty as avenging the sins of the guilty on the innocent, was indecent, if not blasphemous, as it was to represent him acting against the first principles of natural justice, and against the original notions of right and wrong, which he himself had implanted in our minds, by which we were to judge not only in all matters which were not revealed, but even of the truth of revelation itself. He said he knew many held the same principles with the captain on this head, but he was himself firmly convinced to the contrary, and would provide in the same manner for this poor infant, as if a legitimate child had had fortune to have been found in the same place.

While the captain was taking all opportunities to press these and such like arguments, to remove the little foundling from Mr Allworthy's, of whose fondness for him he began to be jealous, Mrs Deborah had made a discovery, which, in its event, threatened at least to prove more fatal to poor Tommy than all the reasonings of the captain.

Whether the insatiable curiosity of this good woman had carried her on to that business, or whether she did it to confirm herself in the good graces of Mrs Blifil, who, notwithstanding her outward behaviour to the foundling, frequently abused the infant in private, and her brother too, for his fondness to it, I will not determine, but she had now, as she conceived, fully detected the father of the foundling.

Now, as this was a discovery of great consequence, it may be necessary to trace it from the fountain-head. We shall therefore very minutely lay open those previous matters by which it was produced, and for that purpose we shall be obliged to reveal all the secrets of a little family with which my reader is at present entirely unacquainted, and of which the economy was so rare and extraordinary, that I fear it will shock the utmost credulity of many married persons.

Chapter Three

The description of a domestic government founded upon rules directly contrary to those of Aristotle

My reader may please to remember he hath been informed that Jenny Jones had lived some years with a certain schoolmaster, who had, at her earnest desire, instructed her in Latin, in which, to do justice to her genius, she had so improved herself, that she was become a better scholar than her master.

Indeed, though this poor man had undertaken a profession to which learning must be allowed necessary, this was the least of his commendations. He was one of the best-natured fellows in the world, and was, at the same time, master of so much pleasantry and humour, that he was reputed the wit of the country. All the neighbouring gentlemen were so desirous of his company, that as denying was not his talent, he spent much time at their houses, which he might, with more emolument, have spent in his school.

It may be imagined that a gentleman so qualified and so disposed, was in no danger of becoming formidable to the learned seminaries of Eton or Westminster. To speak plainly, his scholars were divided into two classes — in the upper of which was a young gentleman, the son of a neighbouring squire, who, at the age of seventeen, was just entered into his Syntaxis, and in the lower was a second son of the same gentleman, who, together with seven parish-boys, was learning to read and write.

The stipend arising hence would hardly have indulged the schoolmaster in the luxuries of life, had he not added to this office those of clerk and barber, and had not Mr Allworthy added to the whole an annuity of ten pounds, which the poor man received every Christmas, and with which he was enabled to cheer his heart during that sacred festival.

Among his other treasures, the pedagogue had a wife, whom he had married out of Mr Allworthy's kitchen for her fortune, viz., twenty pounds, which she had there amassed.

This woman was not very amiable in her person. Whether she sat to my friend Hogarth, or no, I will not determine, but she exactly resembled the young woman who is pouring out her mistress's tea in the third picture of the Harlot's Progress. She was, besides, a professed follower of that noble sect founded by Xantippe of old, by means of which she became more formidable in the school than her husband, for, to confess the truth, he was never master there, or anywhere else, in her presence.

Though her countenance did not denote much natural sweetness of temper, yet this was, perhaps, somewhat soured by a circumstance which generally poisons matrimonial felicity. For children are rightly called the pledges of love, and her husband, though they had been married nine years, had given her no such pledges, a default for which he had no excuse, either from age or health, being not yet thirty years old, and what they call a jolly brisk young man.

Hence arose another evil, which produced no little uneasiness to the poor pedagogue, of whom she maintained so constant a jealousy, that he durst hardly speak to one woman in the parish. The least degree of civility, or even correspondence, with any female, was sure to bring his wife upon her back, and his own.

In order to guard herself against matrimonial injuries in her own house, as she kept one maid-servant, she always took care to choose her out of that order of females whose faces are taken as a kind of security for their virtue, of which number Jenny Jones, as the reader hath been before informed, was one.

As the face of this young woman might be called pretty good security of the before-mentioned kind, and as her behaviour had been always extremely modest, which is the certain consequence of understanding in women, she had passed above four years at Mr Partridge's — for that was the schoolmaster's name — without creating the least suspicion in her mistress. Nay, she had been treated with uncommon kindness, and her mistress had permitted Mr Partridge to give her those instructions which have been before commemorated.

What Mrs Partridge had no way of knowing was what good Squire Allworthy was later to discover for himself, that what Jenny lacked in facial comeliness her body more than compensated for that, and when Mr Partridge had occasion to discipline the girl, he did so with a full heart.

For her part, Jenny discovered a previously unsuspected longing for such discipline, and enjoyed her master's punishments to such an extent that from time to time she provoked it.

Such was a time, when she declined the noun *exercitus* incorrectly on purpose.

Mr Partridge rounded the table they customarily used for their lessons, and leaned over her, saying, "Now, Jenny, you are quite the donkey today, because yesterday you achieved the task flawlessly. It is the most elementary of mistakes. Really, my dear, I fear you must be punished for such an error."

Instead of the doleful countenance that the reader might imagine would accompany these words, Jenny's radiant expression revealed that her subterfuge had resulted in its longed-for conclusion.

Hands crossed before her, and head bowed, she rose from her seat and went on her knees in front of her master. "I beg your pardon, sir," she said in the quiet and reverential tones she used on such occasions, "I would you punished me with the severity my crime deserves."

Partridge touched her chin in the gentlest way imaginable, but he extinguished his tenderness in the next moment, when he crossed the room to the window. By its side, he found the object he sought—a switch, fashioned of broad leather, such that will make a goodly sound and provide an object of stimulation for those who enjoy what is generally known as 'the French way'. Except in France, where contrarily it is known as 'the English way', but our neighbours are always contrary, being deprived of good English beef and the stout spirit our nation is famed for. But perhaps, this time, they had the right of it.

When he turned around, bearing the instrument of punishment, prepared to deliver pleasure to his partner in crime, Jenny was bent over his desk, her skirts pushed up, and her legs open.

For that, he delivered one strike. Jenny gave a small whimper, but the sounds were muffled by the expedient of her sleeve, which she had stuffed into her mouth, lest anyone hear and come to investigate. Although they knew the good parson preferred to punish his pupils in a stringent fashion, the better for them to learn their lessons.

"Decline the noun, Jenny," he said quietly.

In a quavering voice, Jenny obeyed her master, but again made an error at the same spot, for which she received two blows.

Her buttocks quivered and reddened, and Partridge smoothed his palm over the heated mounds, the better to soothe her and prepare her for the next act.

The mistake occurred again, and this time she received three strikes. "You want more?" the man said, his voice quiet.

"Yes, yes, please, sir."

"Then take my hand." He delivered as many blows with his hands as he had with his instrument of torture, which he laid down by her head. "Kiss it, thank it for teaching you such a lesson."

Jenny's ruby lips touched the switch so reverently it might have been a sacred object. "Thank you, sir, for teaching me so well."

Unable to wait a moment longer, the parson unfastened his breeches and found his cock, hard and straining. He brought it to his willing pupil, stroking it along the reddened cheeks, shuddering in his turn as the evidence of his punishment heated his member.

He introduced his cock to her slit, now leaking full measure, and drove it deep, giving Jenny no mercy. His pupil did not object to such rough treatment, but lifted her backside eagerly, the better to receive his punishing strokes.

With trembling fingers, Partridge circled that other opening, that connoisseurs sometimes prefer to the more frequented highway, and plunged two fingers inside, the better to remind Jenny that declensions were the basis of Latin grammar, and she must improve her lessons.

Jenny bit her sleeve in earnest, sinking right through the cloth so that her teeth marked her skin in her effort not to cry out her ecstasy to all who might be listening. But the parson's household contained fewer servants than the Allworthy house, and its good lady was at present visiting the sick, or so she told her husband, although he suspected she was at present seated in the house of one of her closest friends, bemoaning something or other, one of her favourite pastimes.

Her husband was currently engaged in one of his.

He gave his pupil the punishment she so richly deserved, his correction a lesson she would never forget. Occasionally, in this new level of chastisement he would remind her of what had gone before, striking her to encourage that rich blush to continue, the better to stimulate him to more efforts, and her to a higher level by which she should recite her lesson perfectly.

When he felt his time come upon him, Partridge said, in as steady a voice as he could contrive, considering his cock was driving into her, "Now recite the whole declension, Jenny."

"Exercitus, exercitus — an army," she began, and this time completed the lesson without error.

They reached a satisfactory conclusion to the lesson together, and such was their practice that it fell right on the last word of the declension.

Such a culmination had its inevitable conclusion, and the parson, less perspicacious than his friend and mentor the squire, fell over the prone body of his willing and from the rear at least, comely pupil.

Although they were properly attired and demurely absorbed in their lesson when Mrs Partridge arrived home, it did not prevent her suspicions growing apace.

But it is with jealousy as with the gout, when such distempers are in the blood, there is never any security against their breaking out, and that often on the slightest occasions, and when least suspected.

Thus it happened to Mrs Partridge, who had submitted four years to her husband's teaching this young woman, and had suffered her often to neglect her work, in order to pursue her learning in a study that remained firmly locked, the better, Partridge said, to concentrate her mind. For, passing by one day, as the girl was reading, and her master leaning over her, the girl, I know not for what reason, suddenly started up from her chair, and this was the first time that suspicion ever entered into the head of her mistress. This did not, however, at that time discover itself, but lay lurking in her mind, like a concealed enemy, who waits for a reinforcement of additional strength before he openly declares himself and proceeds upon hostile operations, and such additional strength soon arrived to corroborate her suspicion.

Not long after, the husband and wife being at dinner, the master said to his maid, *"Da mihi aliquid potum,"* upon which the poor girl smiled, perhaps at the badness of the Latin, and when her mistress cast her eyes on her, blushed, possibly with a consciousness of having laughed at her master. Mrs Partridge, upon this, immediately fell into a fury, and discharged the trencher on which she was eating, at the head of poor Jenny, crying out, "You impudent whore, do you play tricks with my husband before my face?" and at the same instant rose from her chair with a knife in her hand, with which, most probably, she would have executed very tragical vengeance, had not the girl taken the advantage of being nearer the door than her mistress, and avoided her fury by running away.

For, as to the poor husband, whether surprise had rendered him motionless, or fear—which is full as probable—had restrained him from venturing at any opposition, he sat staring and trembling in his chair. Nor did he once offer to move or speak, till his wife, returning from the pursuit of Jenny, made some defensive measures necessary for his own preservation, and he likewise was obliged to retreat, after the example of the maid.

This good woman was, no more than Othello, of a disposition –

To make a life of jealousy
And follow still the changes of the moon
With fresh suspicions –
With her, as well as him,
To be once in doubt,
Was once to be resolved.

She therefore ordered Jenny immediately to pack up her alls and begone, for that she was determined she should not sleep that night within her walls.

Mr Partridge had profited too much by experience to interpose in a matter of this nature. He therefore had recourse to his usual receipt of patience, for, though he was not a great adept in Latin, he remembered, and well understood, the advice contained in these words — *leve fit quod bene fertur onus,* in English, *a burden becomes lightest when it is well borne* — which he had always in his mouth, and of which, to say the truth, he had often occasion to experience the truth.

Jenny offered to make protestations of her innocence, but the tempest was too strong for her to be heard. She then betook herself to the business of packing, for which a small quantity of brown paper sufficed, and having received her small pittance of wages, she returned home.

The schoolmaster and his consort passed their time unpleasantly enough that evening, but something or other happened before the next morning, which a little abated the fury of Mrs Partridge, and she at length admitted her husband to make his excuses. To which she gave the readier belief, as he had, instead of desiring her to recall Jenny, professed a satisfaction in her being dismissed, saying, she was grown of little use as a servant, spending all her time in reading, and was become, moreover, very pert and obstinate. Indeed, she and her master had lately had frequent disputes in literature, in which, as hath been said, she was become greatly his superior. This, however, he would by no means allow, and as he called her persisting in the right, obstinacy, he began to hate her with no small inveteracy.

Chapter Four

Containing one of the most bloody battles, or rather duels,
that were ever recorded in domestic history

For the reasons mentioned in the preceding chapter,
and from some other matrimonial concessions, well
known to most husbands, and which, like the secrets
of freemasonry, should be divulged to none who are
not members of that honourable fraternity, Mrs
Partridge was pretty well satisfied that she had
condemned her husband without cause, and
endeavoured by acts of kindness to make him amends
for her false suspicion. Her passions were indeed
equally violent, whichever way they inclined, for as
she could be extremely angry, so could she be
altogether as fond.

But though these passions ordinarily succeed each
other, and scarce twenty-four hours ever passed in
which the pedagogue was not, in some degree, the
object of both, yet, on extraordinary occasions, when
the passion of anger had raged very high, the

remission was usually longer. And so was the case at present, for she continued longer in a state of affability, after this fit of jealousy was ended, than her husband had ever known before, and had it not been for some little exercises, which all the followers of Xantippe are obliged to perform daily, Mr Partridge would have enjoyed a perfect serenity of several months. It was unfortunate that Mr Partridge was not of the persuasion that preferred to receive rather than give, for his wife might have punished him in some vigorous form, and then Xantippe could have remained in Athens.

Perfect calms at sea are always suspected by the experienced mariner to be the forerunners of a storm, and I know some persons, who, without being generally the devotees of superstition, are apt to apprehend that great and unusual peace or tranquillity will be attended with its opposite. For which reason the ancients used, on such occasions, to sacrifice to the goddess Nemesis, a deity who was thought by them to look with an invidious eye on human felicity, and to have a peculiar delight in overturning it.

As we are very far from believing in any such heathen goddess, or from encouraging any superstition, so we wish Mr John Fr —, or some other such philosopher, would bestir himself a little, in order to find out the real cause of this sudden transition from good to bad fortune, which hath been so often remarked, and of which we shall proceed to give an instance. For it is our province to relate facts, and we shall leave causes to persons of much higher genius.

Mankind have always taken great delight in knowing and descanting on the actions of others.

Hence there have been, in all ages and nations, certain places set apart for public rendezvous, where the curious might meet and satisfy their mutual curiosity. Among these, the barbers' shops have justly borne the pre-eminence. Among the Greeks, barbers' news was a proverbial expression, and Horace, in one of his epistles, makes honourable mention of the Roman barbers in the same light.

Those of England are known to be no wise inferior to their Greek or Roman predecessors. You there see foreign affairs discussed in a manner little inferior to that with which they are handled in the coffee-houses, and domestic occurrences are much more largely and freely treated in the former than in the latter. But this serves only for the men. Now, whereas the females of this country, especially those of the lower order, do associate themselves much more than those of other nations, our polity would be highly deficient, if they had not some place set apart likewise for the indulgence of their curiosity, seeing they are in this no way inferior to the other half of the species.

In enjoying, therefore, such place of rendezvous, the British fair ought to esteem themselves more happy than any of their foreign sisters, as I do not remember either to have read in history, or to have seen in my travels, anything of the like kind.

This place then is no other than the chandler's shop, the known seat of all the news, or, as it is vulgarly called, gossiping, in every parish in England.

Mrs Partridge being one day at this assembly of females, was asked by one of her neighbours, if she had heard no news lately of Jenny Jones? To which she answered in the negative. Upon this the other replied, with a smile, that the parish was very much obliged to her for having turned Jenny away as she did.

Mrs Partridge, whose jealousy, as the reader well knows, was long since cured, and who had no other quarrel to her maid, answered boldly, she did not know any obligation the parish had to her on that account, for she believed Jenny had scarce left her equal behind her.

"No, truly," said the gossip, "I hope not, though I fancy we have sluts enough too. Then you have not heard, it seems, that she hath been brought to bed of two bastards? But as they are not born here, my husband and the other overseer says we shall not be obliged to keep them."

"Two bastards!" answered Mrs Partridge hastily. "You surprise me! I don't know whether we must keep them, but I am sure they must have been begotten here, for the wench hath not been nine months gone away."

Nothing can be so quick and sudden as the operations of the mind, especially when hope, or fear, or jealousy, to which the two others are but journeymen, set it to work. It occurred instantly to her, that Jenny had scarce ever been out of her own house while she lived with her. The leaning over the chair, the sudden starting up, the Latin, the smile, and many other things, rushed upon her all at once. The satisfaction her husband expressed in the departure of Jenny, appeared now to be only dissembled, again, in the same instant, to be real, but yet to confirm her jealousy, proceeding from satiety, and a hundred other bad causes. In a word, she was convinced of her husband's guilt, and immediately left the assembly in confusion.

As fair Grimalkin, who, though the youngest of the feline family, degenerates not in ferocity from the elder branches of her house, and though inferior in strength, is equal in fierceness to the noble tiger himself, when a little mouse, whom it hath long tormented in sport, escapes from her clutches for a while, frets, scolds, growls, swears, but if the trunk, or box, behind which the mouse lay hid be again removed, she flies like lightning on her prey, and with envenomed wrath, bites, scratches, mumbles, and tears the little animal.

Not with less fury did Mrs Partridge fly on the poor pedagogue. Her tongue, teeth, and hands, fell all upon him at once. His wig was in an instant torn from his head, his shirt from his back, and from his face descended five streams of blood, denoting the number of claws with which nature had unhappily armed the enemy.

Mr Partridge acted for some time on the defensive only. Indeed he attempted only to guard his face with his hands, but as he found that his antagonist abated nothing of her rage, he thought he might, at least, endeavour to disarm her, or rather to confine her arms. In doing which her cap fell off in the struggle, and her hair being too short to reach her shoulders, erected itself on her head. Her stays likewise, which were laced through one single hole at the bottom, burst open, and her breasts, which were much more redundant than her hair, hung down below her middle. Her face was likewise marked with the blood of her husband. Her teeth gnashed with rage, and fire, such as sparkles from a smith's forge, darted from her eyes. So that, altogether, this Amazonian heroine might have been an object of terror to a much bolder man than Mr Partridge.

A bolder man could have taken advantage of her state, for indeed, a powerful fucking would have calmed her and turned her temper instantly, but Mr Partridge merely wished to encourage her to regain control. So although her breasts lashed him and his manhood responded accordingly, he ignored the provocation.

He had, at length, the good fortune, by getting possession of her arms, to render those weapons which she wore at the ends of her fingers useless, which she no sooner perceived, than the softness of her sex prevailed over her rage, and she presently dissolved in tears, which soon after concluded in a fit.

That small share of sense which Mr Partridge had hitherto preserved through this scene of fury, of the cause of which he was hitherto ignorant, now utterly abandoned him. He ran instantly into the street, hallowing out that his wife was in the agonies of death, and beseeching the neighbours to fly with the utmost haste to her assistance. Several good women obeyed his summons, who entering his house, and applying the usual remedies on such occasions, Mrs Partridge was at length, to the great joy of her husband, brought to herself.

As soon as she had a little recollected her spirits, and somewhat composed herself with a cordial, she began to inform the company of the manifold injuries she had received from her husband, who, she said, was not contented to injure her in her bed, but, upon her upbraiding him with it, had treated her in the cruellest manner imaginable—had tore her cap and hair from her head, and her stays from her body, giving her, at the same time, several blows, the marks of which she should carry to the grave. Having been merely restrained, instead of receiving the tribute she believed she deserved, and moreover believing that Jenny Jones had received the bounty which she, as a wife, was more entitled, Mrs Partridge decided on revenge.

The poor man, who bore on his face many more visible marks of the indignation of his wife, stood in silent astonishment at this accusation, which the reader will, I believe, bear witness for him, had greatly exceeded the truth. For indeed he had not struck her once, and this silence being interpreted to be a confession of the charge by the whole court, they all began at once, *una voce*, to rebuke and revile him, repeating often, that none but a coward ever struck a woman in anger.

Mr Partridge bore all this patiently, but when his wife appealed to the blood on her face, as an evidence of his barbarity, he could not help laying claim to his own blood, for so it really was, as he thought it very unnatural, that this should rise up—as we are taught that of a murdered person often doth—in vengeance against him.

To this the women made no other answer, than that it was a pity it had not come from his heart, instead of his face, all declaring, that, if their husbands should lift their hands against them, they would have their hearts' bloods out of their bodies.

After much admonition for what was past, and much good advice to Mr Partridge for his future behaviour, the company at length departed, and left the husband and wife to a personal conference together, in which Mr Partridge soon learned the cause of all his sufferings.

Mrs Partridge wept on her husband's breast, and he soothed her with great patience, and not a little guilt. "There, there, my love, it is nothing. We will henceforth contrive to live in greater harmony. Now come up to the bedchamber and allow me to aid you to rest."

He took her upstairs with every evidence of tenderness, and helped her to disrobe before drawing back the sheets and assisting her in. She held her arms out to him in a beseeching manner, and for the first time, Mr Partridge wondered if she could be brought to share in his predilection for more inventive bed-play.

Accordingly, he ventured to say, as if in jest, "I should find my horsewhip, wife, for your accusations, but I am too fond."

At once her eyes sparkled, and her tears melted away as if they had never been. "Oh, sir, I do not think you should go to such lengths for me. I do not deserve such treatment, indeed I do not."

All this time Partridge was busy divesting himself of his own clothing, because he had been married long enough to recognise the signs of need in his wife and not being averse to such practice, remembered the old adage, 'Kiss and make up', something he had every intention of undertaking.

Retaining his neckcloth, he snapped the length of cloth between his hands, watching closely for her every reaction.

Xanthippe had gone, replaced by the softer Penelope, ever patient and subservient. Taking hold of one hand, he bound the cloth around her wrist, and noted how her eyes gleamed with interest. He wished for no unwilling partners, and the joy he'd found in Jenny Jones was that missing in his wife. If he had looked to her sooner, he would not have committed the sin for which he would spend many hours on his knees begging forgiveness from God.

Now he watched her as he bound her wrists together and bade her open her legs, which she did with much alacrity.

Mr Partridge had never seen his wife completely naked before, and he was pleased by the comeliness of form that she constantly hid under voluminous nightwear and clothes that did not suit her figure. He began to understand why they were so at odds, and vowed it would not happen again.

He set to, ordering her to hold the bed-posts, because he was to give her such a fucking as she would never forget, and would beg him to give her more.

The good lady gave no word of complaint, but when he lay over her, ready to breach her, she arched up, forcing him to press her back down so he could get his cock into her cunt.

For a lady with hands bound together at the wrists, she made a good fight, but the more she fought, the more her husband determined to control her, until their bed became the veritable scene of battle, as much as anything the neighbourhood witnessed. He forced her to compliance, then she fought back, arching her body, thrusting up one knee, compelling him to respond in kind. Soon the blood that had dried from their previous encounter welled up fresh, but they ignored such small matters, for none of the wounds would trouble them above a week or two, and continued to engage in the stimulating exercise that proved to be such pleasure to them both.

Relentlessly, he took her, and equally relentlessly, she countered, so it was closer to the union of Mars and Venus than to Baucis and Philemon, neither submitting their will to the other.

Having left his switch in his study, his cock remained his chief weapon, and Partridge used it to great effect, eventually, and with great travail, bringing her to that state of submission that gave him his weakest moment.

After the encounter, they lay side by side, until, overcome by the emotion of the day, they burst into helpless laughter.

Chapter Five

Containing much matter to exercise the judgement and reflection of the reader

I believe it is a true observation, that few secrets are divulged to one person only, but certainly, it would be next to a miracle that a fact of this kind should be known to a whole parish, and not transpire any further.

And indeed, a very few days had passed, before the country, to use a common phrase, rang of the schoolmaster of Little Baddington, who was said to have beaten his wife in the most cruel manner. Nay, in some places it was reported he had murdered her, in others, that he had broken her arms, in others, her legs. In short, there was scarce an injury which can be done to a human creature, but what Mrs Partridge was somewhere or other affirmed to have received from her husband.

The cause of this quarrel was likewise variously reported, for as some people said that Mrs Partridge had caught her husband in bed with his maid, so many other reasons, of a very different kind, went abroad. Nay, some transferred the guilt to the wife, and the jealousy to the husband.

Mrs Wilkins had long ago heard of this quarrel, but, as a different cause from the true one had reached her ears, she thought proper to conceal it, and the rather, perhaps, as the blame was universally laid on Mr Partridge, and his wife, when she was servant to Mr Allworthy, had in something offended Mrs Wilkins, who was not of a very forgiving temper.

But Mrs Wilkins, whose eyes could see objects at a distance, and who could very well look forward a few years into futurity, had perceived a strong likelihood of Captain Blifil's being hereafter her master. As she plainly discerned that the captain bore no great goodwill to the little foundling, she fancied it would be rendering him an agreeable service, if she could make any discoveries that might lessen the affection which Mr Allworthy seemed to have contracted for this child, and which gave visible uneasiness to the captain, who could not entirely conceal it even before Allworthy himself. Though his wife, who acted her part much better in public, frequently recommended to him her own example, of conniving at the folly of her brother, which, she said, she at least as well perceived, and as much resented, as any other possibly could.

Mrs Wilkins having therefore, by accident, got a true scent of the above story — though long after it had happened, failed not to satisfy herself thoroughly of all the particulars, and then acquainted the captain, that she had at last discovered the true father of the little bastard, which she was sorry, she said, to see her master lose his reputation in the country, by taking so much notice of.

The captain chided her for the conclusion of her speech, as an improper assurance in judging of her master's actions. For if his honour, or his understanding, would have suffered the captain to make an alliance with Mrs Wilkins, his pride would by no means have admitted it. And to say the truth, there is no conduct less politic, than to enter into any confederacy with your friend's servants against their master, for by these means you afterwards become the slave of these very servants, by whom you are constantly liable to be betrayed. And this consideration, perhaps it was, which prevented Captain Blifil from being more explicit with Mrs Wilkins, or from encouraging the abuse which she had bestowed on Allworthy.

But though he declared no satisfaction to Mrs Wilkins at this discovery, he enjoyed not a little from it in his own mind, and resolved to make the best use of it he was able.

He kept this matter a long time concealed within his own breast, in hopes that Mr Allworthy might hear it from some other person, but Mrs Wilkins, whether she resented the captain's behaviour, or whether his cunning was beyond her, and she feared the discovery might displease him, never afterwards opened her lips about the matter.

I have thought it somewhat strange, upon reflection, that the housekeeper never acquainted Mrs Blifil with this news, as women are more inclined to communicate all pieces of intelligence to their own sex, than to ours. The only way, as it appears to me, of solving this difficulty, is, by imputing it to that distance which was now grown between the lady and the housekeeper, whether this arose from a jealousy in Mrs Blifil, that Wilkins showed too great a respect to the foundling. While she was endeavouring to ruin the little infant, in order to ingratiate herself with the captain, she was every day more and more commending it before Allworthy, as his fondness for it every day increased. This, notwithstanding all the care she took at other times to express the direct contrary to Mrs Blifil, perhaps offended that delicate lady, who certainly now hated Mrs Wilkins, and though she did not, or possibly could not, absolutely remove her from her place, she found, however, the means of making her life very uneasy. This Mrs Wilkins, at length, so resented, that she very openly showed all manner of respect and fondness to little Tommy, in opposition to Mrs Blifil.

The captain, therefore, finding the story in danger of perishing, at last took an opportunity to reveal it himself.

He was one day engaged with Mr Allworthy in a discourse on charity, in which the captain, with great learning, proved to Mr Allworthy, that the word charity in Scripture nowhere means beneficence or generosity.

"The Christian religion," he said, "was instituted for much nobler purposes, than to enforce a lesson which many heathen philosophers had taught us long before, and which, though it might perhaps be called a moral virtue, savoured but little of that sublime, Christian-like disposition, that vast elevation of thought, in purity approaching to angelic perfection, to be attained, expressed, and felt only by grace. Those," he said, "came nearer to the Scripture meaning, who understood by it candour, or the forming of a benevolent opinion of our brethren, and passing a favourable judgement on their actions—a virtue much higher, and more extensive in its nature, than a pitiful distribution of alms, which, though we would never so much prejudice, or even ruin our families, could never reach many, whereas charity, in the other and truer sense, might be extended to all mankind."

He said, "Considering who the disciples were, it would be absurd to conceive the doctrine of generosity, or giving alms, to have been preached to them. And, as we could not well imagine this doctrine should be preached by its Divine Author to men who could not practise it, much less should we think it understood so by those who can practise it, and do not.

"But though," continued he, "there is, I am afraid, little merit in these benefactions, there would, I must confess, be much pleasure in them to a good mind, if it was not abated by one consideration. I mean, that we are liable to be imposed upon, and to confer our choicest favours often on the undeserving, as you must own was your case in your bounty to that worthless fellow Partridge, for two or three such examples must greatly lessen the inward satisfaction which a good man would otherwise find in generosity—nay, may even make him timorous in bestowing, lest he should be guilty of supporting vice, and encouraging the wicked. A crime of a very black dye, and for which it will by no means be a sufficient excuse, that we have not actually intended such an encouragement, unless we have used the utmost caution in choosing the objects of our beneficence. A consideration which, I make no doubt, hath greatly checked the liberality of many a worthy and pious man."

Mr Allworthy answered that he could not dispute with the captain in the Greek language, and therefore could say nothing as to the true sense of the word which is translated charity, but that he had always thought it was interpreted to consist in action, and that giving alms constituted at least one branch of that virtue.

As to the meritorious part, he said, he readily agreed with the captain, for where could be the merit of barely discharging a duty? Which, he said, let the word charity have what construction it would, it sufficiently appeared to be from the whole tenor of the New Testament. And as he thought it an indispensable duty, enjoined both by the Christian law, and by the law of nature itself, so was it withal so pleasant, that if any duty could be said to be its own reward, or to pay us while we are discharging it, it was this.

"To confess the truth," said he, "there is one degree of generosity—of charity, I would have called it— which seems to have some show of merit, and that is, where, from a principle of benevolence and Christian love, we bestow on another what we really want ourselves—where, in order to lessen the distresses of another, we condescend to share some part of them, by giving what even our own necessities cannot well spare. This is, I think, meritorious, but to relieve our brethren only with our superfluities, to be charitable— I must use the word—rather at the expense of our coffers than ourselves, to save several families from misery rather than hang up an extraordinary picture in our houses or gratify any other idle ridiculous vanity—this seems to be only being human creatures. Nay, I will venture to go further, it is being in some degree epicures. For what could the greatest epicure wish rather than to eat with many mouths instead of one? Which I think may be predicated of anyone who knows that the bread of many is owing to his own largesses.

"As to the apprehension of bestowing bounty on such as may hereafter prove unworthy objects, because many have proved such. Surely it can never deter a good man from generosity. I do not think a few or many examples of ingratitude can justify a man's hardening his heart against the distresses of his fellow-creatures, nor do I believe it can ever have such effect on a truly benevolent mind. Nothing less than a persuasion of universal depravity can lock up the charity of a good man, and this persuasion must lead him, I think, either into atheism, or enthusiasm, but surely it is unfair to argue such universal depravity from a few vicious individuals. Nor was this, I believe, ever done by a man, who, upon searching his own mind, found one certain exception to the general rule." He then concluded by asking who that Partridge was, whom he had called a worthless fellow?

"I mean," said the captain, "Partridge the barber, the schoolmaster, what do you call him? Partridge, the father of the little child which you found in your bed."

Mr Allworthy expressed great surprise at this account, and the captain as great at his ignorance of it, for he said he had known it above a month, and at length recollected with much difficulty that he was told it by Mrs Wilkins.

Upon this, Wilkins was immediately summoned, who having confirmed what the captain had said, was by Mr Allworthy, by and with the captain's advice, dispatched to Little Baddington, to inform herself of the truth of the fact, for the captain expressed great dislike at all hasty proceedings in criminal matters, and said he would by no means have Mr Allworthy take any resolution either to the prejudice of the child or its father, before he was satisfied that the latter was guilty. For though he had privately satisfied himself of this from one of Partridge's neighbours, yet he was too generous to give any such evidence to Mr Allworthy.

Chapter Six

The trial of Partridge, the schoolmaster, for incontinency. The evidence of his wife. A short reflection on the wisdom of our law, with other grave matters, which those will like best who understand them most

It may be wondered that a story so well known, and which had furnished so much matter of conversation, should never have been mentioned to Mr Allworthy himself, who was perhaps the only person in that country who had never heard of it.

To account in some measure for this to the reader, I think proper to inform him, that there was no one in the kingdom less interested in opposing that doctrine concerning the meaning of the word charity, which hath been seen in the preceding chapter, than our good man. Indeed, he was equally entitled to this virtue in either sense, for as no man was ever more sensible of the wants, or more ready to relieve the distresses of others, so none could be more tender of their characters, or slower to believe anything to their disadvantage.

Scandal, therefore, never found any access to his table. As it hath been long since observed that you may know a man by his companions, so I will venture to say, that, by attending to the conversation at a great man's table, you may satisfy yourself of his religion, his politics, his taste, and indeed of his entire disposition. For though a few odd fellows will utter their own sentiments in all places, yet much the greater part of mankind have enough of the courtier to accommodate their conversation to the taste and inclination of their superiors.

But to return to Mrs Wilkins, who, having executed her commission with great dispatch, though at fifteen miles distance, brought back such a confirmation of the schoolmaster's guilt, that Mr Allworthy determined to send for the criminal, and examine him *viva voce*. Mr Partridge, therefore, was summoned to attend, in order to his defence—if he could make any—against this accusation.

At the time appointed, before Mr Allworthy himself, at Paradise-hall, came as well the said Partridge, with Anne, his wife, as Mrs Wilkins his accuser.

And now Mr Allworthy being seated in the chair of justice, Mr Partridge was brought before him. Having heard his accusation from the mouth of Mrs Wilkins, he pleaded not guilty, making many vehement protestations of his innocence.

Mrs Partridge was then examined, who, after a modest apology for being obliged to speak the truth against her husband, related all the circumstances with which the reader hath already been acquainted, and at last concluded with her husband's confession of his guilt. For since her husband and herself had discovered their mutual pleasure in bed, out of it matters continued ill, and Mrs Partridge had taken counsel of people more known for gossip than for wisdom.

Whether she had forgiven him or no, I will not venture to determine, but it is certain she was an unwilling witness in this cause, and it is probable from certain other reasons, would never have been brought to depose as she did, had not Mrs Wilkins, with great art, fished all out of her at her own house, and had she not indeed made promises, in Mr Allworthy's name, that the punishment of her husband should not be such as might anywise affect his family.

Partridge still persisted in asserting his innocence, though he admitted he had made the above-mentioned confession, which he however endeavoured to account for, by protesting that he was forced into it by the continued importunity she used, who vowed, that, as she was sure of his guilt, she would never leave tormenting him till he had owned it, and faithfully promised, that, in such case, she would never mention it to him more. Hence, he said, he had been induced falsely to confess himself guilty, though he was innocent, and that he believed he should have confessed a murder from the same motive.

Mrs Partridge could not bear this imputation with patience, and having no other remedy in the present place but tears, she called forth a plentiful assistance from them, and then addressing herself to Mr Allworthy, she said, or rather cried, "May it please your worship, there never was any poor woman so injured as I am by that base man, for this is not the only instance of his falsehood to me. No, may it please your worship, he hath injured my bed many's the good time and often. I could have put up with his drunkenness and neglect of his business, if he had not broken one of the sacred commandments. Besides, if it had been out of doors I had not mattered it so much, but with my own servant, in my own house, under my own roof, to defile my own chaste bed, which to be sure he hath, with his beastly stinking whores. Yes, you villain, you have defiled my own bed, you have, and then you have charged me with bullocking you into owning the truth.

"It is very likely, an't please your worship, that I should bullock him? I have marks enough about my body to show of his cruelty to me. If you had been a man, you villain, you would have scorned to injure a woman in that manner. But you an't half a man, you know it. Nor have you been half a husband to me. You need run after whores, you need, when I'm sure — And since he provokes me, I am ready, an't please your worship, to take my bodily oath that I found them a-bed together. What, you have forgot, I suppose, when you beat me into a fit, and made the blood run down my forehead, because I only civilly taxed you with adultery! But I can prove it by all my neighbours. You have almost broke my heart, you have, you have."

Here Mr Allworthy interrupted, and begged her to be pacified, promising her that she should have justice. Then turning to Partridge, who stood aghast, one half of his wits being hurried away by surprise and the other half by fear, he said he was sorry to see there was so wicked a man in the world. He assured him that his prevaricating and lying backward and forward was a great aggravation of his guilt, for which the only atonement he could make was by confession and repentance. He exhorted him, therefore, to begin by immediately confessing the fact, and not to persist in denying what was so plainly proved against him even by his own wife.

Here, reader, I beg your patience a moment, while I make a just compliment to the great wisdom and sagacity of our law, which refuses to admit the evidence of a wife for or against her husband. This, says a certain learned author, who, I believe, was never quoted before in any but a law-book, would be the means of creating an eternal dissension between them. It would, indeed, be the means of much perjury, and of much whipping, fining, imprisoning, transporting, and hanging.

Partridge stood a while silent, till, being bid to speak, he said he had already spoken the truth, and appealed to Heaven for his innocence, and lastly to the girl herself, whom he desired his worship immediately to send for, for he was ignorant, or at least pretended to be so, that she had left that part of the country.

Mr Allworthy, whose natural love of justice, joined to his coolness of temper, made him always a most patient magistrate in hearing all the witnesses which an accused person could produce in his defence, agreed to defer his final determination of this matter till the arrival of Jenny, for whom he immediately dispatched a messenger. Then having recommended peace between Partridge and his wife—though he addressed himself chiefly to the wrong person—he appointed them to attend again the third day, for he had sent Jenny a whole day's journey from his own house.

At the appointed time the parties all assembled, when the messenger returning brought word, that Jenny was not to be found, for that she had left her habitation a few days before, in company with a recruiting officer.

Mr Allworthy was deceived in his faith in Jenny, and feeling not a small portion betrayed by the wench, who had sworn she would visit him once more before she quit the neighbourhood, then declared that the evidence of such a slut as she appeared to be would have deserved no credit. But he said he could not help thinking that, had she been present, and would have declared the truth, she must have confirmed what so many circumstances, together with his own confession, and the declaration of his wife that she had caught her husband in the fact, did sufficiently prove. He therefore once more exhorted Partridge to confess, but he still avowing his innocence, Mr Allworthy declared himself satisfied of his guilt, and that he was too bad a man to receive any encouragement from him. He therefore deprived him of his annuity, and recommended repentance to him on account of another world, and industry to maintain himself and his wife in this.

There were not, perhaps, many more unhappy persons than poor Partridge. He had lost the best part of his income by the evidence of his wife, and yet was daily upbraided by her for having, among other things, been the occasion of depriving her of that benefit, but such was his fortune, and he was obliged to submit to it. For she was such a contrary creature, that dominance in the bedchamber was not enough for her, and she would have it outside as well, and thus lost both.

Though I called him poor Partridge in the last paragraph, I would have the reader rather impute that epithet to the compassion in my temper than conceive it to be any declaration of his innocence. Whether he was innocent or not will perhaps appear hereafter, but if the historic muse hath entrusted me with any secrets, I will by no means be guilty of discovering them till she shall give me leave.

Here therefore the reader must suspend his curiosity. Certain it is that, whatever was the truth of the case, there was evidence more than sufficient to convict him before Allworthy. Indeed, much less would have satisfied a bench of justices on an order of bastardy, and yet, notwithstanding the positiveness of Mrs Partridge, who would have taken the sacrament upon the matter, there is a possibility that the schoolmaster was entirely innocent. Though it appeared clear on comparing the time when Jenny departed from Little Baddington with that of her delivery that she had there conceived this infant, yet it by no means followed of necessity that Partridge must have been its father. For, to omit other particulars, there was in the same house a lad near eighteen, between whom and Jenny there had subsisted sufficient intimacy to found a reasonable suspicion, and yet, so blind is jealousy, this circumstance never once entered into the head of the enraged wife.

Whether Partridge repented or not, according to Mr Allworthy's advice, is not so apparent. Certain it is that his wife repented heartily of the evidence she had given against him, especially when she found Mrs Deborah had deceived her, and refused to make any application to Mr Allworthy on her behalf. She had, however, somewhat better success with Mrs Blifil, who was, as the reader must have perceived, a much better-tempered woman, and very kindly undertook to solicit her brother to restore the annuity, in which, though good-nature might have some share, yet a stronger and more natural motive will appear in the next chapter.

These solicitations were nevertheless unsuccessful, for though Mr Allworthy did not think, with some late writers, that mercy consists only in punishing offenders. Yet he was as far from thinking that it is proper to this excellent quality to pardon great criminals wantonly, without any reason whatever. Any doubtfulness of the fact, or any circumstance of mitigation, was never disregarded, but the petitions of an offender, or the intercessions of others, did not in the least affect him. In a word, he never pardoned because the offender himself, or his friends, were unwilling that he should be punished.

Partridge and his wife were therefore both obliged to submit to their fate, which was indeed severe enough. So far was he from doubling his industry on the account of his lessened income, that he did in a manner abandon himself to despair, and as he was by nature indolent, that vice now increased upon him, by which means he lost the little school he had, so that neither his wife nor himself would have had any bread to eat, had not the charity of some good Christian interposed, and provided them with what was just sufficient for their sustenance.

As this support was conveyed to them by an unknown hand, they imagined, and so, I doubt not, will the reader, that Mr Allworthy himself was their secret benefactor, who, though he would not openly encourage vice, could yet privately relieve the distresses of the vicious themselves, when these became too exquisite and disproportionate to their demerit. In which light their wretchedness appeared now to Fortune herself, for she at length took pity on this miserable couple, and considerably lessened the wretched state of Partridge, by putting a final end to that of his wife, who soon after caught the smallpox, and died.

The justice which Mr Allworthy had executed on Partridge at first met with universal approbation, but no sooner had he felt its consequences, than his neighbours began to relent, and to compassionate his case, and presently after, to blame that as rigour and severity which they before called justice. They now exclaimed against punishing in cold blood, and sang forth the praises of mercy and forgiveness.

These cries were considerably increased by the death of Mrs Partridge, which, though owing to the distemper above mentioned, which is no consequence of poverty or distress, many were not ashamed to impute to Mr Allworthy's severity, or, as they now termed it, cruelty.

Partridge having now lost his wife, his school, and his annuity, and the unknown person having now discontinued the last-mentioned charity, resolved to change the scene, and left the country, where he was in danger of starving, with the universal compassion of all his neighbours.

Chapter Seven

A short sketch of that felicity which prudent couples may extract from hatred, with a short apology for those people who overlook imperfections in their friends

Though the captain had effectually demolished poor Partridge, yet had he not reaped the harvest he hoped for, which was to turn the foundling out of Mr Allworthy's house.

On the contrary, that gentleman grew every day fonder of little Tommy, as if he intended to counterbalance his severity to the father with extraordinary fondness and affection towards the son.

This a good deal soured the captain's temper, as did all the other daily instances of Mr Allworthy's generosity, for he looked on all such largesses to be diminutions of his own wealth. He counted the house as his already, by virtue of the child his wife had borne him.

In this, we have said, he did not agree with his wife, nor, indeed, in anything else, for though an affection placed on the understanding is, by many wise persons, thought more durable than that which is founded on beauty, yet it happened otherwise in the present case. Nay, the understandings of this couple were their principal bone of contention, and one great cause of many quarrels, which from time to time arose between them, and which at last ended, on the side of the lady, in a sovereign contempt for her husband, and on the husband's, in an utter abhorrence of his wife.

As these had both exercised their talents chiefly in the study of divinity, this was, from their first acquaintance, the most common topic of conversation between them. The captain, like a well-bred man, had, before marriage, always given up his opinion to that of the lady, and this, not in the clumsy awkward manner of a conceited blockhead, who, while he civilly yields to a superior in an argument, is desirous of being still known to think himself in the right. The captain, on the contrary, though one of the proudest fellows in the world, so absolutely yielded the victory to his antagonist, that she, who had not the least doubt of his sincerity, retired always from the dispute with an admiration of her own understanding and a love for his.

But though this complacence to one whom the captain thoroughly despised, was not so uneasy to him as it would have been had any hopes of preferment made it necessary to show the same submission to a Hoadley, or to some other of great reputation in the science, yet even this cost him too much to be endured without some motive. Matrimony, therefore, having removed all such motives, he grew weary of this condescension, and began to treat the opinions of his wife with that haughtiness and insolence, which none but those who deserve some contempt themselves can bestow, and those only who deserve no contempt can bear.

When the first torrent of tenderness was over, and when, in the calm and long interval between the fits, reason began to open the eyes of the lady, and she saw this alteration of behaviour in the captain, who at length answered all her arguments only with 'pish' and 'pshaw', she was far from enduring the indignity with a tame submission. Indeed, it at first so highly provoked her, that it might have produced some tragical event, had it not taken a more harmless turn, by filling her with the utmost contempt for her husband's understanding, which somewhat qualified her hatred towards him, though of this likewise she had a pretty moderate share.

The captain's hatred to her was of a purer kind, for as to any imperfections in her knowledge or understanding, he no more despised her for them, than for her not being six feet high. In his opinion of the female sex, he exceeded the moroseness of Aristotle himself. He looked on a woman as on an animal of domestic use, of somewhat higher consideration than a cat, since her offices were of rather more importance, but the difference between these two was, in his estimation, so small, that, in his marriage contracted with Mr Allworthy's lands and tenements, it would have been pretty equal which of them he had taken into the bargain. And yet so tender was his pride, that it felt the contempt which his wife now began to express towards him, and this, added to the surfeit he had before taken of her love, created in him a degree of disgust and abhorrence, perhaps hardly to be exceeded.

One situation only of the married state is excluded from pleasure, and that is, a state of indifference, but as many of my readers, I hope, know what an exquisite delight there is in conveying pleasure to a beloved object, so some few, I am afraid, may have experienced the satisfaction of tormenting one we hate. It is, I apprehend, to come at this latter pleasure, that we see both sexes often give up that ease in marriage which they might otherwise possess, though their mate was never so disagreeable to them. Hence the wife often puts on fits of love and jealousy, nay, even denies herself any pleasure, to disturb and prevent those of her husband, and he again, in return, puts frequent restraints on himself, and stays at home in company which he dislikes, in order to confine his wife to what she equally detests. Hence, too, must flow those tears which a widow sometimes so plentifully sheds over the ashes of a husband with whom she led a life of constant disquiet and turbulency, and whom now she can never hope to torment any more.

But if ever any couple enjoyed this pleasure, it was at present experienced by the captain and his lady. It was always a sufficient reason to either of them to be obstinate in any opinion, that the other had previously asserted the contrary. If the one proposed any amusement, the other constantly objected to it. They never loved or hated, commended or abused, the same person. And for this reason, as the captain looked with an evil eye on the little foundling, his wife began now to caress it almost equally with her own child.

The reader will be apt to conceive, that this behaviour between the husband and wife did not greatly contribute to Mr Allworthy's repose, as it tended so little to that serene happiness which he had designed for all three from this alliance. But the truth is, though he might be a little disappointed in his sanguine expectations, yet he was far from being acquainted with the whole matter, for, as the captain was, from certain obvious reasons, much on his guard before him, the lady was obliged, for fear of her brother's displeasure, to pursue the same conduct.

In fact, it is possible for a third person to be very intimate, nay even to live long in the same house, with a married couple, who have any tolerable discretion, and not even guess at the sour sentiments which they bear to each other. For though the whole day may be sometimes too short for hatred, as well as for love, yet the many hours which they naturally spend together, apart from all observers, furnish people of tolerable moderation with such ample opportunity for the enjoyment of either passion, that, if they love, they can support being a few hours in company without toying, or if they hate, without spitting in each other's faces.

It is possible, however, that Mr Allworthy saw enough to render him a little uneasy, for we are not always to conclude, that a wise man is not hurt because he doth not cry out and lament himself, like those of a childish or effeminate temper. But indeed it is possible he might see some faults in the captain without any uneasiness at all, for men of true wisdom and goodness are contented to take persons and things as they are, without complaining of their imperfections, or attempting to amend them. They can see a fault in a friend, a relation, or an acquaintance, without ever mentioning it to the parties themselves, or to any others, and this often without lessening their affection.

Indeed, unless great discernment be tempered with this overlooking disposition, we ought never to contract friendship but with a degree of folly which we can deceive. I hope my friends will pardon me when I declare, I know none of them without a fault, and I should be sorry if I could imagine I had any friend who could not see mine. Forgiveness of this kind we give and demand in turn. It is an exercise of friendship, and perhaps none of the least pleasant. And this forgiveness we must bestow, without desire of amendment. There is, perhaps, no surer mark of folly, than an attempt to correct the natural infirmities of those we love. The finest composition of human nature, as well as the finest china, may have a flaw in it, and this, I am afraid, in either case, is equally incurable, though, nevertheless, the pattern may remain of the highest value.

Upon the whole, then, Mr Allworthy certainly saw some imperfections in the captain, but as this was a very artful man, and eternally upon his guard before him, these appeared to him no more than blemishes in a good character, which his goodness made him overlook, and his wisdom prevented him from discovering to the captain himself. Very different would have been his sentiments had he discovered the whole, which perhaps would in time have been the case, had the husband and wife long continued this kind of behaviour to each other, but this kind Fortune took effectual means to prevent, by forcing the captain to do that which rendered him again dear to his wife, and restored all her tenderness and affection towards him.

Chapter Eight

A receipt to regain the lost affections of a wife, which hath never been known to fail in the most desperate cases

The captain was made large amends for the unpleasant minutes which he passed in the conversation of his wife — and which were as few as he could contrive to make them — by the pleasant meditations he enjoyed when alone. Indeed, where many men would take the toy donated to them by a gracious nature and deploy it in a way to take most pleasure, the captain gained as much delight by sitting under the great oak and contemplating that which one day he would call his. It would not be too fanciful to state that the pleasures of the flesh were as nothing compared to the joy the captain took in surveying the acres before him. Although he did not hesitate to take both enjoyments at the same time, something that gave him a great deal more satisfaction. He could work his cock and come to a climax merely by contemplating his inheritance, instead of imagining the most beauteous woman in creation.

These meditations were entirely employed on Mr Allworthy's fortune. First, he exercised much thought in calculating, as well as he could, the exact value of the whole, which calculations he often saw occasion to alter in his own favour. And, secondly and chiefly, he pleased himself with intended alterations in the house and gardens, and in projecting many other schemes, as well for the improvement of the estate as of the grandeur of the place. For this purpose he applied himself to the studies of architecture and gardening, and read over many books on both these subjects, for these sciences, indeed, employed his whole time, and formed his only amusement. He at last completed a most excellent plan, and very sorry we are, that it is not in our power to present it to our reader, since even the luxury of the present age, I believe, would hardly match it.

It had, indeed, in a superlative degree, the two principal ingredients which serve to recommend all great and noble designs of this nature, for it required an immoderate expense to execute, and a vast length of time to bring it to any sort of perfection. The former of these, the immense wealth of which the captain supposed Mr Allworthy possessed, and which he thought himself sure of inheriting, promised very effectually to supply, and the latter, the soundness of his own constitution, and his time of life, which was only what is called middle-age, removed all apprehension of his not living to accomplish.

Nothing was wanting to enable him to enter upon the immediate execution of this plan, but the death of Mr Allworthy, in calculating which he had employed much of his own algebra, besides purchasing every book extant that treats of the value of lives, reversions, etc. From all which he satisfied himself, that as he had every day a chance of this happening, so had he more than an even chance of its happening within a few years.

But while the captain was one day busied in deep contemplations of this kind, one of the most unlucky as well as unseasonable accidents happened to him. The utmost malice of Fortune could, indeed, have contrived nothing so cruel, so malapropos, so absolutely destructive to all his schemes. In short, not to keep the reader in long suspense, just at the very instant when his heart was exulting in meditations on the happiness which would accrue to him by Mr Allworthy's death, he himself died of an apoplexy.

This unfortunately befell the captain as he was taking his evening walk by himself, so that nobody was present to lend him any assistance, if indeed, any assistance could have preserved him. He took, therefore, measure of that proportion of soil which was now become adequate to all his future purposes, and he lay dead on the ground, a great, though not a living, example of the truth of that observation of Horace — *tu secanda marmora Locas sub ipsum funus, et sepulchri Immemor, struis domos* — which sentiment I shall thus give to the English reader — "You provide the noblest materials for building, when a pickaxe and a spade are only necessary, and build houses of five hundred by a hundred feet, forgetting that of six by two."

So the captain's ambitions were reduced to a smaller space, and his aspirations reached heavenwards, ignoring the base metal he left behind.

Chapter Nine

A proof of the infallibility of the foregoing receipt, in the lamentations of the widow, with other suitable decorations of death, such as physicians, etc, and an epitaph in the true style

Mr Allworthy, his sister, and another lady, were assembled at the accustomed hour in the supper-room, where, having waited a considerable time longer than usual, Mr Allworthy first declared he began to grow uneasy at the captain's stay—for he was always most punctual at his meals—and gave orders that the bell should be rung without the doors, and especially towards those walks which the captain was wont to use.

All these summons proving ineffectual—for the captain had, by perverse accident, betaken himself to a new walk that evening—Mrs Blifil declared she was seriously frightened. Upon which the other lady, who was one of her most intimate acquaintances, and who well knew the true state of her affections, endeavoured all she could to pacify her, telling her, to be sure she could not help being uneasy, but that she should hope the best. That, perhaps the sweetness of the evening had enticed the captain to go farther than his usual walk, or he might be detained at some neighbour's. Mrs Blifil answered, no, she was sure some accident had befallen him, for that he would never stay out without sending her word, as he must know how uneasy it would make her. The other lady, having no other arguments to use, betook herself to the entreaties usual on such occasions, and begged her not to frighten herself, for it might be of very ill consequence to her own health, and filling out a very large glass of wine, advised, and at last prevailed with her to drink it.

Mr Allworthy now returned into the parlour, for he had been himself in search after the captain. His countenance sufficiently showed the consternation he was under, which, indeed, had a good deal deprived him of speech, but as grief operates variously on different minds, so the same apprehension which depressed his voice, elevated that of Mrs Blifil. She now began to bewail herself in very bitter terms, and floods of tears accompanied her lamentations, which the lady, her companion, declared she could not blame, but at the same time dissuaded her from indulging, attempting to moderate the grief of her friend by philosophical observations on the many disappointments to which human life is daily subject—which, she said, was a sufficient consideration to fortify our minds against any accidents, how sudden or terrible soever. She said her brother's example ought to teach her patience, who, though indeed he could not be supposed as much concerned as herself, yet was, doubtless, very uneasy, though his resignation to the Divine will had restrained his grief within due bounds.

"Mention not my brother," said Mrs Blifil. "I alone am the object of your pity. What are the terrors of friendship to what a wife feels on these occasions? Oh, he is lost! Somebody hath murdered him—I shall never see him more!" Here a torrent of tears had the same consequence with what the suppression had occasioned to Mr Allworthy, and she remained silent.

At this interval a servant came running in, out of breath, and cried out, "The captain is found," and before he could proceed farther, he was followed by two more, bearing the dead body between them.

Here the curious reader may observe another diversity in the operations of grief, for as Mr Allworthy had been before silent, from the same cause which had made his sister vociferous, so did the present sight, which drew tears from the gentleman, put an entire stop to those of the lady, who first gave a violent scream, and presently after fell into a fit.

The room was soon full of servants, some of whom, with the lady visitant, were employed in care of the wife, and others, with Mr Allworthy, assisted in carrying off the captain to a warm bed, where every method was tried, in order to restore him to life.

And glad should we be, could we inform the reader that both these bodies had been attended with equal success, for those who undertook the care of the lady succeeded so well, that, after the fit had continued a decent time, she again revived, to their great satisfaction, but as to the captain, all experiments of bleeding, chafing, dropping, etc, proved ineffectual. Death, that inexorable judge, had passed sentence on him, and refused to grant him a reprieve, though two doctors who arrived, and were fee'd at one and the same instant, were his counsel.

These two doctors, whom, to avoid any malicious applications, we shall distinguish by the names of Dr Y and Dr Z, having felt his pulse — to wit, Dr Y his right arm, and Dr Z his left — both agreed that he was absolutely dead, but as to the distemper, or cause of his death, they differed, Dr Y holding that he died of an apoplexy, and Dr Z of an epilepsy.

Hence arose a dispute between the learned men, in which each delivered the reasons of their several opinions. These were of such equal force, that they served both to confirm either doctor in his own sentiments, and made not the least impression on his adversary.

To say the truth, every physician almost hath his favourite disease, to which he ascribes all the victories obtained over human nature. The gout, the rheumatism, the stone, the gravel, and the consumption, have all their several patrons in the faculty, and none more than the nervous fever, or the fever on the spirits. And here we may account for those disagreements in opinion, concerning the cause of a patient's death, which sometimes occur, between the most learned of the college, and which have greatly surprised that part of the world who have been ignorant of the fact we have above asserted.

The reader may perhaps be surprised, that, instead of endeavouring to revive the patient, the learned gentlemen should fall immediately into a dispute on the occasion of his death, but in reality all such experiments had been made before their arrival, for the captain was put into a warm bed, had his veins scarified, his forehead chafed, and all sorts of strong drops applied to his lips and nostrils.

The physicians, therefore, finding themselves anticipated in everything they ordered, were at a loss how to apply that portion of time which it is usual and decent to remain for their fee, and were therefore necessitated to find some subject or other for discourse, and what could more naturally present itself than that before mentioned?

Our doctors were about to take their leave, when Mr Allworthy, having given over the captain, and acquiesced in the Divine will, began to enquire after his sister, whom he desired them to visit before their departure.

This lady was now recovered of her fit, and to use the common phrase, as well as could be expected for one in her condition. The doctors, therefore, all previous ceremonies being complied with, as this was a new patient, attended, according to desire, and laid hold on each of her hands, as they had before done on those of the corpse.

The case of the lady was in the other extreme from that of her husband, for as he was past all the assistance of physic, so in reality she required none.

There is nothing more unjust than the vulgar opinion by which physicians are misrepresented as friends to death. On the contrary, I believe, if the number of those who recover by physic could be opposed to that of the martyrs to it, the former would rather exceed the latter. Nay, some are so cautious on this head, that, to avoid a possibility of killing the patient, they abstain from all methods of curing, and prescribe nothing but what can neither do good nor harm. I have heard some of these, with great gravity, deliver it as a maxim, that Nature should be left to do her own work, while the physician stands by as it were to clap her on the back, and encourage her when she doth well.

So little then did our doctors delight in death, that they discharged the corpse after a single fee, but they were not so disgusted with their living patient, concerning whose case they immediately agreed, and fell to prescribing with great diligence.

Whether, as the lady had at first persuaded her physicians to believe her ill, they had now, in return, persuaded her to believe herself so, I will not determine, but she continued a whole month with all the decorations of sickness. During this time she was visited by physicians, attended by nurses, and received constant messages from her acquaintance to enquire after her health.

At length the decent time for sickness and immoderate grief being expired, the doctors were discharged, and the lady began to see company, being altered only from what she was before, by that colour of sadness in which she had dressed her person and countenance.

The captain was now interred, and might, perhaps, have already made a large progress towards oblivion, had not the friendship of Mr Allworthy taken care to preserve his memory, by the following epitaph, which was written by a man of as great genius as integrity, and one who perfectly well knew the captain.

Here lies, in expectation of a joyful rising, the body of Captain John Blifil. London had the honour of his birth, Oxford of his education. His parts were an honour to his profession and to his country – his life, to his religion and human nature. He was a dutiful son, a tender husband, an affectionate father, a most kind brother, a sincere friend, a devout Christian, and a good man. His inconsolable widow hath erected this stone, the monument of his virtues and of her affection.

BOOK THREE

Containing the most memorable transactions which passed in the family of Mr Allworthy, from the time when Tommy Jones arrived at the age of fourteen, till he attained the age of nineteen. In this book the reader may pick up some hints concerning the education of children.

Chapter One

Containing little or nothing

The reader will be pleased to remember, that, at the beginning of the second book of this history, we gave him a hint of our intention to pass over several large periods of time, in which nothing happened worthy of being recorded in a chronicle of this kind.

In so doing, we do not only consult our own dignity and ease, but the good and advantage of the reader. Besides that by these means we prevent him from throwing away his time, in reading without either pleasure or emolument, we give him, at all such seasons, an opportunity of employing that wonderful sagacity, of which he is master, by filling up these vacant spaces of time with his own conjectures, for which purpose we have taken care to qualify him in the preceding pages.

For instance, what reader but knows that Mr Allworthy felt, at first, for the loss of his friend, those emotions of grief, which on such occasions enter into all men whose hearts are not composed of flint, or their heads of as solid materials? Again, what reader doth not know that philosophy and religion in time moderated, and at last extinguished, this grief? The former of these teaching the folly and vanity of it, and the latter correcting it as unlawful, and at the same time assuaging it, by raising future hopes and assurances, which enable a strong and religious mind to take leave of a friend, on his deathbed, with little less indifference than if he was preparing for a long journey, and indeed, with little less hope of seeing him again.

Nor can the judicious reader be at a greater loss on account of Mrs Bridget Blifil, who, he may be assured, conducted herself through the whole season in which grief is to make its appearance on the outside of the body, with the strictest regard to all the rules of custom and decency, suiting the alterations of her countenance to the several alterations of her habit. As this changed from weeds to black, from black to grey, from grey to white, so did her countenance change from dismal to sorrowful, from sorrowful to sad, and from sad to serious, till the day came in which she was allowed to return to her former serenity.

We have mentioned these two, as examples only of the task which may be imposed on readers of the lowest class. Much higher and harder exercises of judgement and penetration may reasonably be expected from the upper graduates in criticism. Many notable discoveries will, I doubt not, be made by such, of the transactions which happened in the family of our worthy man, during all the years which we have thought proper to pass over. Though nothing worthy of a place in this history occurred within that period, yet did several incidents happen of equal importance with those reported by the daily and weekly historians of the age, in reading which great numbers of persons consume a considerable part of their time, very little, I am afraid, to their emolument. Now, in the conjectures here proposed, some of the most excellent faculties of the mind may be employed to much advantage, since it is a more useful capacity to be able to foretell the actions of men, in any circumstance, from their characters, than to judge of their characters from their actions. The former, I own, requires the greater penetration, but may be accomplished by true sagacity with no less certainty than the latter.

As we are sensible that much the greatest part of our readers are very eminently possessed of this quality, we have left them a space of twelve years to exert it in, and shall now bring forth our hero, at about fourteen years of age, not questioning that many have been long impatient to be introduced to his acquaintance.

Chapter Two

The hero of this great history appears with very bad omens. A little tale of so low a kind that some may think it not worth their notice. A word or two concerning a squire, and more relating to a gamekeeper and a schoolmaster

As we determined, when we first sat down to write this history, to flatter no man, but to guide our pen throughout by the directions of truth, we are obliged to bring our hero on the stage in a much more disadvantageous manner than we could wish, and to declare honestly, even at his first appearance, that it was the universal opinion of all Mr Allworthy's family that he was certainly born to be hanged.

Indeed, I am sorry to say there was too much reason for this conjecture, the lad having from his earliest years discovered a propensity to many vices, and especially to one which hath as direct a tendency as any other to that fate which we have just now observed to have been prophetically denounced against him. He had been already convicted of three robberies, viz., of robbing an orchard, of stealing a duck out of a farmer's yard, and of picking Master Blifil's pocket of a ball.

The vices of this young man were, moreover, heightened by the disadvantageous light in which they appeared when opposed to the virtues of Master Blifil, his companion, a youth of so different a cast from little Jones, that not only the family but all the neighbourhood resounded his praises. He was, indeed, a lad of a remarkable disposition, sober, discreet, and pious beyond his age, qualities which gained him the love of everyone who knew him, while Tom Jones was universally disliked, and many expressed their wonder that Mr Allworthy would suffer such a lad to be educated with his nephew, lest the morals of the latter should be corrupted by his example.

An incident which happened about this time will set the characters of these two lads more fairly before the discerning reader than is in the power of the longest dissertation.

Tom Jones, who, bad as he is, must serve for the hero of this history, had only one friend among all the servants of the family, for as to Mrs Wilkins, she had long since given him up, and was perfectly reconciled to her mistress. This friend was the gamekeeper, a fellow of a loose kind of disposition, and who was thought not to entertain much stricter notions concerning the difference of *meum* and *tuum* than the young gentleman himself. And hence this friendship gave occasion to many sarcastical remarks among the domestics, most of which were either proverbs before, or at least are become so now, and indeed, the wit of them all may be comprised in that short Latin proverb, *noscitur a socio*, which, I think, is thus expressed in

English, 'You may know him by the company he keeps'.

To say the truth, some of that atrocious wickedness in Jones, of which we have just mentioned three examples, might perhaps be derived from the encouragement he had received from this fellow, who, in two or three instances, had been what the law calls an accessory after the fact, for the whole duck, and great part of the apples, were converted to the use of the gamekeeper and his family. Though, as Jones alone was discovered, the poor lad bore not only the whole smart, but the whole blame, both which fell again to his lot on the following occasion.

Contiguous to Mr Allworthy's estate was the manor of one of those gentlemen who are called preservers of the game. This species of men, from the great severity with which they revenge the death of a hare or partridge, might be thought to cultivate the same superstition with the Bannians in India — many of whom, we are told, dedicate their whole lives to the preservation and protection of certain animals — was it not that our English Bannians, while they preserve them from other enemies, will most unmercifully slaughter whole horse-loads themselves, so that they stand clearly acquitted of any such heathenish superstition.

I have, indeed, a much better opinion of this kind of men than is entertained by some, as I take them to answer the order of Nature, and the good purposes for which they were ordained, in a more ample manner than many others. Now, as Horace tells us that there are a set of human beings *fruges consumere nati*, 'born to consume the fruits of the earth', so I make no manner of doubt but that there are others *feras consumere nati*, 'born to consume the beasts of the field', or, as it is commonly called, the game, and none, I believe, will deny but that those squires fulfil this end of their creation.

Little Jones went one day a shooting with the gamekeeper, when happening to spring a covey of partridges near the border of that manor over which Fortune, to fulfil the wise purposes of Nature, had planted one of the game consumers, the birds flew into it, and were marked — as it is called — by the two sportsmen, in some furze bushes, about two or three hundred paces beyond Mr Allworthy's dominions.

Mr Allworthy had given the fellow strict orders, on pain of forfeiting his place, never to trespass on any of his neighbours, no more on those who were less rigid in this matter than on the lord of this manor. With regard to others, indeed, these orders had not been always very scrupulously kept, but as the disposition of the gentleman with whom the partridges had taken sanctuary was well known, the gamekeeper had never yet attempted to invade his territories. Nor had he done it now, had not the younger sportsman, who was excessively eager to pursue the flying game, over-persuaded him, but Jones being very importunate, the other, who was himself keen enough after the sport, yielded to his persuasions, entered the manor, and shot one of the partridges.

The gentleman himself was at that time on horseback, at a little distance from them, and hearing the gun go off, he immediately made towards the place, and discovered poor Tom, for the gamekeeper had leapt into the thickest part of the furze-brake, where he had happily concealed himself.

The gentleman having searched the lad, and found the partridge upon him, denounced great vengeance, swearing he would acquaint Mr Allworthy. He was as good as his word, for he rode immediately to his house, and complained of the trespass on his manor in as high terms and as bitter language as if his house had been broken open, and the most valuable furniture stole out of it. He added, that some other person was in his company, though he could not discover him, for that two guns had been discharged almost in the same instant. And, said he, "We have found only this partridge, but the Lord knows what mischief they have done."

At his return home, Tom was presently convened before Mr Allworthy. He owned the fact, and alleged no other excuse but what was really true, viz., that the covey was originally sprung in Mr Allworthy's own manor.

Tom was then interrogated who was with him, which Mr Allworthy declared he was resolved to know, acquainting the culprit with the circumstance of the two guns, which had been deposed by the squire and both his servants, but Tom stoutly persisted in asserting that he was alone, yet, to say the truth, he hesitated a little at first, which would have confirmed Mr Allworthy's belief, had what the squire and his servants said wanted any further confirmation.

The gamekeeper, being a suspected person, was now sent for, and the question put to him, but he, relying on the promise which Tom had made him, to take all upon himself, very resolutely denied being in company with the young gentleman, or indeed having seen him the whole afternoon.

Mr Allworthy then turned towards Tom, with more than usual anger in his countenance, and advised him to confess who was with him, repeating, that he was resolved to know. The lad, however, still maintained his resolution, and was dismissed with much wrath by

Mr Allworthy, who told him he should have to the next morning to consider of it, when he should be questioned by another person, and in another manner.

Poor Jones spent a very melancholy night, and the more so, as he was without his usual companion, for Master Blifil was gone abroad on a visit with his mother. Fear of the punishment he was to suffer was on this occasion his least evil, his chief anxiety being, lest his constancy should fail him, and he should be brought to betray the gamekeeper, whose ruin he knew must now be the consequence.

Nor did the gamekeeper pass his time much better. He had the same apprehensions with the youth, for whose honour he had likewise a much tenderer regard than for his skin.

In the morning, when Tom attended the reverend Mr Thwackum, the person to whom Mr Allworthy had committed the instruction of the two boys, he had the same questions put to him by that gentleman which he had been asked the evening before, to which he returned the same answers. The consequence of this was, so severe a whipping, that it possibly fell little short of the torture with which confessions are in some countries extorted from criminals.

Tom bore his punishment with great resolution, and though his master asked him, between every stroke, whether he would not confess, he was contented to be flead rather than betray his friend, or break the promise he had made.

Mr Thwackum, long convinced of the benefits that such exercise could give to the youth and moreover, to his arms, applied the whip with great alacrity, and was so engaged as to desire Tom to draw down his clothes, the better to receive the blows given to him.

The gamekeeper was now relieved from his anxiety, and Mr Allworthy himself began to be concerned at Tom's sufferings, for besides that Mr Thwackum, being highly enraged that he was not able to make the boy say what he himself pleased, had carried his severity much beyond the good man's intention, this latter began now to suspect that the squire had been mistaken, which his extreme eagerness and anger seemed to make probable, and as for what the servants had said in confirmation of their master's account, he laid no great stress upon that. Now, as cruelty and injustice were two ideas of which Mr Allworthy could by no means support the consciousness a single moment, he sent for Tom, and after many kind and friendly exhortations, said, "I am convinced, my dear child, that my suspicions have wronged you. I am sorry that you have been so severely punished on this account." And at last gave him a little horse to make him amends, again repeating his sorrow for what had passed.

Tom's guilt now flew in his face more than any severity could make it. He could more easily bear the lashes of Thwackum, than the generosity of Allworthy. The tears burst from his eyes, and he fell upon his knees, crying, "Oh, sir, you are too good to me. Indeed you are. Indeed I don't deserve it." And at that very instant, from the fullness of his heart, had almost betrayed the secret, but the good genius of the gamekeeper suggested to him what might be the consequence to the poor fellow, and this consideration sealed his lips.

Thwackum did all he could to persuade Allworthy from showing any compassion or kindness to the boy, saying he had persisted in an untruth, and gave some hints, that a second whipping might probably bring the matter to light.

But Mr Allworthy absolutely refused to consent to the experiment. He said, the boy had suffered enough already for concealing the truth, even if he was guilty, seeing that he could have no motive but a mistaken point of honour for so doing.

"Honour!" cried Thwackum, with some warmth. "Mere stubbornness and obstinacy! Can honour teach anyone to tell a lie, or can any honour exist independent of religion?"

This discourse happened at table when dinner was just ended, and there were present Mr Allworthy, Mr Thwackum, and a third gentleman, who now entered into the debate, and whom, before we proceed any further, we shall briefly introduce to our reader's acquaintance.

Chapter Three

The character of Mr Square the philosopher, and of Mr Thwackum the divine, with a dispute concerning –

The name of this gentleman, who had then resided some time at Mr Allworthy's house, was Mr Square. His natural parts were not of the first rate, but he had greatly improved them by a learned education. He was deeply read in the ancients, and a professed master of all the works of Plato and Aristotle. Upon which great models he had principally formed himself, sometimes according with the opinion of the one, and sometimes with that of the other. In morals he was a professed Platonist, and in religion he inclined to be an Aristotelian.

But though he had, as we have said, formed his morals on the Platonic model, yet he perfectly agreed with the opinion of Aristotle, in considering that great man rather in the quality of a philosopher or a speculatist, than as a legislator. This sentiment he carried a great way, indeed, so far, as to regard all virtue as matter of theory only. This, it is true, he never affirmed, as I have heard, to anyone, and yet upon the least attention to his conduct, I cannot help thinking it was his real opinion, as it will perfectly reconcile some contradictions which might otherwise appear in his character.

This gentleman and Mr Thwackum scarce ever met without a disputation, for their tenets were indeed diametrically opposite to each other. Square held human nature to be the perfection of all virtue, and that vice was a deviation from our nature, in the same manner as deformity of body is. Thwackum, on the contrary, maintained that the human mind, since the fall, was nothing but a sink of iniquity, till purified and redeemed by grace. In one point only they agreed, which was, in all their discourses on morality never to mention the word goodness. The favourite phrase of the former, was the natural beauty of virtue – that of the latter, was the divine power of grace. The former measured all actions by the unalterable rule of right, and the eternal fitness of things. The latter decided all matters by authority, but in doing this, he always used the scriptures and their commentators, as the lawyer doth his Coke upon Lyttleton, where the comment is of equal authority with the text.

After this short introduction, the reader will be pleased to remember, that the parson had concluded his speech with a triumphant question, to which he had apprehended no answer, viz., can any honour exist independent on religion?

To this Square answered, that it was impossible to discourse philosophically concerning words, till their meaning was first established, that there were scarce any two words of a more vague and uncertain signification, than the two he had mentioned, for that there were almost as many different opinions concerning honour, as concerning religion. "But," said he, "if by honour you mean the true natural beauty of virtue, I will maintain it may exist independent of any religion whatever. Nay," added he, "you yourself will allow it may exist independent of all but one, so will a Mahometan, a Jew, and all the maintainers of all the different sects in the world."

Thwackum replied, this was arguing with the usual malice of all the enemies to the true Church. He said he doubted not but that all the infidels and heretics in the world would, if they could, confine honour to their own absurd errors and damnable deceptions, "but honour," said he, "is not therefore manifold, because there are many absurd opinions about it. Nor is religion manifold, because there are various sects and heresies in the world. When I mention religion, I mean the Christian religion, and not only the Christian religion, but the Protestant religion, and not only the Protestant religion, but the Church of England. And when I mention honour, I mean that mode of Divine grace which is not only consistent with, but dependent upon, this religion, and is consistent with and dependent upon no other. Now to say that the honour I here mean, and which was, I thought, all the honour I could be supposed to mean, will uphold, much less dictate an untruth, is to assert an absurdity too shocking to be conceived."

"I purposely avoided," said Square, "drawing a conclusion which I thought evident from what I have said, but if you perceived it, I am sure you have not attempted to answer it. However, to drop the article of religion, I think it is plain, from what you have said, that we have different ideas of honour, or why do we not agree in the same terms of its explanation? I have asserted, that true honour and true virtue are almost synonymous terms, and they are both founded on the unalterable rule of right, and the eternal fitness of things, to which an untruth being absolutely repugnant and contrary, it is certain that true honour cannot support an untruth. In this, therefore, I think we are agreed, but that this honour can be said to be founded on religion, to which it is antecedent, if by religion be meant any positive law — "

"I agree," answered Thwackum, with great warmth, "with a man who asserts honour to be antecedent to religion! Mr Allworthy, did I agree — ?"

He was proceeding when Mr Allworthy interposed, telling them very coldly, they had both mistaken his meaning, for that he had said nothing of true honour. It is possible, however, he would not have easily quieted the disputants, who were growing equally warm, had not another matter now fallen out, which put a final end to the conversation at present.

Chapter Four

Containing a necessary apology for the author, and a childish incident, which perhaps requires an apology likewise

Before I proceed further, I shall beg leave to obviate some misconstructions into which the zeal of some few readers may lead them, for I would not willingly give offence to any, especially to men who are warm in the cause of virtue or religion.

I hope, therefore, no man will, by the grossest misunderstanding or perversion of my meaning, misrepresent me, as endeavouring to cast any ridicule on the greatest perfections of human nature, and which do, indeed, alone purify and ennoble the heart of man, and raise him above the brute creation. This, reader, I will venture to say—and by how much the better man you are yourself, by so much the more will you be inclined to believe me—that I would rather have buried the sentiments of these two persons in eternal oblivion, than have done any injury to either of these glorious causes.

On the contrary, it is with a view to their service, that I have taken upon me to record the lives and actions of two of their false and pretended champions. A treacherous friend is the most dangerous enemy, and I will say boldly, that both religion and virtue have received more real discredit from hypocrites than the wittiest profligates or infidels could ever cast upon them. Nay, further, as these two, in their purity, are rightly called the bands of civil society, and are indeed the greatest of blessings, so when poisoned and corrupted with fraud, pretence, and affectation, they have become the worst of civil curses, and have enabled men to perpetrate the most cruel mischiefs to their own species.

Indeed, I doubt not but this ridicule will in general be allowed. My chief apprehension is, as many true and just sentiments often came from the mouths of these persons, lest the whole should be taken together, and I should be conceived to ridicule all alike. Now the reader will be pleased to consider, that, as neither of these men were fools, they could not be supposed to have holden none but wrong principles, and to have uttered nothing but absurdities. What injustice, therefore, must I have done to their characters, had I selected only what was bad! And how horribly wretched and maimed must their arguments have appeared!

Upon the whole, it is not religion or virtue, but the want of them, which is here exposed. Had not Thwackum too much neglected virtue, and Square, religion, in the composition of their several systems, and had not both utterly discarded all natural goodness of heart, they had never been represented as the objects of derision in this history, in which we will now proceed.

This matter then, which put an end to the debate mentioned in the last chapter, was no other than a quarrel between Master Blifil and Tom Jones, the consequence of which had been a bloody nose to the former, for though Master Blifil, notwithstanding he was the younger, was in size above the other's match, yet Tom was much his superior at the noble art of boxing.

Tom, however, cautiously avoided all engagements with that youth, for besides that Tommy Jones was an inoffensive lad amidst all his roguery, and really loved Blifil, Mr Thwackum being always the second of the latter, would have been sufficient to deter him.

But well says a certain author, "No man is wise at all hours". It is therefore no wonder that a boy is not so. A difference arising at play between the two lads, Master Blifil called Tom a beggarly bastard. Upon which the latter, who was somewhat passionate in his disposition, immediately caused that phenomenon in the face of the former, which we have above remembered.

Master Blifil now, with his blood running from his nose, and the tears galloping after from his eyes, appeared before his uncle and the tremendous Thwackum. In which court an indictment of assault, battery, and wounding, was instantly preferred against Tom, who in his excuse only pleaded the provocation, which was indeed all the matter that Master Blifil had omitted.

It is indeed possible that this circumstance might have escaped his memory, for, in his reply, he positively insisted, that he had made use of no such appellation, adding, Heaven forbid such naughty words should ever come out of his mouth!

Tom, though against all form of law, rejoined in affirmance of the words. Upon which Master Blifil said, "It is no wonder. Those who will tell one fib, will hardly stick at another. If I had told my master such a wicked fib as you have done, I should be ashamed to show my face."

"What fib, child?" cried Thwackum pretty eagerly.

"Why, he told you that nobody was with him a shooting when he killed the partridge, but he knows" — here he burst into a flood of tears — "yes, he knows, for he confessed it to me, that Black George the gamekeeper was there. Nay, he said — yes you did — deny it if you can, that you would not have confessed the truth, though master had cut you to pieces."

At this the fire flashed from Thwackum's eyes, and he cried out in triumph. "Oh! Ho! this is your mistaken notion of honour! This is the boy who was not to be whipped again!"

But Mr Allworthy, with a more gentle aspect, turned towards the lad, and said, "Is this true, child? How came you to persist so obstinately in a falsehood?"

Tom said he scorned a lie as much as anyone, but he thought his honour engaged him to act as he did, for he had promised the poor fellow to conceal him, which, he said, he thought himself further obliged to, as the gamekeeper had begged him not to go into the gentleman's manor, and had at last gone himself, in compliance with his persuasions.

He said this was the whole truth of the matter, and he would take his oath of it, and concluded with very passionately begging Mr Allworthy to have compassion on the poor fellow's family, especially as he himself only had been guilty, and the other had been very difficultly prevailed on to do what he did. "Indeed, sir," said he, "it could hardly be called a lie that I told, for the poor fellow was entirely innocent of the whole matter. I should have gone alone after the birds. Nay, I did go at first, and he only followed me to prevent more mischief. Do, pray, sir, let me be punished, take my little horse away again, but pray, sir, forgive poor George."

Mr Allworthy hesitated a few moments, and then dismissed the boys, advising them to live more friendly and peaceably together.

Chapter Five

The opinions of the divine and the philosopher concerning the two boys, with some reasons for their opinions, and other matters

It is probable, that by disclosing this secret, which had been communicated in the utmost confidence to him, young Blifil preserved his companion from a good lashing. The offence of the bloody nose would have been of itself sufficient cause for Thwackum to have proceeded to correction, but now this was totally absorbed in the consideration of the other matter, and with regard to this, Mr Allworthy declared privately, he thought the boy deserved reward rather than punishment, so that Thwackum's hand was withheld by a general pardon.

Thwackum, whose meditations were full of birch, exclaimed against this weak — and as he said he would venture to call it — wicked lenity. To remit the punishment of such crimes was, he said, to encourage them. He enlarged much on the correction of children, and quoted many texts from Solomon, and others, which being to be found in so many other books, shall not be found here. He then applied himself to the vice of lying, on which head he was altogether as learned as he had been on the other.

Square said, he had been endeavouring to reconcile the behaviour of Tom with his idea of perfect virtue, but could not. He owned there was something which at first sight appeared like fortitude in the action, but as fortitude was a virtue, and falsehood a vice, they could by no means agree or unite together. He added, that as this was in some measure to confound virtue and vice, it might be worth Mr Thwackum's consideration, whether a larger castigation might not be laid on upon the account.

As both these learned men concurred in censuring Jones, so were they no less unanimous in applauding Master Blifil. To bring truth to light, was by the parson asserted to be the duty of every religious man and by the philosopher this was declared to be highly conformable with the rule of right, and the eternal and unalterable fitness of things.

All this, however, weighed very little with Mr Allworthy. He could not be prevailed on to sign the warrant for the execution of Jones. There was something within his own breast with which the invincible fidelity which that youth had preserved, corresponded much better than it had done with the religion of Thwackum, or with the virtue of Square. He therefore strictly ordered the former of these gentlemen to abstain from laying violent hands on Tom for what had passed. The pedagogue was obliged to obey those orders, but not without great reluctance, and frequent mutterings that the boy would be certainly spoiled.

Towards the gamekeeper the good man behaved with more severity. He presently summoned that poor fellow before him, and after many bitter remonstrances, paid him his wages, and dismissed him from his service, for Mr Allworthy rightly observed, that there was a great difference between being guilty of a falsehood to excuse yourself, and to excuse another. He likewise urged, as the principal motive to his inflexible severity against this man, that he had basely suffered Tom Jones to undergo so heavy a punishment for his sake, whereas he ought to have prevented it by making the discovery himself.

When this story became public, many people differed from Square and Thwackum, in judging the conduct of the two lads on the occasion. Master Blifil was generally called a sneaking rascal, a poor-spirited wretch, with other epithets of the like kind, whilst Tom was honoured with the appellations of a brave lad, a jolly dog, and an honest fellow. Indeed, his behaviour to Black George much ingratiated him with all the servants, for though that fellow was before universally disliked, yet he was no sooner turned away than he was as universally pitied. The friendship and gallantry of Tom Jones was celebrated by them all with the highest applause, and they condemned Master Blifil as openly as they durst, without incurring the danger of offending his mother. For all this, however, poor Tom smarted in the flesh, for though Thwackum had been inhibited to exercise his arm on the foregoing account, yet, as the proverb says, 'It is easy to find a stick', etc. So was it easy to find a rod, and indeed, the not being able to find one was the only thing which could have kept Thwackum any long time from chastising poor Jones.

"You shall confess, Tom," the man said, before bringing down the whip with a great thwack, raising a pink weal on the surface of the young, sweet skin.

"Oh sir, I cannot!" said Tom, who already knew his part. He would not bring trouble to anyone else's door, even if it should mean he could not sit down for a week or more.

Another blow brought another weal, but such was the pedagogue's skill at this method of punishment, that he did not draw blood, nor did he intend to just yet. Marking the pale, soft skin was his only desire, so that Tom was brought to confess.

But the boy did not, and held fast, and after half a dozen strikes with the switch, Thwackum saved his aching arm and Tom's quivering, rosy flesh, and turned to striking him with a crop, which left intriguing marks on the boy's body. Once or twice, as if by accident, Thwackum caught the more tender parts of Tom's anatomy, the fine end of the crop merely stroking that sack of flesh that is one of the definitions of the male gender, and Tom, much to his shame, discovered the touch less punishment and more of a stimulant to his baser self. He could only assume that his master had intended to do so.

The schoolmaster's breath came shorter, and Tom was afraid he would have an apoplexy, much as his benefactor's brother-in-law had suffered long before, but this breathing seemed more erratic, and the man did not appear to be stressed by his worthy efforts.

Indeed the man became so carried away by his exertions that he struck harder, and more often, until finally he drew the blood that appeared to be the culmination of his ambitions, for he paused, turned away and bade Tom dress and leave the room. "For I have done with you this day," he said sternly. "No, do

Henry Fielding & Lynne Connolly

not look at me. You do not deserve that privilege. Go and pray for forgiveness, and do not return to this room until tomorrow."

Anxious to leave, Tom scurried away, as best he could with hind quarters painfully swollen, informing a maid on the way that he thought Mr Thwackum might be falling ill, and he would not wish that on anyone.

Had the bare delight in the sport been the only inducement to the pedagogue, it is probable Master Blifil would likewise have had his share, but though Mr Allworthy had given him frequent orders to make no difference between the lads, yet was Thwackum altogether as kind and gentle to this youth, as he was harsh, nay even barbarous, to the other. To say the truth, Blifil had greatly gained his master's affections, partly by the profound respect he always showed his person, but much more by the decent reverence with which he received his doctrine, for he had got by heart, and frequently repeated, his phrases, and maintained all his master's religious principles with a zeal which was surprising in one so young, and which greatly endeared him to the worthy preceptor.

Tom Jones, on the other hand, was not only deficient in outward tokens of respect, often forgetting to pull off his hat, or to bow at his master's approach, but was altogether as unmindful both of his master's precepts and example. He was indeed a thoughtless, giddy youth, with little sobriety in his manners, and less in his countenance, and would often very impudently and indecently laugh at his companion for his serious behaviour.

Mr Square had the same reason for his preference of the former lad, for Tom Jones showed no more regard to the learned discourses which this gentleman would sometimes throw away upon him, than to those of Thwackum. He once ventured to make a jest of the rule of right, and at another time said, he believed there was no rule in the world capable of making such a man as his father—for so Mr Allworthy suffered himself to be called.

Master Blifil, on the contrary, had address enough at sixteen to recommend himself at one and the same time to both these opposites. With one he was all religion, with the other he was all virtue. And when both were present, he was profoundly silent, which both interpreted in his favour and in their own.

Nor was Blifil contented with flattering both these gentlemen to their faces. He took frequent occasions of praising them behind their backs to Allworthy, before whom, when they two were alone, and his uncle commended any religious or virtuous sentiment—for many such came constantly from him—he seldom failed to ascribe it to the good instructions he had received from either Thwackum or Square. He knew his uncle repeated all such compliments to the persons for whose use they were meant, and he found by experience the great impressions which they made on the philosopher, as well as on the divine, for, to say the truth, there is no kind of flattery so irresistible as this, at second hand.

The young gentleman, moreover, soon perceived how extremely grateful all those panegyrics on his instructors were to Mr Allworthy himself, as they so loudly resounded the praise of that singular plan of education which he had laid down. This worthy man having observed the imperfect institution of our public schools, and the many vices which boys were there liable to learn, had resolved to educate his nephew, as well as the other lad, whom he had in a manner adopted, in his own house, where he thought their morals would escape all that danger of being corrupted to which they would be unavoidably exposed in any public school or university.

Having, therefore, determined to commit these boys to the tuition of a private tutor, Mr Thwackum was recommended to him for that office, by a very particular friend, of whose understanding Mr Allworthy had a great opinion, and in whose integrity he placed much confidence. This Thwackum was fellow of a college, where he almost entirely resided, and had a great reputation for learning, religion, and sobriety of manners. And these were doubtless the qualifications by which Mr Allworthy's friend had been induced to recommend him, though indeed this friend had some obligations to Thwackum's family, who were the most considerable persons in a borough which that gentleman represented in parliament.

Thwackum, at his first arrival, was extremely agreeable to Allworthy, and indeed he perfectly answered the character which had been given of him. Upon longer acquaintance, however, and more intimate conversation, this worthy man saw infirmities in the tutor, which he could have wished him to have been without, though as those seemed greatly overbalanced by his good qualities, they did not incline Mr Allworthy to part with him, nor would they indeed have justified such a proceeding. For the reader is greatly mistaken, if he conceives that Thwackum appeared to Mr Allworthy in the same light as he doth to him in this history, and he is as much deceived, if he imagines that the most intimate acquaintance which he himself could have had with that divine, would have informed him of those things which we, from our inspiration, are enabled to open and discover. Of readers who, from such conceits as these, condemn the wisdom or penetration of Mr Allworthy, I shall not scruple to say, that they make a very bad and ungrateful use of that knowledge which we have communicated to them.

These apparent errors in the doctrine of Thwackum served greatly to palliate the contrary errors in that of Square, which our good man no less saw and condemned. He thought, indeed, that the different exuberancies of these gentlemen would correct their different imperfections, and that from both, especially with his assistance, the two lads would derive sufficient precepts of true religion and virtue. If the event happened contrary to his expectations, this possibly proceeded from some fault in the plan itself, which the reader hath my leave to discover, if he can, for we do not pretend to introduce any infallible characters into this history, where we hope nothing will be found which hath never yet been seen in human nature.

To return therefore, the reader will not, I think, wonder that the different behaviour of the two lads above commemorated, produced the different effects of which he hath already seen some instance, and besides this, there was another reason for the conduct of the philosopher and the pedagogue, but this being matter of great importance, we shall reveal it in the next chapter.

Chapter Six

Containing a better reason still for the before-mentioned opinions

It is to be known then, that those two learned personages, who have lately made a considerable figure on the theatre of this history, had, from their first arrival at Mr Allworthy's house, taken so great an affection, the one to his virtue, the other to his religion, that they had meditated the closest alliance with him.

For this purpose they had cast their eyes on that fair widow, whom, though we have not for some time made any mention of her, the reader, we trust, hath not forgot. Mrs Blifil was indeed the object to which they both aspired.

It may seem remarkable, that, of four persons whom we have commemorated at Mr Allworthy's house, three of them should fix their inclinations on a lady who was never greatly celebrated for her beauty, and who was, moreover, now a little descended into the vale of years. But in reality bosom friends, and intimate acquaintances, have a kind of natural propensity to particular females at the house of a friend — viz., to his grandmother, mother, sister, daughter, aunt, niece, or cousin, when they are rich, and to his wife, sister, daughter, niece, cousin, mistress, or servant-maid, if they should be handsome.

We would not, however, have our reader imagine, that persons of such characters as were supported by Thwackum and Square, would undertake a matter of this kind, which hath been a little censured by some rigid moralists, before they had thoroughly examined it, and considered whether it was — as Shakespeare phrases it — 'stuff o' th' conscience', or no. Thwackum was encouraged to the undertaking by reflecting that to covet your neighbour's sister is nowhere forbidden, and he knew it was a rule in the construction of all laws, that *'expressum facit cessare tacitum'*, the sense of which is, 'when a lawgiver sets down plainly his whole meaning, we are prevented from making him mean what we please ourselves'. As some instances of women, therefore, are mentioned in the divine law, which forbids us to covet our neighbour's goods, and that of a sister omitted, he concluded it to be lawful. And as to Square, who was in his person what is called a jolly fellow, or a widow's man, he easily reconciled his choice to the eternal fitness of things.

Now, as both of these gentlemen were industrious in taking every opportunity of recommending themselves to the widow, they apprehended one certain method was, by giving her son the constant preference to the other lad. As they conceived the kindness and affection which Mr Allworthy showed the latter, must be highly disagreeable to her, they doubted not but the laying hold on all occasions to degrade and vilify him, would be highly pleasing to her, who, as she hated the boy, must love all those who did him any hurt.

In this Thwackum had the advantage, for while Square could only scarify the poor lad's reputation, he could flea his skin, and indeed, he considered every lash he gave him as a compliment paid to his mistress, so that he could, with the utmost propriety, repeat this old flogging line, *"Castigo te non quod odio habeam, sed quod* amem. I chastise thee not out of hatred, but out of love."* And this, indeed, he often had in his mouth, or rather, according to the old phrase, never more properly applied, at his fingers' ends. Had he but known it, the lady had an interest in such activities, although several years had passed since her last opportunity to practice the English method. But that had not diminished her enthusiasm for the sport.

For this reason, principally, the two gentlemen concurred, as we have seen above, in their opinion concerning the two lads, this being, indeed, almost the only instance of their concurring on any point, for, beside the difference of their principles, they had both long ago strongly suspected each other's design, and hated one another with no little degree of inveteracy.

This mutual animosity was a good deal increased by their alternate successes, for Mrs Blifil knew what they would be at long before they imagined it, or, indeed, intended she should, for they proceeded with great caution, lest she should be offended, and acquaint Mr Allworthy. But they had no reason for any such fear, she was well enough pleased with a passion, of which she intended none should have any fruits but herself. And the only fruits she designed for herself were, flattery and courtship, for which purpose she soothed them by turns, and a long time equally.

Every day first one gentleman and then the other assaulted her with sweet words and courtship, and while she enjoyed both, she never gave any preference over the other.

One morning, she was walking by her favourite oak when Mr Square accosted her with "What? Have the Muses finally descended to earth, embodied in one person?" He granted her an indulgent smile, as if he made a jest they both could share.

Mrs Blifil returned the smile, but waited for more, as more there would undoubtedly be. She might not have the learning of the good philosopher, but she had a great deal more commonsense.

She was not long in waiting. "Your beauty dazzles the sun," Square animadverted. "Dare I approach such a creature?" His smile became less avuncular, more predatory as he moved closer and touched her hand. "Perhaps I was wrong," he said, stroking her. "Perhaps Venus herself has come down to earth."

When the lady remained in place, he moved closer, taking a most deliberate step to her side, before dipping his head to feather a gentle kiss over her shoulder. Although she had donned a light gown and fichu that morning, she allowed herself to shiver, to give him some encouragement. Such flirtation worked well in lieu of the pleasures she preferred. At least she could thank her late husband for introducing her to such delights. She had since perfected the practice with person or persons unknown to your poor narrator, and knew her preferences. However, Square had shown no inclination to enjoy her attentions, and she had to move carefully, lest he take fright and move away. However, the prize was one she understood only too well.

She turned her head away, as if to modestly hide her blushes, but she allowed her hand to remain in Square's, and his person to linger in close proximity to hers. A sweet kiss on the cheek was her reward and then, as if by accident, when she turned her head, his lips brushed hers. The plentiful exercise Square afforded his mouth and tongue added to the soft texture and dexterity, which he employed to full extent in the interlude that followed, so much that before the end of their first flurry of kisses, he had her turned towards him and her full breasts in his hands. Indeed, before she quit the house that morning intent on her morning constitutional, Mrs Blifil had ensured that anyone laying hands on her person would find her more intimate parts more accessible than usual, by lacing her stays in a particular way, and wearing the lightest of petticoats. She had employed such tactics before with her late husband to great effect. It would work as well with her new swains.

Enchanted by the lady's charms, Square set to kissing and caressing, comparing her with a newly blossomed rose, presented to the great Zeus himself by Hera, his wife.

Having thus put himself in the place of the King of the gods of Olympus, Mr Square set to more earthly concerns, bending his head to kiss and suckle her breasts, as eager as any infant.

He urged her to lean back on that sturdy bench that had witnessed many happy scenes before this, and not merely from the lady and her swains. Willingly, she obeyed, and glancing up, perceived a pair of eyes concealed in the thick roof of leaves above her head. Those eyes belonged to a body she had reason to know, but no sooner had she identified the orbs as being owned by Mr Thwackum, than Mr Square, unaware of their peeping Tom, was upon her, and spreading kisses over her uncovered bosom, to the great satisfaction of them both.

She did not attempt to prevent his ingress under her skirts, indeed she had left off her hoops that morning for that very purpose, and wore instead a quilted petticoat which served to soften the hard surface on which she lay.

She did not avoid the hard, unblinking stare of the man perched above them, but stared directly at him, letting him know that she, at least, was in perfect knowledge that the great oak harboured an invader. Not a partridge, as the old rhyme would have it, but a parson. A parson in an oak tree.

Mr Square continued on his journey of discovery, his hand reaching that sweet pearl of flesh between her legs, sheltered by the bush of hair cultivated to protect a woman's most delicate parts. For a philosopher, he had a dexterous touch, most gratifying, and Mrs Blifil thought that if she could persuade him to submit to her ungentle hand, he might be the choice she would make. If she wished for another lord and master.

Mr Blifil insinuated his digits into that sweet space guaranteed to bring the most pleasure to a poor female who had not known a foreign touch in that place for some time. She sighed under his ministrations, and savoured his skill. He used her most assiduously, drawing his fingers out then thrusting in with a vigour that rivalled that part of his anatomy that pushed insistently against the fall of his sturdy country breeches.

All the while their interloper watched, and Mrs Blifil allowed it, enjoying the attentions of one admirer and the worshipful stare of another, for the lady always savoured the interest of more than one gentleman, being ever hungry for notice.

The sounds of his work permeated the atmosphere, a wet, sucking sound, punctuated by the lady's frequent sighs and moans, the better to encourage the man in his exertions.

He brought her to one great sigh, in which she cried her pleasure out to the heavens and the man above them, and allowed Mr Square to caress her for a while before he helped to restore her person to respectability.

Such was his ambition to secure her body and all that went with it in a binding manner that Square chose to forego his own pleasure, and instead offered her his arm in support to escort her back to the house, so she might recover from her exertions in her chamber. And all the time he remained unaware of the man in the tree, watching them with an avidity that could not have been bettered by a magpie lusting after a bright trinket.

The two men pleased Mrs Blifil so much that day that she resolved to take one or the other, but when the matter came to a decision, she could not make up her mind.

She was, indeed, rather inclined to favour the parson's principles, but Square's person was more agreeable to her eye, for he was a comely man, whereas the pedagogue did in countenance very nearly resemble that gentleman, who, in the Harlot's Progress, is seen correcting the ladies in Bridewell.

Whether Mrs Blifil had been surfeited with the sweets of marriage, or disgusted by its bitters, or from what other cause it proceeded, I will not determine, but she could never be brought to listen to any second proposals. However, she at last conversed with Square with such a degree of inadvisable intimacy that malicious tongues began to whisper things of her, to which, as well for the sake of the lady, as that they were highly disagreeable to the rule of right and the fitness of things, we will give no more credit, and therefore shall not blot our paper further with them. The pedagogue, 'tis certain, whipped on, without getting a step nearer to his journey's end.

Indeed he had committed a great error, and that Square discovered much sooner than himself. Mrs Blifil—as, perhaps, the reader may have formerly guessed—was not over and above pleased with the behaviour of her husband. Nay, to be honest, she absolutely hated him, till his death at last a little reconciled him to her affections. It will not be therefore greatly wondered at, if she had not the most violent regard to the offspring she had by him. And, in fact, she had so little of this regard, that in his infancy she seldom saw her son, or took any notice of him, and hence she acquiesced, after a little reluctance, in all the favours which Mr Allworthy showered on the foundling, whom the good man called his own boy, and in all things put on an entire equality with Master Blifil.

This acquiescence in Mrs Blifil was considered by the neighbours, and by the family, as a mark of her condescension to her brother's humour, and she was imagined by all others, as well as Thwackum and Square, to hate the foundling in her heart. Nay, the more civility she showed him, the more they conceived she detested him, and the surer schemes she was laying for his ruin, for as they thought it her interest to hate him, it was very difficult for her to persuade them she did not.

Thwackum was the more confirmed in his opinion, as she had more than once slyly caused him to whip Tom Jones, when Mr Allworthy, who was an enemy to this exercise, was abroad, whereas she had never given any such orders concerning young Blifil. He noted the pleasure she gained by such an act, and exerted himself mightily to give her what she wished for, and so cause the lad much pain. And this had likewise imposed upon Square. In reality, though she certainly hated her own son — of which, however monstrous it appears, I am assured she is not a singular instance — she appeared, notwithstanding all her outward compliance, to be in her heart sufficiently displeased with all the favour shown by Mr Allworthy to the foundling. She frequently complained of this behind her brother's back, and very sharply censured him for it, both to Thwackum and Square. Nay, she would throw it in the teeth of Allworthy himself, when a little quarrel, or miff, as it is vulgarly called, arose between them.

However, when Tom grew up, and gave tokens of that gallantry of temper which greatly recommends men to women, this disinclination which she had discovered to him when a child, by degrees abated, and at last she so evidently demonstrated her affection to him to be much stronger than what she bore her own son, that it was impossible to mistake her any longer. She was so desirous of often seeing him, and discovered such satisfaction and delight in his company, that before he was eighteen years old he was become a rival to both Square and Thwackum, and what is worse, the whole country began to talk as loudly of her inclination to Tom, as they had before done of that which she had shown to Square, on which account the philosopher conceived the most implacable hatred for our poor hero.

Chapter Seven

In which the author himself makes his appearance on the stage

Though Mr Allworthy was not of himself hasty to see things in a disadvantageous light, and was a stranger to the public voice, which seldom reaches to a brother or a husband, though it rings in the ears of all the neighbourhood, yet was this affection of Mrs Blifil to Tom, and the preference which she too visibly gave him to her own son, of the utmost disadvantage to that youth.

For such was the compassion which inhabited Mr Allworthy's mind, that nothing but the steel of justice could ever subdue it. To be unfortunate in any respect was sufficient, if there was no demerit to counterpoise it, to turn the scale of that good man's pity, and to engage his friendship and his benefaction.

When therefore he plainly saw Master Blifil was absolutely detested — for that he was — by his own mother, he began, on that account only, to look with an eye of compassion upon him, and what the effects of compassion are, in good and benevolent minds, I need not here explain to most of my readers.

Henceforward he saw every appearance of virtue in the youth through the magnifying end, and viewed all his faults with the glass inverted, so that they became scarce perceptible. And this perhaps the amiable temper of pity may make commendable, but the next step the weakness of human nature alone must excuse, for he no sooner perceived that preference which Mrs Blifil gave to Tom, than that poor youth, however innocent, began to sink in his affections as he rose in hers. This, it is true, would of itself alone never have been able to eradicate Jones from his bosom, but it was greatly injurious to him, and prepared Mr Allworthy's mind for those impressions which afterwards produced the mighty events that will be contained hereafter in this history, and to which, it must be confessed, the unfortunate lad, by his own wantonness, wildness, and want of caution, too much contributed.

In recording some instances of these, we shall, if rightly understood, afford a very useful lesson to those well-disposed youths who shall hereafter be our readers, for they may here find, that goodness of heart, and openness of temper, though these may give them great comfort within, and administer to an honest pride in their own minds, will by no means, alas, do their business in the world. Prudence and circumspection are necessary even to the best of men. They are indeed, as it were, a guard to Virtue, without which she can never be safe. It is not enough that your designs, nay, that your actions, are intrinsically good, you must take care they shall appear so. If your inside be never so beautiful, you must preserve a fair outside also. This must be constantly looked to, or malice and envy will take care to blacken it so, that the sagacity and goodness of an Allworthy will not be able to see through it, and to discern the beauties within.

Let this, my young readers, be your constant maxim, that no man can be good enough to enable him to neglect the rules of prudence, nor will Virtue herself look beautiful, unless she be bedecked with the outward ornaments of decency and decorum. And this precept, my worthy disciples, if you read with due attention, you will, I hope, find sufficiently enforced by examples in the following pages.

I ask pardon for this short appearance, by way of chorus, on the stage. It is in reality for my own sake, that, while I am discovering the rocks on which innocence and goodness often split, I may not be misunderstood to recommend the very means to my worthy readers, by which I intend to show them they will be undone. And this, as I could not prevail on any of my actors to speak, I myself was obliged to declare.

Chapter Eight

A childish incident, in which, however, is seen a good-natured disposition in Tom Jones

The reader may remember that Mr Allworthy gave Tom Jones a little horse, as a kind of smart-money for the punishment which he imagined he had suffered innocently.

This horse Tom kept above half a year, and then rode him to a neighbouring fair, and sold him.

At his return, being questioned by Thwackum what he had done with the money for which the horse was sold, he frankly declared he would not tell him.

"Oho!" said Thwackum. "You will not! Then I will have it out of your breeches," that being the place to which he always applied for information on every doubtful occasion.

Tom was now mounted on the back of a footman, and everything prepared for execution, when Mr Allworthy, entering the room, gave the criminal a reprieve, and took him with him into another apartment, where, being alone with Tom, he put the same question to him which Thwackum had before asked him.

Tom answered, he could in duty refuse him nothing, but as for that tyrannical rascal, he would never make him any other answer than with a cudgel, with which he hoped soon to be able to pay him for all his barbarities.

Mr Allworthy very severely reprimanded the lad for his indecent and disrespectful expressions concerning his master, but much more for his avowing an intention of revenge. He threatened him with the entire loss of his favour, if he ever heard such another word from his mouth, for, he said, he would never support or befriend a reprobate. By these and the like declarations, he extorted some compunction from Tom, in which that youth was not over-sincere, for he really meditated some return for all the smarting favours he had received at the hands of the pedagogue. He was, however, brought by Mr Allworthy to express a concern for his resentment against Thwackum, and then the good man, after some wholesome admonition, permitted him to proceed, which he did as follows.

"Indeed, my dear sir, I love and honour you more than all the world, I know the great obligations I have to you, and should detest myself if I thought my heart was capable of ingratitude. Could the little horse you gave me speak, I am sure he could tell you how fond I was of your present, for I had more pleasure in feeding him than in riding him. Indeed, sir, it went to my heart to part with him, nor would I have sold him upon any other account in the world than what I did. You yourself, sir, I am convinced, in my case, would have done the same, for none ever so sensibly felt the misfortunes of others. What would you feel, dear sir, if you thought yourself the occasion of them? Indeed, sir, there never was any misery like theirs."

"Like whose, child?" said Allworthy. "What do you mean?"

"Oh, sir!" answered Tom. "Your poor gamekeeper, with all his large family, ever since your discarding him, have been perishing with all the miseries of cold and hunger, I could not bear to see these poor wretches naked and starving, and at the same time know myself to have been the occasion of all their sufferings. I could not bear it, sir, upon my soul, I could not." Here the tears ran down his cheeks, and he thus proceeded, "It was to save them from absolute destruction I parted with your dear present, notwithstanding all the value I had for it, I sold the horse for them, and they have every farthing of the money."

Mr Allworthy now stood silent for some moments, and before he spoke the tears started from his eyes. He at length dismissed Tom with a gentle rebuke, advising him for the future to apply to him in cases of distress, rather than to use extraordinary means of relieving them himself.

This affair was afterwards the subject of much debate between Thwackum and Square. Thwackum held, that this was flying in Mr Allworthy's face, who had intended to punish the fellow for his disobedience. He said, in some instances, what the world called charity appeared to him to be opposing the will of the Almighty, which had marked some particular persons for destruction, and that this was in like manner acting in opposition to Mr Allworthy, concluding, as usual, with a hearty recommendation of birch.

Square argued strongly on the other side, in opposition perhaps to Thwackum, or in compliance with Mr Allworthy, who seemed very much to approve what Jones had done. As to what he urged on this occasion, as I am convinced most of my readers will be much abler advocates for poor Jones, it would be impertinent to relate it. Indeed it was not difficult to reconcile to the rule of right an action which it would have been impossible to deduce from the rule of wrong.

Chapter Nine

Containing an incident of a more heinous kind, with the comments of Thwackum and Square

It hath been observed by some man of much greater reputation for wisdom than myself, that misfortunes seldom come single. An instance of this may, I believe, be seen in those gentlemen who have the misfortune to have any of their rogueries detected, for here discovery seldom stops till the whole is come out. Thus it happened to poor Tom, who was no sooner pardoned for selling the horse, than he was discovered to have some time before sold a fine Bible which Mr Allworthy gave him, the money arising from which sale he had disposed of in the same manner. This Bible Master Blifil had purchased, though he had already such another of his own, partly out of respect for the book, and partly out of friendship to Tom, being unwilling that the Bible should be sold out of the family at half-price. He therefore deposited the said half-price himself, for he was a very prudent lad, and so careful of his money, that he had laid up almost every penny which he had received from Mr Allworthy.

Some people have been noted to be able to read in no book but their own. On the contrary, from the time when Master Blifil was first possessed of this Bible, he never used any other. Nay, he was seen reading in it much oftener than he had before been in his own. Now, as he frequently asked Thwackum to explain difficult passages to him, that gentleman unfortunately took notice of Tom's name, which was written in many parts of the book. This brought on an inquiry, which obliged Master Blifil to discover the whole matter.

Thwackum was resolved a crime of this kind, which he called sacrilege, should not go unpunished. He therefore proceeded immediately to castigation, and not contented with that he acquainted Mr Allworthy, at their next meeting, with this monstrous crime, as it appeared to him, inveighing against Tom in the most bitter terms, and likening him to the buyers and sellers who were driven out of the temple.

Square saw this matter in a very different light. He said, he could not perceive any higher crime in selling one book than in selling another. That to sell Bibles was strictly lawful by all laws both Divine and human, and consequently there was no unfitness in it. He told Thwackum, that his great concern on this occasion brought to his mind the story of a very devout woman, who, out of pure regard to religion, stole Tillotson's Sermons from a lady of her acquaintance.

This story caused a vast quantity of blood to rush into the parson's face, which of itself was none of the palest, and he was going to reply with great warmth and anger, had not Mrs Blifil, who was present at this debate, interposed. That lady declared herself absolutely of Mr Square's side. She argued, indeed, very learnedly in support of his opinion, and concluded with saying, if Tom had been guilty of any fault, she must confess her own son appeared to be equally culpable, for that she could see no difference between the buyer and the seller, both of whom were alike to be driven out of the temple.

Mrs Blifil having declared her opinion, put an end to the debate. Square's triumph would almost have stopped his words, had he needed them, and Thwackum, who, for reasons before-mentioned, durst not venture at disobliging the lady, was almost choked with indignation. As to Mr Allworthy, he said, since the boy had been already punished he would not deliver his sentiments on the occasion, and whether he was or was not angry with the lad, I must leave to the reader's own conjecture.

Soon after this, an action was brought against the gamekeeper by Squire Western—the gentleman in whose manor the partridge was killed—for depredations of the like kind. This was a most unfortunate circumstance for the fellow, as it not only of itself threatened his ruin, but actually prevented Mr Allworthy from restoring him to his favour. For as that gentleman was walking out one evening with Master Blifil and young Jones, the latter slyly drew him to the habitation of Black George, where the family of that poor wretch, namely, his wife and children, were found in all the misery with which cold, hunger, and nakedness, can affect human creatures, for as to the money they had received from Jones, former debts had consumed almost the whole.

Such a scene as this could not fail of affecting the heart of Mr Allworthy. He immediately gave the mother a couple of guineas, with which he bid her clothe her children. The poor woman burst into tears at this goodness, and while she was thanking him, could not refrain from expressing her gratitude to Tom, who had, she said, long preserved both her and hers from starving. "We have not," said she, "had a morsel to eat, nor have these poor children had a rag to put on, but what his goodness hath bestowed on us." For, indeed, besides the horse and the Bible, Tom had sacrificed a night-gown, and other things, to the use of this distressed family.

On their return home, Tom made use of all his eloquence to display the wretchedness of these people, and the penitence of Black George himself, and in this he succeeded so well, that Mr Allworthy said, he thought the man had suffered enough for what was past, that he would forgive him, and think of some means of providing for him and his family.

Jones was so delighted with this news, that, though it was dark when they returned home, he could not help going back a mile, in a shower of rain, to acquaint the poor woman with the glad tidings. But, like other hasty divulgers of news, he only brought on himself the trouble of contradicting it, for the ill fortune of Black George made use of the very opportunity of his friend's absence to overturn all again.

Tom, disheartened, stopped at the ale house, the better to restore his spirits, and found a party of strangers stopped there overnight, after losing a wheel from their travelling carriage. Two ladies, very well set up, on their way, they said, to London. Tom had promised himself a trip to London before too long had passed, and they fell to talking, Tom abandoning his customary companions to sit at their table and keep them company during their dinner.

He found the ladies excellent company, and discovered the older, very well formed and with all her own teeth, owned an establishment in the region of Covent Garden, a place well known for the fresh produce it sold in the morning and the not-so-fresh produce on offer at night times.

After assuring him that they were returning from their holiday, and they would not be recommencing their business in his part of the world, the ladies invited him to join them for a small libation in their bedchamber, the better to aid their sleep, for, as one lady said, "We do not sleep well in any bed but our own, and we find the addition of a small quantity of brandy at bedtime aids slumber."

The younger lady, who had informed him her name was Anne, agreed with her mentor and added, "We have found your conversation so stimulating, we would prefer to discuss it further in the privacy of our own bedchamber. Do come up!" And she gave him the sweetest smile, so that Tom had no choice but to accompany them upstairs.

The ladies had bespoken the finest room in the house, a spacious chamber containing a large four-poster bed, which, the local wits would have it, was there before the inn was built, having belonged to a great king in the past ages, who had left it there when he had no need of it any more.

Now the company hiring it for a night had need, for no sooner had they latched the door than the ladies were on him, saying what a fine, well-set-up young man he was, how much maturity became him, Tom having reached the age of eighteen, and what a strong body and comely limbs he owned. The younger,

Anne, did not delay in divesting him of his coat. Tom thought they might wish to steal his money, but they would have poor pickings from him, as he had given all he had to the gamekeeper's family. The innkeeper knew him well enough to set up an account in his name, so he had not even the wherewithal to pay him until the morrow.

But the thought passed through his mind and left it as if it never was, because the ladies would not stop touching his person, and Tom, much though he preferred to keep his body to himself, enjoyed their attentions.

They drew him closer to the bed, and so slow was their progress that by the time they reached its lofty heights, for it was one of those old erections that the occupant must climb up to reach the sleeping-surface, Tom had lost his coat, neckcloth and shirt, Anne keeping him occupied beforehand, while the older lady, Mary, attended to the stripping, displaying her expertise and revealing the fact that she had done so several times before.

"Oh, sir, I have lost count of the times I have aided gentlemen in just such a way!" Mary exclaimed. "I do not, as a rule, undergo such exercise these days, having retired from the field to make way for my younger sisters, but Anne here is from the provinces and not used to our ways. You would oblige us both by engaging in that activity that will heretofore become her career."

Tom, being an obliging lad, readily agreed to her suggestion, and the ladies promptly discarded any attempt at modesty, unhooking and unlacing until their gowns lay in heaps on the chair, their hoops with them. Tom watched the show with great interest. He had not indulged in a great deal of such activity in his time, his benefactor indulging him with the maxim of never engaging in intimacy with any of the household servants, and the village being such a centre of gossip that he dared not pay too much attention to anyone hereabouts. But, as young men do, he had managed.

This would be an experience beyond his capabilities, and had not the ladies been skilled, he would have brought the matter to a conclusion far earlier than they would have liked, but such was their teasing that they gave him pause to recompose himself, and have at it with a stronger spirit.

The ladies walked around him, the better to admire the comeliness of his form, which, they assured him, would tempt a saint into sin. "Such strong shoulders!" Anne declared, running her hand along the impressive breadth.

When Tom gave a shrug, she shuddered in delight. "I love a strong man."

Mary laughed and declared herself in accord with her friend. "We have only had each other for company on this journey. It's a pleasure to share our bed with a man once more."

"And such a man!" Anne's tone was almost cooing, sharing its gentle sweetness with the dove, but the seductive note was all her own, as sweet as the song of the thrush on a summer morning.

The young woman coyly lowered her shift and revealed her breasts, which were thrust high by the tight-lacing of her stays. Tom understood that many ladies preferred to travel with their stays looser than they customarily used, but such was not the case here, because Mary came around to stand next to her, and favour him with a similar display.

Truly, Tom could not decide whether he preferred the smooth, sweet apples of Anne, or the larger fruit

Mary offered, so he took hold of both, the better to judge. Much laughter ensued, and then kisses, first one and then the other, and then Mary indulged Anne with a long kiss of her own, displaying to an astonished Tom the way ladies could take pleasure in each other when they did not have a man nearby.

Their breasts pressed together in a display that could only stir Tom to further exertions. If he had imagined that both were an enticement, together they created a temptation no youth could resist, and Tom fell to, kissing and sucking until they laughingly bade him stop so they could climb on to that high mattress where they intended to take the play to its inevitable conclusion.

Tom helped one lady, and then the other, and they did not object when his hand slipped higher than was strictly polite. The rewards awaiting him were considerable, lush, wet paradise at the apex of each lady's thighs, so similar and yet so different.

When he clambered up to join them, he took care to disturb their already scanty shifts, so that the beauties of their forms were exposed to his avid stare. By which he discovered that Anne was a natural blonde beauty, and Mary had lush, auburn curls which almost matched the hair on her head. Nothing loath, they spread their legs and exposed themselves for his viewing pleasure. That small pearl of flesh stood prominently on each, and he couldn't resist a small taste, so lusciously inviting did they appear, but he did not linger, too eager to bring the banquet to its main course.

Like the greatest course in an earl's mansion, the ladies had much to offer, and the difference of their tastes only enhanced their similarities for Tom. Undecided which to favour first, they helped him on his way by unbuttoning the fall of his breeches and unfastening the buckles at his knees, so he could strip the offending garment from his body, the better to show them he was more than ready to indulge them in any way they wished.

Mary, declaring herself more than ready, pushed him down on to the bed, so he lay recumbent, and before he could regain his balance, straddled him, opening her body to him fully so he could touch and get hold of her bosom, now swinging before his face in delightful invitation. She lowered herself on to that organ that stood prepared to accede to her demands, and as she enclosed him in female flesh, he gave out such a groan, that had he been listening, the squire would have known his activity. Tom could only be glad that the inn was a mile or more distant from his customary abode, for he could not control his delight.

Anne, laughing as she saw his reaction to her mistress's sudden claiming, watched them, and why this would happen Tom did not know, but her observation added to his pleasure, driving him to exert his body in greater efforts to please Mary and bring her to that conclusion that he had experienced but a few times before in a woman's body. Instinct gave him the experience he in reality lacked, and he bucked against her, feeling her body grow hotter and more insistent. Her breasts bounced in harmony with her actions, and none of them heeded the creaking of the sturdy bed as Mary cried out, "Oh God, my death has come!" as her quim contracted around him and she collapsed on to the bed with great moaning and sweet sighs.

No sooner had she pulled away, exposing that sensitive part of Tom to the cooler air, than Anne was upon him, taking the place of the other woman. Anne had less expertise, but more energy, her smaller bosom nonetheless jiggling in a most distracting manner as she rode him in the manner of a man riding a horse on the hunting field.

Tom could take no more. He exploded with a great cry, his cock rigid inside the young woman, who smiled down at him in an almost angelic manner, as she took all he bestowed upon her, before dismounting and lying on the bed next to him.

But then, "My sweet," Mary said caressingly to her young charge, "You have not come to that sweet climax women are entitled to expect. While I can understand our young friend lacking the stamina on an initial encounter, allow me to aid you to that oblivion."

So saying, she took the tiny pearl of flesh between the girl's legs between two fingers, delicately pressing and tweaking until Anne moaned most delightfully, and turned her head to Tom, allowing him to sip at her lips. He had the notion that Mary would accept a little aid, and while he recovered the tumescent state the ladies preferred, he used his fingers, pushing them inside his new friend's most intimate recess while Mary worked her other parts. Anne still held evidence of Tom's recent activity within her person, but this was released as their exertions reached their natural conclusion. Tom could not help but admire the neat way nearly all the creamy essence of their previous encounter was expelled from Anne as she cried out and came, after which Mary used Anne's shift to sop up the juices and prepare her for a new invasion.

So it was that Tom spent the night in such enjoyable activity that he did not reach his home until light was dawning the next morning, having seen his delectable companions on their journey, with many promises of visits in the future. He was not so innocent that he did not understand that a free sample of the joys they could offer could be expected to entice him to visit the establishment Mary assured him was discreet and genteel, but that did not prevent him vowing to himself that he would pay them a call if he ever found himself in the region of Covent Garden. After all, it was only polite to return such a visit.

Chapter Ten

In which Master Blifil and Jones appear in different lights

Master Blifil fell very short of his companion in the amiable quality of mercy, but he as greatly exceeded him in one of a much higher kind, namely, in justice, in which he followed both the precepts and example of Thwackum and Square. Though they would both make frequent use of the word mercy, yet it was plain that in reality Square held it to be inconsistent with the rule of right, and Thwackum was for doing justice, and leaving mercy to heaven. The two gentlemen did indeed somewhat differ in opinion concerning the objects of this sublime virtue, by which Thwackum would probably have destroyed one half of mankind, and Square the other half.

Master Blifil then, though he had kept silence in the presence of Jones, yet, when he had better considered the matter, could by no means endure the thought of suffering his uncle to confer favours on the undeserving. He therefore resolved immediately to acquaint him with the fact which we have above slightly hinted to the readers. The truth of which was as follows.

The gamekeeper, about a year after he was dismissed from Mr Allworthy's service, and before Tom's selling the horse, being in want of bread, either to fill his own mouth or those of his family, as he passed through a field belonging to Mr Western espied a hare sitting in her form. This hare he had basely and barbarously knocked on the head, against the laws of the land, and no less against the laws of sportsmen.

The higgler to whom the hare was sold, being unfortunately taken many months after with a quantity of game upon him, was obliged to make his peace with the squire, by becoming evidence against some poacher. And now Black George was pitched upon by him, as being a person already obnoxious to Mr Western, and one of no good fame in the country. He was, besides, the best sacrifice the higgler could make, as he had supplied him with no game since, and by this means the witness had an opportunity of screening his better customers, for the squire, being charmed with the power of punishing Black George, whom a single transgression was sufficient to ruin, made no further enquiry.

Had this fact been truly laid before Mr Allworthy, it might probably have done the gamekeeper very little mischief. But there is no zeal blinder than that which is inspired with the love of justice against offenders. Master Blifil had forgot the distance of the time. He varied likewise in the manner of the fact, and by the hasty addition of the single letter 'S' he considerably altered the story, for he said that George had wired hares. These alterations might probably have been set right, had not Master Blifil unluckily insisted on a promise of secrecy from Mr Allworthy before he revealed the matter to him, but by that means the poor gamekeeper was condemned without having an opportunity to defend himself, for as the fact of killing the hare, and of the action brought, were certainly true, Mr Allworthy had no doubt concerning the rest.

Short-lived then was the joy of these poor people, for Mr Allworthy the next morning declared he had fresh reason, without assigning it, for his anger, and strictly forbade Tom to mention George any more, though as for his family, he said he would endeavour to keep them from starving, but as to the fellow himself, he would leave him to the laws, which nothing could keep him from breaking.

Tom could by no means divine what had incensed Mr Allworthy, for of Master Blifil he had not the least suspicion. However, as his friendship was to be tired out by no disappointments, he now determined to try another method of preserving the poor gamekeeper from ruin.

Jones was lately grown very intimate with Mr Western. He had so greatly recommended himself to that gentleman, by leaping over five-barred gates, and by other acts of sportsmanship, that the squire had declared Tom would certainly make a great man if he had but sufficient encouragement. He often wished he had himself a son with such parts, and one day very solemnly asserted at a drinking bout, that Tom should hunt a pack of hounds for a thousand pound of his money, with any huntsman in the whole country.

By such kind of talents he had so ingratiated himself with the squire, that he was a most welcome guest at his table, and a favourite companion in his sport, everything which the squire held most dear, to wit, his guns, dogs, and horses, were now as much at the command of Jones, as if they had been his own. He resolved therefore to make use of this favour on behalf of his friend Black George, whom he hoped to introduce into Mr Western's family, in the same capacity in which he had before served Mr Allworthy.

The reader, if he considers that this fellow was already obnoxious to Mr Western, and if he considers further the weighty business by which that gentleman's displeasure had been incurred, will perhaps condemn this as a foolish and desperate undertaking, but if he should totally condemn young Jones on that account, he will greatly applaud him for strengthening himself with all imaginable interest on so arduous an occasion.

For this purpose, then, Tom applied to Mr Western's daughter, a young lady of about seventeen years of age, whom her father, next after those necessary implements of sport just before mentioned, loved and esteemed above all the world. Now, as she had some influence on the squire, so Tom had some little influence on her. But this being the intended heroine of this work, a lady with whom we ourselves are greatly in love, and with whom many of our readers will probably be in love too, before we part, it is by no means proper she should make her appearance at the end of a book.

BOOK FOUR

Containing the time of a year.

Chapter One

Containing five pages of paper

As truth distinguishes our writings from those idle romances which are filled with monsters — the productions, not of nature, but of distempered brains, and which have been therefore recommended by an eminent critic to the sole use of the pastry-cook — so, on the other hand, we would avoid any resemblance to that kind of history which a celebrated poet seems to think is no less calculated for the emolument of the brewer, as the reading it should be always attended with a tankard of good ale —

While history with her comrade ale,
Soothes the sad series of her serious tale.

For as this is the liquor of modern historians, nay, perhaps their muse, if we may believe the opinion of Butler, who attributes inspiration to ale, it ought likewise to be the potation of their readers, since every book ought to be read with the same spirit and in the same manner as it is writ. Thus the famous author of Hurlothrumbo told a learned bishop, that the reason his lordship could not taste the excellence of his piece was, that he did not read it with a fiddle in his hand, which instrument he himself had always had in his own, when he composed it.

That our work, therefore, might be in no danger of being likened to the labours of these historians, we have taken every occasion of interspersing through the whole sundry similes, descriptions, and other kind of poetical embellishments. These are, indeed, designed to supply the place of the said ale, and to refresh the mind, whenever those slumbers, which in a long work are apt to invade the reader as well as the writer, shall begin to creep upon him. Without interruptions of this kind, the best narrative of plain matter of fact must overpower every reader, for nothing but the everlasting watchfulness, which Homer has ascribed only to Jove himself, can be proof against a newspaper of many volumes.

We shall leave to the reader to determine with what judgement we have chosen the several occasions for inserting those ornamental parts of our work. Surely it will be allowed that none could be more proper than the present, where we are about to introduce a considerable character on the scene, no less, indeed, than the heroine of this heroic, historical, prosaic poem. Here, therefore, we have thought proper to prepare the mind of the reader for her reception, by filling it with every pleasing image which we can draw from the face of nature. And for this method we plead many precedents. First, this is an art well known to, and much practised by, our tragic poets, who seldom fail to prepare their audience for the reception of their principal characters.

Thus the hero is always introduced with a flourish of drums and trumpets, in order to rouse a martial spirit in the audience, and to accommodate their ears to bombast and fustian, which Mr Locke's blind man would not have grossly erred in likening to the sound of a trumpet. Again, when lovers are coming forth, soft music often conducts them on the stage, either to soothe the audience with the softness of the tender passion, or to lull and prepare them for that gentle slumber in which they will most probably be composed by the ensuing scene.

And not only the poets, but the masters of these poets, the managers of playhouses, seem to be in this secret, for, besides the aforesaid kettle-drums, etc, which denote the hero's approach, he is generally ushered on the stage by a large troop of half a dozen scene-shifters, and how necessary these are imagined to his appearance, may be concluded from the following theatrical story.

King Pyrrhus was at dinner at an ale-house bordering on the theatre, when he was summoned to go on the stage. The hero, being unwilling to quit his shoulder of mutton, and as unwilling to draw on himself the indignation of Mr Wilks, his brother-manager, for making the audience wait, had bribed these his harbingers to be out of the way. While Mr Wilks, therefore, was thundering out, "Where are the carpenters to walk on before King Pyrrhus?" that monarch very quietly ate his mutton, and the audience, however impatient, were obliged to entertain themselves with music in his absence.

To be plain, I much question whether the politician, who hath generally a good nose, hath not scented out somewhat of the utility of this practice. I am convinced that awful magistrate my lord-mayor contracts a good deal of that reverence which attends him through the year, by the several pageants which precede his pomp. Nay, I must confess, that even I myself, who am not remarkably liable to be captivated with show, have yielded not a little to the impressions of much preceding state. When I have seen a man strutting in a procession, after others whose business was only to walk before him, I have conceived a higher notion of his dignity than I have felt on seeing him in a common situation.

But there is one instance, which comes exactly up to my purpose. This is the custom of sending on a basket-woman, who is to precede the pomp at a coronation, and to strew the stage with flowers, before the great personages begin their procession. The ancients would certainly have invoked the goddess Flora for this purpose, and it would have been no difficulty for their priests, or politicians to have persuaded the people of the real presence of the deity, though a plain mortal had personated her and performed her office. But we have no such design of imposing on our reader, and therefore those who object to the heathen theology, may, if they please, change our goddess into the above-mentioned basket-woman.

Our intention, in short, is to introduce our heroine with the utmost solemnity in our power, with an elevation of style, and all other circumstances proper to raise the veneration of our reader. Indeed we would, for certain causes, advise those of our male readers who have any hearts, to read no further, were we not well assured, that how amiable soever the picture of our heroine will appear, as it is really a copy from nature, many of our fair countrywomen will be found worthy to satisfy any passion, and to answer any idea of female perfection which our pencil will be able to raise.

And now, without any further preface, we proceed to our next chapter.

Chapter Two

A short hint of what we can do in the sublime, and a description of Miss Sophia Western

Hushed be every ruder breath. May the heathen ruler of the winds confine in iron chains the boisterous limbs of noisy Boreas, and the sharp-pointed nose of bitter-biting Eurus. Do thou, sweet Zephyrus, rising from thy fragrant bed, mount the western sky, and lead on those delicious gales, the charms of which call forth the lovely Flora from her chamber, perfumed with pearly dews, when on the first of June, her birthday, the blooming maid, in loose attire, gently trips it over the verdant mead, where every flower rises to do her homage, till the whole field becomes enamelled, and colours contend with sweets which shall ravish her most.

So charming may she now appear! And you, the feathered choristers of nature, whose sweetest notes not even Handel can excel, tune your melodious throats to celebrate her appearance. From love proceeds your music, and to love it returns. Awaken therefore that gentle passion in every swain, for lo! Adorned with all the charms in which nature can array her, bedecked with beauty, youth, sprightliness, innocence, modesty, and tenderness, breathing sweetness from her rosy lips, and darting brightness from her sparkling eyes, the lovely Sophia comes!

Reader, perhaps thou hast seen the statue of the *Venus de Medicis*. Perhaps, too, thou hast seen the gallery of beauties at Hampton Court. Thou may'st remember each bright Churchill of the galaxy, and all the toasts of the Kit-cat. Or, if their reign was before thy times, at least thou hast seen their daughters, the no less dazzling beauties of the present age, whose names, should we here insert, we apprehend they would fill the whole volume.

Now if thou hast seen all these, be not afraid of the rude answer which Lord Rochester once gave to a man who had seen many things. No. If thou hast seen all these without knowing what beauty is, thou hast no eyes, if without feeling its power, thou hast no heart.

Yet is it possible, my friend, that thou mayest have seen all these without being able to form an exact idea of Sophia, for she did not exactly resemble any of them. She was most like the picture of Lady Ranelagh, and I have heard, more still to the famous duchess of Mazarin, but most of all she resembled one whose image never can depart from my breast, and whom, if thou dost remember, thou hast then, my friend, an adequate idea of Sophia.

But lest this should not have been thy fortune, we will endeavour with our utmost skill to describe this paragon, though we are sensible that our highest abilities are very inadequate to the task.

Sophia, then, the only daughter of Mr Western, was a middle-sized woman, but rather inclining to tall. Her shape was not only exact, but extremely delicate, and the nice proportion of her arms promised the truest symmetry in her limbs. Her hair, which was black, was so luxuriant, that it reached her middle, before she cut it to comply with the modern fashion, and it was now curled so gracefully in her neck, that few could believe it to be her own. If envy could find any part of the face which demanded less commendation than the rest, it might possibly think her forehead might have been higher without prejudice to her. Her eyebrows were full, even, and arched beyond the power of art to imitate. Her black eyes had a lustre in them, which all her softness could not extinguish. Her nose was exactly regular, and her mouth, in which were two rows of ivory, exactly answered Sir John Suckling's description in those lines —

Her lips were red, and one was thin,
Compar'd to that was next her chin.
Some bee had stung it newly.

Her cheeks were of the oval kind, and in her right she had a dimple, which the least smile discovered. Her chin had certainly its share in forming the beauty of her face, but it was difficult to say it was either large or small, though perhaps it was rather of the former kind. Her complexion had rather more of the lily than of the rose, but when exercise or modesty increased her natural colour, no vermilion could equal it. Then one might indeed cry out with the celebrated Dr Donne —

Her pure and eloquent blood
Spoke in her cheeks, and so distinctly wrought
That one might almost say her body thought.

Her neck was long and finely turned, and here, if I was not afraid of offending her delicacy, I might justly say, the highest beauties of the famous *Venus de Medicis* were outdone. Here was whiteness which no lilies, ivory, nor alabaster could match. The finest cambric might indeed be supposed from envy to cover that bosom which was much whiter than itself. It was indeed *nitor splendens Pario marmore purius* — a gloss shining beyond the purest brightness of Parian marble.

Such was the outside of Sophia, nor was this beautiful frame disgraced by an inhabitant unworthy of it. Her mind was every way equal to her person, nay, the latter borrowed some charms from the former, for when she smiled, the sweetness of her temper diffused that glory over her countenance which no regularity of features can give. But as there are no perfections of the mind which do not discover themselves in that perfect intimacy to which we intend to introduce our reader with this charming young creature, so it is needless to mention them here, nay, it is a kind of tacit affront to our reader's understanding, and may also rob him of that pleasure which he will receive in forming his own judgement of her character.

It may, however, be proper to say, that whatever mental accomplishments she had derived from nature, they were somewhat improved and cultivated by art, for she had been educated under the care of an aunt, who was a lady of great discretion, and was thoroughly acquainted with the world, having lived in her youth about the court, whence she had retired some years since into the country. By her conversation and instructions, Sophia was perfectly well bred, though perhaps she wanted a little of that ease in her behaviour which is to be acquired only by habit, and living within what is called the polite circle. But this, to say the truth, is often too dearly purchased, and though it hath charms so inexpressible, that the French, perhaps, among other qualities, mean to express this, when they declare they know not what it is, yet its absence is well compensated by innocence, nor can good sense and a natural gentility ever stand in need of it.

Chapter Three

Wherein the history goes back to commemorate a trifling incident that happened some years since, but which, trifling as it was, had some future consequences

The amiable Sophia was now in her eighteenth year, when she is introduced into this history. Her father, as hath been said, was fonder of her than of any other human creature. To her, therefore, Tom Jones applied, in order to engage her interest on the behalf of his friend the gamekeeper.

But before we proceed to this business, a short recapitulation of some previous matters may be necessary.

Though the different tempers of Mr Allworthy and of Mr Western did not admit of a very intimate correspondence, yet they lived upon what is called a decent footing together, by which means the young people of both families had been acquainted from their infancy, and as they were all near of the same age, had been frequent playmates together.

The gaiety of Tom's temper suited better with Sophia, than the grave and sober disposition of Master Blifil. And the preference which she gave the former of these, would often appear so plainly, that a lad of a more passionate turn than Master Blifil was, might have shown some displeasure at it.

As he did not, however, outwardly express any such disgust, it would be an ill office in us to pay a visit to the inmost recesses of his mind, as some scandalous people search into the most secret affairs of their friends, and often pry into their closets and cupboards, only to discover their poverty and meanness to the world.

However, as persons who suspect they have given others cause of offence, are apt to conclude they are offended, so Sophia imputed an action of Master Blifil to his anger, which the superior sagacity of Thwackum and Square discerned to have arisen from a much better principle.

Tom Jones, when very young, had presented Sophia with a little bird, which he had taken from the nest, had nursed up, and taught to sing.

Of this bird, Sophia, then about thirteen years old, was so extremely fond, that her chief business was to feed and tend it, and her chief pleasure to play with it. By these means little Tommy, for so the bird was called, was become so tame, that it would feed out of the hand of its mistress, would perch upon the finger, and lie contented in her bosom, where it seemed almost sensible of its own happiness, though she always kept a small string about its leg, nor would ever trust it with the liberty of flying away.

One day, when Mr Allworthy and his whole family dined at Mr Western's, Master Blifil, being in the garden with little Sophia, and observing the extreme fondness that she showed for her little bird, desired her to trust it for a moment in his hands. Sophia presently complied with the young gentleman's request, and after some previous caution, delivered him her bird, of which he was no sooner in possession, than he slipped the string from its leg and tossed it into the air.

The foolish animal no sooner perceived itself at liberty, than forgetting all the favours it had received from Sophia, it flew directly from her, and perched on a bough at some distance.

Sophia, seeing her bird gone, screamed out so loud, that Tom Jones, who was at a little distance, immediately ran to her assistance.

He was no sooner informed of what had happened, than he cursed Blifil for a pitiful malicious rascal, and then immediately stripping off his coat he applied himself to climbing the tree to which the bird escaped.

Tom had almost recovered his little namesake, when the branch on which it was perched, and that hung over a canal, broke, and the poor lad plumped over head and ears into the water.

Sophia's concern now changed its object. And as she apprehended the boy's life was in danger, she screamed ten times louder than before, and indeed Master Blifil himself now seconded her with all the vociferation in his power.

The company, who were sitting in a room next the garden, were instantly alarmed, and came all forth, but just as they reached the canal, Tom, for the water was luckily pretty shallow in that part, arrived safely on shore.

Thwackum fell violently on poor Tom, who stood dripping and shivering before him, when Mr Allworthy desired him to have patience, and turning to Master Blifil, said, "Pray, child, what is the reason of all this disturbance?"

Master Blifil answered, "Indeed, uncle, I am very sorry for what I have done, I have been unhappily the occasion of it all. I had Miss Sophia's bird in my hand, and thinking the poor creature languished for liberty, I own I could not forbear giving it what it desired, for I always thought there was something very cruel in confining anything. It seemed to be against the law of nature, by which everything hath a right to liberty, nay, it is even unchristian, for it is not doing what we would be done by, but if I had imagined Miss Sophia would have been so much concerned at it, I am sure I never would have done it. Nay, if I had known what would have happened to the bird itself—for when Master Jones, who climbed up that tree after it, fell into the water, the bird took a second flight, and presently a nasty hawk carried it away."

Poor Sophia, who now first heard of her little Tommy's fate—for her concern for Jones had prevented her perceiving it when it happened—shed a shower of tears. These Mr Allworthy endeavoured to assuage, promising her a much finer bird, but she declared she would never have another. Her father chided her for crying so for a foolish bird, but could not help telling young Blifil, if he was a son of his, his backside should be well flead.

Sophia now returned to her chamber, the two young gentlemen were sent home, and the rest of the company returned to their bottle, where a conversation ensued on the subject of the bird, so curious, that we think it deserves a chapter by itself.

Chapter Four

Containing such very deep and grave matters, that some readers, perhaps, may not relish it

Square had no sooner lighted his pipe, than, addressing himself to Allworthy, he thus began, "Sir, I cannot help congratulating you on your nephew, who, at an age when few lads have any ideas but of sensible objects, is arrived at a capacity of distinguishing right from wrong. 'To confine anything, seems to me against the law of nature, by which everything hath a right to liberty.' These were his words, and the impression they have made on me is never to be eradicated. Can any man have a higher notion of the rule of right, and the eternal fitness of things? I cannot help promising myself, from such a dawn, that the meridian of this youth will be equal to that of either the elder or the younger Brutus."

Here Thwackum hastily interrupted, and spilling some of his wine, and swallowing the rest with great eagerness, answered, "From another expression he made use of, I hope he will resemble much better men. The law of nature is a jargon of words, which means nothing. I know not of any such law, nor of any right which can be derived from it. To do as we would be done by, is indeed a Christian motive, as the boy well expressed himself, and I am glad to find my instructions have borne such good fruit."

"If vanity was a thing fit," said Square, "I might indulge some on the same occasion, for whence only he can have learnt his notions of right or wrong, I think is pretty apparent. If there be no law of nature, there is no right nor wrong."

"How!" said the parson. "Do you then banish revelation? Am I talking with a deist or an atheist?"

"Drink about," said Western. "Pox of your laws of nature! I don't know what you mean, either of you, by right and wrong. To take away my girl's bird was wrong, in my opinion, and my neighbour Allworthy may do as he pleases, but to encourage boys in such practices, is to breed them up to the gallows."

Allworthy answered, that he was sorry for what his nephew had done, but could not consent to punish him, as he acted rather from a generous than unworthy motive. He said, if the boy had stolen the bird, none would have been more ready to vote for a severe chastisement than himself, but it was plain that was not his design, and indeed, it was as apparent to him, that he could have no other view but what he had himself avowed. For as to that malicious purpose which Sophia suspected, it never once entered into the head of Mr Allworthy. He at length concluded with again blaming the action as inconsiderate, and which, he said, was pardonable only in a child.

Square had delivered his opinion so openly, that if he was now silent, he must submit to have his judgement censured. He said, therefore, with some warmth, that Mr Allworthy had too much respect to the dirty consideration of property. That in passing our judgements on great and mighty actions, all private regards should be laid aside, for by adhering to those narrow rules, the younger Brutus had been condemned of ingratitude, and the elder of parricide.

"And if they had been hanged too for those crimes," cried Thwackum, "they would have had no more than their deserts. A couple of heathenish villains! Heaven be praised we have no Brutuses nowadays! I wish, Mr Square, you would desist from filling the minds of my pupils with such antichristian stuff, for the consequence must be, while they are under my care, its being well scourged out of them again. There is your disciple Tom almost spoiled already. I overheard him the other day disputing with Master Blifil that there was no merit in faith without works. I know that is one of your tenets, and I suppose he had it from you."

"Don't accuse me of spoiling him," said Square. "Who taught him to laugh at whatever is virtuous and decent, and fit and right in the nature of things? He is your own scholar, and I disclaim him. No, no, Master Blifil is my boy. Young as he is, that lad's notions of moral rectitude I defy you ever to eradicate."

Thwackum put on a contemptuous sneer at this, and replied, "Ay, ay, I will venture him with you. He is too well grounded for all your philosophical cant to hurt. No, no, I have taken care to instil such principles into him—"

"And I have instilled principles into him too," cried Square. "What but the sublime idea of virtue could inspire a human mind with the generous thought of giving liberty? And I repeat to you again, if it was a fit thing to be proud, I might claim the honour of having infused that idea."

"And if pride was not forbidden," said Thwackum, "I might boast of having taught him that duty which he himself assigned as his motive."

"So between you both," said the squire, "the young gentleman hath been taught to rob my daughter of her bird. I find I must take care of my partridge-mew. I shall have some virtuous religious man or other set all my partridges at liberty." Then slapping a gentleman of the law, who was present, on the back until he choked, he cried out, "What say you to this, Mr Counsellor? Is not this against law?"

After recovering his dignity, the lawyer with great gravity delivered himself as follows.

"If the case be put of a partridge, there can be no doubt but an action would lie, for though this be *ferae naturae*, yet being reclaimed, property vests, but being the case of a singing bird, though reclaimed, as it is a thing of base nature, it must be considered as *nullius in bonis*. In this case, therefore, I conceive the plaintiff must be non-suited, and I should disadvise the bringing any such action."

"Well," said the squire, "if it be *nullus bonus*, let us drink about, and talk a little of the state of the nation, or some such discourse that we all understand, for I am sure I don't understand a word of this. It may be learning and sense for aught I know, but you shall never persuade me into it. Pox! You have neither of you mentioned a word of that poor lad who deserves to be commended, to venture breaking his neck to oblige my girl was a generous-spirited action, I have learning enough to see that. Damn me, here's Tom's health! I shall love the boy for it the longest day I have to live."

Thus was the debate interrupted, but it would probably have been soon resumed, had not Mr Allworthy presently called for his coach, and carried off the two combatants.

Such was the conclusion of this adventure of the bird, and of the dialogue occasioned by it, which we could not help recounting to our reader, though it happened some years before that stage or period of time at which our history is now arrived.

It is often said that the character of a person is better demonstrated by deeds, not words, but this the reader will have to judge for himself.

Chapter Five

Containing matter accommodated to every taste

"*Parva leves capiunt animos* —Small things affect light minds," was the sentiment of a great master of the passion of love. And certain it is, that from this day Sophia began to have some little kindness for Tom Jones, and no little aversion for his companion.

Many accidents from time to time improved both these passions in her breast, which, without our recounting, the reader may well conclude, from what we have before hinted of the different tempers of these lads, and how much the one suited with her own inclinations more than the other. To say the truth, Sophia, when very young, discerned that Tom, though an idle, thoughtless, rattling rascal, was nobody's enemy but his own, and that Master Blifil, though a prudent, discreet, sober young gentleman, was at the same time strongly attached to the interest only of one single person, and who that single person was the reader will be able to divine without any assistance of ours.

These two characters are not always received in the world with the different regard which seems severally due to either, and which one would imagine mankind, from self-interest, should show towards them. But perhaps there may be a political reason for it. In finding one of a truly benevolent disposition, men may very reasonably suppose they have found a treasure, and be desirous of keeping it, like all other good things, to themselves. Hence they may imagine, that to trumpet forth the praises of such a person, would, in the vulgar phrase, be crying roast-meat, and calling in partakers of what they intend to apply solely to their own use. If this reason does not satisfy the reader, I know no other means of accounting for the little respect which I have commonly seen paid to a character which really does great honour to human nature, and is productive of the highest good to society. But it was otherwise with Sophia. She honoured Tom Jones, and scorned Master Blifil, almost as soon as she knew the meaning of those two words.

Sophia had been absent upwards of three years with her aunt, during all which time she had seldom seen either of these young gentlemen. She dined, however, once, together with her aunt, at Mr Allworthy's. This was a few days after the adventure of the partridge, before commemorated. Sophia heard the whole story at table, where she said nothing, nor indeed could her aunt get many words from her as she returned home, but her maid, when undressing her, happening to say, "Well, miss, I suppose you have seen young Master Blifil today?"

She answered with much passion, "I hate the name of Master Blifil, as I do whatever is base and treacherous, and I wonder Mr Allworthy would suffer that old barbarous schoolmaster to punish a poor boy so cruelly for what was only the effect of his good-nature." She then recounted the story to her maid, and concluded with saying, "Don't you think he is a boy of noble spirit?"

This young lady was now returned to her father, who gave her the command of his house, and placed her at the upper end of his table, where Tom—who for his great love of hunting was become a great favourite of the squire—often dined. Young men of open, generous dispositions are naturally inclined to gallantry, which, if they have good understandings, as was in reality Tom's case, exerts itself in an obliging complacent behaviour to all women in general. This greatly distinguished Tom from the boisterous brutality of mere country squires on the one hand, and from the solemn and somewhat sullen deportment of Master Blifil on the other, and he began now, at twenty, to have the name of a pretty fellow among all the women in the neighbourhood.

Tom behaved to Sophia with no particularity, unless perhaps by showing her a higher respect than he paid to any other. This distinction her beauty, fortune, sense, and amiable carriage, seemed to demand, but as to design upon her person he had none, for which we shall at present suffer the reader to condemn him of stupidity, but perhaps we shall be able indifferently well to account for it hereafter.

Sophia, with the highest degree of innocence and modesty, had a remarkable sprightliness in her temper. This was so greatly increased whenever she was in company with Tom, that had he not been very young and thoughtless, he must have observed it, or had not Mr Western's thoughts been generally either in the field, the stable, or the dog-kennel, it might have perhaps created some jealousy in him. But so far was the good gentleman from entertaining any such suspicions, that he gave Tom every opportunity with his daughter which any lover could have wished, and this Tom innocently improved to better advantage, by following only the dictates of his natural gallantry and good-nature, than he might perhaps have done had he had the deepest designs on the young lady.

But indeed it can occasion little wonder that this matter escaped the observation of others, since poor Sophia herself never remarked it, and her heart was irretrievably lost before she suspected it was in danger.

Matters were in this situation, when Tom, one afternoon, finding Sophia alone, began, after a short apology, with a very serious face, to acquaint her that he had a favour to ask of her which he hoped her goodness would comply with.

Though neither the young man's behaviour, nor indeed his manner of opening this business, were such as could give her any just cause of suspecting he intended to make love to her, yet whether Nature whispered something into her ear, or from what cause it arose I will not determine, certain it is, some idea of that kind must have intruded itself. Her colour forsook her cheeks, her limbs trembled, and her tongue would have faltered, had Tom stopped for an answer. But he soon relieved her from her perplexity, by proceeding to inform her of his request, which was to solicit her interest on behalf of the gamekeeper, whose own ruin, and that of a large family, must be, he said, the consequence of Mr Western's pursuing his action against him.

Sophia presently recovered her confusion, and with a smile full of sweetness, said, "Is this the mighty favour you asked with so much gravity? I will do it with all my heart. I really pity the poor fellow, and no longer ago than yesterday sent a small matter to his wife." This small matter was one of her gowns, some linen, and ten shillings in money, of which Tom had heard, and it had, in reality, put this solicitation into his head.

Our youth, now, emboldened with his success, resolved to push the matter further, and ventured even to beg her recommendation of him to her father's service, protesting that he thought him one of the honestest fellows in the country, and extremely well qualified for the place of a gamekeeper, which luckily then happened to be vacant.

Sophia answered, "Well, I will undertake this too, but I cannot promise you as much success as in the former part, which I assure you I will not quit my father without obtaining. However, I will do what I can for the poor fellow, for I sincerely look upon him and his family as objects of great compassion. And now, Mr Jones, I must ask you a favour."

"A favour, madam!" cried Tom. "If you knew the pleasure you have given me in the hopes of receiving a command from you, you would think by mentioning it you did confer the greatest favour on me, for by this dear hand I would sacrifice my life to oblige you."

He then snatched her hand, and eagerly kissed it, which was the first time his lips had ever touched her. The blood, which before had forsaken her cheeks, now made her sufficient amends, by rushing all over her face and neck with such violence, that they became all of a scarlet colour. She now first felt a sensation to which she had been before a stranger, and which, when she had leisure to reflect on it, began to acquaint her with some secrets, which the reader, if he doth not already guess them, will know in due time.

Tom had always loved the lady, but now saw something anew in the beauty of this woman. He newly acquired maturity had given him fresh insights into the ways of the world, and the matters of deep delight that exist between a man and a woman. Sophia was as unspoiled as dewfall, as sweet as honey just collected from the comb, and he felt a strong desire, heretofore unknown, to taste that adorable flavour. Her beauty amazed him, just as his previous ignorance of his sentiments towards her took him by surprise.

He proceeded to kiss her forearm, after pushing back the lace at her elbow, and caressed the soft skin inside that joint with his tongue. Sophia shivered delightfully in response, and gave Tom cause to believe she would not find his attentions unwelcome, so he touched his lips to her throat, which tasted dulcet enough for him to linger there some moments before landing on her mouth.

He retained control of his natural appetites, for he wished only to give her pleasure and take a little for himself, but it delighted Tom that Sophia encouraged his attentions. She nestled into his arms like a shy bird, reminding him of that incident long ago when he had delighted her with the tame creature. She needed as careful handling and as gentle tethering. Her lips, ripe as cherries, returned his salute with a tentative caress, as soft as a feather, and as lovely. Tom thirsted for more, and when she opened her mouth, he touched his tongue to her lower lip, as gently as he could manage, to introduce her to the pleasures of his kiss.

She gave a little chuckle which fully enchanted him, and if he had not been wholly bespelled by her sweetness, he would have been after that adorable sound.

Entering into the spirit of the occasion, Sophia settled more closely into his arms, and tilted her head back, so that Tom could push his fingers into the long fall of her silky hair, and insinuate his tongue deeper into her mouth, imitating that action he ached to complete with her, but knew he should not. His cock worked hard to escape the confines of his breeches, but he did his best to ignore the wayward creature, although it became more difficult by the minute, and Tom was not known for his forbearance.

He kissed her for he knew not how long, and she rewarded him with sighs and responses, but he durst not take her farther along the road, much though he longed to. When she tried to speak, he kissed her again, and emboldened by her eager participation, he stroked her bosom, where it emerged from her stays.

She put a hand to her stomacher. "Dear sir, what are you about?"

Tom immediately ceased his assiduous attentions. "I would not distress you for the world, dearest ma'am. But I wished to please you and so please myself. I will show you the best of delights, but I swear I will do no harm."

Sophia was a country girl, and not ignorant of his intentions, since she had glimpsed such goings-on from time to time, and once her best friend explained his desires she wanted nothing more than to aid him in his objective.

When she sighed and nodded, he ventured deeper, after unhooking the top part of her gown to allow himself farther ingress. Her response was to sigh more, so Tom left her mouth to caress her throat with his tongue, and then to press fervent kisses against her bosom, before he dared to venture lower, and take that sweet peak into his mouth, to harden it with his attentions and taste her completely.

He would have gone more, but her shudders told him that he must treat her gently and with respect, so he slowly reversed what he had achieved, tucking her away to her satisfaction, and vowing that no one but him would introduce sweet Sophia to the pleasures of the flesh. All the time he spoke to her soothingly, so by the time he found her little lace cap to tie over her still-disordered curls, they were discussing family matters once more and she was in complete amity with him.

Sophia, as soon as she could speak, which was not instantly, informed him that the favour she had to desire of him was, not to lead her father through so many dangers in hunting, for that, from what she had heard, she was terribly frightened every time they went out together, and expected some day or other to see her father brought home with broken limbs. She therefore begged him, for her sake, to be more cautious, and as he well knew Mr Western would follow him, not to ride so madly, nor to take those dangerous leaps for the future.

Tom promised faithfully to obey her commands, and after thanking her for her kind compliance with his request, took his leave, and departed highly charmed with his success.

Poor Sophia was charmed too, but in a very different way. Her sensations, however, the reader's heart — if he or she have any — will better represent than I can, if I had as many mouths as ever poet wished for, to eat, I suppose, those many dainties with which he was so plentifully provided.

It was Mr Western's custom every afternoon, as soon as he was drunk, to hear his daughter play on the harpsichord, for he was a great lover of music, and perhaps, had he lived in town, might have passed for a connoisseur, for he always excepted against the finest compositions of Mr Handel. He never relished any music but what was light and airy, and indeed his most favourite tunes were Old Sir Simon the King, St George he was for England, Bobbing Joan, and some others.

His daughter, though she was a perfect mistress of music, and would never willingly have played any but Handel's, was so devoted to her father's pleasure, that she learnt all those tunes to oblige him. However, she would now and then endeavour to lead him into her own taste, and when he required the repetition of his ballads, would answer with a "Nay, dear sir," and would often beg him to suffer her to play something else.

This evening, however, when the gentleman was retired from his bottle, she played all his favourites three times over without any solicitation. This so pleased the good squire, that he started from his couch, gave his daughter a kiss, and swore her hand was greatly improved. She took this opportunity to execute her promise to Tom, in which she succeeded so well, that the squire declared, if she would give him t'other bout of Old Sir Simon, he would give the gamekeeper his deputation the next morning. Sir Simon was played again and again, till the charms of the music soothed Mr Western to sleep. In the morning Sophia did not fail to remind him of his engagement, and his attorney was immediately sent for, ordered to stop any further proceedings in the action, and to make out the deputation.

Tom's success in this affair soon began to ring over the country, and various were the censures passed upon it, some greatly applauding it as an act of good nature, others sneering, and saying, "No wonder that one idle fellow should love another." Young Blifil was greatly enraged at it. He had long hated Black George in the same proportion as Jones delighted in him, not from any offence which he had ever received, but from his great love to religion and virtue – for Black George had the reputation of a loose kind of a fellow. Blifil therefore represented this as flying in Mr Allworthy's face, and declared, with great concern, that it was impossible to find any other motive for doing good to such a wretch.

Thwackum and Square likewise sang to the same tune. They were now, especially the latter, become greatly jealous of young Jones with the widow, for he now approached the age of twenty, was really a fine young fellow, and that lady, by her encouragements to him, seemed daily more and more to think him so.

Allworthy was not, however, moved with their malice. He declared himself very well satisfied with what Jones had done. He said the perseverance and integrity of his friendship was highly commendable, and he wished he could see more frequent instances of that virtue.

But Fortune, who seldom greatly relishes such sparks as my friend Tom, perhaps because they do not pay more ardent addresses to her, gave now a very different turn to all his actions, and showed them to

Mr Allworthy in a light far less agreeable than that gentleman's goodness had hitherto seen them in.

Chapter Six

An apology for the insensibility of Mr Jones to all the charms of the lovely Sophia, in which possibly we may, in a considerable degree, lower his character in the estimation of those men of wit and gallantry who approve the heroes in most of our modern comedies

There are two sorts of people, who, I am afraid, have already conceived some contempt for my hero, on account of his behaviour to Sophia. The former of these will blame his prudence in neglecting an opportunity to possess himself of Mr Western's fortune, and the latter will no less despise him for his backwardness to so fine a girl, who seemed ready to fly into his arms forever, if he would open them to receive her. Her willingness itself mitigated against his determination, for the ancient laws of hospitality and gentility forbade that he should persuade a woman in devotion to him without her guardian being aware of the eventuality. He could not steal her away without the complicity and blessing of her father. For Sophia not only represented a beauteous body and form, but her father, whose heir she was, had other responsibilities to his people, his county and even his country, that Tom, wayward lad though he was, could not bring himself to shatter by breaking that protocol.

Now, though I shall not perhaps be able absolutely to acquit him of either of these charges — for want of prudence admits of no excuse, and what I shall produce against the latter charge will, I apprehend, be scarce satisfactory — yet, as evidence may sometimes be offered in mitigation, I shall set forth the plain matter of fact, and leave the whole to the reader's determination.

Mr Jones had somewhat about him, which, though I think writers are not thoroughly agreed in its name, doth certainly inhabit some human breasts, whose use is not so properly to distinguish right from wrong, as to prompt and incite them to the former, and to restrain and withhold them from the latter.

This somewhat may be indeed resembled to the famous trunk-maker in the playhouse, for, whenever the person who is possessed of it doth what is right, no ravished or friendly spectator is so eager or so loud in his applause, on the contrary, when he doth wrong, no critic is so apt to hiss and explode him.

To give a higher idea of the principle I mean, as well as one more familiar to the present age, it may be considered as sitting on its throne in the mind, like the Lord High Chancellor of this kingdom in his court, where it presides, governs, directs, judges, acquits, and condemns according to merit and justice, with a knowledge which nothing escapes, a penetration which nothing can deceive, and an integrity which nothing can corrupt.

This active principle may perhaps be said to constitute the most essential barrier between us and our neighbours the brutes, for if there be some in the human shape who are not under any such dominion, I choose rather to consider them as deserters from us to our neighbours, among whom they will have the fate of deserters, and not be placed in the first rank.

Our hero, whether he derived it from Thwackum or Square I will not determine, was very strongly under the guidance of this principle, for though he did not always act rightly, yet he never did otherwise without feeling and suffering for it. It was this which taught him, that to repay the civilities and little friendships of hospitality by robbing the house where you have received them, is to be the basest and meanest of thieves. He did not think the baseness of this offence lessened by the height of the injury committed, on the contrary, if to steal another's plate deserved death and infamy, it seemed to him difficult to assign a punishment adequate to the robbing a man of his whole fortune, and of his child into the bargain.

This principle, therefore, prevented him from any thought of making his fortune by such means—for this, as I have said, is an active principle, and doth not content itself with knowledge or belief only. Had he been greatly enamoured of Sophia, he possibly might have thought otherwise, but give me leave to say, there is great difference between running away with a man's daughter from the motive of love, and doing the same thing from the motive of theft.

Now, though this young gentleman was not insensible of the charms of Sophia, though he greatly liked her beauty, and esteemed all her other qualifications, she had made, however, no deep impression on his heart, for which, as it renders him liable to the charge of stupidity, or at least of want of taste, we shall now proceed to account. His previous encounter with her notwithstanding, the youth was fully aware of the difference between head and heart, and he esteemed Sophia so highly that he would not counterfeit either to possess that which he felt he had no right to own. He persuaded himself that he could easily separate himself from her, and although her charms were beauteous in the extreme, he reasoned that many other women existed, and he wished to explore the world further so that he could be sure of his choice. Any other excuse must be put down to his youth, and a profound misunderstanding of his own sensibilities.

The truth then is, his heart was in the possession of another woman. Here I question not but the reader will be surprised at our long taciturnity as to this matter, and quite at a loss to divine who this woman was, since we have hitherto not dropped a hint of anyone likely to be a rival to Sophia. As to Mrs Blifil, though we have been obliged to mention some suspicions of her affection for Tom, we have not hitherto given the least latitude for imagining that he had any for her, and indeed, I am sorry to say it, but the youth of both sexes are too apt to be deficient in their gratitude for that regard with which persons more advanced in years are sometimes so kind to honour them.

That the reader may be no longer in suspense, he will be pleased to remember, that we have often mentioned the family of George Seagrim – commonly called Black George, the gamekeeper – which consisted at present of a wife and five children.

The second of these children was a daughter, whose name was Molly, and who was esteemed one of the handsomest girls in the whole country.

Congreve well says there is in true beauty something which vulgar souls cannot admire, so can no dirt or rags hide this something from those souls which are not of the vulgar stamp.

The beauty of this girl made, however, no impression on Tom, till she grew towards the age of sixteen, when Tom, who was near three years older, began first to cast the eyes of affection upon her. And this affection he had fixed on the girl long before he could bring himself to attempt the possession of her person, for though his constitution urged him greatly to this, his principles no less forcibly restrained him. To debauch a young woman, however low her condition was, appeared to him a very heinous crime, and the good-will he bore the father, with the compassion he had for his family, very strongly corroborated all such sober reflections, so that he once resolved to get the better of his inclinations, and he actually abstained three whole months without ever going to Seagrim's house, or seeing his daughter. To dally with one such as Sophia, albeit without bringing their play to a natural conclusion, was one thing, but Sophia could expect a happy future with a gentleman of her and her father's choice, while Molly had fewer prospects and no fortune to support her good looks.

Now, though Molly was, as we have said, generally thought a very fine girl, and in reality she was so, yet her beauty was not of the most amiable kind. It had, indeed, very little of feminine in it, and would have become a man at least as well as a woman, for, to say the truth, youth and florid health had a very considerable share in the composition.

Nor was her mind more effeminate than her person. As this was tall and robust, so was that bold and forward. So little had she of modesty, that Jones had more regard for her virtue than she herself. And as most probably she liked Tom as well as he liked her, so when she perceived his backwardness she herself grew proportionably forward, and when she saw he had entirely deserted the house, she found means of throwing herself in his way, and behaved in such a manner that the youth must have had very much or very little of the hero if her endeavours had proved unsuccessful. In a word, she soon triumphed over all the virtuous resolutions of Jones, for though she behaved at last with all decent reluctance, yet I rather choose to attribute the triumph to her, since, in fact, it was her design which succeeded.

On the final day of her determined campaign, she tracked down her target as he passed through the village on his way home, but wily Molly waited until he had gone out of sight of any of the houses, for she wanted no witnesses to the outcome but herself, and gave Tom no opportunity to refuse her offer.

He seemed pleased to see her. "Well, Molly, I thought you were occupied with your mother today. But I cannot deny you add unexpected pleasure to my walk."

"Thank you, sir." Molly dipped a curtsey which Tom gratifyingly helped her out of when she stumbled on the uneven ground. She gave him a shy smile in thanks, which brought the roses to his cheeks. Obviously touched by her deference and sweetness, he retained her hand when perhaps he should have dropped it. Molly let it remain where it was, remembering the old adage about birds in the hand.

However, she refrained from pushing her advantage, knowing Tom would not take it in good part, but consider her too forward. Instead, she started, as if suddenly made aware of the intimacy, and made to withdraw her hand. Such tactics work well with young men with more hair than wit, and it worked with Tom. Instead of allowing her to withdraw, in which case she would have left the field, regrouped and come back on another flank, but his sudden motion, jerking her forward, gave her the occasion to stumble. She stumbled right into his arms.

Startled, Tom closed his arms around her, the better to steady her, but when she turned up her dewy young face, and allowed her cheeks to gain that sweet flush that conveyed her apparent innocence to his dazzled eyes, she quite captured him entirely.

Before he could reconsider his actions, he kissed her, so well and so thoroughly that she exclaimed, once he had done, "Why sir, I am quite breathless!" She allowed her fichu, always an unstable part of her attire, to slip, and breathed deeply, the better to display her fine bosom. Her mother had declared it her greatest asset, but Molly had reason to believe otherwise.

He glanced down, and she panted most distressingly. "May I rest for a moment? I declare I am quite overcome."

Nothing loath, Tom helped her to recline on the grassy bank that lay conveniently behind them, both providing the bed of nature and concealing their activities from prying eyes, for there are no such avaricious gossips as you might find in a village. In London you may be in the centre of the city, and yet men will not concern you if you do not wish them to. So involved with their own lives, they have no heed for another's. In a village, everyone knows everybody else's business, and after church on Sundays is a fine time to discuss the latest scandal.

Molly wished above all things to avoid becoming the subject of such post-sermon discussions, so like the Senate of small matters, knowing she would not escape public condemnation, so she had chosen the scene for this little play carefully, hence the grassy bank.

Tom helped her down most tenderly, and it was not his fault that in laying her supine, her skirts rode a little high and her gown low, and heaven knew where her fichu lay—most likely under her, where it would come to least harm. She had gartered her stockings above her knees with her prettiest garters, which a lady of fashion would disdain, but Molly treasured, only deploying them when she wished to make the greatest effect on her audience. Unfortunately washing had rendered their rich blue hue paler now, but they still showed to effect, with roses adorning the strings.

Tom took hold of her skirts, no doubt intending to restore the girl's modesty, but somehow the opposite occurred and they rose even higher on her legs. She parted her thighs a small amount, the better to cool her heated body.

"Molly..." Tom swallowed. "I would not harm you for the world, but my dear girl, you must know that I love you with the greatest passion imaginable. My kiss—"

She fanned her face with her hand. "Quite overwhelmed me, sir. I have been kissed before"— here she lowered her gaze, and avoided his fiery stare—"but never in that way. And I want to be kissed by no one else from now on. I do not understand why."

"I do." With those words, spoken in such a passionate tone that she gave a cry of delight, Tom raised his body over hers, and fumbled with his falls, the better to get out his instrument of torture. He had known ladies declare it such, because of its formidable size, at least they had told him so and it gave him satisfaction to allow himself to believe the statements.

Holding his fleshy rod in his hand, he guided it to the wet, hot centre of her desire. Her quim throbbed against him, and she gave another cry, as if afraid of what he would do, but reached for him. "I am at your mercy," she said, submitting to a great general. His grace the late Duke of Marlborough could not have taken the defeat of his enemies so graciously, indeed having been found buck naked in the bedroom of one of his adversaries early in his career, he did not hesitate to take the quickest route to victory, viz, defenestration.

There being no window close by, Molly could only press her fist to her mouth to subdue her cries. To be sure, she had to put a great deal of effort into her sobs of maidenly modesty and surprise, when she would have rather cried out her pleasure.

Tom treated her most gently, thinking she was the maiden he assumed her to be, and Molly gave him no reason to doubt that assumption, since gentlemen prefer to think they have the right of things.

No doubt Tom, flattered by her deference to his superior prowess in the field of amour, felt this maid deserved his protection. At least, after he had presented her with his best efforts, and to this end he worked hard and made all the effort his body and hers demanded of him.

Breathless but triumphant, Tom aided Molly to that pinnacle, when all is lost and then all is won, victory within their grasp.

Molly gave Tom every evidence of her wonder and amazement at his skill and strength, praising him with many kisses and sweet words. Dazed by her words, and the delight her untutored body gave him, Tom devoted himself henceforth to her pleasure, which incidentally, also contained his.

In the conduct of this matter, I say, Molly so well played her part, that Jones attributed the conquest entirely to himself, and considered the young woman as one who had yielded to the violent attacks of his passion. He likewise imputed her yielding to the ungovernable force of her love towards him, and this the reader will allow to have been a very natural and probable supposition, as we have more than once mentioned the uncommon comeliness of his person, and indeed, he was one of the handsomest young fellows in the world.

As there are some minds whose affections, like Master Blifil's, are solely placed on one single person, whose interest and indulgence alone they consider on every occasion, regarding the good and ill of all others as merely indifferent, any further than as they contribute to the pleasure or advantage of that person, so there is a different temper of mind which borrows a degree of virtue even from self-love. Such can never receive any kind of satisfaction from another, without loving the creature to whom that satisfaction is owing, and without making its well-being in some sort necessary to their own ease.

Of this latter species was our hero. He considered this poor girl as one whose happiness or misery he had caused to be dependent on himself. Her beauty was still the object of desire, though greater beauty, or a fresher object, might have been more so, but the little abatement which fruition had occasioned to this was highly overbalanced by the considerations of the affection which she visibly bore him, and of the situation into which he had brought her. The former of these created gratitude, the latter compassion, and both, together with his desire for her person, raised in him a passion which might, without any great violence to the word, be called love, though, perhaps, it was at first not very judiciously placed.

This, then, was the true reason of that insensibility which he had shown to the charms of Sophia, and that behaviour in her which might have been reasonably enough interpreted as an encouragement to his addresses, for as he could not think of abandoning his Molly, poor and destitute as she was, so no more could he entertain a notion of betraying such a creature as Sophia. His goodness of heart would not allow him to consider abandoning one so wanting in support and the good will of society. And surely, had he given the least encouragement to any passion for that young lady, he must have been absolutely guilty of one or other of those crimes, either of which would, in my opinion, have very justly subjected him to that fate, which, at his first introduction into this history, I mentioned to have been generally predicted as his certain destiny.

Chapter Seven

Being the shortest chapter in this book

Her mother first perceived the alteration in the shape of Molly, and in order to hide it from her neighbours, she foolishly clothed her in that sacque gown which Sophia had sent her, though, indeed, that young lady had little apprehension that the poor woman would have been weak enough to let any of her daughters wear it in that form.

Molly was charmed with the first opportunity she ever had of showing her beauty to advantage, for though she could very well bear to contemplate herself in the glass, even when dressed in rags, and though she had in that dress conquered the heart of Jones, and perhaps of some others, yet she thought the addition of finery would much improve her charms, and extend her conquests.

Molly, therefore, having dressed herself out in this sacque, with a new laced cap, and some other ornaments which Tom had given her, repaired to church with her fan in her hand the very next Sunday. The great are deceived if they imagine they have appropriated ambition and vanity to themselves. These noble qualities flourish as notably in a country church and churchyard as in the drawing-room, or in the closet. Schemes have indeed been laid in the vestry which would hardly disgrace the conclave. Here is a ministry, and here is an opposition. Here are plots and circumventions, parties and factions, equal to those which are to be found in courts.

Nor are the women here less practised in the highest feminine arts than their fair superiors in quality and fortune. Here are prudes and coquettes. Here are dressing and ogling, falsehood, envy, malice, scandal, in short, everything which is common to the most splendid assembly, or politest circle. Let those of high life, therefore, no longer despise the ignorance of their inferiors, nor the vulgar any longer rail at the vices of their betters.

Molly had seated herself some time before she was known by her neighbours. And then a whisper ran through the whole congregation, "Who is she?" but when she was discovered, such sneering, giggling, tittering, and laughing ensued among the women, that Mr Allworthy was obliged to exert his authority to preserve any decency among them.

Chapter Eight

*A battle sung by the muse in the Homerican style, and
which none but the classical reader can taste*

Mr Western had an estate in this parish, and as his
house stood at little greater distance from this church
than from his own, he very often came to Divine
Service here, and both he and the charming Sophia
happened to be present at this time.

Sophia was much pleased with the beauty of the girl,
whom she pitied for her simplicity in having dressed
herself in that manner, as she saw the envy which it
had occasioned among her equals. She no sooner came
home than she sent for the gamekeeper, and ordered
him to bring his daughter to her, saying she would
provide for her in the family, and might possibly place
the girl about her own person, when her own maid,
who was now going away, had left her.

Poor Seagrim was thunderstruck at this, for he was
no stranger to the fault in the shape of his daughter.
He answered, in a stammering voice, that he was

afraid Molly would be too awkward to wait on her ladyship, as she had never been at service.

"No matter for that," said Sophia, "she will soon improve. I am pleased with the girl, and am resolved to try her."

Black George now repaired to his wife, on whose prudent counsel he depended to extricate him out of this dilemma, but when he came thither he found his house in some confusion. So great envy had this sacque occasioned, that when Mr Allworthy and the other gentry were gone from church, the rage, which had hitherto been confined, burst into an uproar, and having vented itself at first in opprobrious words, laughs, hisses, and gestures, betook itself at last to certain missile weapons—which, though from their plastic nature they threatened neither the loss of life or of limb, were however sufficiently dreadful to a well-dressed lady. Molly had too much spirit to bear this treatment tamely. Having therefore—but hold, as we are diffident of our own abilities, let us here invite a superior power to our assistance.

Ye Muses, then, whoever ye are, who love to sing battles, and principally thou who whilom didst recount the slaughter in those fields where Hudibras and Trulla fought, if thou wert not starved with thy friend Butler, assist me on this great occasion. All things are not in the power of all.

As a vast herd of cows in a rich farmer's yard, if, while they are milked, they hear their calves at a distance, lamenting the robbery which is then committing, roar and bellow, so roared forth the Somersetshire mob an hallaloo, made up of almost as many squalls, screams, and other different sounds as there were persons, or indeed passions among them, some were inspired by rage, others alarmed by fear, and others had nothing in their heads but the love of fun, but chiefly Envy, the sister of Satan, and his constant companion, rushed among the crowd, and blew up the fury of the women, who no sooner came up to Molly than they pelted her with dirt and rubbish.

Molly, having endeavoured in vain to make a handsome retreat, faced about, and laying hold of ragged Bess, who advanced in the front of the enemy, she at one blow felled her to the ground. The whole army of the enemy — though near a hundred in number — seeing the fate of their general, gave back many paces, and retired behind a new-dug grave, for the churchyard was the field of battle, where there was to be a funeral that very evening. Molly pursued her victory, and catching up a skull which lay on the side of the grave, discharged it with such fury, that having hit a tailor on the head, the two skulls sent equally forth a hollow sound at their meeting, and the tailor took presently measure of his length on the ground, where the skulls lay side by side, and it was doubtful which was the more valuable of the two. Molly then, taking a thigh-bone in her hand, fell in among the flying ranks, and dealing her blows with great liberality on either side, overthrew the carcass of many a mighty hero and heroine.

Recount, O Muse, the names of those who fell on this fatal day. First, Jemmy Tweedle felt on his hinder head the direful bone. Him the pleasant banks of sweetly-winding Stour had nourished, where he first learnt the vocal art, with which, wandering up and down at wakes and fairs, he cheered the rural nymphs and swains, when upon the green they interweaved the sprightly dance, while he himself stood fiddling and jumping to his own music. How little now avails his fiddle! He thumps the verdant floor with his carcass.

Next, old Echepole, the sowgelder, received a blow in his forehead from our Amazonian heroine, and immediately fell to the ground. He was a swinging fat fellow, and fell with almost as much noise as a house. His tobacco-box dropped at the same time from his pocket, which Molly took up as lawful spoils.

Then Kate of the Mill tumbled unfortunately over a tombstone, which catching hold of her ungartered stocking inverted the order of nature, and gave her heels the superiority to her head and the gentlemen a rare sight of Kate's nether regions, which paused the ferocity of the battle for full ten seconds.

Betty Pippin, with young Roger her lover, fell both to the ground, where, oh perverse fate, she salutes the earth, and he the sky.

Tom Freckle, the smith's son, was the next victim to her rage. He was an ingenious workman, and made excellent pattens, nay, the very patten with which he was knocked down was his own workmanship. Had he been at that time singing psalms in the church, he would have avoided a broken head.

Miss Crow, the daughter of a farmer, John Giddish, himself a farmer, Nan Slouch, Esther Codling, Will Spray, Tom Bennet, the three Misses Potter, whose father keeps the sign of the Red Lion, Betty Chambermaid, Jack Ostler, and many others of inferior note, lay rolling among the graves.

Not that the strenuous arm of Molly reached all these, for many of them in their flight overthrew each other.

But now Fortune, fearing she had acted out of character, and had inclined too long to the same side, especially as it was the right side, hastily turned about, for now Goody Brown—whom Zekiel Brown caressed in his arms, nor he alone, but half the parish besides, so famous was she in the fields of Venus, nor indeed less in those of Mars. The trophies of both these her husband always bore about on his head and face, for if ever human head did by its horns display the amorous glories of a wife, Zekiel's did, nor did his well-scratched face less denote her talents—or rather talons—of a different kind.

No longer bore this Amazon the shameful flight of her party. She stopped short, and calling aloud to all who fled, spoke as follows. "Ye Somersetshire men, or rather ye Somersetshire women, are ye not ashamed thus to fly from a single woman? But if no other will oppose her, I myself and Joan Top here will have the honour of the victory." Having thus said, she flew at Molly Seagrim, and easily wrenched the thigh-bone from her hand, at the same time clawing off her cap from her head. Then laying hold of the hair of Molly with her left hand, she attacked her so furiously in the face with the right, that the blood soon began to trickle from her nose.

Molly was not idle this while. She soon removed the clout from the head of Goody Brown, and then fastening on her hair with one hand, with the other she caused another bloody stream to issue forth from the nostrils of the enemy.

When each of the combatants had borne off sufficient spoils of hair from the head of her antagonist, the next rage was against the garments. In this attack they exerted so much violence, that in a very few minutes they were both naked to the middle.

It is lucky for the women that the seat of fisticuff war is not the same with them as among men, but though they may seem a little to deviate from their sex, when they go forth to battle, yet I have observed, they never so far forget, as to assail the bosoms of each other, where a few blows would be fatal to most of them. This, I know, some derive from their being of a more bloody inclination than the males. On which account they apply to the nose, as to the part whence blood may most easily be drawn, but this seems a far-fetched as well as ill-natured supposition.

Goody Brown had great advantage of Molly in this particular, for the former had indeed no breasts, her bosom, if it may be so called, as well in colour as in many other properties, exactly resembling an ancient piece of parchment, upon which anyone might have drummed a considerable while without doing her any great damage.

Molly, beside her present unhappy condition, was differently formed in those parts, and might, perhaps, have tempted the envy of Brown to give her a fatal blow, had not the lucky arrival of Tom Jones at this instant put an immediate end to the bloody scene.

This accident was luckily owing to Mr Square, for he, Master Blifil, and Jones, had mounted their horses, after church, to take the air, and had ridden about a quarter of a mile, when Square, changing his mind — not idly, but for a reason which we shall unfold as soon as we have leisure — desired the young gentlemen to ride with him another way than they had at first purposed. This motion being complied with, brought them of necessity back again to the churchyard.

Master Blifil, who rode first, seeing such a mob assembled, and two women in the posture in which we left the combatants, stopped his horse to enquire what was the matter. A country fellow, scratching his head, answered him, "I don't know, measter, un't I, an't please your honour, here hath been a vight, I think, between Goody Brown and Moll Seagrim."

"Who, who?" cried Tom, but without waiting for an answer, having discovered the features of his Molly through all the discomposure in which they now were, he hastily alighted, turned his horse loose, and leaping over the wall, ran to her. She now, first bursting into tears, told him how barbarously she had been treated. Upon which, forgetting the sex of Goody Brown, or perhaps not knowing it in his rage—for, in reality, she had no feminine appearance but a petticoat, which he might not observe—he gave her a lash or two with his horsewhip, and then flying at the mob, who were all accused by Moll, he dealt his blows so profusely on all sides, that unless I would again invoke the muse—which the good-natured reader may think a little too hard upon her, as she hath so lately been violently sweated—it would be impossible for me to recount the horse-whipping of that day.

Having scoured the whole coast of the enemy, as well as any of Homer's heroes ever did, or as Don Quixote or any knight-errant in the world could have done, he returned to Molly, whom he found in a condition which must give both me and my reader pain, was it to be described here. Tom raved like a madman, beat his breast, tore his hair, stamped on the ground, and vowed the utmost vengeance on all who had been concerned. He then pulled off his coat, and buttoned it round her, put his hat upon her head, wiped the blood from her face as well as he could with his handkerchief, and called out to the servant to ride as fast as possible for a side-saddle, or a pillion, that he might carry her safe home.

Master Blifil objected to the sending away the servant, as they had only one with them, but as Square seconded the order of Jones, he was obliged to comply.

The servant returned in a very short time with the pillion, and Molly, having collected her rags as well as she could, was placed behind him. In which manner she was carried home, Square, Blifil, and Jones attending.

Here Jones having received his coat, given her a sly kiss, and whispered her, that he would return in the evening, quitted his Molly, and rode on after his companions.

Chapter Nine

Containing matter of no very peaceable colour

Molly had no sooner apparelled herself in her accustomed rags, than her sisters began to fall violently upon her, particularly her eldest sister, who told her she was well enough served. How had she the assurance to wear a gown which young Madam Western had given to mother! "If one of us was to wear it, I think," said she, "I myself have the best right, but I warrant you think it belongs to your beauty. I suppose you think yourself more handsomer than any of us."

"Hand her down the bit of glass from over the cupboard," cried another, "I'd wash the blood from my face before I talked of my beauty."

"You'd better have minded what the parson says," cried the eldest, "and not a-harkened after men voke."

"Indeed, child, and so she had," said the mother, sobbing, "she hath brought a disgrace upon us all. She's the vurst of the vamily that ever was a whore."

"You need not upbraid me with that, mother," cried Molly, "you yourself was brought-to-bed of sister there, within a week after you was married."

"Yes, hussy," answered the enraged mother, "so I was, and what was the mighty matter of that? I was made an honest woman then, and if you was to be made an honest woman, I should not be angry, but you must have to doing with a gentleman, you nasty slut, you will have a bastard, hussy, you will, and that I defy anyone to say of me."

In this situation Black George found his family, when he came home for the purpose before mentioned. As his wife and three daughters were all of them talking together, and most of them crying, it was some time before he could get an opportunity of being heard, but as soon as such an interval occurred, he acquainted the company with what Sophia had said to him.

Goody Seagrim then began to revile her daughter afresh. "Here," said she, "you have brought us into a fine quandary indeed. What will madam say to that big belly? Oh that ever I should live to see this day!"

Molly answered with great spirit, "And what is this mighty place which you have got for me, father?" For he had not well understood the phrase used by Sophia of being about her person. "I suppose it is to be under the cook, but I shan't wash dishes for anybody. My gentleman will provide better for me. See what he hath given me this afternoon. He hath promised I shall never want money, and you shan't want money neither, mother, if you will hold your tongue, and know when you are well." And so saying, she pulled out several guineas, and gave her mother one of them.

The good woman no sooner felt the gold within her palm, than her temper began—such is the efficacy of that panacea — to be mollified. "Why, husband," said she, "would any but such a blockhead as you not have enquired what place this was before he had accepted it? Perhaps, as Molly says, it may be in the kitchen, and truly I don't care my daughter should be a scullion wench, for, poor as I am, I am a gentlewoman. And thof I was obliged, as my father, who was a clergyman, died worse than nothing, and so could not give me a shilling of *portion*, to undervalue myself by marrying a poor man, yet I would have you to know, I have a spirit above all them things.

"Marry come up! It would better become Madam Western to look at home, and remember who her own grandfather was. Some of my family, for aught I know, might ride in their coaches, when the grandfathers of some voke walked a-voot. I warrant she fancies she did a mighty matter, when she sent us that old gownd, some of my family would not have picked up such rags in the street, but poor people are always trampled upon. The parish need not have been in such a fluster with Molly. You might have told them, child, your grandmother wore better things new out of the shop."

"Well, but consider," cried George, "what answer shall I make to madam?"

"I don't know what answer," said she, "you are always bringing your family into one quandary or other. Do you remember when you shot the partridge, the occasion of all our misfortunes? Did not I advise you never to go into Squire Western's manor? Did not I tell you many a good year ago what would come of it? But you would have your own headstrong ways, yes, you would, you villain."

Black George was, in the main, a peaceable kind of fellow, and nothing choleric nor rash, yet did he bear about him something of what the ancients called the irascible, and which his wife, if she had been endowed with much wisdom, would have feared. He had long experienced, that when the storm grew very high, arguments were but wind, which served rather to increase, than to abate it. He was therefore seldom unprovided with a small switch, a remedy of wonderful force, as he had often essayed, and which the word villain served as a hint for his applying.

No sooner, therefore, had this symptom appeared, than he had immediate recourse to the said remedy, which though, as it is usual in all very efficacious medicines, it at first seemed to heighten and inflame the disease, soon produced a total calm, and restored the patient to perfect ease and tranquillity.

This is, however, a kind of horse-medicine, which requires a very robust constitution to digest, and is therefore proper only for the vulgar, unless in one single instance, viz., where superiority of birth breaks out. In which case, we should not think it very improperly applied by any husband whatever, if the application was not in itself so base, that, like certain applications of the physical kind which need not be mentioned, it so much degrades and contaminates the hand employed in it, that no gentleman should endure the thought of anything so low and detestable.

The whole family were soon reduced to a state of perfect quiet, for the virtue of this medicine, like that of electricity, is often communicated through one person to many others, who are not touched by the instrument. To say the truth, as they both operate by friction, it may be doubted whether there is not something analogous between them, of which Mr Freke would do well to enquire, before he publishes the next edition of his book.

A council was now called, in which, after many debates, Molly still persisting that she would not go to service, it was at length resolved, that Goody Seagrim herself should wait on Miss Western, and endeavour to procure the place for her eldest daughter, who declared great readiness to accept it, but Fortune, who seems to have been an enemy of this little family, afterwards put a stop to her promotion.

That evening appeared Tom, as promised, trysting with her in the fields where they first met, eager to comfort his Molly and console her for the loss of the fine gown.

Knowing the ways of gentlemen, Molly appeared as fine as she could manage, and had even washed her face, but when he appeared she rinsed it more with a libation of lachrymose qualities the finest actress on the London stage would have been proud to display.

Tom, having not had the fortune to see the great Mrs Clive or any other of her kind on stage, had no conception of the thespian skills of the fairer sex, and took Molly into his arms, comforting her as gently as he knew how to do.

The tender actions soon had their desired result, and soon Tom and Molly were lying on the riverbank consoling each other. When Tom rolled over Molly, her skirts somehow lifted, revealing her finest charms, and the ones she prided herself on the most of all. It is said that infinite variety is the way to keep matters fresh between a couple used to each other, but Molly believed in using the methods she had practised and discovered to be true. He expressed great delight in the sight, and sat back on his heels, the better to view her beauties, moving her ragged petticoat out of the way. Obligingly, Molly opened her legs, her white thighs now framing the wet entrance to her feminine paradise. Those parts of her that seldom saw the sun were as fine and well-made as any that ever tramped the boards or danced in the finest drawing-rooms in London.

Tom appreciated the sight before him and took his time viewing the masterpiece, before he began to explore it with hands and mouth. Knowing the preferences of the gentry, Molly had been sure to wash the parts of her person she assumed Tom would take more interest in, and the scent that rose was as fresh and sweet as the finest courtesan's.

Thus, he ventured to sample his mistress's most intimate effluvium, and found it to his taste. While Molly made a great show of thrashing and moaning, Tom savoured her flavour, and took great satisfaction from exploring the crevices and peaks of her cunny. When he delved inside, he discovered the most sweet secrets of her body, and Molly eagerly granted him access, bunching her skirts under her body to bring her backside higher.

When she moaned his name in a most gratifying manner, he looked up, to see her watching him, the gleam of desire in her eyes. Somehow her breasts had come loose from their gentle restraints, and bounced, full and ruddy, for his eyes to feast on, as his mouth had feasted on her willing slit.

He could wait no more to seat his aching prick in her body, for much as he would have liked to delay the dalliance, the eagerness of youth took him full measure, and if he had waited overlong, he would not have experienced the pleasure of her sweet body.

Although he had prepared Molly, and not being a novice to these pleasures, she was fully ready to receive his homage, he pressed in with some difficulty. This did not give Molly any concern. "My, you are a big fellow," she purred. "But we will get there."

Sure enough, a little more exertion proved that Molly's faith in Tom wasn't unfounded, and he sank deep inside her to the very hilt.

Tom was compelled to take a few deep breaths to ensure he wouldn't spill his climax too quickly, then he was ready to pleasure Molly, a task he was determined to accomplish and with as much finesse as he could muster.

For a beginner, Tom proved so adept at his chosen task, that Molly cried out before five minutes were done, and Tom, now perspiring mightily, could give himself to his own pleasure, and bucked as he delivered a full measure of his endowment before collapsing in a sweaty confusion of limbs on top of her.

He soon recollected his position, and after putting himself to rights, he lay down and took Molly into his arms, returning to his original intention of soothing her after her ordeal that day.

For her part, Molly, well satisfied with her lover, allowed him to comfort her so agreeably that they decided on a repeat performance before they went their separate ways later that night. She liked him well, but she knew she could never hope to keep him, although, if she worked hard, she could become an important part of his life.

Chapter Ten

A story told by Mr Supple, the curate. The penetration of Squire Western. His great love for his daughter, and the return to it made by her

The next morning Tom Jones hunted with Mr Western, and was at his return invited by that gentleman to dinner.

The lovely Sophia shone forth that day with more gaiety and sprightliness than usual. Her battery was certainly levelled at our hero, though, I believe, she herself scarce yet knew her own intention, but if she had any design of charming him, she now succeeded.

Mr Supple, the curate of Mr Allworthy's parish, made one of the company. He was a good-natured, worthy man, but chiefly remarkable for his great taciturnity at table, though his mouth was never shut at it. In short, he had one of the best appetites in the world. However, the cloth was no sooner taken away, than he always made sufficient amends for his silence, for he was a very hearty fellow, and his conversation was often entertaining, never offensive.

At his first arrival, which was immediately before the entrance of the roast beef, he had given an intimation that he had brought some news with him, and was beginning to tell, that he came that moment from Mr Allworthy's, when the sight of the roast beef struck him dumb, permitting him only to say grace, and to declare he must pay his respect to the baronet, for so he called the sirloin.

When dinner was over, being reminded by Sophia of his news, he began as follows. "I believe, lady, your ladyship observed a young woman at church yesterday at evensong, who was dressed in one of your outlandish garments. I think I have seen your ladyship in such a one. However, in the country, such dresses are *rara avis in terris, nigroque simillima cygno.* That is, madam, as much as to say, 'A rare bird upon the earth, and very like a black swan'. The verse is in Juvenal.

"But to return to what I was relating. I was saying such garments are rare sights in the country, and perchance, too, it was thought the more rare, respect being had to the person who wore it, who, they tell me, is the daughter of Black George, your worship's gamekeeper, whose sufferings, I should have opined, might have taught him more wit, than to dress forth his wenches in such gaudy apparel. She created so much confusion in the congregation, that if Squire Allworthy had not silenced it, it would have interrupted the service, for I was once about to stop in the middle of the first lesson.

"Howbeit, nevertheless, after prayer was over, and I was departed home, this occasioned a battle in the churchyard, where, amongst other mischief, the head of a travelling fiddler was very much broken. This morning the fiddler came to Squire Allworthy for a warrant, and the wench was brought before him. The squire was inclined to have compounded matters, when, lo! On a sudden the wench appeared—I ask your ladyship's pardon—to be, as it were, at the eve of bringing forth a bastard. The squire demanded of her who was the father? But she pertinaciously refused to make any response. So that he was about to make her mittimus to Bridewell when I departed."

"And is a wench having a bastard all your news, doctor?" cried Western. "I thought it might have been some public matter, something about the nation."

"I am afraid it is too common, indeed," answered the parson, "but I thought the whole story altogether deserved commemorating. As to national matters, your worship knows them best. My concerns extend no farther than my own parish."

"Why, ay," said the squire, "I believe I do know a little of that matter, as you say. But, come, Tommy, drink about, the bottle stands with you."

Tom begged to be excused, for that he had particular business, and getting up from table, escaped the clutches of the squire, who was rising to stop him, and went off with very little ceremony.

The squire gave him a good curse at his departure, and then turning to the parson, he cried out, "I smoke it, I smoke it. Tom is certainly the father of this bastard. Zooks, parson, you remember how he recommended the veather o' her to me. Damn un, what a sly b—ch 'tis. Ay, ay, as sure as two-pence, Tom is the veather of the bastard."

"I should be very sorry for that," says the parson.

"Why sorry," cries the squire, "Where is the mighty matter o't? What, I suppose dost pretend that thee hast never got a bastard? Pox! More good luck's thine? For I warrant hast a done a *therefore* many's the good time and often."

"Your worship is pleased to be jocular," answered the parson, "but I do not only animadvert on the sinfulness of the action—though that surely is to be greatly deprecated—but I fear his unrighteousness may injure him with Mr Allworthy. And truly I must say, though he hath the character of being a little wild, I never saw any harm in the young man, nor can I say I have heard any, save what your worship now mentions. I wish, indeed, he was a little more regular in his responses at church, but altogether he seems *ingenui vultus puer ingenuique pudoris.* That is a classical line, young lady, and being rendered into English, is, 'a lad of an ingenuous countenance, and of an ingenuous modesty', for this was a virtue in great repute both among the Latins and Greeks. I must say, the young gentleman—for so I think I may call him, notwithstanding his birth—appears to me a very modest, civil lad, and I should be sorry that he should do himself any injury in Squire Allworthy's opinion."

"Poogh!" says the squire, "Injury, with Allworthy! Why, Allworthy loves a wench himself. Doth not all the country know whose son Tom is? You must talk to another person in that manner. I remember Allworthy at college."

"I thought," said the parson, "he had never been at the university."

"Yes, yes, he was," says the squire, "and many a wench have we two had together. As arrant a whore-master as any within five miles o'un. No, no. It will do'n no harm with he, assure yourself, nor with anybody else. Ask Sophy there—You have not the worse opinion of a young fellow for getting a bastard, have you, girl? No, no, the women will like un the better for't."

This was a cruel question to poor Sophia. She had observed Tom's colour change at the parson's story, and that, with his hasty and abrupt departure, gave her sufficient reason to think her father's suspicion not groundless. Her heart now at once discovered the great secret to her which it had been so long disclosing by little and little, and she found herself highly interested in this matter.

In such a situation, her father's malapert question rushing suddenly upon her, produced some symptoms which might have alarmed a suspicious heart, but, to do the squire justice, that was not his fault. When she rose therefore from her chair, and told him a hint from him was always sufficient to make her withdraw, he suffered her to leave the room, and then with great gravity of countenance remarked, that it was better to see a daughter over-modest than over-forward. A sentiment which was highly applauded by the parson.

There now ensued between the squire and the parson a most excellent political discourse, framed out of newspapers and political pamphlets, in which they made a libation of four bottles of wine to the good of their country, and then, the squire being fast asleep, the parson lighted his pipe, mounted his horse, and rode home.

When the squire had finished his half-hour's nap, he summoned his daughter to her harpsichord, but she begged to be excused that evening, on account of a violent headache. This remission was presently granted, for indeed she seldom had occasion to ask him twice, as he loved her with such ardent affection, that, by gratifying her, he commonly conveyed the highest gratification to himself.

She was really, what he frequently called her, his little darling, and she well deserved to be so, for she returned all his affection in the most ample manner. She had preserved the most inviolable duty to him in all things, and this her love made not only easy, but so delightful, that when one of her companions laughed at her for placing so much merit in such scrupulous obedience, as that young lady called it, Sophia answered, "You mistake me, madam, if you think I value myself upon this account, for besides that I am barely discharging my duty, I am likewise pleasing myself. I can truly say I have no delight equal to that of contributing to my father's happiness, and if I value myself, my dear, it is on having this power, and not on executing it."

This was a satisfaction, however, which poor Sophia was incapable of tasting this evening. She therefore not only desired to be excused from her attendance at the harpsichord, but likewise begged that he would suffer her to absent herself from supper. To this request likewise the squire agreed, though not without some reluctance, for he scarce ever permitted her to be out of his sight, unless when he was engaged with his horses, dogs, or bottle. Nevertheless he yielded to the desire of his daughter, though the poor man was at the same time obliged to avoid his own company — if I may so express myself — by sending for a neighbouring farmer to sit with him.

Chapter Eleven

The narrow escape of Molly Seagrim, with some observations for which we have been forced to dive pretty deep into nature

Tom Jones had ridden one of Mr Western's horses that morning in the chase, so that having no horse of his own in the squire's stable, he was obliged to go home on foot, this he did so expeditiously that he ran upwards of three miles within the half-hour.

Just as he arrived at Mr Allworthy's outward gate, he met the constable and company with Molly in their possession, whom they were conducting to that house where the inferior sort of people may learn one good lesson, viz., respect and deference to their superiors, since it must show them the wide distinction Fortune intends between those persons who are to be corrected for their faults, and those who are not—which lesson if they do not learn, I am afraid they very rarely learn any other good lesson, or improve their morals, at the house of correction.

A lawyer may perhaps think Mr Allworthy exceeded his authority a little in this instance. And, to say the truth, I question, as here was no regular information before him, whether his conduct was strictly regular. However, as his intention was truly upright, he ought to be excused in *foro conscientiae*, since so many arbitrary acts are daily committed by magistrates who have not this excuse to plead for themselves.

Tom was no sooner informed by the constable whither they were proceeding—indeed he pretty well guessed it of himself—than he caught Molly in his arms, and embracing her tenderly before them all, swore he would murder the first man who offered to lay hold of her. He bid her dry her eyes and be comforted, for, wherever she went, he would accompany her. Then turning to the constable, who stood trembling with his hat off, he desired him, in a very mild voice, to return with him for a moment only to his father—for so he now called Allworthy—for he durst, he said, be assured, that, when he had alleged what he had to say in her favour, the girl would be discharged.

The constable, who, I make no doubt, would have surrendered his prisoner had Tom demanded her, very readily consented to this request. So back they all went into Mr Allworthy's hall, where Tom desired them to stay till his return, and then went himself in pursuit of the good man. As soon as he was found, Tom threw himself at his feet, and having begged a patient hearing, confessed himself to be the father of the child of which Molly was then big. He entreated him to have compassion on the poor girl, and to consider, if there was any guilt in the case, it lay principally at his door.

"If there is any guilt in the case!" answered Allworthy warmly. "Are you then so profligate and abandoned a libertine to doubt whether the breaking the laws of God and man, the corrupting and ruining a poor girl be guilt? I own, indeed, it doth lie principally upon you, and so heavy it is, that you ought to expect it should crush you."

"Whatever may be my fate," says Tom, "let me succeed in my intercessions for the poor girl. I confess I have corrupted her! But whether she shall be ruined, depends on you. For Heaven's sake, sir, revoke your warrant, and do not send her to a place which must unavoidably prove her destruction."

Allworthy bid him immediately call a servant. Tom answered there was no occasion, for he had luckily met them at the gate, and relying upon his goodness, had brought them all back into his hall, where they now waited his final resolution, which upon his knees he besought him might be in favour of the girl, that she might be permitted to go home to her parents, and not be exposed to a greater degree of shame and scorn than must necessarily fall upon her. "I know," said he, "that is too much. I know I am the wicked occasion of it. I will endeavour to make amends, if possible, and if you shall have hereafter the goodness to forgive me, I hope I shall deserve it."

Allworthy hesitated some time, and at last said, "Well, I will discharge my mittimus. You may send the constable to me." He was instantly called, discharged, and so was the girl.

It will be believed that Mr Allworthy failed not to read Tom a very severe lecture on this occasion, but it is unnecessary to insert it here, as we have faithfully transcribed what he said to Jenny Jones in the first book, most of which may be applied to the men, equally with the women. So sensible an effect had these reproofs on the young man, who was no hardened sinner, that he retired to his own room, where he passed the evening alone, in much melancholy contemplation. The pleasures of the flesh were difficult to resist, but the physical animadversions he had added to his stern lecture must, he hoped, have aided Jenny to take more care with the person to whom she granted the use of her body.

Allworthy was sufficiently offended by this transgression of Jones, for notwithstanding the assertions of Mr Western, it is certain this worthy man had never indulged himself in any loose pleasures with women, and greatly condemned the vice of incontinence in others. He discounted from this consideration his occasional dalliances with willing females, for both parties were cognisant and agreeable to what was indeed of only private concern. His personal indulgences he considered necessary for his health and the female's, and he never took what was not freely offered, or took that which belonged to another. A public confession of loose behaviour would necessarily condemn his people too, and Mr Allworthy had no desire to intimate that kind of behaviour.

Indeed, there is much reason to imagine that there was not the least truth in what Mr Western affirmed, especially as he laid the scene of those impurities at the university, where Mr Allworthy had never been. In fact, the good squire was a little too apt to indulge that kind of pleasantry which is generally called rodomontade, but which may, with as much propriety, be expressed by a much shorter word, and perhaps we too often supply the use of this little monosyllable by others, since very much of what frequently passes in the world for wit and humour, should, in the strictest purity of language, receive that short appellation, which, in conformity to the well-bred laws of custom, I here suppress.

But whatever detestation Mr Allworthy had to this or to any other vice, he was not so blinded by it but that he could discern any virtue in the guilty person, as clearly indeed as if there had been no mixture of vice in the same character. While he was angry therefore with the incontinence of Jones, he was no less pleased with the honour and honesty of his self-accusation. He began now to form in his mind the same opinion of this young fellow, which, we hope, our reader may have conceived. And in balancing his faults with his perfections, the latter seemed rather to preponderate.

It was to no purpose, therefore, that Thwackum, who was immediately charged by Mr Blifil with the story, unbended all his rancour against poor Tom. Allworthy gave a patient hearing to their invectives, and then answered coldly, that young men of Tom's complexion were too generally addicted to this vice, but he believed that youth was sincerely affected with what he had said to him on the occasion, and he hoped he would not transgress again. So that, as the days of whipping were at an end, the tutor had no other vent but his own mouth for his gall, the usual poor resource of impotent revenge.

But Square, who was less violent, was a much more artful man, and as he hated Jones more perhaps than Thwackum himself did, so he contrived to do him more mischief in the mind of Mr Allworthy.

The reader must remember the several little incidents of the partridge, the horse, and the Bible, which were recounted in the second book. By all which Jones had rather improved than injured the affection which Mr Allworthy was inclined to entertain for him. The same, I believe, must have happened to him with every other person who hath any idea of friendship, generosity, and greatness of spirit, that is to say, who hath any traces of goodness in his mind.

Square himself was not unacquainted with the true impression which those several instances of goodness had made on the excellent heart of Allworthy, for the philosopher very well knew what virtue was, though he was not always perhaps steady in its pursuit. But as for Thwackum, from what reason I will not determine, no such thoughts ever entered into his head. He saw Jones in a bad light, and he imagined Allworthy saw him in the same, but that he was resolved, from pride and stubbornness of spirit, not to give up the boy whom he had once cherished, since by so doing, he must tacitly acknowledge that his former opinion of him had been wrong.

Square therefore embraced this opportunity of injuring Jones in the tenderest part, by giving a very bad turn to all these before-mentioned occurrences. "I am sorry, sir," said he, "to own I have been deceived as well as yourself. I could not, I confess, help being pleased with what I ascribed to the motive of friendship, though it was carried to an excess, and all excess is faulty and vicious, but in this I made allowance for youth. Little did I suspect that the sacrifice of truth, which we both imagined to have been made to friendship, was in reality a prostitution of it to a depraved and debauched appetite.

"You now plainly see whence all the seeming generosity of this young man to the family of the gamekeeper proceeded. He supported the father in order to corrupt the daughter, and preserved the family from starving, to bring one of them to shame and ruin. This is friendship! This is generosity! As Sir Richard Steele says, 'Gluttons who give high prices for delicacies, are very worthy to be called generous.' In short I am resolved, from this instance, never to give way to the weakness of human nature more, nor to think anything virtue which doth not exactly quadrate with the unerring rule of right."

The goodness of Allworthy had prevented those considerations from occurring to himself, yet were they too plausible to be absolutely and hastily rejected, when laid before his eyes by another. Indeed what Square had said sank very deeply into his mind, and the uneasiness which it there created was very visible to the other, though the good man would not acknowledge this, but made a very slight answer, and forcibly drove off the discourse to some other subject. It was well perhaps for poor Tom, that no such suggestions had been made before he was pardoned, for they certainly stamped in the mind of Allworthy the first bad impression concerning Jones.

Chapter Twelve

Containing much clearer matters, but which flowed from the same fountain with those in the preceding chapter

The reader will be pleased, I believe, to return with me to Sophia. She passed the night, after we saw her last, in no very agreeable manner. Sleep befriended her but little, and dreams less. In the morning, when Mrs Honour, her maid, attended her at the usual hour, she was found already up and dressed.

Persons who live two or three miles' distance in the country are considered as next-door neighbours, and transactions at the one house fly with incredible celerity to the other. Mrs Honour, therefore, had heard the whole story of Molly's shame, which she, being of a very communicative temper, had no sooner entered the apartment of her mistress, than she began to relate in the following manner.

"La, ma'am, what doth your la'ship think? The girl that your la'ship saw at church on Sunday, whom you thought so handsome, though you would not have thought her so handsome neither, if you had seen her nearer, but to be sure she hath been carried before the justice for being big with child. She seemed to me to look like a confident slut, and to be sure she hath laid the child to young Mr Jones. And all the parish says Mr Allworthy is so angry with young Mr Jones, that he won't see him.

"To be sure, one can't help pitying the poor young man, and yet he doth not deserve much pity neither, for demeaning himself with such kind of trumpery. Yet he is so pretty a gentleman, I should be sorry to have him turned out of doors. I dares to swear the wench was as willing as he, for she was always a forward kind of body. And when wenches are so coming, young men are not so much to be blamed neither, for to be sure they do no more than what is natural. Indeed it is beneath them to meddle with such dirty draggle-tails, and whatever happens to them, it is good enough for them. And yet, to be sure, the vile baggages are most in fault. I wishes, with all my heart, they were well to be whipped at the cart's tail, for it is pity they should be the ruin of a pretty young gentleman, and nobody can deny but that Mr Jones is one of the most handsomest young men that ever—"

She was running on thus, when Sophia, with a more peevish voice than she had ever spoken to her in before, cried, "Prithee, why dost thou trouble me with all this stuff? What concern have I in what Mr Jones doth? I suppose you are all alike. And you seem to me to be angry it was not your own case."

"I, ma'am!" answered Mrs Honour. "I am sorry your ladyship should have such an opinion of me. I am sure nobody can say any such thing of me. All the young fellows in the world may go to the devil for me. Because I said he was a handsome man? Everybody says it as well as I. To be sure, I never thought as it was any harm to say a young man was handsome, but to be sure I shall never think him so any more now, for handsome is that handsome does. A beggar wench!"

"Stop thy torrent of impertinence," cries Sophia, stamping her pretty foot, "and see whether my father wants me at breakfast."

Mrs Honour then flung out of the room, muttering much to herself, of which "Marry come up, I assure you," was all that could be plainly distinguished.

Whether Mrs Honour really deserved that suspicion, of which her mistress gave her a hint, is a matter which we cannot indulge our reader's curiosity by resolving. We will, however, make him amends in disclosing what passed in the mind of Sophia.

The reader will be pleased to recollect, that a secret affection for Mr Jones had insensibly stolen into the bosom of this young lady. That it had there grown to a pretty great height before she herself had discovered it. When she first began to perceive its symptoms, the sensations were so sweet and pleasing, that she had not resolution sufficient to check or repel them, and thus she went on cherishing a passion of which she never once considered the consequences. Their sweet dalliance remained long on her mind, and she would go to sleep in the evening dreaming of it many a time.

Once her maid had gone to her own rest, Sophia touched her breasts the way Tom had done, and although she found not the same enjoyment as she had when he had taken hold, still, it was not a disagreeable experience. She lifted her night rail and touched them, gently at first, then taking her nipples between finger and thumb in a twirling motion, until they hardened and peaked.

She found the experience interesting but it also sent sensations through her, such that she wished to know more. After all, how could she please a man if she did not know her own body first? She decided that a woman deserved to feel just as content as her partner after making the two-backed beast, and proceeded to explore what God had generously bestowed on her.

Her soft belly was as yet little rounded, but that sweet pillow a man could lay his head on would come in time, she was sure. She touched it, felt the place where, one day, she would feel her child grow, then continued to explore.

Her legs were of that milky white that ladies aspired to, and would apply all manner of concoctions to achieve, but Sophia had it as a birthright. She would drive a man mad with the perfection of her form.

Between her legs lay a soft covering of hair that she had before not concerned herself with, once her maid assured her that all ladies developed such a bush. Beneath the patch of dark blonde curls lay the area Tom had toyed with so delightfully, and which she had rarely done anything with except to keep clean.

Now she inserted one exploratory finger into the cleft that delved beneath two plump cushions of flesh. She gasped at the intensity of the sensation, but dared to continue, discovering that her fingers became coated with liquid that came from her own body.

She nestled the pad of her forefinger by the opening that was exuding the liquid and discovered it warm to her touch, warmer than the rest of her body, but not of a feverish nature. She dared to insert her finger into the small space, but did not venture very far, because this place was where her virginity resided, such as it was, for Mrs Honour had informed her that riding would reduce the tightness of her womb and Sophia spent a great deal of time in the saddle. Perhaps, Mrs Honour had said with a wink and a smile, in time she would spend as long in a different saddle, the one belonging to a man, as well as the one on the back of a horse.

Returning to her slit, Sophia slid her finger to the top and was surprised by the sensation that shot through her body, like a pleasurable bolt of lightning. Continuing her manipulations, she discovered that pressing the knot of flesh she found there increased her delight, until she was arching up and working her fingers as if nature had intended her to discover such a thing.

The sensations increased and Sophia discovered such joy there that she continued until her body went into spasms of intense delight, bright and sweet.

She went to sleep, enraptured that she could please herself in such a way and determined to understand her body even more thoroughly before it should please her father to bestow her hand in marriage to a worthy suitor.

In the meantime, she could take care of her own desires and needs. That knowledge gave her great satisfaction.

This incident relating to Molly first opened her eyes. She now first perceived the weakness of which she had been guilty, and though it caused the utmost perturbation in her mind, yet it had the effect of other nauseous physic, and for the time expelled her distemper. Its operation indeed was most wonderfully quick, and in the short interval, while her maid was absent, so entirely removed all symptoms, that when Mrs Honour returned with a summons from her father, she was become perfectly easy, and had brought herself to a thorough indifference for Mr

Jones. If she meant so little to him, then why should she repine? And with her newfound discoveries, she needed no man to help her to paradise.

The diseases of the mind do in almost every particular imitate those of the body. For which reason, we hope, that learned faculty, for whom we have so profound a respect, will pardon us the violent hands we have been necessitated to lay on several words and phrases, which of right belong to them, and without which our descriptions must have been often unintelligible.

Now there is no one circumstance in which the distempers of the mind bear a more exact analogy to those which are called bodily, than that aptness which both have to a relapse. This is plain in the violent diseases of ambition and avarice. I have known ambition, when cured at court by frequent disappointments, which are the only physic for it, to break out again in a contest for foreman of the grand jury at an assizes. I have heard of a man who had so far conquered avarice, as to give away many a sixpence, that comforted himself, at last, on his deathbed, by making a crafty and advantageous bargain concerning his ensuing funeral, with an undertaker who had married his only child.

In the affair of love, which, out of strict conformity with the Stoic philosophy, we shall here treat as a disease, this proneness to relapse is no less conspicuous. Thus it happened to poor Sophia, upon whom, the very next time she saw young Jones, all the former symptoms returned, and from that time cold and hot fits alternately seized her heart.

The situation of this young lady was now very different from what it had ever been before. That passion which had formerly been so exquisitely delicious, became now a scorpion in her bosom. She resisted it therefore with her utmost force, and summoned every argument her reason—which was surprisingly strong for her age—could suggest, to subdue and expel it. In this she so far succeeded, that she began to hope from time and absence a perfect cure. She resolved therefore to avoid Tom Jones as much as possible, for which purpose she began to conceive a design of visiting her aunt, to which she made no doubt of obtaining her father's consent.

But Fortune, who had other designs in her head, put an immediate stop to any such proceeding, by introducing an accident, which will be related in the next chapter.

Chapter Thirteen

A dreadful accident which befell Sophia. The gallant behaviour of Jones, and the more dreadful consequence of that behaviour to the young lady, with a short digression in favour of the female sex

Mr Western grew every day fonder and fonder of Sophia, insomuch that his beloved dogs themselves almost gave place to her in his affections, but as he could not prevail on himself to abandon these, he contrived very cunningly to enjoy their company, together with that of his daughter, by insisting on her riding a hunting with him.

Sophia, to whom her father's word was a law, readily complied with his desires, though she had not the least delight in a sport, which was of too rough and masculine a nature to suit with her disposition. She had however another motive, beside her obedience, to accompany the old gentleman in the chase, for by her presence she hoped in some measure to restrain his impetuosity, and to prevent him from so frequently exposing his neck to the utmost hazard.

The strongest objection was that which would have formerly been an inducement to her, namely, the frequent meeting with young Jones, whom she had determined to avoid, but as the end of the hunting season now approached, she hoped, by a short absence with her aunt, to reason herself entirely out of her unfortunate passion, and had not any doubt of being able to meet him in the field the subsequent season without the least danger.

On the second day of her hunting, as she was returning from the chase, and was arrived within a little distance from Mr Western's house, her horse, whose mettlesome spirit required a better rider, fell suddenly to prancing and capering in such a manner that she was in the most imminent peril of falling. Tom Jones, who was at a little distance behind, saw this, and immediately galloped up to her assistance. As soon as he came up, he leapt from his own horse, and caught hold of hers by the bridle. The unruly beast presently reared himself an end on his hind legs, and threw his lovely burden from his back, and Jones caught her in his arms. Only a wince on his handsome face betrayed any inconvenience, but Sophia, not being in her right mind, immediately pressed her lips to his and gave him a deep, penetrating kiss. Tom responded in kind, opening his mouth against hers and plunging his tongue into her mouth, but he drew back with a kind of gasp she didn't think was entirely from the bliss of holding her.

She was so affected with the fright, that she was not immediately able to satisfy Jones, who was very solicitous to know whether she had received any hurt. She soon after, however, recovered her spirits, assured him she was safe, and thanked him for the care he had taken of her. Jones answered, "If I have preserved you, madam, I am sufficiently repaid, for I promise you, I would have secured you from the least harm at the expense of a much greater misfortune to myself than I have suffered on this occasion."

"What misfortune?" replied Sophia eagerly. "I hope you have come to no mischief?"

"Be not concerned, madam," answered Jones. "Heaven be praised you have escaped so well, considering the danger you was in. If I have broke my arm, I consider it as a trifle, in comparison of what I feared upon your account."

Sophia then screamed out, "Broke your arm! Heaven forbid."

"I am afraid I have, madam," says Jones, "but I beg you will suffer me first to take care of you. I have a right hand yet at your service, to help you into the next field, whence we have but a very little walk to your father's house." His sincerity in this could not be denied, Sophia saw the truth in his eyes before she turned her eyes to his limb.

Sophia seeing his left arm dangling by his side, while he was using the other to lead her, no longer doubted of the truth. She now grew much paler than her fears for herself had made her before. All her limbs were seized with a trembling, insomuch that Jones could scarce support her, and as her thoughts were in no less agitation, she could not refrain from giving Jones a look so full of tenderness, that it almost argued a stronger sensation in her mind, than even gratitude and pity united can raise in the gentlest female bosom, without the assistance of a third more powerful passion.

Overwhelmed by the hurt he had taken on her behalf, she pressed her lips to his once more, and at that moment, had he wished it, she would have given him anything he desired, including that precious commodity that should clearly belong to the man who took her in marriage. Not being backwards in his apprehension, Tom responded in full measure, once again taking her in a considerably passionate kiss.

Mr Western, who was advanced at some distance when this accident happened, was now returned, as were the rest of the horsemen. Sophia immediately acquainted them with what had befallen Jones, and begged them to take care of him. Upon which Western, who had been much alarmed by meeting his daughter's horse without its rider, and was now overjoyed to find her unhurt, cried out, "I am glad it is no worse. If Tom hath broken his arm, we will get a joiner to mend un again."

The squire alighted from his horse, and proceeded to his house on foot, with his daughter and Jones. An impartial spectator, who had met them on the way, would, on viewing their several countenances, have concluded Sophia alone to have been the object of compassion, for as to Jones, he exulted in having probably saved the life of the young lady, at the price only of a broken bone, and Mr Western, though he was not unconcerned at the accident which had befallen Jones, was, however, delighted in a much higher degree with the fortunate escape of his daughter.

The generosity of Sophia's temper construed this behaviour of Jones into great bravery, and it made a deep impression on her heart, for certain it is, that there is no one quality which so generally recommends men to women as this—proceeding, if we believe the common opinion, from that natural timidity of the sex, which is, says Mr Osborne, "so great, that a woman is the most cowardly of all the creatures God ever made". A sentiment more remarkable for its bluntness than for its truth.

Aristotle, in his Politics, doth them, I believe, more justice, when he says, "The modesty and fortitude of men differ from those virtues in women, for the fortitude which becomes a woman, would be cowardice in a man, and the modesty which becomes a man, would be pertness in a woman." Nor is there, perhaps, more of truth in the opinion of those who derive the partiality which women are inclined to show to the brave, from this excess of their fear. Mr Bayle—I think, in his article of Helen—imputes this, and with greater probability, to their violent love of glory, for the truth of which, we have the authority of him who of all others saw farthest into human nature, and who introduces the heroine of his Odyssey, the great pattern of matrimonial love and constancy, assigning the glory of her husband as the only source of her affection towards him.

However this be, certain it is that the accident operated very strongly on Sophia, and indeed, after much enquiry into the matter, I am inclined to believe, that, at this very time, the charming Sophia made no less impression on the heart of Jones. To say truth, he had for some time become sensible of the irresistible power of her charms.

Chapter Fourteen

The arrival of a surgeon. His operations, and a long dialogue between Sophia and her maid

When they arrived at Mr Western's hall, Sophia, who had tottered along with much difficulty, sunk down in her chair, but by the assistance of hartshorn and water, she was prevented from fainting away, and had pretty well recovered her spirits, when the surgeon who was sent for to Jones appeared. Mr Western, who imputed these symptoms in his daughter to her fall, advised her to be presently blooded by way of prevention. In this opinion he was seconded by the surgeon, who gave so many reasons for bleeding, and quoted so many cases where persons had miscarried for want of it, that the squire became very importunate, and indeed insisted peremptorily that his daughter should be blooded.

Sophia soon yielded to the commands of her father, though entirely contrary to her own inclinations, for she suspected, I believe, less danger from the fright, than either the squire or the surgeon. She then stretched out her beautiful arm, and the operator began to prepare for his work.

While the servants were busied in providing materials, the surgeon, who imputed the backwardness which had appeared in Sophia to her fears, began to comfort her with assurances that there was not the least danger, for no accident, he said, could ever happen in bleeding, but from the monstrous ignorance of pretenders to surgery, which he pretty plainly insinuated was not at present to be apprehended. Sophia declared she was not under the least apprehension, adding, "If you open an artery, I promise you I'll forgive you."

"Will you?" cries Western. "Damn me, if I will. If he does thee the least mischief, damn me if I don't ha' the heart's blood o'un out."

The surgeon assented to bleed her upon these conditions, and then proceeded to his operation, which he performed with as much dexterity as he had promised, and with as much quickness, for he took but little blood from her, saying, it was much safer to bleed again and again, than to take away too much at once.

Sophia, when her arm was bound up, retired, for she was not willing — nor was it, perhaps, strictly decent — to be present at the operation on Jones. Indeed, one objection which she had to bleeding, though she did not make it, was the delay which it would occasion to setting the broken bone. For Western, when Sophia was concerned, had no consideration but for her, and as for Jones himself, he "sat like patience on a monument smiling at grief". To say the truth, when he saw the blood springing from the lovely arm of

Sophia, he scarce thought of what had happened to himself.

The surgeon now ordered his patient to be stripped to his shirt, and then entirely baring the arm, he began to stretch and examine it, in such a manner that the tortures he put him to caused Jones to make several wry faces, which the surgeon observing, greatly wondered at, crying, "What is the matter, sir? I am sure it is impossible I should hurt you." And then holding forth the broken arm, he began a long and very learned lecture of anatomy, in which simple and double fractures were most accurately considered, and the several ways in which Jones might have broken his arm were discussed, with proper annotations showing how many of these would have been better, and how many worse than the present case.

Having at length finished his laboured harangue – with which the audience, though it had greatly raised their attention and admiration, were not much edified, as they really understood not a single syllable of all he had said – he proceeded to business, which he was more expeditious in finishing, than he had been in beginning.

Jones was then ordered into a bed, which Mr Western compelled him to accept at his own house, and sentence of water-gruel was passed upon him.

Among the good company which had attended in the hall during the bone-setting, Mrs Honour was one, who being summoned to her mistress as soon as it was over, and asked by her how the young gentleman did, presently launched into extravagant praises on the magnanimity, as she called it, of his behaviour, which, she said, "was so charming in so pretty a creature". She then burst forth into much warmer encomiums on the beauty of his person, enumerating many particulars, and ending with the whiteness of his skin.

This discourse had an effect on Sophia's countenance, which would not perhaps have escaped the observance of the sagacious waiting-woman, had she once looked her mistress in the face, all the time she was speaking. But as a looking-glass, which was most commodiously placed opposite to her, gave her an opportunity of surveying those features, in which, of all others, she took most delight, so she had not once removed her eyes from that amiable object during her whole speech.

Mrs Honour was so entirely wrapped up in the subject on which she exercised her tongue, and the object before her eyes, that she gave her mistress time to conquer her confusion, which having done, she smiled on her maid, and told her, she was certainly in love with this young fellow.

"I in love, madam!" answers she. "Upon my word, ma'am, I assure you, ma'am, upon my soul, ma'am, I am not."

"Why, if you was," cries her mistress, "I see no reason that you should be ashamed of it, for he is certainly a pretty fellow."

"Yes, ma'am," answered the other, "that he is, the most handsomest man I ever saw in my life. Yes, to be sure, that he is, and as your ladyship says, I don't know why I should be ashamed of loving him, though he is my betters. To be sure, gentlefolks are but flesh and blood no more than us servants. Besides, as for Mr Jones, thof Squire Allworthy hath made a gentleman of him, he was not so good as myself by birth, for thof I am a poor body, I am an honest person's child, and my father and mother were married, which is more than some people can say, as high as they hold their heads. Marry, come up! I assure you, my dirty cousin! Thof his skin be so white, and to be sure it is the most whitest that ever was seen, I am a Christian as well as he, and nobody can say that I am base born. My grandfather was a clergyman, and would have been very angry, I believe, to have thought any of his family should have taken up with Molly Seagrim's dirty leavings."

Perhaps Sophia might have suffered her maid to run on in this manner, from wanting sufficient spirits to stop her tongue, which the reader may probably conjecture was no very easy task, for certainly there were some passages in her speech which were far from being agreeable to the lady. However, she now checked the torrent, as there seemed no end of its flowing. "I wonder," says she, "at your assurance in daring to talk thus of one of my father's friends. As to the wench, I order you never to mention her name to me. And with regard to the young gentleman's birth, those who can say nothing more to his disadvantage, may as well be silent on that head, as I desire you will be for the future."

"I am sorry I have offended your ladyship," answered Mrs Honour. "I am sure I hate Molly Seagrim as much as your ladyship can, and as for abusing Squire Jones, I can call all the servants in the house to witness, that whenever any talk hath been about bastards, I have always taken his part, for which of you, says I to the footmen, would not be a bastard, if he could, to be made a gentleman of? And, says I, I am sure he is a very fine gentleman, and he hath one of the whitest hands in the world, for to be sure so he hath, and says I, one of the sweetest temperedest, best naturedest men in the world he is, and says I, all the servants and neighbours all round the country loves him. And, to be sure, I could tell your ladyship something, but that I am afraid it would offend you."

"What could you tell me, Honour?" says Sophia.

"Nay, ma'am, to be sure he meant nothing by it, therefore I would not have your ladyship be offended."

"Prithee tell me," says Sophia, "I will know it this instant."

"Why, ma'am," answered Mrs Honour, "he came into the room one day last week when I was at work, and there lay your ladyship's muff on a chair, and to be sure he put his hands into it, that very muff your ladyship gave me but yesterday. 'La!' says I, 'Mr Jones, you will stretch my lady's muff, and spoil it,' but he still kept his hands in it, and then he kissed it — to be sure I hardly ever saw such a kiss in my life as he gave it."

"I suppose he did not know it was mine," replied Sophia, nose in the air, but she blushed at the words. Although, as a well-brought-up young lady, she was supposed to know nothing of cant, she could not help sometimes but hear the rude jokes of people who customarily resided below-stairs. For those pretty curls between her legs were oft referred to in such a manner, and the desire of Tom to kiss her muff could not be denied. Or of Sophia to have him do so, and she was not referring to the muff she used to warm her hands in cold weather.

"Your ladyship shall hear, ma'am. He kissed it again and again, and said it was the prettiest muff in the world. 'La! Sir,' says I, 'you have seen it a hundred times.' 'Yes, Mrs Honour,' cried he, 'but who can see anything beautiful in the presence of your lady but herself?' Nay, that's not all neither, but I hope your ladyship won't be offended, for to be sure he meant nothing.

"One day, as your ladyship was playing on the harpsichord to my master, Mr Jones was sitting in the next room, and methought he looked melancholy. 'La!' says I, 'Mr Jones, what's the matter? A penny for your thoughts,' says I. 'Why, hussy,' says he, starting up from a dream, 'what can I be thinking of, when that angel your mistress is playing?' And then squeezing me by the hand, 'Oh! Mrs Honour, says he, how happy will that man be!' And then he sighed. Upon my troth, his breath is as sweet as a nosegay.

"But to be sure he meant no harm by it. So I hope your ladyship will not mention a word, for he gave me a crown never to mention it, and made me swear upon a book, but I believe, indeed, it was not the Bible."

Till something of a more beautiful red than vermilion be found out, I shall say nothing of Sophia's colour on this occasion. "Honour," says she, "I—if you will not mention this any more to me—nor to anybody else, I will not betray you—I mean, I will not be angry, but I am afraid of your tongue. Why, my girl, will you give it such liberties?"

"Nay, ma'am," answered she, "to be sure, I would sooner cut out my tongue than offend your ladyship. To be sure I shall never mention a word that your ladyship would not have me."

"Why, I would not have you mention this any more," said Sophia, "for it may come to my father's ears, and he would be angry with Mr Jones, though I really believe, as you say, he meant nothing. I should be very angry myself, if I imagined—"

"Nay, ma'am," says Honour, "I protest I believe he meant nothing. I thought he talked as if he was out of his senses, nay, he said he believed he was beside himself when he had spoken the words. 'Ay, sir,' says I, 'I believe so too.' 'Yes,' says he, 'Honour —' But I ask your ladyship's pardon, I could tear my tongue out for offending you."

"Go on," says Sophia, "you may mention anything you have not told me before."

"'Yes, Honour,' says he — this was some time afterwards, when he gave me the crown —'I am neither such a coxcomb, or such a villain, as to think of her in any other delight but as my goddess, as such I will always worship and adore her while I have breath.' This was all, ma'am, I will be sworn, to the best of my remembrance. I was in a passion with him myself, till I found he meant no harm."

"Indeed, Honour," says Sophia, "I believe you have a real affection for me. I was provoked the other day when I gave you warning, but if you have a desire to stay with me, you shall."

"To be sure, ma'am," answered Mrs Honour, "I shall never desire to part with your ladyship. To be sure, I almost cried my eyes out when you gave me warning. It would be very ungrateful in me to desire to leave your ladyship, because as why, I should never get so good a place again. I am sure I would live and die with your ladyship, for, as poor Mr Jones said, happy is the man —"

Here the dinner bell interrupted a conversation which had wrought such an effect on Sophia, that she was, perhaps, more obliged to her bleeding in the morning, than she, at the time, had apprehended she should be. As to the present situation of her mind, I shall adhere to a rule of Horace, by not attempting to describe it, from despair of success. Most of my readers will suggest it easily to themselves, and the few who cannot, would not understand the picture, or at least would deny it to be natural, if ever so well drawn.

I will add, however, that Sophia took some time going downstairs after Mrs Honour left her alone to complete her preparations and she placed her fingers in that other muff, that was perhaps the one Tom was considering when he, as Mrs Honour would have it, was worshipping the other. She felt such pressure there that she knew she would not be comfortable until she had relieved herself of that agitation. So she worked the sweet pearl of flesh that she had discovered and soon brought herself to a conclusion, having imagined all the while Tom's fingers there, and even his mouth, kissing her as he had her outer muff.

BOOK FIVE

Containing a portion of time somewhat longer than half a year.

Chapter One

Of the serious in writing, and for what purpose it is introduced

Peradventure there may be no parts in this prodigious work which will give the reader less pleasure in the perusing, than those which have given the author the greatest pains in composing. Among these probably may be reckoned those initial essays which we have prefixed to the historical matter contained in every book, and which we have determined to be essentially necessary to this kind of writing, of which we have set ourselves at the head.

For this our determination we do not hold ourselves strictly bound to assign any reason, it being abundantly sufficient that we have laid it down as a rule necessary to be observed in all prosai-comi-epic writing. Whoever demanded the reasons of that nice unity of time or place which is now established to be so essential to dramatic poetry? What critic hath been ever asked, why a play may not contain two days as well as one? Or why the audience—provided they travel, like electors, without any expense—may not be wafted fifty miles as well as five? Hath any commentator well accounted for the limitation which an ancient critic hath set to the drama, which he will have contain neither more nor less than five acts? Or hath anyone living attempted to explain what the modern judges of our theatres mean by that word *low*, by which they have happily succeeded in banishing all humour from the stage, and have made the theatre as dull as a drawing-room!

Upon all these occasions the world seems to have embraced a maxim of our law, viz., *cuicunque in arte sua perito credendum est,* for it seems perhaps difficult to conceive that anyone should have had enough of impudence to lay down dogmatical rules in any art or science without the least foundation. In such cases, therefore, we are apt to conclude there are sound and good reasons at the bottom, though we are unfortunately not able to see so far.

Now, in reality, the world have paid too great a compliment to critics, and have imagined them men of much greater profundity than they really are. From this complacence, the critics have been emboldened to assume a dictatorial power, and have so far succeeded, that they are now become the masters, and have the assurance to give laws to those authors from whose predecessors they originally received them.

The critic, rightly considered, is no more than the clerk, whose office it is to transcribe the rules and laws laid down by those great judges whose vast strength of genius hath placed them in the light of legislators, in the several sciences over which they presided. This office was all which the critics of old aspired to, nor did they ever dare to advance a sentence, without supporting it by the authority of the judge from whence it was borrowed.

But in process of time, and in ages of ignorance, the clerk began to invade the power and assume the dignity of his master. The laws of writing were no longer founded on the practice of the author, but on the dictates of the critic. The clerk became the legislator, and those very peremptorily gave laws whose business it was, at first, only to transcribe them.

Hence arose an obvious, and perhaps an unavoidable error, for these critics being men of shallow capacities, very easily mistook mere form for substance. They acted as a judge would, who should adhere to the lifeless letter of law, and reject the spirit. Little circumstances, which were perhaps accidental in a great author, were by these critics considered to constitute his chief merit, and transmitted as essentials to be observed by all his successors. To these encroachments, time and ignorance, the two great supporters of imposture, gave authority, and thus many rules for good writing have been established, which have not the least foundation in truth or nature, and which commonly serve for no other purpose than to curb and restrain genius, in the same manner as it would have restrained the dancing-master, had the many excellent treatises on that art laid it down as an essential rule that every man must dance in chains.

To avoid, therefore, all imputation of laying down a rule for posterity, founded only on the authority of *ipse dixit*—for which, to say the truth, we have not the profoundest veneration—we shall here waive the privilege above contended for, and proceed to lay before the reader the reasons which have induced us to intersperse these several digressive essays in the course of this work.

And here we shall of necessity be led to open a new vein of knowledge, which if it hath been discovered, hath not, to our remembrance, been wrought on by any ancient or modern writer. This vein is no other than that of contrast, which runs through all the works of the creation, and may probably have a large share in constituting in us the idea of all beauty, as well natural as artificial, for what demonstrates the beauty and excellence of anything but its reverse? Thus the beauty of day, and that of summer, is set off by the horrors of night and winter. And, I believe, if it was possible for a man to have seen only the two former, he would have a very imperfect idea of their beauty.

But to avoid too serious an air, can it be doubted, but that the finest woman in the world would lose all benefit of her charms in the eye of a man who had never seen one of another cast? The ladies themselves seem so sensible of this, that they are all industrious to procure foils, nay, they will become foils to themselves, for I have observed — at Bath particularly — that they endeavour to appear as ugly as possible in the morning, in order to set off that beauty which they intend to show you in the evening.

Most artists have this secret in practice, though some, perhaps, have not much studied the theory. The jeweller knows that the finest brilliant requires a foil, and the painter, by the contrast of his figures, often acquires great applause.

A great genius among us will illustrate this matter fully. I cannot, indeed, range him under any general head of common artists, as he hath a title to be placed among those *inventas qui vitam excoluere per artes*, 'who by invented arts have life improved'. I mean here the inventor of that most exquisite entertainment, called the English Pantomime.

This entertainment consisted of two parts, which the inventor distinguished by the names of the serious and the comic. The serious exhibited a certain number of heathen gods and heroes, who were certainly the worst and dullest company into which an audience was ever introduced, and — which was a secret known to few — were actually intended so to be, in order to contrast the comic part of the entertainment, and to display the tricks of harlequin to the better advantage.

This was, perhaps, no very civil use of such personages, but the contrivance was, nevertheless, ingenious enough, and had its effect. And this will now plainly appear, if, instead of serious and comic, we supply the words duller and dullest, for the comic was certainly duller than anything before shown on the stage, and could be set off only by that superlative degree of dullness which composed the serious. So intolerably serious, indeed, were these gods and heroes, that harlequin — though the English gentleman of that name is not at all related to the French family, for he is of a much more serious disposition — was always welcome on the stage, as he relieved the audience from worse company.

Judicious writers have always practised this art of contrast with great success. I have been surprised that Horace should cavil at this art in Homer, but indeed he contradicts himself in the very next line —

Indignor quandoque bonus dormitat Homerus,
Verum opere in longo fas est obrepere somnum.
I grieve if e'er great Homer chance to sleep,
Yet slumbers on long works have right to creep.

For we are not here to understand, as perhaps some have, that an author actually falls asleep while he is writing. It is true, that readers are too apt to be so overtaken, but if the work was as long as any of Oldmixon, the author himself is too well entertained to be subject to the least drowsiness. He is, as Mr Pope observes, 'Sleepless himself to give his readers sleep'.

To say the truth, these soporific parts are so many scenes of serious artfully interwoven, in order to contrast and set off the rest, and this is the true meaning of a late facetious writer, who told the public that whenever he was dull they might be assured there was a design in it.

In this light, then, or rather in this darkness, I would have the reader to consider these initial essays. And after this warning, if he shall be of opinion that he can find enough of serious in other parts of this history, he may pass over these, in which we profess to be laboriously dull, and begin the following books at the second chapter.

Chapter Two

In which Mr Jones receives many friendly visits during his confinement, with some fine touches of the passion of love, scarce visible to the naked eye

Tom Jones had many visitors during his confinement, though some, perhaps, were not very agreeable to him. Mr Allworthy saw him almost every day, but though he pitied Tom's sufferings, and greatly approved the gallant behaviour which had occasioned them, yet he thought this was a favourable opportunity to bring him to a sober sense of his indiscreet conduct, and that wholesome advice for that purpose could never be applied at a more proper season than at the present, when the mind was softened by pain and sickness, and alarmed by danger, and when its attention was unembarrassed with those turbulent passions which engage us in the pursuit of pleasure.

At all seasons, therefore, when the good man was alone with the youth, especially when the latter was totally at ease, he took occasion to remind him of his former miscarriages, but in the mildest and tenderest manner, and only in order to introduce the caution which he prescribed for his future behaviour. On which alone, he assured him, would depend his own felicity, and the kindness which he might yet promise himself to receive at the hands of his father by adoption, unless he should hereafter forfeit his good opinion, for as to what had passed, he said, it should be all forgiven and forgotten. He therefore advised him to make a good use of this accident, that so in the end it might prove a visitation for his own good.

Thwackum was likewise pretty assiduous in his visits, and he too considered a sick-bed to be a convenient scene for lectures. His style, however, was more severe than Mr Allworthy's. He told his pupil, that he ought to look on his broken limb as a judgement from heaven on his sins. That it would become him to be daily on his knees, pouring forth thanksgivings that he had broken his arm only, and not his neck, which latter, he said, was very probably reserved for some future occasion, and that, perhaps, not very remote.

For his part, he said, he had often wondered some judgement had not overtaken him before, but it might be perceived by this, that Divine punishments, though slow, are always sure. Hence likewise he advised him, to foresee, with equal certainty, the greater evils which were yet behind, and which were as sure as this of overtaking him in his state of reprobacy. "These are," said he, "to be averted only by such a thorough and sincere repentance as is not to be expected or hoped for from one so abandoned in his youth, and whose mind, I am afraid, is totally corrupted. It is my duty, however, to exhort you to this repentance, though I too well know all exhortations will be vain and fruitless. But *liberavi animam meam.* I can accuse my own conscience of no neglect, though it is at the same time with the utmost concern I see you travelling on to certain misery in this world, and to as certain damnation in the next."

Square talked in a very different strain. He said, such accidents as a broken bone were below the consideration of a wise man. That it was abundantly sufficient to reconcile the mind to any of these mischances, to reflect that they are liable to befall the wisest of mankind, and are undoubtedly for the good of the whole. He said, it was a mere abuse of words to call those things evils, in which there was no moral unfitness, that pain, which was the worst consequence of such accidents, was the most contemptible thing in the world, with more of the like sentences, extracted out of the second book of Tully's Tusculan questions, and from the great Lord Shaftesbury.

In pronouncing these he was one day so eager, that he unfortunately bit his tongue, and in such a manner, that it not only put an end to his discourse, but created much emotion in him, and caused him to mutter an oath or two, but what was worst of all, this accident gave Thwackum, who was present, and who held all such doctrine to be heathenish and atheistical, an opportunity to clap a judgement on his back. Now this was done with so malicious a sneer, that it totally unhinged—if I may so say—the temper of the philosopher, which the bite of his tongue had somewhat ruffled, and as he was disabled from venting his wrath at his lips, he had possibly found a more violent method of revenging himself, had not the surgeon, who was then luckily in the room, contrary to his own interest, interposed and preserved the peace.

Mr Blifil visited his friend Jones but seldom, and never alone. This worthy young man, however, professed much regard for him, and as great concern at his misfortune, but cautiously avoided any intimacy, lest, as he frequently hinted, it might contaminate the sobriety of his own character, for which purpose he had constantly in his mouth that proverb in which Solomon speaks against evil communication. Not that he was so bitter as Thwackum, for he always expressed some hopes of Tom's reformation, which, he said, the unparalleled goodness shown by his uncle on this occasion, must certainly effect in one not absolutely abandoned, but concluded, "If Mr Jones ever offends hereafter, I shall not be able to say a syllable in his favour."

As to Squire Western, he was seldom out of the sick-room, unless when he was engaged either in the field or over his bottle. Nay, he would sometimes retire hither to take his beer, and it was not without difficulty that he was prevented from forcing Jones to take his beer too, for no quack ever held his nostrum to be a more general panacea than he did this, which, he said, had more virtue in it than was in all the physic in an apothecary's shop. He was, however, by much entreaty, prevailed on to forbear the application of this medicine, but from serenading his patient every hunting morning with the horn under his window, it was impossible to withhold him. Nor did he ever lay aside that "Hallo!" with which he entered into all companies, when he visited Jones, without any regard to the sick person's being at that time either awake or asleep.

This boisterous behaviour, as it meant no harm, so happily it effected none, and was abundantly compensated to Jones, as soon as he was able to sit up, by the company of Sophia, whom the squire then brought to visit him. Nor was it, indeed, long before Jones was able to attend her to the harpsichord, where she would kindly condescend, for hours together, to charm him with the most delicious music, unless when the squire thought proper to interrupt her, by insisting on Old Sir Simon, or some other of his favourite pieces.

Notwithstanding the nicest guard which Sophia endeavoured to set on her behaviour, she could not avoid letting some appearances now and then slip forth, for love may again be likened to a disease in this, that when it is denied a vent in one part, it will certainly break out in another. What her lips, therefore, concealed, her eyes, her blushes, and many little involuntary actions, betrayed.

She even allowed Tom a few maidenly favours, sitting by him and allowing him privileges which by rights would have him paying his respects to her father, but neither of them spoke of this. Instead, a few kisses, and Sophia allowed Tom to remind her of the delights of opening her mouth under his and allowing him to caress her inside, as well as on her cherry-red lips. Sighing, she allowed him to touch her bosom, introducing his good hand to the softness of her breasts, by which he enhanced and deepened the pleasures of their kisses.

One day, when Sophia was playing on the harpsichord, and Jones was attending, the squire came into the room, crying, "There, Tom, I have had a battle for thee below-stairs with thick parson Thwackum. He hath been a-telling Allworthy, before my face, that the broken bone was a judgement upon thee. 'Damn it,' says I, 'how can that be? Did he not come by it in defence of a young woman?' A judgement indeed! Pox, if he never doth anything worse, he will go to heaven sooner than all the parsons in the country. He hath more reason to glory in it than to be ashamed of it." It was fortunate that the squire had not thought to study the people in the room before he began his intemperate diatribe, because Tom was not placed in an entirely decorous position where Sophia was concerned.

The speech gave Tom enough time to remove his hand and to restore Sophia to some semblance of respectability, drawing her kerchief back over her breasts. Such was the squire's passion that he did not remark Tom's close proximity to his daughter. "Indeed, sir," says Jones, "I have no reason for either, but if it preserved Miss Western, I shall always think it the happiest accident of my life."

"And to gu," said the squire, "to zet Allworthy against thee vor it! Damn un, if the parson had unt his petticuoats on, I should have lent un o flick, for I love thee dearly, my boy, and damn me if there is anything in my power which I won't do for thee. Sha't take thy choice of all the horses in my stable tomorrow morning, except only the Chevalier and Miss Slouch."

Jones thanked him, but declined accepting the offer.

"Nay," added the squire, "sha't ha the sorrel mare that Sophy rode. She cost me fifty guineas, and comes six years old this grass."

"If she had cost me a thousand," cries Jones passionately, "I would have given her to the dogs."

"Pooh! Pooh!" answered Western. "What! Because she broke thy arm? Shouldst forget and forgive. I thought hadst been more a man than to bear malice against a dumb creature."

Here Sophia interposed, and put an end to the conversation, by desiring her father's leave to play to him, a request which he never refused.

The countenance of Sophia had undergone more than one change during the foregoing speeches, and probably she imputed the passionate resentment which Jones had expressed against the mare, to a different motive from that from which her father had derived it. Her spirits were at this time in a visible flutter, and she played so intolerably ill, that had not Western soon fallen asleep, he must have remarked it.

Jones, however, who was sufficiently awake, and was not without an ear any more than without eyes, made some observations, which being joined to all which the reader may remember to have passed formerly, gave him pretty strong assurances, when he came to reflect on the whole, that all was not well in the tender bosom of Sophia. An opinion which many young gentlemen will, I doubt not, extremely wonder at his not having been well confirmed in long ago. To confess the truth, he had rather too much diffidence in himself, and was not forward enough in seeing the formal advances of a young lady, a misfortune which can be cured only by that early town education, which is at present so generally in fashion.

While Tom felt exceeding fond towards Sophia, he had two considerations on his mind. First, Molly, penniless and friendless. He had some obligation to her and while the woman, pregnant and alone, needed him he had convinced himself he should be there to stand her friend. Secondly, his future was by no means assured. He would not court Sophia without some confirmation of his prospects, and fully aware of his humble birth, would not presume on the good squire too far. However, he could not deny that his friendship with the lovely Sophia was fast turning into something more.

When these thoughts had fully taken possession of Jones, they occasioned a perturbation in his mind, which, in a constitution less pure and firm than his, might have been, at such a season, attended with very dangerous consequences. He was truly sensible of the great worth of Sophia. He extremely liked her person, no less admired her accomplishments, and tenderly loved her goodness. In reality, as he had never once entertained any thought of possessing her, nor had ever given the least voluntary indulgence to his inclinations after that first occasion, he had a much stronger passion for her than he himself was acquainted with. His heart now brought forth the full secret, at the same time that it assured him the adorable object returned his affection.

However, before he quit the room, Sophia pressed a note into his hand. She had spent some time putting away her music, and he could only conclude that she had contrived to draw one up while her father had been in full flow.

The note contained two words, viz – 'Orchard, midnight'.

How Sophia would contrive to elude her faithful duenna and the maids who lurked in the kitchen day and night Tom did not know, and at the appointed hour entered the orchard with no great expectations of seeing her.

Therefore he was agreeably surprised when a figure, gowned in a white night rail and heavy cloak, accosted him. The orchard faced the day rooms and nobody habited these quarters after dark, preferring the drawing room and dining room at the other side of the house. The trees offered other concealment, so they were safe.

Tom caught her shoulders, and gazed into her eyes. "How did you get here?" quoth he.

"The catch to the window on the breakfast room has lately failed, and my father has yet to have it repaired, although he will have it done tomorrow or the day after," she replied, turning her lovely face up to his. "I wished to see you alone, Tom, and we have precious little opportunity during the day, even though my father likes and trusts you."

"But I cannot," Tom said, groaning his despair. "I can at present offer you nothing for certain, Sophia, although my father has promised much. I must speak to him before I can call you mine. If you should wish it, of course," he added hastily.

"Tom, I would like it above all others!" She looked down, away from him, until he tucked a finger under her chin and urged her to lift her head so he could see her again.

"I cannot imagine not wanting that, Sophia," he said softly, and he kissed her.

She went into his arms as sweetly as a bird nestling against the person it most trusted. She felt soft and sweet and Tom, being an impetuous lad, became totally overwhelmed by her proximity in so few garments. He stroked her breast, and she pushed it into his hand, such a sweet morsel of flesh that he longed to taste it.

He sank to the soft grass under them, inviting her to lie by him. She spread her cloak on the ground, leaving her clad in her thin night rail, and nestled close so he could kiss her again. They shared increasingly passionate embraces, until he had undone the ribbon at the top of her night rail and inserted his hand into the resultant opening so he could stroke and caress her bare breast.

Sweetly, he kissed her, careful not to alarm her by too much passion, but she seemed intent on discovering more, her curiosity overcoming the natural modesty maidens are customarily subject to.

Her eagerness to touch him convinced Tom that she was ready to exchange more intimate caresses. Accordingly, he aided her to sit, and drew off her night rail, laughing softly when she wished to perform the same office to him, so they were soon naked, his coat bundled up to form a pillow, her cloak below them and his stockings, breeches, shirt and drawers laid aside together with both their pairs of shoes.

Sky formed their blanket on this temperate night. After all, if they were discovered, they might be compelled into the condition both of them wished for, viz, marriage. For they could no longer hide their passion from each other.

"I want no-one but you," he murmured, kissing first one nipple, then the other. She sighed in happiness, and stroked his strong shoulders, then as much of his back as she could reach.

Sophia watched her Tom as he gave her all the pleasure he knew without breaching that part of her that they would both wait to experience together. When his mouth fastened on that part she had lately discovered, she covered her mouth with her hand, realising why a woman might need a man to perform this office for her. It felt so much better, she thought, than doing the thing herself, good though that felt. This experience surpassed the other, and as Tom kissed her most intimate parts, she let him take her to paradise.

She cried out into her palm and then he returned to her, sharing her taste with her when he kissed her. Sophia lapped eagerly at his mouth, wanting to experience what he did, and then to give him the same as he had granted her. So she rolled over him as he lay on his back and dared to explore his body, strong, young and exciting. His skin was firm and she could feel the muscles gained from healthy country living as she kissed down his body, preparing for a closer encounter with the principal difference between the sexes.

Tom touched her hair, which had somehow come loose from its night-time braids and now flowed around her. He wound locks of the mass around his fingers, and held on while she kissed and caressed the proof of his manhood, now hard and leaking for her.

He tasted of salt and a touch of sweetness, like some exotic spice she had yet to discover. When she sucked, he moaned her name and liking the sound, she continued, daring to touch the heavy balls that customarily swung under his manhood. He moaned a little louder, then hushed as if remembering they might be overheard.

Sophia wanted to bring him all the pleasure he had lately given her, so she continued her ministrations, and licked him to gather his taste before she sucked again.

Tom, while not completely inexperienced, could not resist the lure of the lady he was swiftly coming to imagine as his for long, and sooner than he thought he started shooting ribbons of his tribute down the throat of his temptress.

They lay there, panting, for a full five minutes before she moved and returned to him. Swiftly, they helped each other dress, for they dared not tarry much longer, for who knew when Mrs Honour would take it into her head to check on her precious charge? Standing, once again fully clothed, Tom took both her hands in his. He wished to devote himself to her alone, but he could not, for he had already pledged himself to Molly, in an intimate moment when she had, as always, overcome him with passion. He was helpless in Molly's expert hands, but in innocent Sophia, he had found a desire for constancy and protection he had not experienced before.

"You must go in, sweet Sophia, for it cannot be safe for much longer."

After ensuring she was safely within the house, Tom took his leave, his mind still in turmoil, for when he was with Molly, he wished for her above all women, but Sophia affected him in the same way, and Tom, while lusty, did not have the experience or the knowledge to know one woman's intent from another.

Chapter Three

Which all who have no heart will think to contain much ado about nothing

The reader will perhaps imagine the sensations which now arose in Jones to have been so sweet and delicious, that they would rather tend to produce a cheerful serenity in the mind, than any of those dangerous effects which we have mentioned. In fact, sensations of this kind, however delicious, are, at their first recognition, of a very tumultuous nature, and have very little of the opiate in them. They were, moreover, in the present case, embittered with certain circumstances, which being mixed with sweeter ingredients, tended altogether to compose a draught that might be termed bitter-sweet, than which, as nothing can be more disagreeable to the palate, so nothing, in the metaphorical sense, can be so injurious to the mind.

For first, though he had sufficient foundation to flatter himself in what he had observed in Sophia, he was not yet free from doubt of misconstruing compassion, or at best, esteem, into a warmer regard. He was far from a sanguine assurance that Sophia had any such affection towards him, as might promise his inclinations that harvest, which, if they were encouraged and nursed, they would finally grow up to require. Besides, if he could hope to find no bar to his happiness from the daughter, he thought himself certain of meeting an effectual bar in the father, who, though he was a country squire in his diversions, was perfectly a man of the world in whatever regarded his fortune, had the most violent affection for his only daughter, and had often signified, in his cups, the pleasure he proposed in seeing her married to one of the richest men in the county.

Jones was not so vain and senseless a coxcomb as to expect, from any regard which Western had professed for him, that he would ever be induced to lay aside these views of advancing his daughter. He well knew that fortune is generally the principal, if not the sole, consideration, which operates on the best of parents in these matters, for friendship makes us warmly espouse the interest of others, but it is very cold to the gratification of their passions. Indeed, to feel the happiness which may result from this, it is necessary we should possess the passion ourselves.

As he had therefore no hopes of obtaining her father's consent, so he thought to endeavour to succeed without it, and by such means to frustrate the great point of Mr Western's life, was to make a very ill use of his hospitality, and a very ungrateful return to the many little favours received — however roughly — at his hands. If he saw such a consequence with horror and disdain, how much more was he shocked with what regarded Mr Allworthy, to whom, as he had more than filial obligations, so had he for him more than filial piety! He knew the nature of that good man to be so averse to any baseness or treachery, that the least attempt of such a kind would make the sight of the guilty person for ever odious to his eyes, and his name a detestable sound in his ears. The appearance of such insurmountable difficulties was sufficient to have inspired him with despair, however ardent his wishes had been, but even these were controlled by compassion for another woman.

The idea of lovely Molly now intruded itself before him. He had sworn eternal constancy in her arms, and she had as often vowed never to out-live his deserting her. He now saw her in all the most shocking postures of death—nay, he considered all the miseries of prostitution to which she would be liable, and of which he would be doubly the occasion, first by seducing, and then by deserting her. For he well knew the hatred which all her neighbours, and even her own sisters, bore her, and how ready they would all be to tear her to pieces.

Indeed, he had exposed her to more envy than shame, or rather to the latter by means of the former, for many women abused her for being a whore, while they envied her her lover, and her finery, and would have been themselves glad to have purchased these at the same rate. The ruin, therefore, of the poor girl must, he foresaw, unavoidably attend his deserting her, and this thought stung him to the soul. Poverty and distress seemed to him to give none a right of aggravating those misfortunes. The meanness of her condition did not represent her misery as of little consequence in his eyes, nor did it appear to justify, or even to palliate, his guilt, in bringing that misery upon her. But why do I mention justification? His own heart would not suffer him to destroy a human creature who, he thought, loved him, and had to that love sacrificed her innocence. His own good heart pleaded her cause, not as a cold venal advocate, but as one interested in the event, and which must itself deeply share in all the agonies its owner brought on another.

When this powerful advocate had sufficiently raised the pity of Jones, by painting poor Molly in all the circumstances of wretchedness, it artfully called in the assistance of another passion, and represented the girl in all the amiable colours of youth, health, and beauty, as one greatly the object of desire, and much more so, at least to a good mind, from being, at the same time, the object of compassion.

Amidst these thoughts, poor Jones passed a long sleepless night, and in the morning the result of the whole was to abide by Molly, and to think no more of Sophia.

In this virtuous resolution he continued all the next day till the evening, cherishing the idea of Molly, and driving Sophia from his thoughts, but in the fatal evening, a very trifling accident set all his passions again on float, and worked so total a change in his mind, that we think it decent to communicate it in a fresh chapter.

Chapter Four

A little chapter, in which is contained a little incident

Among other visitants, who paid their compliments to the young gentleman in his confinement, Mrs Honour was one. The reader, perhaps, when he reflects on some expressions which have formerly dropped from her, may conceive that she herself had a very particular affection for Mr Jones, but, in reality, it was no such thing. Tom was a handsome young fellow, and for that species of men Mrs Honour had some regard, but this was perfectly indiscriminate, for having being crossed in the love which she bore a certain nobleman's footman, who had basely deserted her after a promise of marriage, she had so securely kept together the broken remains of her heart, that no man had ever since been able to possess himself of any single fragment. She viewed all handsome men with that equal regard and benevolence which a sober and virtuous mind bears to all the good. She might indeed be called a lover of men, as Socrates was a lover of mankind, preferring one to another for corporeal, as he for mental qualifications, but never carrying this preference so far as to cause any perturbation in the philosophical serenity of her temper.

The day after Mr Jones had that conflict with himself which we have seen in the preceding chapter, Mrs Honour came into his room, and finding him alone, began in the following manner. "La, sir, where do you think I have been? I warrants you, you would not guess in fifty years, but if you did guess, to be sure I must not tell you neither."

"Nay, if it be something which you must not tell me," said Jones, "I shall have the curiosity to enquire, and I know you will not be so barbarous to refuse me."

"I don't know," cries she, "why I should refuse you neither, for that matter, for to be sure you won't mention it any more. And for that matter, if you knew where I have been, unless you knew what I have been about, it would not signify much. Nay, I don't see why it should be kept a secret for my part, for to be sure she is the best lady in the world."

Upon this, Jones began to beg earnestly to be let into this secret, and faithfully promised not to divulge it.

She then proceeded thus. "Why, you must know, sir, my young lady sent me to enquire after Molly Seagrim, and to see whether the wench wanted anything. To be sure, I did not care to go, methinks, but servants must do what they are ordered. How could you undervalue yourself so, Mr Jones? So my lady bid me go and carry her some linen, and other things. She is too good. If such forward sluts were sent to Bridewell, it would be better for them. I told my lady, says I, madam, your la'ship is encouraging idleness."

"And was my Sophia so good?" says Jones.

"My Sophia! I assure you, marry come up," answered Honour. "And yet if you knew all—indeed, if I was as Mr Jones, I should look a little higher than such trumpery as Molly Seagrim."

"What do you mean by these words," replied Jones, "if I knew all?"

"I mean what I mean," says Honour. "Don't you remember putting your hands in my lady's muff once? I vow I could almost find in my heart to tell, if I was certain my lady would never come to the hearing on't."

Jones then made several solemn protestations, understanding that Honour might have seen more than she should, servants considering it a natural part of their income to press vails on their betters if they see or hear more than their friends might consider proper.

And Honour proceeded. "Then to be sure, my lady gave me that muff, and afterwards, upon hearing what you had done—"

"Then you told her what I had done?" interrupted Jones.

"If I did, sir," answered she, "you need not be angry with me. Many's the man would have given his head to have had my lady told, if they had known—for, to be sure, the biggest lord in the land might be proud—but, I protest, I have a great mind not to tell you."

Jones fell to entreaties, and soon prevailed on her to go on thus. "You must know then, sir, that my lady had given this muff to me, but about a day or two after I had told her the story, she quarrels with her new muff, and to be sure it is the prettiest that ever was seen. 'Honour,' says she, 'this is an odious muff, it is too big for me, I can't wear it, till I can get another, you must let me have my old one again, and you may have this in the room on't' — for she's a good lady, and scorns to give a thing and take a thing, I promise you that. So to be sure I fetched it her back again, and I believe, she hath worn it upon her arm almost ever since, and I warrants hath given it many a kiss when nobody hath seen her."

Here the conversation was interrupted by Mr Western himself, who came to summon Jones to the harpsichord, whither the poor young fellow went all pale and trembling. This Western observed, but, on seeing Mrs Honour, imputed it to a wrong cause, and having given Jones a hearty curse between jest and earnest, he bid him beat abroad, and not poach up the game in his warren.

Sophia looked this evening with more than usual beauty, and we may believe it was no small addition to her charms, in the eye of Mr Jones, that she now happened to have on her right arm this very muff.

She was playing one of her father's favourite tunes, and he was leaning on her chair, when the muff fell over her fingers, and put her out. This so disconcerted the squire, that he snatched the muff from her, and with a hearty curse threw it into the fire. Sophia instantly started up, and with the utmost eagerness recovered it from the flames.

Though this incident will probably appear of little consequence to many of our readers, yet, trifling as it was, it had so violent an effect on poor Jones, that we thought it our duty to relate it. In reality, there are many little circumstances too often omitted by injudicious historians, from which events of the utmost importance arise. The world may indeed be considered as a vast machine, in which the great wheels are originally set in motion by those which are very minute, and almost imperceptible to any but the strongest eyes.

Thus, not all the charms of the incomparable Sophia, not all the dazzling brightness, and languishing softness of her eyes, the harmony of her voice, and of her person, not all her wit, good-humour, greatness of mind, or sweetness of disposition, had been able so absolutely to conquer and enslave the heart of poor Jones, as this little incident of the muff. Thus the poet sweetly sings of Troy —

Captique dolis lachrymisque coacti
Quos neque Tydides, nec Larissaeus Achilles,
Non anni domuere decem, non mille Carinae.
What Diomede or Thetis' greater son,
A thousand ships, nor ten years' siege had done
False tears and fawning words the city won.

The citadel of Jones was now taken by surprise. All those considerations of honour and prudence which our hero had lately with so much military wisdom placed as guards over the avenues of his heart, ran away from their posts, and the god of love marched in, in triumph.

Chapter Five

A very long chapter, containing a very great incident

But though this victorious deity easily expelled his avowed enemies from the heart of Jones, he found it more difficult to supplant the garrison which he himself had placed there. To lay aside all allegory, the concern for what must become of poor Molly greatly disturbed and perplexed the mind of the worthy youth. The superior merit of Sophia totally eclipsed, or rather extinguished, all the beauties of the poor girl, but compassion instead of contempt succeeded to love.

He was convinced the girl had placed all her affections, and all her prospect of future happiness, in him only. For this he had, he knew, given sufficient occasion, by the utmost profusion of tenderness towards her, a tenderness which he had taken every means to persuade her he would always maintain.

She, on her side, had assured him of her firm belief in his promise, and had with the most solemn vows declared, that on his fulfilling or breaking these promises, it depended, whether she should be the happiest or most miserable of womankind. And to be the author of this highest degree of misery to a human being, was a thought on which he could not bear to ruminate a single moment.

He considered this poor girl as having sacrificed to him everything in her little power, as having been at her own expense the object of his pleasure, as sighing and languishing for him even at that very instant. 'Shall then,' says he, 'my recovery, for which she hath so ardently wished, shall my presence, which she hath so eagerly expected, instead of giving her that joy with which she hath flattered herself, cast her at once down into misery and despair? Can I be such a villain?' Here, when the genius of poor Molly seemed triumphant, the love of Sophia towards him, which now appeared no longer dubious, rushed upon his mind, and bore away every obstacle before it.

At length it occurred to him, that he might possibly be able to make Molly amends another way, namely, by giving her a sum of money. This, nevertheless, he almost despaired of her accepting, when he recollected the frequent and vehement assurances he had received from her, that the world put in balance with him would make her no amends for his loss. However, her extreme poverty, and chiefly her egregious vanity—somewhat of which hath been already hinted to the reader—gave him some little hope, that, notwithstanding all her avowed tenderness, she might in time be brought to content herself with a fortune superior to her expectation, and which might indulge her vanity, by setting her above all her equals. He resolved therefore to take the first opportunity of making a proposal of this kind.

One day, accordingly, when his arm was so well recovered that he could walk easily with it slung in a sash, he stole forth, at a season when the squire was engaged in his field exercises, and visited his fair one. Her mother and sisters, whom he found taking their tea, informed him first that Molly was not at home, but afterwards the eldest sister acquainted him, with a malicious smile, that she was above stairs a-bed. Tom had no objection to this situation of his mistress, and immediately ascended the ladder which led towards her bed-chamber, but when he came to the top, he, to his great surprise, found the door fast, nor could he for some time obtain any answer from within, for Molly, as she herself afterwards informed him, was fast asleep.

The extremes of grief and joy have been remarked to produce very similar effects, and when either of these rushes on us by surprise, it is apt to create such a total perturbation and confusion, that we are often thereby deprived of the use of all our faculties. It cannot therefore be wondered at, that the unexpected sight of Mr Jones should so strongly operate on the mind of Molly, and should overwhelm her with such confusion, that for some minutes she was unable to express the great raptures, with which the reader will suppose she was affected on this occasion. As for Jones, he was so entirely possessed, and as it were enchanted, by the presence of his beloved object, that he for a while forgot Sophia, and consequently the principal purpose of his visit.

"Molly, I have an important matter to discuss with you," said he, before spying his erstwhile lover, one breast peeking artfully over the low neckline of her shift, and her hair down around her shoulders.

His mind was so overcome to find his inamorata in such delightful undress, that he completed what her surprise had begun, and soon separated Molly from the greater part of her clothing, and somehow, in the turmoil of mind to which he found himself, his clothing disappeared too, along with his modesty.

He fell on her with all the finesse of a ravaging pirate, sucking at the twin peaks of her bosom one after the other, so hardening them, while lifting them with his hands, noting how plumply delicious they had become in the time since her condition altered.

The milky skin she carefully hid from the sun, Molly disdained to hide from Tom, for what was done could not be undone, and she did not wish to turn him away before hearing what he wished to tell her. Transported by delight, she spread her white thighs when he demanded it of her, and aided him to push his weapon home, sheathing it in the snuggest of protectors. As if undecided, and preparing itself for further action, Tom drove home again and again, moaning the while, since he had not had occasion to perform this mode of exercise for some time, except for gentle dalliance with the lovely Sophia, a name that would mean little to him had Molly repeated it now, something she was extremely careful not to test.

However, she joined him on his journey of pleasure with alacrity, and her first transports quenched by a peak of exquisite ecstasy, willingly aided Tom to his own pinnacle, by which he drowned her in the essence which he'd been storing up for just such an occasion.

Paradise obtained, Tom lay by her side and recalled who he was and what had brought him here. He dressed quickly, afraid he would be tempted to repeat the action had he remained buff naked.

The reason for his visit, however, soon recurred to his memory, and after the first transports of their meeting were over, he found means by degrees to introduce a discourse on the fatal consequences which must attend their amour, if Mr Allworthy, who had strictly forbidden him ever seeing her more, should discover that he still carried on this commerce. Such a discovery, which his enemies gave him reason to think would be unavoidable, must, he said, end in his ruin, and consequently in hers.

Since therefore their hard fates had determined that they must separate, he advised her to bear it with resolution, and swore he would never omit any opportunity, through the course of his life, of showing her the sincerity of his affection, by providing for her in a manner beyond her utmost expectation, or even beyond her wishes, if ever that should be in his power — concluding at last, that she might soon find some man who would marry her, and who would make her much happier than she could be by leading a disreputable life with him.

Molly remained a few moments in silence, and then bursting into a flood of tears, she began to upbraid him in the following words. "And this is your love for me, to forsake me in this manner, now you have ruined me! How often, when I have told you that all men are false and perjury alike, and grow tired of us as soon as ever they have had their wicked wills of us, how often have you sworn you would never forsake me! And can you be such a perjury man after all? What signifies all the riches in the world to me without you, now you have gained my heart, so you have — you have — ? Why do you mention another man to me? I can never love any other man as long as I live. All other men are nothing to me. If the greatest squire in all the country would come a-suiting to me tomorrow, I would not give my company to him. No, I shall always hate and despise the whole sex for your sake."

She was proceeding thus, when an accident put a stop to her tongue, before it had run out half its career. The room, or rather garret, in which Molly lay, being up one pair of stairs, that is to say, at the top of the house, was of a sloping figure, resembling the great Delta of the Greeks. The English reader may perhaps form a better idea of it, by being told that it was impossible to stand upright anywhere but in the middle. Now, as this room wanted the conveniency of a closet, Molly had, to supply that defect, nailed up an old rug against the rafters of the house, which enclosed a little hole where her best apparel, such as the remains of that sacque which we have formerly mentioned, some caps, and other things with which she had lately provided herself, were hung up and secured from the dust.

This enclosed place exactly fronted the foot of the bed, to which, indeed, the rug hung so near, that it served in a manner to supply the want of curtains. Now, whether Molly, in the agonies of her rage, pushed this rug with her feet, or Jones might touch it, or whether the pin or nail gave way of its own accord, I am not certain, but as Molly pronounced those last words, which are recorded above, the wicked rug got loose from its fastening, and discovered everything hid behind it, where among other female utensils appeared — with shame I write it, and with sorrow will it be read — the philosopher Square, in a posture, for the place would not near admit his standing upright, as ridiculous as can possibly be conceived.

The posture, indeed, in which he stood, was not greatly unlike that of a soldier who is tied neck and heels, or rather resembling the attitude in which we often see fellows in the public streets of London, who are not suffering but deserving punishment by so standing. He had a nightcap belonging to Molly on his head, and his two large eyes, the moment the rug fell, stared directly at Jones, so that when the idea of philosophy was added to the figure now discovered, it would have been very difficult for any spectator to have refrained from immoderate laughter.

I question not but the surprise of the reader will be here equal to that of Jones, as the suspicions which must arise from the appearance of this wise and grave man in such a place, may seem so inconsistent with that character which he hath, doubtless, maintained hitherto, in the opinion of everyone.

But to confess the truth, this inconsistency is rather imaginary than real. Philosophers are composed of flesh and blood as well as other human creatures, and however sublimated and refined the theory of these may be, a little practical frailty is as incident to them as to other mortals. It is, indeed, in theory only, and not in practice, as we have before hinted, that consists the difference, for though such great beings think much better and more wisely, they always act exactly like other men. They know very well how to subdue all appetites and passions, and to despise both pain and pleasure, and this knowledge affords much delightful contemplation, and is easily acquired, but the practice would be vexatious and troublesome, and therefore, the same wisdom which teaches them to know this, teaches them to avoid carrying it into execution.

Mr Square happened to be at church on that Sunday, when, as the reader may be pleased to remember, the appearance of Molly in her sacque had caused all that disturbance. Here he first observed her, and was so pleased with her beauty, that he prevailed with the young gentlemen to change their intended ride that evening, that he might pass by the habitation of Molly, and by that means might obtain a second chance of seeing her. This reason, however, as he did not at that time mention to any, so neither did we think proper to communicate it then to the reader.

Among other particulars which constituted the unfitness of things in Mr Square's opinion, danger and difficulty were two. The difficulty therefore which he apprehended there might be in corrupting this young wench, and the danger which would accrue to his character on the discovery, were such strong dissuasives, that it is probable he at first intended to have contented himself with the pleasing ideas which the sight of beauty furnishes us with. These the gravest men, after a full meal of serious meditation, often allow themselves by way of dessert, for which purpose, certain books and pictures find their way into the most private recesses of their study, and a certain liquorish part of natural philosophy is often the principal subject of their conversation.

But when the philosopher heard, a day or two afterwards, that the fortress of virtue had already been subdued, he began to give a larger scope to his desires. His appetite was not of that squeamish kind which cannot feed on a dainty because another hath tasted it. In short, he liked the girl the better for the want of that chastity, which, if she had possessed it, must have been a bar to his pleasures. He pursued and obtained her.

The reader will be mistaken, if he thinks Molly gave Square the preference to her younger lover. On the contrary, had she been confined to the choice of one only, Tom Jones would undoubtedly have been, of the two, the victorious person. Nor was it solely the consideration that two are better than one—though this had its proper weight—to which Mr Square owed his success. The absence of Jones during his confinement was an unlucky circumstance, and in that interval some well-chosen presents from the philosopher so softened and unguarded the girl's heart, that a favourable opportunity became irresistible, and Square triumphed over the poor remains of virtue which subsisted in the bosom of Molly.

It was now about a fortnight since this conquest, when Jones paid the above-mentioned visit to his mistress, at a time when she and Square were in bed together. This was the true reason why the mother denied her as we have seen, for as the old woman shared in the profits arising from the iniquity of her daughter, she encouraged and protected her in it to the utmost of her power. But such was the envy and hatred which the elder sister bore towards Molly, that, notwithstanding she had some part of the booty, she would willingly have parted with this to ruin her sister and spoil her trade. Hence she had acquainted Jones with her being above-stairs in bed, in hopes that he might have caught her in Square's arms. This, however, Molly found means to prevent, as the door was fastened, which gave her an opportunity of conveying her lover behind that rug or blanket where he now was unhappily discovered.

Square no sooner made his appearance than Molly flung herself back in her bed, cried out she was undone, and abandoned herself to despair. This poor girl, who was yet but a novice in her business, had not arrived to that perfection of assurance which helps off a town lady in any extremity, and either prompts her with an excuse, or else inspires her to brazen out the matter with her husband, who, from love of quiet, or out of fear of his reputation — and sometimes, perhaps, from fear of the gallant, who, like Mr Constant in the play, wears a sword — is glad to shut his eyes, and content to put his horns in his pocket. Molly, on the contrary, was silenced by this evidence, and very fairly gave up a cause which she had hitherto maintained with so many tears, and with such solemn and vehement protestations of the purest love and constancy.

As to the gentleman behind the arras, he was not in much less consternation. He stood for a while motionless, and seemed equally at a loss what to say, or whither to direct his eyes. Jones, though perhaps the most astonished of the three, first found his tongue, and being immediately recovered from those uneasy sensations which Molly by her upbraidings had occasioned, he burst into a loud laughter, and then saluting Mr Square, advanced to take him by the hand, and to relieve him from his place of confinement.

Square being now arrived in the middle of the room, in which part only he could stand upright, looked at Jones with a very grave countenance, and said to him, "Well, sir, I see you enjoy this mighty discovery, and I dare swear, take great delight in the thoughts of exposing me, but if you will consider the matter fairly, you will find you are yourself only to blame. I am not guilty of corrupting innocence. I have done nothing for which that part of the world which judges of matters by the rule of right, will condemn me. Fitness is governed by the nature of things, and not by customs, forms, or municipal laws. Nothing is indeed unfit which is not unnatural."

"Well reasoned, old boy," answered Jones, "but why dost thou think that I should desire to expose thee? I promise thee, I was never better pleased with thee in my life, and unless thou hast a mind to discover it thyself, this affair may remain a profound secret for me."

"Nay, Mr Jones," replied Square, "I would not be thought to undervalue reputation. Good fame is a species of the Kalon, and it is by no means fitting to neglect it. Besides, to murder one's own reputation is a kind of suicide, a detestable and odious vice. If you think proper, therefore, to conceal any infirmity of mine—for such I may have, since no man is perfectly perfect—I promise you I will not betray myself. Things may be fitting to be done, which are not fitting to be boasted of, for by the perverse judgement of the world, that often becomes the subject of censure, which is, in truth, not only innocent but laudable."

"Right!" cries Jones. "What can be more innocent than the indulgence of a natural appetite? Or what more laudable than the propagation of our species?"

"To be serious with you," answered Square, "I profess they always appeared so to me."

"And yet," said Jones, "you was of a different opinion when my affair with this girl was first discovered."

"Why, I must confess," says Square, "as the matter was misrepresented to me, by that parson Thwackum, I might condemn the corruption of innocence, it was that, sir, it was that—and that—for you must know, Mr Jones, in the consideration of fitness, very minute circumstances, sir, very minute circumstances cause great alteration."

"Well," cries Jones, "be that as it will, it shall be your own fault, as I have promised you, if you ever hear any more of this adventure. Behave kindly to the girl, and I will never open my lips concerning the matter to anyone. And, Molly, do you be faithful to your friend, and I will not only forgive your infidelity to me, but will do you all the service I can." So saying, he took a hasty leave, and slipping down the ladder, retired with much expedition, relieved to have escaped from the affair with the tatters of his honour clasped around him.

Square was rejoiced to find this adventure was likely to have no worse conclusion, and as for Molly, being recovered from her confusion, she began at first to upbraid Square with having been the occasion of her loss of Jones, but that gentleman soon found the means of mitigating her anger, partly by caresses, and partly by a small nostrum from his purse, of wonderful and approved efficacy in purging off the ill humours of the mind, and in restoring it to a good temper.

Square, being of robust constitution and an equally robust mind, recollected that he had Molly to himself now, and he should make the most of it, since the enemy had retreated, leaving him in possession of the field. Feeling the vanquishing warrior, new vigour filled his body with strength he thought he'd exerted earlier in the evening, and he pushed Molly down to her pallet, and fell over her in an excess of energy.

Although Molly pushed at Square, the better to breathe, she did not dislodge him completely, for she felt she needed some consolation after her recent fright, so she invited him to set to.

Besides, it would provide further proof of his complicity in her condition. That had not escaped the calculating Molly's notice. The consolation Square could bring her might ameliorate the distress of losing her most promising prospect.

She then poured forth a vast profusion of tenderness towards her new lover, turned all she had said to Jones, and Jones himself, into ridicule, and vowed, though he once had the possession of her person, that none but Square had ever been master of her heart.

Believing her assurances, Square set to, and opening her legs roughly with one hand, inserted his cock into the depths of her cunt, plunging in deeply in one motion, and grunting his approval of her state of readiness.

Although he had not the eagerness of youth or the consideration that Tom had brought to her bed, Molly thought he would do well enough. Square plunged and puffed above her, as she caressed him and told him that he was the best lover she'd ever known, that Jones was nothing compared to a mature, strong, masterful man, and soon she brought him to the state where he was sweating and pushing. Although Square did not bring Molly to her culmination, she had not expected it and was well enough content with his attentions, particularly as later that night she made him repeat the exercise, although he protested he'd rather sleep, and this time he managed to please her better.

Chapter Six

By comparing which with the former, the reader may possibly correct some abuse which he hath formerly been guilty of in the application of the word love

The infidelity of Molly, which Jones had now discovered, would perhaps have vindicated a much greater degree of resentment than he expressed on the occasion, and if he had abandoned her directly from that moment, very few, I believe, would have blamed him.

Certain, however, it is, that he saw her in the light of compassion, and though his love to her was not of that kind which could give him any great uneasiness at her inconstancy, yet was he not a little shocked on reflecting that he had himself originally corrupted her innocence, for to this corruption he imputed all the vice into which she appeared now so likely to plunge herself.

This consideration gave him no little uneasiness, till Betty, the elder sister, was so kind, some time afterwards, entirely to cure him by a hint, that one Will Barnes, and not himself, had been the first seducer of Molly, and that the little child, which he had hitherto so certainly concluded to be his own, might very probably have an equal title, at least, to claim Barnes for its father.

Jones eagerly pursued this scent when he had first received it, and in a very short time was sufficiently assured that the girl had told him truth, not only by the confession of the fellow, but at last by that of Molly herself.

This Will Barnes was a country gallant, and had acquired as many trophies of this kind as any ensign or attorney's clerk in the kingdom. He had, indeed, reduced several women to a state of utter profligacy, had broken the hearts of some, and had the honour of occasioning the violent death of one poor girl, who had either drowned herself, or, what was rather more probable, had been drowned by him.

Among other of his conquests, this fellow had triumphed over the heart of Betty Seagrim. He had made love to her long before Molly was grown to be a fit object of that pastime, but had afterwards deserted her, and applied to her sister, with whom he had almost immediate success. Now Will had, in reality, the sole possession of Molly's affection, while Jones and Square were almost equally sacrifices to her interest and to her pride.

Hence had grown that implacable hatred which we have before seen raging in the mind of Betty, though we did not think it necessary to assign this cause sooner, as envy itself alone was adequate to all the effects we have mentioned.

Jones was become perfectly easy by possession of this secret with regard to Molly, but as to Sophia, he was far from being in a state of tranquillity, nay, indeed, he was under the most violent perturbation. His heart was now, if I may use the metaphor, entirely evacuated, and Sophia took absolute possession of it. He loved her with an unbounded passion, and plainly saw the tender sentiments she had for him, yet could not this assurance lessen his despair of obtaining the consent of her father, nor the horrors which attended his pursuit of her by any base or treacherous method.

The injury which he must thus do to Mr Western, and the concern which would accrue to Mr Allworthy, were circumstances that tormented him all day, and haunted him on his pillow at night. His life was a constant struggle between honour and inclination, which alternately triumphed over each other in his mind. He often resolved, in the absence of Sophia, to leave her father's house, and to see her no more, and as often, in her presence, forgot all those resolutions, and determined to pursue her at the hazard of his life, and at the forfeiture of what was much dearer to him.

This conflict began soon to produce very strong and visible effects, for he lost all his usual sprightliness and gaiety of temper, and became not only melancholy when alone, but dejected and absent in company. Nay, if ever he put on a forced mirth, to comply with Mr Western's humour, the constraint appeared so plain, that he seemed to have been giving the strongest evidence of what he endeavoured to conceal by such ostentation.

It may, perhaps, be a question, whether the art which he used to conceal his passion, or the means which honest nature employed to reveal it, betrayed him most. For while art made him more than ever reserved to Sophia, and forbade him to address any of his discourse to her, nay, to avoid meeting her eyes, with the utmost caution, nature was no less busy in counterplotting him. Hence, at the approach of the young lady, he grew pale, and if this was sudden, started. If his eyes accidentally met hers, the blood rushed into his cheeks, and his countenance became all over scarlet. If common civility ever obliged him to speak to her, as to drink her health at table, his tongue was sure to falter. If he touched her, his hand, nay his whole frame, trembled. And if any discourse tended, however remotely, to raise the idea of love, an involuntary sigh seldom failed to steal from his bosom. Most of which accidents nature was wonderfully industrious to throw daily in his way.

All these symptoms escaped the notice of the squire, but not so of Sophia. She soon perceived these agitations of mind in Jones, and was at no loss to discover the cause, for indeed she recognised it in her own breast. And this recognition is, I suppose, that sympathy which hath been so often noted in lovers, and which will sufficiently account for her being so much quicker-sighted than her father.

But, to say the truth, there is a more simple and plain method of accounting for that prodigious superiority of penetration which we must observe in some men over the rest of the human species, and one which will serve not only in the case of lovers, but of all others. From whence is it that the knave is generally so quick-sighted to those symptoms and operations of knavery, which often dupe an honest man of a much better understanding? There surely is no general sympathy among knaves, nor have they, like freemasons, any common sign of communication. In reality, it is only because they have the same thing in their heads, and their thoughts are turned the same way. Thus, that Sophia saw, and that Western did not see, the plain symptoms of love in Jones can be no wonder, when we consider that the idea of love never entered into the head of the father, whereas the daughter, at present, thought of nothing else.

When Sophia was well satisfied of the violent passion which tormented poor Jones, and no less certain that she herself was its object, she had not the least difficulty in discovering the true cause of his present behaviour. This highly endeared him to her, and raised in her mind two of the best affections which any lover can wish to raise in a mistress — these were, esteem and pity — for sure the most outrageously rigid among her sex will excuse her pitying a man whom she saw miserable on her own account, nor can they blame her for esteeming one who visibly, from the most honourable motives, endeavoured to smother a flame in his own bosom, which, like the famous Spartan theft, was preying upon and consuming his very vitals.

Thus his backwardness, his shunning her, his coldness, and his silence, were the forwardest, the most diligent, the warmest, and most eloquent advocates, and wrought so violently on her sensible and tender heart, that she soon felt for him all those gentle sensations which are consistent with a virtuous and elevated female mind. In short, all which esteem, gratitude, and pity, can inspire in such towards an agreeable man — indeed, all which the nicest delicacy can allow. In a word, she was in love with him to distraction.

One day this young couple accidentally met in the garden, at the end of the two walks which were both bounded by that canal in which Jones had formerly risked drowning to retrieve the little bird that Sophia had there lost.

This place had been of late much frequented by Sophia. Here she used to ruminate, with a mixture of pain and pleasure, on an incident which, however trifling in itself, had possibly sown the first seeds of that affection which was now arrived to such maturity in her heart.

Here then this young couple met. They were almost close together before either of them knew anything of the other's approach. A bystander would have discovered sufficient marks of confusion in the countenance of each, but they felt too much themselves to make any observation.

As soon as Jones had a little recovered his first surprise, he accosted the young lady with some of the ordinary forms of salutation, which she in the same manner returned, and their conversation began, as usual, on the delicious beauty of the morning. Hence they passed to the beauty of the place, on which Jones launched forth very high encomiums. When they came to the tree whence he had formerly tumbled into the canal, Sophia could not help reminding him of that accident, and said, "I fancy, Mr Jones, you have some little shuddering when you see that water."

"I assure you, madam," answered Jones, "the concern you felt at the loss of your little bird will always appear to me the highest circumstance in that adventure. Poor little Tommy! There is the branch he stood upon. How could the little wretch have the folly to fly away from that state of happiness in which I had the honour to place him? His fate was a just punishment for his ingratitude."

"Upon my word, Mr Jones," said she, "your gallantry very narrowly escaped as severe a fate. Sure the remembrance must affect you."

"Indeed, madam," answered he, "if I have any reason to reflect with sorrow on it, it is, perhaps, that the water had not been a little deeper, by which I might have escaped many bitter heartaches that Fortune seems to have in store for me."

"Fie, Mr Jones!" replied Sophia, much shocked. "I am sure you cannot be in earnest now. This affected contempt of life is only an excess of your complacence to me. You would endeavour to lessen the obligation of having twice ventured it for my sake. Beware the third time." She spoke these last words with a smile, and a softness inexpressible.

Jones answered with a sigh that he feared it was already too late for caution, and then looking tenderly and steadfastly on her, he cried, "Oh, Miss Western! Can you desire me to live? Can you wish me so ill?"

Sophia, looking down on the ground, answered with some hesitation, "Indeed, Mr Jones, I do not wish you ill."

"Oh, I know too well that heavenly temper," cries Jones, "that divine goodness, which is beyond every other charm."

"Nay, now," answered she, "I understand you not. I can stay no longer."

"I—I would not be understood!" cries he. "Nay, I can't be understood. I know not what I say. Meeting you here so unexpectedly, I have been unguarded. For Heaven's sake pardon me, if I have said anything to offend you. I did not mean it. Indeed, I would rather have died—nay, the very thought would kill me."

"You surprise me," answered she. "How can you possibly think you have offended me?"

"Fear, madam," says he, "easily runs into madness, and there is no degree of fear like that which I feel of offending you. How can I speak then? Nay, don't look angrily at me, one frown will destroy me. I mean nothing. Blame my eyes, or blame those beauties. What am I saying? Pardon me if I have said too much. My heart overflowed. I have struggled with my love to the utmost, and have endeavoured to conceal a fever which preys on my vitals, and will, I hope, soon make it impossible for me ever to offend you more."

Mr Jones now fell a trembling as if he had been shaken with the fit of an ague. Sophia, who was in a situation not very different from his, answered in these words, "Mr Jones, I will not affect to misunderstand you, indeed, I understand you too well, but, for Heaven's sake, if you have any affection for me, let me make the best of my way into the house. I wish I may be able to support myself thither."

Jones, who was hardly able to support himself, offered her his arm, which she condescended to accept, but begged he would not mention a word more to her of this nature at present. He promised he would not, insisting only on her forgiveness of what love, without the leave of his will, had forced from him. This, she told him, he knew how to obtain by his future behaviour, and thus this young pair tottered and trembled along, the lover not once daring to squeeze the hand of his mistress, though it was locked in his.

Sophia immediately retired to her chamber, where Mrs Honour and the hartshorn were summoned to her assistance. As to poor Jones, the only relief to his distempered mind was an unwelcome piece of news, which, as it opens a scene of different nature from those in which the reader hath lately been conversant, will be communicated to him in the next chapter.

Chapter Seven

In which Mr Allworthy appears on a sick-bed

Mr Western was become so fond of Jones that he was unwilling to part with him, though his arm had been long since cured, and Jones, either from the love of sport, or from some other reason, was easily persuaded to continue at his house, which he did sometimes for a fortnight together without paying a single visit at Mr Allworthy's, nay, without ever hearing from thence.

Mr Allworthy had been for some days indisposed with a cold, which had been attended with a little fever. This he had, however, neglected, as it was usual with him to do all manner of disorders which did not confine him to his bed, or prevent his several faculties from performing their ordinary functions — a conduct which we would by no means be thought to approve or recommend to imitation. Surely the gentlemen of the Aesculapian art are in the right in advising, that the moment the disease has entered at one door, the physician should be introduced at the other. What else is meant by that old adage, *Venienti occurrite morbo?* 'Oppose a distemper at its first approach.'

Thus the doctor and the disease meet in fair and equal conflict, whereas, by giving time to the latter, we often suffer him to fortify and entrench himself, like a French army, so that the learned gentleman finds it very difficult, and sometimes impossible, to come at the enemy. Nay, sometimes by gaining time the disease applies to the French military politics, and corrupts nature over to his side, and then all the powers of physic must arrive too late. Agreeable to these observations was, I remember, the complaint of the great Doctor Misaubin, who used very pathetically to lament the late applications which were made to his skill, saying, "Bygar, me believe my pation take me for de undertaker, for dey never send for me till de physicion have kill dem."

Mr Allworthy's distemper, by means of this neglect, gained such ground, that, when the increase of his fever obliged him to send for assistance, the doctor at his first arrival shook his head, wished he had been sent for sooner, and intimated that he thought him in very imminent danger. Mr Allworthy, who had settled all his affairs in this world, and was as well prepared as it is possible for human nature to be for the other, received this information with the utmost calmness and unconcern. He could, indeed, whenever he laid himself down to rest, say with Cato in the tragical poem —

Let guilt or fear
Disturb man's rest, Cato knows neither of them,
Indifferent in his choice to sleep or die.

In reality, he could say this with ten times more reason and confidence than Cato, or any other proud fellow among the ancient or modern heroes, for he was not only devoid of fear, but might be considered as a faithful labourer, when at the end of harvest he is summoned to receive his reward at the hands of a bountiful master.

The good man gave immediate orders for all his family to be summoned round him. None of these were then abroad, but Mrs Blifil, who had been some time in London, and Mr Jones, whom the reader hath just parted from at Mr Western's, and who received this summons just as Sophia had left him.

The news of Mr Allworthy's danger — for the servant told him he was dying — drove all thoughts of love out of his head. He hurried instantly into the chariot which was sent for him, and ordered the coachman to drive with all imaginable haste, nor did the idea of Sophia, I believe, once occur to him on the way.

And now the whole family, namely, Mr Blifil, Mr Jones, Mr Thwackum, Mr Square, and some of the servants — for such were Mr Allworthy's orders — being all assembled round his bed, the good man sat up in it, and was beginning to speak, when Blifil fell to blubbering, and began to express very loud and bitter lamentations.

Upon this Mr Allworthy shook him by the hand, and said, "Do not sorrow thus, my dear nephew, at the most ordinary of all human occurrences. When misfortunes befall our friends we are justly grieved, for those are accidents which might often have been avoided, and which may seem to render the lot of one man more peculiarly unhappy than that of others. But death is certainly unavoidable, and is that common lot in which alone the fortunes of all men agree, nor is the time when this happens to us very material.

"If the wisest of men hath compared life to a span, surely we may be allowed to consider it as a day. It is my fate to leave it in the evening, but those who are taken away earlier have only lost a few hours, at the best little worth lamenting, and much oftener hours of labour and fatigue, of pain and sorrow. One of the Roman poets, I remember, likens our leaving life to our departure from a feast—a thought which hath often occurred to me when I have seen men struggling to protract an entertainment, and to enjoy the company of their friends a few moments longer. Alas! How short is the most protracted of such enjoyments! How immaterial the difference between him who retires the soonest, and him who stays the latest! This is seeing life in the best view, and this unwillingness to quit our friends is the most amiable motive from which we can derive the fear of death, and yet the longest enjoyment which we can hope for of this kind is of so trivial a duration, that it is to a wise man truly contemptible.

"Few men, I own, think in this manner, for, indeed, few men think of death till they are in its jaws. However gigantic and terrible an object this may appear when it approaches them, they are nevertheless incapable of seeing it at any distance—nay, though they have been ever so much alarmed and frightened when they have apprehended themselves in danger of dying, they are no sooner cleared from this apprehension than even the fears of it are erased from their minds. But, alas! He who escapes from death is not pardoned, he is only reprieved, and reprieved to a short day.

"Grieve, therefore, no more, my dear child, on this occasion, an event which may happen every hour, which every element, nay, almost every particle of matter that surrounds us is capable of producing, and which must and will most unavoidably reach us all at last, ought neither to occasion our surprise nor our lamentation.

"My physician having acquainted me — which I take very kindly of him — that I am in danger of leaving you all very shortly, I have determined to say a few words to you at this our parting, before my distemper, which I find grows very fast upon me, puts it out of my power.

"But I shall waste my strength too much. I intended to speak concerning my will, which, though I have settled long ago, I think proper to mention such heads of it as concern any of you, that I may have the comfort of perceiving you are all satisfied with the provision I have there made for you.

"Nephew Blifil, I leave you the heir to my whole estate, except only five hundred pounds a year, which is to revert to you after the death of your mother, and except one other estate of five hundred pounds a year, and the sum of six thousand pounds, which I have bestowed in the following manner.

"The estate of five hundred pounds a year I have given to you, Mr Jones, and as I know the inconvenience which attends the want of ready money, I have added one thousand pounds in specie. In this I know not whether I have exceeded or fallen short of your expectation. Perhaps you will think I have given you too little, and the world will be as ready to condemn me for giving you too much — but the latter censure I despise, and as to the former, unless you should entertain that common error which I have often heard in my life pleaded as an excuse for a total want of charity, namely, that instead of raising gratitude by voluntary acts of bounty, we are apt to raise demands, which of all others are the most boundless and most difficult to satisfy. Pardon me the bare mention of this, I will not suspect any such thing."

Jones flung himself at his benefactor's feet, and taking eagerly hold of his hand, assured him his goodness to him, both now and all other times, had so infinitely exceeded not only his merit but his hopes, that no words could express his sense of it. "And I assure you, sir," said he, "your present generosity hath left me no other concern than for the present melancholy occasion. Oh, my friend, my father!" Here his words choked him, and he turned away to hide a tear which was starting from his eyes.

Allworthy then gently squeezed his hand, and proceeded thus. "I am convinced, my child, that you have much goodness, generosity, and honour, in your temper. If you will add prudence and religion to these, you must be happy, for the three former qualities, I admit, make you worthy of happiness, but they are the latter only which will put you in possession of it.

"One thousand pounds I have given to you, Mr Thwackum, a sum I am convinced which greatly exceeds your desires, as well as your wants. However, you will receive it as a memorial of my friendship, and whatever superfluities may redound to you, that piety which you so rigidly maintain will instruct you how to dispose of them.

"A like sum, Mr Square, I have bequeathed to you. This, I hope, will enable you to pursue your profession with better success than hitherto. I have often observed with concern, that distress is more apt to excite contempt than commiseration, especially among men of business, with whom poverty is understood to indicate want of ability. But the little I have been able to leave you will extricate you from those difficulties with which you have formerly struggled, and then I doubt not but you will meet with sufficient prosperity to supply what a man of your philosophical temper will require.

"I find myself growing faint, so I shall refer you to my will for my disposition of the residue. My servants will there find some tokens to remember me by, and there are a few charities which, I trust, my executors will see faithfully performed. Bless you all. I am setting out a little before you."

Here a footman came hastily into the room, and said there was an attorney from Salisbury who had a particular message, which he said he must communicate to Mr Allworthy himself, that he seemed in a violent hurry, and protested he had so much business to do, that, if he could cut himself into four quarters, all would not be sufficient.

"Go, child," said Allworthy to Blifil, "see what the gentleman wants. I am not able to do any business now, nor can he have any with me, in which you are not at present more concerned than myself. Besides, I really am—I am incapable of seeing anyone at present, or of any longer attention." He then saluted them all, saying, perhaps he should be able to see them again, but he should be now glad to compose himself a little, finding that he had too much exhausted his spirits in discourse.

Some of the company shed tears at their parting, and even the philosopher Square wiped his eyes, albeit unused to the melting mood. As to Mrs Wilkins, she dropped her pearls as fast as the Arabian trees their medicinal gums, for this was a ceremonial which that gentlewoman never omitted on a proper occasion.

After this Mr Allworthy again laid himself down on his pillow, and endeavoured to compose himself to rest.

Chapter Eight

Containing matter rather natural than pleasing

Besides grief for her master, there was another source for that briny stream which so plentifully rose above the two mountainous cheek-bones of the housekeeper. She was no sooner retired, than she began to mutter to herself in the following pleasant strain.

"Sure master might have made some difference, methinks, between me and the other servants. I suppose he hath left me mourning, but, i'fackins! If that be all, the devil shall wear it for him, for me. I'd have his worship know I am no beggar. I have saved five hundred pound in his service, and after all to be used in this manner. It is a fine encouragement to servants to be honest, and to be sure, if I have taken a little something now and then, others have taken ten times as much, and now we are all put in a lump together. If so be that it be so, the legacy may go to the devil with him that gave it.

"No, I won't give it up neither, because that will please some folks. No, I'll buy the gayest gown I can get, and dance over the old curmudgeon's grave in it. This is my reward for taking his part so often, when all the country have cried shame of him, for breeding up his bastard in that manner, but he is going now where he must pay for all. It would have become him better to have repented of his sins on his deathbed, than to glory in them, and give away his estate out of his own family to a misbegotten child. Found in his bed, forsooth! A pretty story! Ay, ay, those that hide know where to find. Lord forgive him! I warrant he hath many more bastards to answer for, if the truth was known. One comfort is, they will all be known where he is a going now. 'The servants will find some token to remember me by.'

"Those were the very words, I shall never forget them, if I was to live a thousand years. Ay, ay, I shall remember you for huddling me among the servants. One would have thought he might have mentioned my name as well as that of Square, but he is a gentleman forsooth, though he had not cloths on his back when he came hither first. Marry come up with such gentlemen! Though he hath lived here this many years, I don't believe there is arrow a servant in the house ever saw the colour of his money. The devil shall wait upon such a gentleman for me." Much more of the like kind she muttered to herself, but this taste shall suffice to the reader.

Neither Thwackum nor Square were much better satisfied with their legacies. Though they breathed not their resentment so loud, yet from the discontent which appeared in their countenances, as well as from the following dialogue, we collect that no great pleasure reigned in their minds.

About an hour after they had left the sick-room, Square met Thwackum in the hall and accosted him thus. "Well, sir, have you heard any news of your friend since we parted from him?"

"If you mean Mr Allworthy," answered Thwackum, "I think you might rather give him the appellation of your friend, for he seems to me to have deserved that title."

"The title is as good on your side," replied Square, "for his bounty, such as it is, hath been equal to both."

"I should not have mentioned it first," cries Thwackum, "but since you begin, I must inform you I am of a different opinion. There is a wide distinction between voluntary favours and rewards. The duty I have done in his family, and the care I have taken in the education of his two boys, are services for which some men might have expected a greater return. I would not have you imagine I am therefore dissatisfied, for St Paul hath taught me to be content with the little I have. Had the modicum been less, I should have known my duty. But though the Scriptures obliges me to remain contented, it doth not enjoin me to shut my eyes to my own merit, nor restrain me from seeing when I am injured by an unjust comparison."

"Since you provoke me," returned Square, "that injury is done to me, nor did I ever imagine Mr Allworthy had held my friendship so light, as to put me in balance with one who received his wages. I know to what it is owing, it proceeds from those narrow principles which you have been so long endeavouring to infuse into him, in contempt of everything which is great and noble. The beauty and loveliness of friendship is too strong for dim eyes, nor can it be perceived by any other medium than that unerring rule of right, which you have so often endeavoured to ridicule, that you have perverted your friend's understanding."

"I wish," cries Thwackum, in a rage, "I wish, for the sake of his soul, your damnable doctrines have not perverted his faith. It is to this I impute his present behaviour, so unbecoming a Christian. Who but an atheist could think of leaving the world without having first made up his account? Without confessing his sins, and receiving that absolution which he knew he had one in the house duly authorised to give him? He will feel the want of these necessaries when it is too late, when he is arrived at that place where there is wailing and gnashing of teeth. It is then he will find in what mighty stead that heathen goddess, that virtue, which you and all other deists of the age adore, will stand him. He will then summon his priest, when there is none to be found, and will lament the want of that absolution, without which no sinner can be safe."

"If it be so material," says Square, "why don't you present it him of your own accord?"

"It hath no virtue," cries Thwackum, "but to those who have sufficient grace to require it. But why do I talk thus to a heathen and an unbeliever? It is you that taught him this lesson, for which you have been well rewarded in this world, as I doubt not your disciple will soon be in the other."

"I know not what you mean by reward," said Square, "but if you hint at that pitiful memorial of our friendship, which he hath thought fit to bequeath me, I despise it, and nothing but the unfortunate situation of my circumstances should prevail on me to accept it."

The physician now arrived, and began to inquire of the two disputants, how we all did above-stairs?

"In a miserable way," answered Thwackum.

"It is no more than I expected," cries the doctor, "but pray what symptoms have appeared since I left you?"

"No good ones, I am afraid," replied Thwackum, "after what passed at our departure, I think there were little hopes." The bodily physician, perhaps, misunderstood the curer of souls, and before they came to an explanation, Mr Blifil came to them with a most melancholy countenance, and acquainted them that he brought sad news, that his mother was dead at Salisbury, that she had been seized on the road home with the gout in her head and stomach, which had carried her off in a few hours.

"Good-lack-a-day!" says the doctor. "One cannot answer for events, but I wish I had been at hand, to have been called in. The gout is a distemper which it is difficult to treat, yet I have been remarkably successful in it."

Thwackum and Square both condoled with Mr Blifil for the loss of his mother, which the one advised him to bear like a man, and the other like a Christian. The young gentleman said he knew very well we were all mortal, and he would endeavour to submit to his loss as well as he could. That he could not, however, help complaining a little against the peculiar severity of his fate, which brought the news of so great a calamity to him by surprise, and that at a time when he hourly expected the severest blow he was capable of feeling from the malice of fortune. He said, the present occasion would put to the test those excellent rudiments which he had learnt from Mr Thwackum and Mr Square, and it would be entirely owing to them, if he was enabled to survive such misfortunes.

It was now debated whether Mr Allworthy should be informed of the death of his sister. This the doctor violently opposed, in which, I believe, the whole college would agree with him, but Mr Blifil said, he had received such positive and repeated orders from his uncle, never to keep any secret from him for fear of the disquietude which it might give him, that he durst not think of disobedience, whatever might be the consequence. He said, for his part, considering the religious and philosophic temper of his uncle, he could not agree with the doctor in his apprehensions. He was therefore resolved to communicate it to him, for if his uncle recovered – as he heartily prayed he might – he knew he would never forgive an endeavour to keep a secret of this kind from him.

The physician was forced to submit to these resolutions, which the two other learned gentlemen very highly commended. So together moved Mr Blifil and the doctor towards the sick-room, where the physician first entered, and approached the bed, in order to feel his patient's pulse, which he had no sooner done, than he declared he was much better, that the last application had succeeded to a miracle, and had brought the fever to intermit, so that, he said, there appeared now to be as little danger as he had before apprehended there were hopes.

To say the truth, Mr Allworthy's situation had never been so bad as the great caution of the doctor had represented it, but as a wise general never despises his enemy, however inferior that enemy's force may be, so neither doth a wise physician ever despise a distemper, however inconsiderable. As the former preserves the same strict discipline, places the same guards, and employs the same scouts, though the enemy be never so weak, so the latter maintains the same gravity of countenance, and shakes his head with the same significant air, let the distemper be never so trifling. And both, among many other good ones, may assign this solid reason for their conduct, that by these means the greater glory redounds to them if they gain the victory, and the less disgrace if by any unlucky accident they should happen to be conquered.

Mr Allworthy had no sooner lifted up his eyes, and thanked Heaven for these hopes of his recovery, than Mr Blifil drew near, with a very dejected aspect, and having applied his handkerchief to his eye, either to wipe away his tears, or to do as Ovid somewhere expresses himself on another occasion—

Si nullus erit, tamen excute nullum.

If there be none, then wipe away that none.

—he communicated to his uncle what the reader hath been just before acquainted with.

Allworthy received the news with concern, with patience, and with resignation. He dropped a tender tear, then composed his countenance, and at last cried, "The Lord's will be done in everything."

He now enquired for the messenger, but Blifil told him it had been impossible to detain him a moment, for he appeared by the great hurry he was in to have some business of importance on his hands, that he complained of being hurried and driven and torn out of his life, and repeated many times, that if he could divide himself into four quarters, he knew how to dispose of everyone.

Allworthy then desired Blifil to take care of the funeral. He said, he would have his sister deposited in his own chapel, and as to the particulars, he left them to his own discretion, only mentioning the person whom he would have employed on this occasion.

Chapter Nine

Which, among other things, may serve as a comment on that saying of Aeschines, that "drunkenness shows the mind of a man, as a mirror reflects his person"

The reader may perhaps wonder at hearing nothing of Mr Jones in the last chapter. In fact, his behaviour was so different from that of the persons there mentioned, that we chose not to confound his name with theirs.

When the good man had ended his speech, Jones was the last who deserted the room. Thence he retired to his own apartment, to give vent to his concern, but the restlessness of his mind would not suffer him to remain long there, he slipped softly therefore to Allworthy's chamber-door, where he listened a considerable time without hearing any kind of motion within, unless a violent snoring, which at last his fears misrepresented as groans.

This so alarmed him, that he could not forbear entering the room, where he found the good man in the bed, in a sweet composed sleep, and his nurse snoring in the above mentioned hearty manner, at the bed's feet. He immediately took the only method of silencing this thorough bass, whose music he feared might disturb Mr Allworthy, and then sitting down by the nurse, he remained motionless till Blifil and the doctor came in together and waked the sick man, in order that the doctor might feel his pulse, and that the other might communicate to him that piece of news, which, had Jones been apprised of it, would have had great difficulty of finding its way to Mr Allworthy's ear at such a season.

When he first heard Blifil tell his uncle this story, Jones could hardly contain the wrath which kindled in him at the other's indiscretion, especially as the doctor shook his head, and declared his unwillingness to have the matter mentioned to his patient. But as his passion did not so far deprive him of all use of his understanding, as to hide from him the consequences which any violent expression towards Blifil might have on the sick, this apprehension stilled his rage at the present, and he grew afterwards so satisfied with finding that this news had, in fact, produced no mischief, that he suffered his anger to die in his own bosom, without ever mentioning it to Blifil.

The physician dined that day at Mr Allworthy's, and having after dinner visited his patient, he returned to the company, and told them, that he had now the satisfaction to say, with assurance, that his patient was out of all danger, that he had brought his fever to a perfect intermission, and doubted not by throwing in the bark to prevent its return.

This account so pleased Jones, and threw him into such immoderate excess of rapture, that he might be truly said to be drunk with joy — an intoxication which greatly forwards the effects of wine, and as he was very free too with the bottle on this occasion, for he drank many bumpers to the doctor's health, as well as to other toasts, he became very soon literally drunk.

Jones had naturally violent animal spirits, these being set on float and augmented by the spirit of wine, produced most extravagant effects. He kissed the doctor, and embraced him with the most passionate endearments, swearing that next to Mr Allworthy himself, he loved him of all men living. "Doctor," added he, "you deserve a statue to be erected to you at the public expense, for having preserved a man, who is not only the darling of all good men who know him, but a blessing to society, the glory of his country, and an honour to human nature. Damn me if I don't love him better than my own soul."

"More shame for you," cries Thwackum. "Though I think you have reason to love him, for he hath provided very well for you. And perhaps it might have been better for some folks that he had not lived to see just reason of revoking his gift."

Jones now looking on Thwackum with inconceivable disdain, answered, "And doth thy mean soul imagine that any such considerations could weigh with me? No, let the earth open and swallow her own dirt — if I had millions of acres I would say it — rather than swallow up my dear glorious friend."

Quis desiderio sit pudor aut modus Tam chari capitis? What modesty or measure can set bounds to our desire of so dear a friend?

The doctor now interposed, and prevented the effects of a wrath which was kindling between Jones and Thwackum, after which the former gave a loose to mirth, sang two or three amorous songs, and fell into every frantic disorder which unbridled joy is apt to inspire. But so far was he from any disposition to quarrel, that he was ten times better humoured, if possible, than when he was sober.

To say truth, nothing is more erroneous than the common observation, that men who are ill-natured and quarrelsome when they are drunk, are very worthy persons when they are sober. For drink, in reality, doth not reverse nature, or create passions in men which did not exist in them before. It takes away the guard of reason, and consequently forces us to produce those symptoms, which many, when sober, have art enough to conceal. It heightens and inflames our passions — generally indeed that passion which is uppermost in our mind — so that the angry temper, the amorous, the generous, the good-humoured, the avaricious, and all other dispositions of men, are in their cups heightened and exposed.

And yet as no nation produces so many drunken quarrels, especially among the lower people, as England — for indeed, with them, to drink and to fight together are almost synonymous terms — I would not, methinks, have it thence concluded, that the English are the worst-natured people alive. Perhaps the love of glory only is at the bottom of this, so that the fair conclusion seems to be, that our countrymen have more of that love, and more of bravery, than any other plebeians. And this the rather, as there is seldom anything ungenerous, unfair, or ill-natured, exercised on these occasions — nay, it is common for the combatants to express good-will for each other even at the time of the conflict, and as their drunken mirth generally ends in a battle, so do most of their battles end in friendship.

But to return to our history. Though Jones had shown no design of giving offence, yet Mr Blifil was highly offended at a behaviour which was so inconsistent with the sober and prudent reserve of his own temper. He bore it too with the greater impatience, as it appeared to him very indecent at this season, when, as he said, the house was a house of mourning, on the account of his dear mother. If it had pleased Heaven to give him some prospect of Mr Allworthy's recovery, it would become them better to express the exultations of their hearts in thanksgiving, than in drunkenness and riots, which were properer methods to increase the Divine wrath, than to avert it.

Thwackum, who had swallowed more liquor than Jones, but without any ill effect on his brain, seconded the pious harangue of Blifil, but Square, for reasons which the reader may probably guess, was totally silent.

Wine had not so totally overpowered Jones, as to prevent his recollecting Mr Blifil's loss, the moment it was mentioned. As no person, therefore, was more ready to confess and condemn his own errors, he offered to shake Mr Blifil by the hand, and begged his pardon, saying, his excessive joy for Mr Allworthy's recovery had driven every other thought out of his mind.

Blifil scornfully rejected his hand, and with much indignation answered, it was little to be wondered at, if tragical spectacles made no impression on the blind, but, for his part, he had the misfortune to know who his parents were, and consequently must be affected with their loss.

Jones, who, notwithstanding his good humour, had some mixture of the irascible in his constitution, leapt hastily from his chair, and catching hold of Blifil's collar, cried out, "Damn you for a rascal, do you insult me with the misfortune of my birth?" He accompanied these words with such rough actions, that they soon got the better of Mr Blifil's peaceful temper, and a scuffle immediately ensued, which might have produced mischief, had it not been prevented by the interposition of Thwackum and the physician. For the philosophy of Square rendered him superior to all emotions, and he very calmly smoked his pipe, as was his custom in all broils, unless when he apprehended some danger of having it broken in his mouth.

The combatants being now prevented from executing present vengeance on each other, betook themselves to the common resources of disappointed rage, and vented their wrath in threats and defiance. In this kind of conflict, Fortune, which, in the personal attack, seemed to incline to Jones, was now altogether as favourable to his enemy.

A truce, nevertheless, was at length agreed on, by the mediation of the neutral parties, and the whole company again sat down at the table, where Jones being prevailed on to ask pardon, and Blifil to give it, peace was restored, and everything seemed *in statu quo*.

But though the quarrel was, in all appearance, perfectly reconciled, the good humour which had been interrupted by it, was by no means restored. All merriment was now at an end, and the subsequent discourse consisted only of grave relations of matters of fact, and of as grave observations upon them, a species of conversation, in which, though there is much of dignity and instruction, there is but little entertainment. As we presume therefore to convey only this last to the reader, we shall pass by whatever was said, till the rest of the company having by degrees dropped off, left only Square and the physician together. At which time the conversation was a little heightened by some comments on what had happened between the two young gentlemen, both of whom the doctor declared to be no better than scoundrels, to which appellation the philosopher, very sagaciously shaking his head, agreed.

Chapter Ten

Showing the truth of many observations of Ovid, and of other more grave writers, who have proved beyond contradiction, that wine is often the forerunner of incontinency

Jones retired from the company, in which we have seen him engaged, into the fields, where he intended to cool himself by a walk in the open air before he attended Mr Allworthy. There, whilst he renewed those meditations on his dear Sophia, which the dangerous illness of his friend and benefactor had for some time interrupted, an accident happened, which with sorrow we relate, and with sorrow doubtless will it be read. However, that historic truth to which we profess so inviolable an attachment, obliges us to communicate it to posterity.

It was now a pleasant evening in the latter end of June, when our hero was walking in a most delicious grove, where the gentle breezes fanning the leaves, together with the sweet trilling of a murmuring stream, and the melodious notes of nightingales, formed altogether the most enchanting harmony.

In this scene, so sweetly accommodated to love, he meditated on his dear Sophia.

Stroking that part of his anatomy he considered most tender, he felt the rod straighten and become the iron staff by which he dealt blows that sent maidens into languishing swoons of desire. But none being by, he had only his own digits to satisfy the paroxysms of desire that thinking of Sophia sent him into. He would touch her breasts, taste the fountains of beauty and trace their form with tongue and fingers, before curving his hand around the delicate indent of her waist, and the proud swell of her buttocks, ending with a sly delve into the paradise waiting for him between the pillars of Venus, viz, her thighs.

Thinking of those milky columns made liquid escape from the eye of his shaft, and he watched it overspill before smoothing it over the head of his cock, to increase his pleasure as he took that instrument of delight in his hand and pumped it hard, much as he might encourage it to harden for a young lady.

Sophia would receive him sweetly, as her lively, but modest nature allowed, by waiting for him to urge her legs apart, then to lie down on the bower of her bed and bend her knees for him, the better to allow him ingress between those soft pathways to love. He would push his eager member deep inside her, waiting for that soft sigh that indicated her agreement to such an intimate contact.

Her tight, hot glove was exactly fashioned for him, a place no one would ever see, taste or enjoy but Tom himself. He would work her, until her passage softened and melted with the liquid they made to ease their efforts, and she came to meet him with every stroke of his body into hers.

Such would be the deep union. He would take her lips with his, give his tongue the same work as his rod, urging her to trust her delicate sensibilities into his care, and she would.

The climax came, his imaginary love cried his name repeatedly as she found the apogee of her passion, and he, similarly, cried her name as if she had forgotten it and asked him to repeat it until she should remember.

While his wanton fancy roamed unbounded over all her beauties, and his lively imagination painted the charming maid in various ravishing forms, his warm heart melted with tenderness, and at length, throwing himself on the ground, by the side of a gently murmuring brook, he broke forth into the following ejaculation.

"O Sophia, would Heaven give thee to my arms, how blessed would be my condition! Cursed be that fortune which sets a distance between us. Was I but possessed of thee, one only suit of rags thy whole estate, is there a man on earth whom I would envy! How contemptible would the brightest Circassian beauty, dressed in all the jewels of the Indies, appear to my eyes! But why do I mention another woman? Could I think my eyes capable of looking at any other with tenderness, these hands should tear them from my head. No, my Sophia, if cruel fortune separates us forever, my soul shall dote on thee alone. The chastest constancy will I ever preserve to thy image. Though I should never have possession of thy charming person, still shalt thou alone have possession of my thoughts, my love, my soul. Oh! My fond heart is so wrapped in that tender bosom, that the brightest beauties would for me have no charms, nor would a hermit be colder in their embraces. Sophia, Sophia alone shall be mine. What raptures are in that name! I will engrave it on every tree."

At these words he started up, and beheld – not his Sophia – no, nor a Circassian maid richly and elegantly attired for the grand Signior's seraglio. No, without a gown, in a shift that was somewhat of the coarsest, and none of the cleanest, bedewed likewise with some odoriferous effluvia, the produce of the day's labour, with a pitchfork in her hand, Molly Seagrim approached.

Our hero had his penknife in his hand, which he had drawn for the before-mentioned purpose of carving on the bark, when the girl coming near him, cried out with a smile, "You don't intend to kill me, squire, I hope!"

"Why should you think I would kill you?" answered Jones.

"Nay," replied she, with a coy look at him, "after your cruel usage of me when I saw you last, killing me would, perhaps, be too great kindness for me to expect." She manufactured a tear in her eyes, which Tom, ever the gentleman, essayed to assuage.

Here ensued a parley, which, as I do not think myself obliged to relate it, I shall omit. It is sufficient that it lasted a full quarter of an hour, at the conclusion of which they retired into the thickest part of the grove.

Molly had resorted to tears, finding that tactic the best to engage the interest of her erstwhile swain, and Tom, thinking they would not wish to be disturbed, took her to the grove and then into his arms. Molly, a clever wench who could nevertheless never keep a clout about her, found her shift slip to the ground, a convenient place to swoon when Tom showed signs of helping her back into her recently discarded clothing.

Still turgid from the thoughts of another, Tom tried to hide his burgeoning stiffness, but Molly saw it and remembering the delights he had brought her, decided she wanted to experience it again.

Consequently, she sat on the shift, inviting him to join her and allowing her tears to subside to mere pathetic sniffs. Tom, seeing Molly's beauty, found himself unable to resist her charms, and in the way of young men everywhere, holding her close sent him into paroxysms of wanting. He could not go forever without relieving his tender sensibilities. Although he loved Sophia, he had already given her up in despair, because he considered the matter hopeless with her. "For old times' sake, Molly," he said, and she nodded eagerly.

"I have missed you, Tom."

No sooner had she said this than he joined their lips in that dear congress that comes so swiftly to the young, and he omitted to recall anything but the breasts pressing against his chest and the quim so open and wet for him.

Such a flattering invitation could hardly be ignored, and Tom was not long in unfastening his breeches' fall and allowing his cock free access to Molly, to do with as it would. He sat, crossed his legs and displayed his member proudly, standing free of his clothes in query.

Molly, being more experienced than she had even allowed to Tom, leant forward and licked his cock before sucking him in and skilfully bringing him to the point at which he might shoot into her mouth, except she drew back, because she wanted him too, this not being an entirely selfless act. Squatting over him, she gradually sank down on to that instrument that, she knew full well, would bring her the greatest pleasure.

Tom surprised her by inserting one finger into the smaller passage behind, and urging her to move in time with his thrusts.

Molly discovered she enjoyed this new treat, it adding sensations inside her body she had rarely experienced before, and she wondered how it would feel to allow a cock in that part, but for now she retained it where it was, knowing how to please him best that way, and rode him much as a man might ride a horse at full gallop, vigorously and with little in the way of subtlety. But neither Molly nor Tom wished for delicacy at this time, neither being connoisseurs of the art of love, and to their great mutual satisfaction, they romped to a finish.

Some of my readers may be inclined to think this event unnatural. However, the fact is true, and perhaps may be sufficiently accounted for by suggesting, that Jones probably thought one woman better than none, and Molly as probably imagined two men to be better than one. Besides the before-mentioned motive assigned to the present behaviour of Jones, the reader will be likewise pleased to recollect in his favour, that he was not at this time perfect master of that wonderful power of reason, which so well enables grave and wise men to subdue their unruly passions, and to decline any of these prohibited amusements.

Wine now had totally subdued this power in Jones. He was, indeed, in a condition, in which, if reason had interposed, though only to advise, she might have received the answer which one Cleostratus gave many years ago to a silly fellow, who asked him, if he was not ashamed to be drunk? "Are not you," said Cleostratus, "ashamed to admonish a drunken man?"

To say the truth, in a court of justice drunkenness must not be an excuse, yet in a court of conscience it is greatly so, and therefore Aristotle, who commends the laws of Pittacus, by which drunken men received double punishment for their crimes, allows there is more of policy than justice in that law. Now, if there are any transgressions pardonable from drunkenness, they are certainly such as Mr Jones was at present guilty of, on which head I could pour forth a vast profusion of learning, if I imagined it would either entertain my reader, or teach him anything more than he knows already. For his sake therefore I shall keep my learning to myself, and return to my history.

It hath been observed, that Fortune seldom doth things by halves. To say truth, there is no end to her freaks whenever she is disposed to gratify or displease. No sooner had our hero retired with his Dido, but—*speluncam* Blifil *dux et divinus eandem deveniunt*—the parson and the young squire, who were taking a serious walk, arrived at the stile which leads into the grove, and the latter caught a view of the lovers just as they were sinking out of sight.

Blifil knew Jones very well, though he was at above a hundred yards' distance, and he was as positive to the sex of his companion, though not to the individual person. He started, blessed himself, and uttered a very solemn ejaculation.

Thwackum expressed some surprise at these sudden emotions, and asked the reason of them. To which Blifil answered, he was certain he had seen a fellow and wench retire together among the bushes, which he doubted not was with some wicked purpose. As to the name of Jones, he thought proper to conceal it, and why he did so must be left to the judgement of the sagacious reader, for we never choose to assign motives to the actions of men, when there is any possibility of our being mistaken.

The parson, who was not only strictly chaste in his own person, but a great enemy to the opposite vice in all others, fired at this information. He desired Mr Blifil to conduct him immediately to the place, which as he approached he breathed forth vengeance mixed with lamentations. Nor did he refrain from casting some oblique reflections on Mr Allworthy, insinuating that the wickedness of the country was principally owing to the encouragement he had given to vice, by having exerted such kindness to a bastard, and by having mitigated that just and wholesome rigour of the law which allots a very severe punishment to loose wenches.

The way through which our hunters were to pass in pursuit of their game was so beset with briars, that it greatly obstructed their walk, and caused besides such a rustling, that Jones had sufficient warning of their arrival before they could surprise him. Nay, indeed, so incapable was Thwackum of concealing his indignation, and such vengeance did he mutter forth every step he took, that this alone must have abundantly satisfied Jones that he was—to use the language of sportsmen—found sitting.

Chapter Eleven

In which a simile in Mr Pope's period of a mile introduces as bloody a battle as can possibly be fought without the assistance of steel or cold iron

As in the season of rutting—an uncouth phrase, by which the vulgar denote that gentle dalliance, which in the well-wooded forest of Hampshire, passes between lovers of the ferine kind—if, while the lofty-crested stag meditates the amorous sport, a couple of puppies, or any other beasts of hostile note, should wander so near the temple of Venus Ferina that the fair hind should shrink from the place, touched with that somewhat, either of fear or frolic, of nicety or skittishness, with which nature hath bedecked all females, or hath at least instructed them how to put it on, lest, through the indelicacy of males, the Samean mysteries should be pried into by unhallowed eyes, for, at the celebration of these rites, the female priestess cries out with her in Virgil—who was then, probably, hard at work on such celebration—

Procul, o procul este, profani,

Proclamat vates, totoque absistite luco.
Far hence be souls profane,
The sibyl cry'd, and from the grove abstain.

If, I say, while these sacred rites, which are in common to *genus omne animantium,* are in agitation between the stag and his mistress, any hostile beasts should venture too near, on the first hint given by the frighted hind, fierce and tremendous rushes forth the stag to the entrance of the thicket. There stands he sentinel over his love, stamps the ground with his foot, and with his horns brandished aloft in air, proudly provokes the apprehended foe to combat.

Thus, and more terrible, when he perceived the enemy's approach, leapt forth our hero. Many a step advanced he forwards, in order to conceal the trembling hind, and if possible, to secure her retreat. And now Thwackum, having first darted some livid lightning from his fiery eyes, began to thunder forth, "Fie upon it! Fie upon it! Mr Jones. Is it possible you should be the person?"

"You see," answered Jones, "it is possible I should be here."

"And who," said Thwackum, "is that wicked slut with you?"

"If I have any wicked slut with me," cries Jones, "it is possible I shall not let you know who she is."

"I command you to tell me immediately," says Thwackum, "and I would not have you imagine, young man, that your age, though it hath somewhat abridged the purpose of tuition, hath totally taken away the authority of the master. The relation of the master and scholar is indelible, as, indeed, all other relations are, for they all derive their original from heaven. I would have you think yourself, therefore, as much obliged to obey me now, as when I taught you your first rudiments."

"I believe you would," cries Jones, "but that will not happen, unless you had the same birchen argument to convince me."

"Then I must tell you plainly," said Thwackum, "I am resolved to discover the wicked wretch."

"And I must tell you plainly," returned Jones, "I am resolved you shall not." Thwackum then offered to advance, and Jones laid hold of his arms, which Mr Blifil endeavoured to rescue, declaring, he would not see his old master insulted.

Jones now finding himself engaged with two, thought it necessary to rid himself of one of his antagonists as soon as possible. He therefore applied to the weakest first, and letting the parson go, he directed a blow at the young squire's breast, which luckily taking place, reduced him to measure his length on the ground.

Thwackum was so intent on the discovery, that, the moment he found himself at liberty, he stepped forward directly into the fern, without any great consideration of what might in the meantime befall his friend. But he had advanced a very few paces into the thicket, before Jones, having defeated Blifil, overtook the parson, and dragged him backward by the skirt of his coat.

This parson had been a champion in his youth, and had won much honour by his fist, both at school and at the university. He had now indeed, for a great number of years, declined the practice of that noble art, yet was his courage full as strong as his faith, and his body no less strong than either. He was moreover, as the reader may perhaps have conceived, somewhat irascible in his nature. When he looked back, therefore, and saw his friend stretched out on the ground, and found himself at the same time so roughly handled by one who had formerly been only passive in all conflicts between them — a circumstance which highly aggravated the whole — his patience at length gave way. He threw himself into a posture of offence, and collecting all his force, attacked Jones in the front with as much impetuosity as he had formerly attacked him in the rear.

Our hero received the enemy's attack with the most undaunted intrepidity, and his bosom resounded with the blow. This he presently returned with no less violence, aiming likewise at the parson's breast, but he dexterously drove down the fist of Jones, so that it reached only his belly, where two pounds of beef and as many of pudding were then deposited, and whence consequently no hollow sound could proceed. Many lusty blows, much more pleasant as well as easy to have seen, than to read or describe, were given on both sides. At last a violent fall, in which Jones had thrown his knees into Thwackum's breast, so weakened the latter, that victory had been no longer dubious, had not Blifil, who had now recovered his strength, again renewed the fight, and by engaging with Jones, given the parson a moment's time to shake his ears, and to regain his breath.

And now both together attacked our hero, whose blows did not retain that force with which they had fallen at first, so weakened was he by his combat with Thwackum. For though the pedagogue chose rather to play solos on the human instrument, and had been lately used to those only, yet he still retained enough of his ancient knowledge to perform his part very well in a duet.

The victory, according to modern custom, was like to be decided by numbers, when, on a sudden, a fourth pair of fists appeared in the battle, and immediately paid their compliments to the parson, and the owner of them at the same time crying out, "Are not you ashamed, and be damn'd to you, to fall two of you upon one?"

The battle, which was of the kind that for distinction's sake is called royal, now raged with the utmost violence during a few minutes, till Blifil being a second time laid sprawling by Jones, Thwackum condescended to apply for quarter to his new antagonist, who was now found to be Mr Western himself, for in the heat of the action none of the combatants had recognised him.

In fact, that honest squire, happening, in his afternoon's walk with some company, to pass through the field where the bloody battle was fought, and having concluded, from seeing three men engaged, that two of them must be on a side, he hastened from his companions, and with more gallantry than policy, espoused the cause of the weaker party. By which generous proceeding he very probably prevented Mr Jones from becoming a victim to the wrath of Thwackum, and to the pious friendship which Blifil bore his old master, for, besides the disadvantage of such odds, Jones had not yet sufficiently recovered the former strength of his broken arm. This reinforcement, however, soon put an end to the action, and Jones with his ally obtained the victory.

Chapter Twelve

In which is seen a more moving spectacle than all the blood in the bodies of Thwackum and Blifil, and of twenty other such, is capable of producing

The rest of Mr Western's company were now come up, being just at the instant when the action was over. These were the honest clergyman, whom we have formerly seen at Mr Western's table, Mrs Western, the aunt of Sophia, and lastly, the lovely Sophia herself.

At this time, the following was the aspect of the bloody field. In one place lay on the ground, all pale, and almost breathless, the vanquished Blifil. Near him stood the conqueror Jones, almost covered with blood, part of which was naturally his own, and part had been lately the property of the Reverend Mr Thwackum. In a third place stood the said Thwackum, like King Porus, sullenly submitting to the conqueror. The last figure in the piece was Western the Great, most gloriously forbearing the vanquished foe.

Blifil, in whom there was little sign of life, was at first the principal object of the concern of everyone, and particularly of Mrs Western, who had drawn from her pocket a bottle of hartshorn, and was herself about to apply it to his nostrils, when on a sudden the attention of the whole company was diverted from poor Blifil, whose spirit, if it had any such design, might have now taken an opportunity of stealing off to the other world, without any ceremony.

For now a more melancholy and a more lovely object lay motionless before them. This was no other than the charming Sophia herself, who, from the sight of blood, or from fear for her father, or from some other reason, had fallen down in a swoon, before anyone could get to her assistance.

Mrs Western first saw her and screamed. Immediately two or three voices cried out, "Miss Western is dead." Hartshorn, water, every remedy was called for, almost at one and the same instant.

The reader may remember, that in our description of this grove we mentioned a murmuring brook, which brook did not come there, as such gentle streams flow through vulgar romances, with no other purpose than to murmur. No! Fortune had decreed to ennoble this little brook with a higher honour than any of those which wash the plains of Arcadia ever deserved.

Jones was rubbing Blifil's temples, for he began to fear he had given him a blow too much, when the words, 'Miss Western' and 'dead', rushed at once on his ear. He started up, left Blifil to his fate, and flew to Sophia, whom, while all the rest were running against each other, backward and forward, looking for water in the dry paths, he caught up in his arms, and then ran away with her over the field to the rivulet above mentioned, where, plunging himself into the water, he contrived to besprinkle her face, head, and neck very plentifully.

Happy was it for Sophia that the same confusion which prevented her other friends from serving her, prevented them likewise from obstructing Jones. He had carried her half ways before they knew what he was doing, and he had actually restored her to life before they reached the waterside. She stretched out her arms, opened her eyes, and cried, "Oh! Heavens!" just as her father, aunt, and the parson came up.

Jones, who had hitherto held this lovely burden in his arms, now relinquished his hold, but gave her at the same instant a tender caress, which, had her senses been then perfectly restored, could not have escaped her observation. His hand passed over her breast and remained there, as if solicitous for her heartbeat, but once he felt the heavy throb he lingered. As she expressed, therefore, no displeasure at this freedom, we suppose she was not sufficiently recovered from her swoon at the time.

This tragical scene was now converted into a sudden scene of joy. In this our hero was certainly the principal character, for as he probably felt more ecstatic delight in having saved Sophia than she herself received from being saved. Neither were the congratulations paid to her equal to what were conferred on Jones, especially by Mr Western himself, who, after having once or twice embraced his daughter, fell to hugging and kissing Jones. He called him the preserver of Sophia, and declared there was nothing, except her, or his estate, which he would not give him, but upon recollection, he afterwards excepted his fox-hounds, the Chevalier, and Miss Slouch—for so he called his favourite mare.

All fears for Sophia being now removed, Jones became the object of the squire's consideration. "Come, my lad," says Western, "d'off thy quoat and wash thy feace, for att in a devilish pickle, I promise thee. Come, come, wash thyself, and shat go huome with me, and we'l zee to vind thee another quoat."

Jones immediately complied, threw off his coat, went down to the water, and washed both his face and bosom, for the latter was as much exposed and as bloody as the former. But though the water could clear off the blood, it could not remove the black and blue marks which Thwackum had imprinted on both his face and breast, and which, being discerned by Sophia, drew from her a sigh and a look full of inexpressible tenderness.

Jones received this full in his eyes, and it had infinitely a stronger effect on him than all the contusions which he had received before. An effect, however, widely different, for so soft and balmy was it, that, had all his former blows been stabs, it would for some minutes have prevented his feeling their smart.

The company now moved backwards, and soon arrived where Thwackum had got Mr Blifil again on his legs. Here we cannot suppress a pious wish, that all quarrels were to be decided by those weapons only with which Nature, knowing what is proper for us, hath supplied us, and that cold iron was to be used in digging no bowels but those of the earth. Then would war, the pastime of monarchs, be almost inoffensive, and battles between great armies might be fought at the particular desire of several ladies of quality, who, together with the kings themselves, might be actual spectators of the conflict. Then might the field be this moment well strewed with human carcasses, and the next, the dead men, or infinitely the greatest part of them, might get up, like Mr Bayes' troops, and march off either at the sound of a drum or fiddle, as should be previously agreed on.

I would avoid, if possible, treating this matter ludicrously, lest grave men and politicians, whom I know to be offended at a jest, may cry pish at it, but, in reality, might not a battle be as well decided by the greater number of broken heads, bloody noses, and black eyes, as by the greater heaps of mangled and murdered human bodies? Might not towns be contended for in the same manner? Indeed, this may be thought too detrimental a scheme to the French interest, since they would thus lose the advantage they have over other nations in the superiority of their engineers, but when I consider the gallantry and generosity of that people, I am persuaded they would never decline putting themselves upon a par with their adversary, or, as the phrase is, making themselves his match.

But such reformations are rather to be wished than hoped for, I shall content myself, therefore, with this short hint, and return to my narrative.

Western began now to enquire into the original rise of this quarrel. To which neither Blifil nor Jones gave any answer, but Thwackum said surlily, "I believe the cause is not far off, if you beat the bushes well you may find her."

"Find her?" replied Western. "What! have you been fighting for a wench?"

"Ask the gentleman in his waistcoat there," said Thwackum, "he best knows."

"Nay then," cries Western, "it is a wench certainly. Ah, Tom, Tom, thou art a liquorish dog. But come, gentlemen, be all friends, and go home with me, and make final peace over a bottle."

"I ask your pardon, sir," says Thwackum, "it is no such slight matter for a man of my character to be thus injuriously treated, and buffeted by a boy, only because I would have done my duty, in endeavouring to detect and bring to justice a wanton harlot, but, indeed, the principal fault lies in Mr Allworthy and yourself, for if you put the laws in execution, as you ought to do, you will soon rid the country of these vermin."

"I would as soon rid the country of foxes," cries Western. "I think we ought to encourage the recruiting those numbers which we are every day losing in the war. But where is she? Prithee, Tom, show me." He then began to beat about, in the same language and in the same manner as if he had been beating for a hare, and at last cried out, "Soho! Puss is not far off. Here's her form, upon my soul, I believe I may cry stole away." And indeed so he might, for he had now discovered the place whence the poor girl had, at the beginning of the fray, stolen away, upon as many feet as a hare generally uses in travelling.

Sophia now desired her father to return home, saying she found herself very faint, and apprehended a relapse. The squire immediately complied with his daughter's request, for he was the fondest of parents. He earnestly endeavoured to prevail with the whole company to go and sup with him, but Blifil and Thwackum absolutely refused, the former saying, there were more reasons than he could then mention, why he must decline this honour, and the latter declaring — perhaps rightly — that it was not proper for a person of his function to be seen at any place in his present condition.

Jones was incapable of refusing the pleasure of being with his Sophia, so on he marched with Squire Western and his ladies, the parson bringing up the rear. This had, indeed, offered to tarry with his brother Thwackum, professing his regard for the cloth would not permit him to depart, but Thwackum would not accept the favour, and with no great civility, pushed him after Mr Western.

Thus ended this bloody fray, and thus shall end the fifth book of this history.

About the Author

Lynne Connolly has been in epublishing since the Wild West days. She's holding on, and these days she writes for several epublishers. After a varied career in business in which she sold baby nappies, coffee and beer, she took a break, and ended up writing instead. She lives in England, but tries to visit the US at least once a year. She lives in the North West of England with her family and her mews, Jack.

Lynne Connolly loves to hear from readers. You can find her contact information, website details and author profile page at http://www.total-e-bound.com.

Total-E-Bound Publishing

www.total-e-bound.com

Take a look at our exciting range of literagasmic™
erotic romance titles and discover pure quality
at Total-E-Bound.

www.ingramcontent.com/pod-product-compliance
Lightning Source LLC
Chambersburg PA
CBHW020838030726
47496CB00001B/261